"A must-read."

"Spicy and sweet, *Cross the Line* is an adorable brother's-best-friend sports romance that had me grinning from ear to ear!"
— Chloe Liese, *USA Today* bestselling author
of the Bergman Brothers series

"Fast, furious, and unforgettable. [Soltani] seamlessly blends real emotion, diversity, and a Bollywood-esque love story into the exhilarating world of Formula 1. This high-speed romance promises a heartfelt journey that leaves you wanting more, even after crossing the finish line."
— Bal Khabra, international bestselling author of *Collide*

"Simone Soltani cured my F1 off-season blues with this sweet and spicy brother's-best-friend romance. *Cross the Line* is all the fun and drama of *Drive to Survive* but with way more kissing. An absolute delight!"
— Sarah Adler, *USA Today* bestselling author of *Happy Medium*

"Formula 1 fans, this one's for you."   — *US Weekly*

"Soltani's debut is perfect for fans of Netflix's *Formula 1: Drive to Survive* docuseries and brings a unique subcategory and delightful addition to the sports romance genre."
— *Library Journal* (starred review)

"Soltani's sensitive, diverse take on the typical sports romance is a breath of fresh air, helmed by a sexy cinnamon roll hero. . . . Readers looking for gentle sports romance will want to check this out."
— *Publishers Weekly*

TITLES BY SIMONE SOLTANI

Cross the Line
Ride with Me

RIDE WITH ME

SIMONE SOLTANI

Berkley Romance
New York

BERKLEY ROMANCE
Published by Berkley
An imprint of Penguin Random House LLC
1745 Broadway, New York, NY 10019
penguinrandomhouse.com

Book design by Jenni Surasky

Library of Congress Cataloging-in-Publication Data

Names: Soltani, Simone, author.
Title: Ride with me / Simone Soltani.
Description: First edition. | New York: Berkley Romance, 2025. |
Series: Lights Out; 2
Identifiers: LCCN 2024044541 (print) | LCCN 2024044542 (ebook) |
ISBN 9780593818169 (trade paperback) | ISBN 9780593818176 (ebook)
Subjects: LCGFT: Romance fiction. | Novels.
Classification: LCC PS3619.O43957 R54 2025 (print) |
LCC PS3619.O43957 (ebook) | DDC 813/.6—dc23/eng/20240125
LC record available at https://lccn.loc.gov/2024044541
LC ebook record available at https://lccn.loc.gov/2024044542

First Edition: May 2025

Printed in the United States of America
1st Printing

The authorized representative in the EU for product safety and compliance is
Penguin Random House Ireland, Morrison Chambers, 32 Nassau Street,
Dublin D02 YH68, Ireland, https://eu-contact.penguin.ie.

For anyone who knows they deserve more than
what they've been given.

And for Mom D. Please don't read this one.

FORMULA 1 RACE SCHEDULE

~~Bahrain • March 3–5~~

~~Saudi Arabia • March 17–19~~

~~Australia • March 31–April 2~~

~~Azerbaijan • April 28–30~~

~~United States (Miami) • May 5–7~~

~~Italy (Imola) • May 19–21~~

~~Monaco • May 26–28~~

~~Spain • June 2–4~~

~~Canada • June 16–18~~

~~Austria • June 30–July 2~~

~~Great Britain • July 7–9~~

~~Hungary • July 21–23~~

~~Belgium • July 28–30~~

~~Summer Break~~

~~Netherlands • August 25–27~~

~~Italy (Monza) • September 1–3~~

~~Singapore • September 15–17~~

~~Japan • September 22–24~~

~~Qatar • October 6–8~~

~~United States (Austin) • October 20–22~~

~~Mexico • October 27–29~~

~~Brazil • November 3–5~~

United States (Las Vegas) • November 16–18

Abu Dhabi • November 24–26

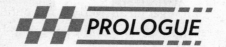 **PROLOGUE**

THOMAS

September
Singapore

I'm watching a crash in slow motion.

In my mirrors, I can't tell exactly how many cars are mangled in the barriers behind me, flames flickering around them. All I know for certain is that no one is going to walk away from it unscathed—if they walk away at all.

"Red flag, Thomas," my race engineer says needlessly over the radio. "Repeat, red flag. Make your way to the pit lane."

I don't reply. I can't do anything but gaze back at the black plumes and the flashing lights and the horror continuing to unfold, amazed that I'm not in it. I so nearly was.

It's easy to forget how dangerous Formula 1 can be. So few of us die on-track these days that we sometimes dismiss the risks we take every time we climb into the car. But lives can so easily be lost. And death isn't always the worst fate.

"Are they out?" I ask when I find my voice. I won't press for more details. I don't want to know. Not yet.

The man is silent. My thundering heart is the only sound in my ears.

"Come on, tell me." I'm tracking team colors as I drive to

the pit lane entrance, but I don't see enough of any. "Are they out of the cars?"

Again, I get no answer. It's not until I'm parked and trying to wrench myself out of the cockpit to better see who else has pulled in that he speaks to me.

"Two of them are out," he finally replies. "Zaid Yousef. And Axel Bergmüller. They're with the medics."

A sick rush of relief hits me, and it's compounded when I spot the other McMorris car behind me. My teammate didn't get caught up in the chaos.

"And the others?" I push. I can't put it off any longer. "Who else was involved?"

His answer comes quickly this time. "Dev Anderson, but he avoided the worst of it. He's okay. Managed to walk away on his own."

I'm still scanning cars and drivers, trying to figure out who's missing. There's only twenty of us. It shouldn't be hard.

I clock it then. "And Lorenzo?"

My engineer exhales long and slow, leaving my stomach to drop. I've had trouble with Lorenzo Castellucci in the past. He's earned his reputation for being an on-track terrorist time and time again. I've been a victim of his reckless driving and his hunger to prove himself as the son of a four-time world champion, resulting in crashes and far too many close calls. Deep down, I've always hated him for it.

But I'd never wish this on him. On anyone.

Except I did. I said as much in a moment when I didn't think anyone malicious was listening. But they were. Of course they were. Now it's out there in the worst possible way, set to haunt me forever, whether Lorenzo is okay or not.

I've cursed us both. And I don't know if either one of us is going to survive it.

 **CHAPTER 1**

THOMAS

Two months later, November
Las Vegas, Nevada

It's not easy being the most hated man in motorsport.

Some days, I wonder if I'm exaggerating. I know I'm not the *most* hated, but I'm definitely in the top five for a lot of people—people who are currently here or will be arriving soon for next weekend's Las Vegas Grand Prix. But then there are days like this one when I have the privilege of experiencing firsthand that I'm definitely *not* exaggerating.

"Fuck you," the red-faced man in front of me spits, skin almost the same shade as the Scuderia D'Ambrosi kit he's wearing, Lorenzo Castellucci's number emblazoned on the front. "*You* did this to him. *You* ruined his life."

Considering I literally wasn't involved in the crash that reportedly left Castellucci paralyzed, the man's facts are a little off. There's no telling him that it was all down to his favorite driver's recklessness, though. I'm public enemy number one, all because of something I said.

I take a breath to settle my nerves and glance over his shoulder, searching for escape routes from this unfortunate conversation, but he's standing between me and the place I need to be—a party bus idling at the curb ten meters away. I didn't think I'd have to face down an angry Castellucci fan before joining a stag do, but this is just my luck these days.

As the other guests climb aboard, I'm trapped on the sidewalk outside my hotel as the man continues his ranting. I can't walk away if I don't want another scathing article hitting the press tomorrow morning, but maybe I *should* just let him think the worst of me. It's not like Formula 1 is a stranger to scandal, from spying and cheating to shady deals and dirty money changing hands. The sport has a history steeped in it, and we drivers are no different. I can't think of a single one of us, past or present, who *hasn't* had something blow up in our faces.

Take Dev Anderson and his antibiotic-resistant STD for example, which was a rumor started by his ex–social media manager when she quit in a blaze of fury. It took months and a complete image overhaul to fix his reputation and convince sponsors he wasn't a liability—and that he didn't actually have an STD. There are still some "family-friendly" brands refusing to work with him, all because of the lies that were spread. It was a nightmare situation, and he's still climbing out of the ashes.

But I'd take Dev's fake STD any day over people knowing I wished death upon a fellow driver.

The worst part is that I actually did it. There were no made-up rumors by vengeful ex-employees or edited sound clips to make me look bad. I said what I said, even if I immediately wanted to take the words back. They were blurted in a moment of anger after nearly being killed on-track by the man I was complaining about.

Besides, I've been wrapped up in this world long enough to know that someone is always listening. And in this case, someone in our garage recorded every single furious word that tumbled from my lips. I don't know who was responsible for it being shot and uploaded to social media, but within the hour, it was all over the internet.

It got some attention at the time, and I got my fair share of hate, but it wasn't until the crash in Singapore two months ago that I officially became the most hated man in F1.

I understand why, and I can't fault anyone for it. I may not believe in the whole woo-woo *be careful what you speak into existence* bullshit, but I know some people do, and they blame me and my outburst for the accident happening. I'm the scapegoat who's getting hourly death threats.

I need to give Dev a call and ask him how he fixed the mess he was in. Maybe I can hire the same social media manager he did, the one who shifted public opinion back in his favor. Last I heard, she's working for Reid Coleman, Scuderia D'Ambrosi's number one driver these days, but I'd say I need her in my corner more than Reid does. Although, considering D'Ambrosi was—*is*—Lorenzo's team, I don't think they'd take kindly to me poaching her.

The people I have in place are doing their best to make me look a little less like a complete twat, so I can only wait until the next scandal is unveiled and the heat moves off me. For my sake, hopefully someone will show up with a secret baby in the next few weeks. I'm keeping my fingers crossed.

"I understand your concerns," I interrupt as diplomatically as I can, desperate to get on the bus. "And I will certainly be more cognizant of my words and actions in the future."

He stares at me like I've grown a second head before the

raging begins again, starting with me being a *fucking pretentious Brit* and ending with a stiff finger repeatedly poking into my chest. All I can do is sigh.

As much as I'd like to run, I doubt there's a safe space for me to go in all of Las Vegas, aside from the McMorris F1 Team motorhome with their top-notch security. I've had to tolerate this in every grand prix location since Singapore—five races of pure torture. Unfortunately, it'll be a few days before I can escape to the protection of my team and the paddock, which means I have to grin and bear this.

I shouldn't even be out tonight. I'm not the Maxwell-Brown sibling who's supposed to be here. It should be Andrew, my older brother and the groom's childhood best friend, but his wife is weeks away from giving birth to their first child. There was no way he'd risk missing it, even for this, so I was volunteered as the next best thing, a stand-in to represent our family at tomorrow's wedding since my race schedule happens to align. I wasn't expecting a stag do invitation to go along with it, but Andrew made it clear I wasn't to say no.

I get a much-needed distraction from being screamed at when my phone buzzes in my pocket, and I pull it out to see a text from my best mate. Still alive? Joshua's message reads, and it takes everything in me not to snort as I type back, Currently being accosted, actually. To that he replies, As long as it doesn't end up in the news, you'll be fine.

At least someone cares.

"Are you even *listening* to me?" the Castellucci fan roars, and I glance up to see he's somehow turned a darker shade of crimson.

To save him from the forthcoming stroke and me from having my mental health destroyed more than it already is, I flash a tight smile and take a large step to the side. "I'm terribly sorry, but there's somewhere I need to be. Take care, yeah?"

There's only a brief moment of silence before he's yelling at my retreating back, but I'm not about to turn around to suffer more of his abuse. Thankfully, he doesn't follow, and then I'm bounding up the steps of the bus, taking a moment once I'm inside to let my eyes adjust to the low light and flashing strobes. Once they do, I freeze.

My brain does its best to compute what I'm seeing. If this is a stag do . . . why are there so many women here? Jesus Christ, why is the *bride* here?

The answer hits a second later. This isn't just a stag do—it's a combination stag *and* hen do.

"Sit down, mate!" someone calls over the booming music, and I look down at a man who's glassy-eyed and grinning, a drink clutched in his hand. "Party's starting!"

Looks like it already started. I briefly consider stepping off the bus, weighing whether I would be better off here or on the streets, but the closing doors decide for me.

Just as the bus lurches away from the curb, I squeeze in beside a few other tuxedoed men. I thought it was odd when Ron, the groom, asked us to wear them tonight, and it appears the bride has requested that the women wear white dresses. With the wardrobe choice, any one of us could be the happy couple, although they've accessorized with silk sashes and crowns to differentiate themselves.

I dare to glance around to see if anyone else is as thrown by this turn of events as I am, but everyone seems to be having the time of their lives. Well, no, that's not quite true—there's one woman near the back who looks like she'd rather be run over by the bus than be on it. But even while miserable, she's stunning.

I'm forced to look away from her when a glass of champagne is shoved into my hand and I'm met with chants to chug it down. I do as I'm told, mostly to get the noise to stop, but also because I have a feeling I'm going to need the alcohol to get through tonight.

Guess I'm along for the ride.

# CHAPTER 2

STELLA

Joint bachelor and bachelorette parties should be illegal.

The Canadians call them *buck and doe parties*, but as an American, I just call them *a waste of my fucking time*. I must have been drunk when I agreed to this, because in no world would I soberly choose to subject myself to sitting on a party bus with a bunch of leering men and screeching women, watching the bride- and groom-to-be paw at each other while leaning against a stripper pole.

I'm barely keeping the grimace off my face as I take it all in, upper lip twitching every few seconds before I press it firmly against my bottom one. I'd be worried about my lipstick smudging if I didn't already know it's practically bombproof, put to the test through rounds of recipe development and tastings. If it can withstand buttercream frosting dolloped on top of a cupcake that you practically have to unhinge your jaw to take a bite of, it can hold up to my sneering.

God, I shouldn't be here. I *should* have been just stepping off a flight from my honeymoon, glowing after days spent in a Maldives over-water bungalow and getting my back blown out by the love of my life, but that plan went to shit when he left me at the altar. The man literally *ran away* when it came time to say his vows while I stood there like a mannequin, watching him burst out of the church like a bat out of hell.

Instead, I'm here: on a party bus in Las Vegas, surrounded by forty-odd people I barely know and wishing I could throw myself out the doors and into the street—wishing I'd never brightly agreed when my favorite cousin convinced me to come along to get my mind off my runaway fiancé.

Yeah, I was definitely drunk when I agreed to this. For the first few days after my failed wedding, wine was my best friend. I haven't been much of a drinker lately, so those bold pinot noirs and piss-adjacent chardonnays went straight to my head.

Who knows what else I agreed to during that time. It's a good thing I don't handle the day-to-day business at my company, or else I might be staring down the face of financial ruin. Although, shit, I think I do remember emailing my head chef at an ungodly hour to ask if we could put a red wine–flavored macaron on the menu at Stella Margaux's.

And then there was that little viral video . . .

"Stella!" a high-pitched voice crows from across the bus, dragging me out of my sulking.

It's Daphne, another of my cousins, a woman I wish I could physically remove from our family tree. Her blunt chin-length bob barely shifts when she reaches forward to grab my hand, her bloodred nails perfectly done. She looks like a Black Stepford Wife whose hobbies include witchcraft and eating the souls of children, and if she didn't annoy the ever-loving shit out of me, I'd adore her vibe.

Unfortunately, she's a gossip-hungry monster who I'm pretty sure leaked all the gory details of my wedding-gone-wrong to the press. I would have thought a thirty-five-year-old mother of two and renowned plastic surgeon would have better things to do with her time than talk shit about a jilted bride seven years her junior, but hey, I guess we all have our vices.

"It's so good you made it!" Daphne gushes, dark eyes boring into me. "How are you feeling? Doing okay after . . . everything?"

That seems to be everyone's favorite question these days. I'd love to say that in the two weeks since my fiancé left I've been the best ever. It's what they'd rather hear. But I can't lie, considering the evidence of my despair is splashed all over the internet.

Someone should have taken my phone from me, or at least changed the passwords to my social media accounts. Maybe that would have stopped me from going live on Instagram and drunkenly raving to the world that love isn't real, men are trash, and the French can get fucked.

"I'm getting through the days," I shout over the music. "Super glad to be here, though! So happy for Janelle and Ron!"

She stares at me like she doesn't believe me for a second, but then she flashes a wide, fake smile. Her teeth are so startlingly white and straight that they have to be veneers. God, they look amazing. "Good for you, being out tonight. Gotta get back on that horse!"

"That's right! Just call me a cowgirl!" I quip back, and I immediately want to shoot myself.

She drops my hand when the bus shudders to a stop and excited shrieks go up around us. At the front, Janelle taps on a microphone, trying to get everyone's attention. The sound makes me wince, and I'm tempted to cover my ears, but I don't want to look like that much of a party pooper this early in the night.

"What's up, wedding squad!" Janelle shouts into the mic. "How we doing tonight?"

There are hoots and hollers, and I have to dodge getting elbowed in the face by the woman sitting next to me, who has already gone a little too hard on the champagne. In comparison, I'm still nursing my first glass, despite wanting to grab the nearest bottle and chug it.

"Well, now that I know y'all are enjoying yourselves," Janelle continues, "I thought we'd go over the itinerary for the night."

The timeline of events is gambling, an eight-course dinner, a strip club where we ladies have the opportunity to get lap dance lessons from the professionals, and then dancing the night away. Normally, I'd be on board for all of those things. I'll hustle anyone at a poker table, I love good food, and the idea of learning how to give a proper lap dance sounds like a hell of a time. But I can't work up the necessary enthusiasm for any of it. I haven't been able to for ages. And it fucking *sucks*.

I miss feeling like myself. I miss being joyful instead of bitter. I miss being the life of the party and the first person to accept a dare, consequences be damned. I miss who I was before the man I loved and trusted left me high and dry.

I miss being *me*—Stella goddamn Baldwin. But who knows when she'll be back.

Tonight, I'll take solace in the fact that I don't seem to be the only one having a shit time. As we disembark from the bus, I fall in line behind a dark-haired man who heaves a weary sigh as we shuffle toward the door, his broad shoulders hunched.

Yeah, bud, I feel you.

I scowl when Daphne bumps my shoulder, stepping in front of me and dragging another woman along with her. I'm tempted to "accidentally" slosh the last of my champagne on them, but considering we're all wearing white at Janelle's behest, it would only make the fabric see-through and lead to me being in trouble. Tragic.

I won't deny that I look good in tonight's dress—a short, silky number with a feathered hem. I always look amazing in white by virtue of being a darker-skinned Black woman. But I also can't deny that the ex-bride inside me is triggered by the sight.

An all too familiar pang of hurt shoots through my chest. I try to drown it by finishing off my champagne, praying Janelle and Ron have paid for open bars in all the places we're hitting. I need to get shit-faced to make it through this. As long as someone stops me from pulling out my phone and recording another rant, I should be fine.

I draw in a steeling breath as we step off the bus, grateful my ankle doesn't roll in my insensible strappy stilettos with little glitter stars on them. They make my legs look a mile long, but they were made for sitting more than walking. Or for throwing over the shoulders of a very attractive man. Not that I've done that recently or have any plans to. Who knew getting my heart broken would throw my libido into the gutter?

"We're gonna have so much fun tonight!" Sydney, one of the bridesmaids, screeches from behind me as we make our way into the lavish casino. "Do any of us even know how to, like, *play* cards, though?"

"Who cares," Rachel, another bridesmaid, replies before cackling. "It's an excuse to watch hot guys in tuxes lose a bunch of money!"

They rush past me in a fit of laughter, nearly toppling over as they attempt to move around the man who was briefly in front of me on the bus.

"Shit, sorry!" Sydney blurts, grabbing at his arm as she stumbles.

The man turns, his hand going to her elbow and holding firm. "You're all right," he says, and I swear I catch a hint of an English accent. It's unsurprising, considering the groom grew up in London and most of his groomsmen are his childhood friends or Premier League footballers. "Careful, though, yeah? Don't think Ron and Janelle want anyone to end up in hospital tonight."

The accent is obvious now, even over the din of trilling slot machines, and the phrasing of his sentence confirms it. But it's his expression that really drives it home. He's smiling in that stereotypical tight-lipped white British way that looks closer to a grimace than an expression of joy. It's polite and deferential but somehow patronizing at the same time. He'd make a great member of parliament with a smile like that.

But speaking of lips . . . the man's got nice ones, the kind where there's actually something to kiss, and I can tell he knows what lip balm is. Not that I'm—not that I'm thinking about *kissing* him. Patronizing men who look too good in tuxes aren't my type. At least, they shouldn't be, because that's exactly who fucked up my entire life.

But I can't deny that this one's handsome.

Under the warm casino lights, his hair is a deep shade of chestnut. A wavy lock of it, perfectly disheveled, sweeps across his forehead, though I have no doubt he styled it that way with some sort of expensive pomade. His eyes, a piercing blue, are framed by thick lashes, the kind I'd be jealous of if I didn't have the best lash tech in the world on speed dial. And while his skin can probably verge on Snow White levels of paleness, he has just enough of a golden undertone that I'm sure he spent the summer letting the sun beat down on him.

If all of that wasn't enough, his features are so perfectly chiseled it's like some classical sculptor birthed him from a slab of marble. Straight nose, high cheekbones, ungodly sharp jaw. He looks . . . regal. The man might as well be out of a fairy tale.

I keep staring as the women titter and giggle and bat their lashes some more. I can't blame them. If I had the opportunity to get that close to him, I might be doing the same. The old Stella—back when I was single, wild, and carefree—wouldn't have missed a beat. But the current version . . .

"God, they're embarrassing."

I glance to my right to find Daphne beside me, sneering at the same scene I'm looking at. Except her focus is on the two women pawing at Prince Charming, not the man himself.

"Rachel and Sydney can never keep it in their pants," she complains, shaking her head like she's witnessing a true shame. "That man better be ready to get mauled."

I won't fault a woman for her desire to maul a man—been there, done that—so I don't deign to answer Daphne's chiding. I *do*, however, let my gaze linger on him. No harm in admiring a little eye candy.

One thing about no longer being in a relationship is that I can look at whoever the hell I want whenever I want. I'm a single woman for the first time in five years. I'm *free*. It's just a shame that *free* means I want to break down about every ten minutes.

As determined as I am to move on, I'm still mourning the loss of my relationship and the life we built together, and I know I will be for a while. But I also know that this could have been so much worse if I'd been just a little more in love with him.

That's not to say I didn't love Étienne. God, far from it. But over the past year, our relationship had been . . . strained. I blamed it on wedding planning and being busy with work, the typical things that could tax a couple, but something else was going on. I ignored it at the time, blamed his emotional distance on everything in the book other than him losing interest in me. But in the end, that's what it came down to.

I just don't want to be with you anymore, Stella.

I really should have seen it coming. We hadn't had sex in four months. Every kiss was barely a peck. Once he even pulled his hand away when I tried to hold it, making the excuse that he was just shocked by how cold my fingers were. It would have been a perfect moment to grab my hand and warm it between his palms, maybe even press a kiss to my freezing knuckles. But no. He'd just shoved his hands into his pockets and let me trail behind him as we walked on. I should have known we were doomed. I just wish I'd opened my eyes to it sooner.

They're open now, though, and they're staring straight at a man who I wouldn't have looked twice at a couple of weeks ago.

"I'm so glad you're not like them," Daphne says, pulling me out of my thoughts. There's a saccharine note to her words that I do not like. "You've been so graceful and dignified throughout all of . . . *you know.* You could have been out in the streets, doing the absolute most to make up for those years you lost to Étienne, but you're not. Those two could really learn something from you instead of acting like nasty little sluts."

I nearly trip at the insult, my heel catching on some invisible bump in the carpet, but I manage to keep my footing. "Excuse me?"

Daphne waves a hand, brushing off her awful comment. "I know it's crude, but women like that are truly a breed of their own. I have no respect for them."

"Are you saying you wouldn't respect me if I'd done that?" I challenge, unable to resist cupping that little spark of anger and fanning the flame. If I have to give Daphne credit for anything, this is the first time I've felt more than bone-crushing despair or numbness since my wedding day.

"Of course not," she scolds, looping her arm through mine and pulling me close. "But I might have viewed you a little differently. Besides, you never would have. That's so out of character for you."

"Oh, really?" We may be family, but it's clear she doesn't know me. Or maybe she's just forgotten what I was like before an intense career and a crumbling relationship slowly sapped away my energy and personality.

She seems to think I've been *graceful* and *dignified* after having my entire life blown up. Last I checked those weren't synonyms for *grieving* and *depressed*. If she's under the impression that any of that is who I really am, then she's sorely mistaken.

"Yeah," Daphne confirms, giving my arm a little squeeze that makes me want to punch her in return. "It's just not you, Stella."

Something snaps in my chest, opening the floodgates of every emotion I've kept locked away and refused to feel lately. Who the hell is she to tell me who I am? How could she possibly know me better than I know myself? And why does she think she has the right to judge how I or anyone else lives their life? It's not like it affects hers.

But okay. All right. If that's what she thinks, then fuck it. Fuck *her*. I'll show her who I really am underneath it all. I'll show her the chaos I can inspire now that I have no one to answer to.

The old Stella's coming back tonight. And she's going to cause a riot.

# CHAPTER 3

THOMAS

All right, so maybe I'm not as hated as I thought.

At least, not by the women at this party. The two currently hanging off me don't seem to mind me. In fact, they seem to like me *very* much.

"You're *such* a gentleman," the one on my left gushes, staring up at me with hearts in her eyes.

After saving her from taking a tumble in the middle of the casino, I've become her—and her friend's—knight in shining armor. I think her name is Rachel . . . or maybe this one's Sydney. I wasn't paying much attention as they introduced themselves, too busy bracing for another possible assault as we made our way through the casino floor and toward the lifts. Getting off the party bus and walking through throngs of people was stressful enough, but so far everything has been fine.

"Genuinely the sweetest," the one to my right coos, pressing closer as we and ten others cram into the metal box. "I bet everyone you meet immediately loves you."

If only they knew.

"I'm a fan favorite," I lie, basking in their smiles and breathy laughs.

They're both pretty and around my age, if not a little older, but that's never bothered me before, and I'll entertain their advances for as long as they're interested. Other than that, though, I'm not looking for anything to happen.

It's not that I don't want it to, but my reputation is so bruised that I can't risk another misstep. I have to keep myself out of trouble. And no offense to these women, but I'm getting the distinct vibe that any escapade with them—either one alone or both together—would end up as tabloid fodder tomorrow.

"Ladies first," I say when the doors reopen.

I get more batted lashes and giggles before they step out behind the rest of the crowd, joining the group that's just gotten off the other lift. We've been dumped in what I assume is the high rollers' room, and I swear I've seen the same one in a James Bond movie. There are poker, blackjack, and craps tables dotted around the expansive black-carpeted, mood-lit space. A sleek mirrored bar lines one wall, with intimate booth seating placed opposite it. And I'm sure the wall of glass on the far side of the room overlooks the Strip, but the space is so vast that all I can see out the darkened windows is the glow of the fake Eiffel Tower and top floors of the hotels across the boulevard.

I'm barely in the room before a waitress approaches with a tray of champagne and a gentle guiding hand, leading me to the section of the room where the other men are gathering. It's a little disappointing to be separated from my two-woman hype squad, but it's probably for the best.

"Gather round, lads," Ron calls over the music, which is slightly less headache-inducing than whatever techno monstrosity was playing on the bus. "I want to make a toast before tonight's debauchery begins."

Not sure how much debauchery can happen with his bride-to-be on the other side of the room, but all right.

"To my countrymen," Ron begins, lifting his champagne glass as his eyes dart around to the handful of us also from the UK. "Thank you for making the trek halfway across the world to be here tonight. And to the rest of you, I'm glad to see your ugly mugs here too. It means the world that you're here celebrating my last night as an unmarried man. Who would've thought I'd settle down?"

Certainly not me. When he was a Premier League footballer, Ron was known for having a different woman on his arm every week. Guess that all changed when he retired last year and met the love of his life. I really am happy for him, but I won't be surprised if his bride gets her heart broken down the line.

It's a cynical take. And maybe they have a chance of making it now that he's stepped out of the limelight. But from what I've seen before and know of my fellow athletes, being faithful is not their strong suit.

Not me, though. Can't cheat if you've never been in a relationship.

"To Ron and Janelle!" a man standing next to me cheers.

I missed the last bit of Ron's toast, but I lift my glass and join the chorus celebrating his impending nuptials. Then it's off to the races.

More specifically, Ron tells us to have the night of our fucking lives and to enjoy the next hour of gambling before we move on to dinner. I've never been much for card games or losing money, so this is wasted on me, but there's no use wallowing in a place like this. I'm safe from prying eyes and cameras, and no one here seems to care about who I am. There are more than enough other stars here, and in the ranking of sports popularity, I'm pretty sure footballers beat F1 drivers—even if the city is about to revolve around us.

Finishing my champagne, I set the empty glass down on a passing waitress's tray and turn for the bar, ready for something stronger. I don't typically drink during the season, except for the celebrations after a placing on the podium, but I'm making an exception this weekend. I deserve it.

Janelle must have finished her own toast before Ron, because the women have dispersed around the room. I smile my way past a group huddled around a tray of shots and stop short when another bunch rushes past to get to the closest blackjack table. Once it's safe, I continue on, but I slow when I spot a woman on her own—the same one I glimpsed on the bus.

Most of them are paired off or in groups, but she's removed from the bedlam, lingering at the far end of the bar. She sits with her back to it, one elbow resting on the marble top, leaning back enough to put the slender line of her body on display. Her long, rich brown legs are crossed at the knee, one stiletto hooked over the bottom rung of the stool while the other slowly bounces to the beat of the song playing. Each time, the feathered hem of her little white dress inches higher.

She's holding a champagne flute loosely against her stomach, posture relaxed, but the look in her eyes tells a different story.

There's no other way to put it: she's prowling.

I keep still when her attention lands on me. She gives me a quick up-and-down glance at first, nothing more than an assessing flick, but it lingers when she reaches my face again. Our gazes meet and hold, and a tense beat passes before her full lips curl into a smile. It beckons me like she's spoken, commanding me to come her way.

And who am I to tell a lady no?

Sidling up to the empty section of bar next to her, I focus on getting the bartender's attention, ordering a bourbon old-fashioned before turning to her. She's even prettier up close, easily the most attractive woman here—sorry to the bride—with flawless skin, wide brown eyes, and a devastating mouth that I'd happily let ruin me.

"Would you like something other than champagne?" I ask. It's not a great opening line, but I'm not trying to pick her up. I'm here to talk to a beautiful woman for as long as she'll let me.

Her gaze cuts in my direction, and I get another quick once-over before she nods. "I'll have the same. But rye, not bourbon."

I relay her order to the bartender, then slide onto the neighboring barstool, watching her from the corner of my eye. She's still facing the rest of the room, continuing the hunt, but I'll consider it my own personal challenge to get her to focus on me.

"So," I prompt. "How do you know the bride?"

A beat passes before her eyes drag back in my direction. I don't have her full attention, probably not even half of it, but it's a start.

"Janelle's my cousin," she answers. She could leave it there and force me to keep the conversation going, but blessedly she asks, "How do you know the groom?"

"He's the son of an old family friend," I answer, leaving out the part about him being my brother's friend. "We're not particularly close."

Judging by the way her head turns another inch, that's piqued her interest. She senses there's a story behind it all. That there might be something a little interesting about me. "And yet you're here anyway."

Unfortunately.

"Have to represent the family," I reply with an easy shrug.

"Plus, I have to be here for work next week, so it fit into my schedule."

She turns a fraction more, shoulders shifting this time. She's not all the way on the hook, but she's considering it. "Do you travel a lot for your job?"

"You could say that."

She waits for me to elaborate, her stare unwavering when I give her nothing else. "You wanna share with the class what it is that you do?"

"You don't know who I am?" I ask before I can stop myself. But it's a genuine question, not one meant to make me sound like a prick, even though her coolly lifted brow indicates that's how she's taking it.

"Am I supposed to?" she tosses back.

Something loosens in my chest at the lack of recognition on her face. She's not pretending—she has no idea who I am. Nice as it is not having to explain who I am and what I do, it's even nicer to encounter someone with zero knowledge of me. Right now, I'm just some bloke at an over-the-top prewedding party chatting her up.

"Have you looked at a single billboard around here recently?"

Something flares in her eyes before she gives a dramatic gasp, champagne glass clutched mock-demurely to her chest. But even though she's clearly about to make fun of me, I've got the outcome I wanted—her attention's all mine.

"Oh my God," she says breathlessly, knee bumping mine as she straightens and turns in her seat. "Are you a dancer with Thunder from Down Under? I *love* you guys." She leans in conspiratorially before asking in a loud whisper, "Can I see your abs?"

I have to bite the inside of my cheek to keep from laughing.

From her polished looks and self-assured body language, I had a feeling she'd be sharp underneath it all, but her humor has me thrown. "Sadly, I'm English, not Australian." I'd happily take my shirt off for her, though.

She heaves a disappointed sigh. "That's a shame. I was looking forward to a private show. You probably have a lot going on under that tux."

She may be taking the piss, but she's bold. Her dark eyes still haven't left mine, a challenge shining in their depths, but again, for just a moment, there's something else in them.

"Wait," she says before I can tease her back. "Are you part of the reason why the roads are such a mess around here?"

I flash a wry grin. Half of this city is about to be shut down to accommodate the race, and she's not wrong about it already being a mess. "Guilty as charged."

Her Mona Lisa–esque smile comes alive in a new way. "So you're a *race car driver*," she says slowly, putting the pieces together, and I swear she presses her knee a little harder against mine. "I don't think I've ever met one of those."

I'm in possession of her full attention now, and it's . . . potent. Pinning me down. Like I couldn't tear myself away from her even if I wanted to. I've made myself into the perfect prey to sink her teeth into, and now she's ready to toy with her food.

"Happy to be your first," I say.

"Mm, I'm sure you are." Finally, she sticks a hand out for me to shake, having made up her mind that I'm worthy of her time. "I'm Stella."

I wrap my fingers around hers, the warmth of her soft palm seeping into mine. "Thomas. Pleasure to meet you."

We drop hands when the bartender sets our drinks down, eye contact breaking. When it does, the rest of the room comes rushing back. I don't remember it fading away, slowly blurring around the edges, but I have to blink to make sense of it again.

"So, Thomas," she says, and the way my name snaps off her tongue with the sharp consonants of her American accent is surprisingly sexy. "Are you winning the championship so far?"

That really goes to show she's unaware of me, because I'm so far away from winning the Drivers' Championship it's comical. Seventh in the points isn't bad by any means, but it sure isn't first.

It would be impossible to quickly explain the ins and outs of this season so far, so I answer with, "No, but I did make it onto the podium in the last race."

"Ah," she murmurs sagely. "So you're a loser."

She's prodded at a sore spot, but I keep the well-practiced smile on my face. "Some might call me that."

"You don't seem like a loser to me." She eyes me carefully again before necking the rest of her champagne. She sets the empty flute down a little too hard, then curls her fingers around the new rocks glass. "If anyone's a loser here, it's me."

It's an odd slip in the confidence she's been radiating, and she flinches when she realizes what she's said. "God, sorry." She exhales a wavering laugh. "I'm just a little bitter. Don't mind me."

I can feel her struggling to regain her previous bearing even as she shakes out her hair and pushes her shoulders back. Part of me is almost tempted to walk away—I don't need to get sucked into someone else's pity party—but the fact that she's fighting to break free of it keeps me in my seat. And all right, I'll admit it . . . I'm curious what could rattle a woman like this.

I wait until she's taken a long swig of her drink before asking, "Any particular reason for the bitterness?"

She swallows, and to her credit, she doesn't wince at the burn of liquor. "You don't read the gossip rags?" she drawls, side-eyeing me. "Check DeuxMoi every morning with your cup of Earl Grey?"

"You're famous enough for that?" I gently lob back with a crooked smile, though it's interesting that I'm talking to someone who's well-known enough to make it into the gossip pages.

Thankfully, it gets her to laugh, and some of the tension in her posture seeps away again. "Way to keep my ego in check."

"To be fair, you didn't know who I was either."

"Touché. Well, if you really want to know my deep, dark story . . . I got left at the altar two weeks ago."

It takes a beat before her words hit me, but my jaw quickly goes slack. Someone left *this* woman on their wedding day? Seems unbelievable having only known her for five minutes, though maybe underneath the good looks and intense charm is a monster. Still, I thought that kind of thing only happened in movies. "You're joking."

"Sadly, no." She flashes a tight smile. "Five years of my life, down the drain in the span of a few seconds."

"My God," I exhale, gut-punched on her behalf. Even if she's some sort of demon, I couldn't imagine waiting so long to break up with someone that you left it until you were about to say your vows. I may not have any relationship experience, but at least I know better than to do *that*. "That's devastating."

"Yes, thank you for the reminder," she says with fake cheer.

I shrug, nonchalant, even though there's a chance I've already made her regret her choice to talk to me. But I'm not going to hold back or lie. "I'd say sorry, but it seems you've dodged a bullet."

She freezes, glass once again halfway to her lips. "How so?"

It's a good sign she's still willing to entertain me, and I mean it when I say, "Any man who'd leave on your biggest day is a cunt you wouldn't want to be tied to for the rest of your life."

Her eyes go wide, a beat passing where I wonder if she'll tell me to fuck off . . . but then she laughs. The sound is a rumble in the air. It's full-throated and genuine, nothing melodic about it. Nothing sweet or put on. And I like it far more than I should.

"Breaking out the *C-word*. I barely know you, mister."

"It seemed fitting."

"You're absolutely right about that," she agrees, lifting her glass a little higher. "How about we toast to it?"

I wrap my hand around my drink and bring it up to hers, gently tapping the rims against each other as I catch her gaze. "To cunts," I announce grandly. "May they stay out of our lives."

She takes a sip of her drink, her tongue swiping across her vermilion-painted bottom lip as she lowers the glass again. The action has my eyes flicking to her mouth, and if her spreading smile is anything to go by, she's noticed.

"You know," she says as she sets her glass down. "I hoped you'd be a little more vulgar with it."

"Yeah?" I prompt as I move to drink more. I need to catch up with her. I also need a distraction from the sinfulness of her lips. "What did you want me to say?"

"Oh, maybe something more along the lines of *The only cunt I'm interested in is the one between your legs.*"

I nearly choke on the whiskey. Coughing, I pound a fist to my chest to clear away the errant liquor. "*Christ*, woman."

I could tell she was bold, but this is a level I didn't expect. It's not unpleasant or unwelcome—not in the slightest. It's compelling and downright entertaining. I like women with no filters, the ones who speak their minds and go after what they want. Demureness is boring.

And besides, she wasn't wrong to hope I'd say something a little more indecent. Under different circumstances, I'd be more than happy to give her exactly what she wanted.

She twirls a lock of hair around her finger, the picture of innocence, but warm amusement rolls off her. She's playing with me. There's something else with it, though, something a little hotter, and it's starting to burn in me as well.

"Was that too much?" she asks coyly.

I already swore I was going to keep myself out of trouble tonight, to be content to just sit here and chat. That was supposed to be enough. But Stella's mouth—in more ways than one—is about to have me going back on my word.

"No," I say, almost surprised that it comes out as more than a rasp. "Just enough."

 **CHAPTER 4**

STELLA

Old Stella is back.

I've hooked a man in five minutes flat, which isn't a new record, but it's on par with the woman I used to be. And God, it feels good.

"Just enough," I echo him, not daring to look away lest I lose the confidence I've regained. But his gaze is so intense that I'm not sure I could even if I wanted to. "All right, if you say so."

I know I pressed my luck with Prince Charming here. He could have found me and my little adjustment of his toast crude and off-putting. I wouldn't have been surprised, given his aggressively posh bearing, but when he looked at my lips like he was imagining them doing something more than talking, I figured I might as well try.

And am I glad I did, because the way his eyes lit up after he recovered was worth the risk. A win I desperately needed. The spark it sent through my blood was only a bonus.

It's nice to feel wanted again. Nice to know my allure hasn't completely vanished. It's been hard not to think I've completely lost it, considering I couldn't keep my fiancé's attention in the final months of our relationship, but this is proof that I can still draw people in. That I can still be lusted after.

Unfortunately, it doesn't do much to close the gaping hole that lingers in my chest, but this is like a Band-Aid pulling the edges together. I'll take it over having nothing.

"I promise it's a compliment," Thomas says, fingertips skimming over my bare knee. "I appreciate boldness."

His touch leaves a trail of heat in its wake, stirring something to life inside me. But I don't get the chance to give it a name, because the feeling is devoured by sharp, gut-churning guilt. Guilt that I've betrayed my fiancé by shamelessly flirting with this man.

I have to quickly remind myself that I don't have a fiancé anymore. I'm not in a relationship. I have no one to be loyal to. No one to cheat on. And I said I was going to cause a riot tonight, didn't I? A girl can't do that if she's holding herself back.

But if I really want to inspire the most chaos—and prove to Daphne that I'm not the saint she thinks I am—it's time for me to lure in my next victim. This one was only supposed to be a stop along the way, my first of many conquests tonight.

Except . . . I don't really want to find another.

First of all, I'm comfortable here at the bar, away from the shrill screams of winning women and the shouted curses of losing men coming from around the room. Second, Thomas is actually putting the *charm* into the Prince Charming nickname—boy can banter. And third . . . maybe Old Stella doesn't need to come *all* the way back. I've already proved to myself that she's still here, that she's just been hibernating. That matters more than proving anything to some mean girl.

And all right, he's easily the hottest man in the room. Why would I leave just to find someone less appealing?

"Good," I tell Thomas, and then I toss back the rest of my

old-fashioned. When I set down the empty glass, I level him with a smile as the whiskey warms my veins. "Then you can get me another drink."

He laughs, deep and low, but he's already lifting a hand to signal to the bartender. It gives me a chance to sneakily assess him again. He's prettier than I first thought, with the lightest smattering of freckles across his nose and a few faint laugh lines around his eyes. He might have been wearing that grimace earlier, but this is a man who smiles often.

When he finishes ordering, he looks back at me, an expectant lift to his brow. "Any ideas for what our next toast should be?"

I pretend to think, tapping a finger against my jaw. "How about to the absolutely ridiculous bride and groom who thought a combined bachelor and bachelorette party was a good idea?"

The corners of his lips twitch up, his gaze sliding out to the crowd where I'm sure Janelle and Ron are acting like fools. "Did you know in Canada they have a name for this kind of thing? 'Buck and doe.'"

How funny that I'd been thinking about that same trivia tidbit earlier. I won't read into it, but it's a fraction of a point in his favor. Instead, I shake my head in disgust. "I *knew* there was something off about the Canadians."

He laughs again, the sound wrapping around me like a warm embrace. "I feel the need to stick up for a Commonwealth nation, but I fear this is indefensible."

"I'm just kidding," I say breezily, eyes flicking to the bartender as he sets down our next round. "I love Canada. My most successful store is in Vancouver. Beautiful city."

"Store?"

"Ah, that's right," I muse, cocking my head to the side as I smile sweetly at him. "You still don't know who I am."

My eyes track his movements as he reaches for his glass and—Lord have mercy, man's got big hands. Long fingers and broad palms, the kind I could imagine doing wicked things.

Too soon, Stella. You're not ready for that.

"Then tell me."

I have to take a sip of my drink to wet my suddenly dry mouth before I can reply. "I'm an entrepreneur."

It's a vague answer, but there's not much else that sums up my career and all the things that make it up.

Of course he calls me out on it. "That doesn't explain why you're famous."

"Not famous, per se," I correct. "Well-known in certain circles."

He shakes his head, almost like he's disappointed in me for playing coy. He must not have been lying about liking boldness.

"Give me more than that." He leans in, our eyes catching again. There's a curiosity in his gaze that takes me aback because I can't remember the last time a man looked at me with such interest. "Tell me who you are."

My heart's beating faster. This isn't a competition, but it still feels like I'm losing the upper hand. He's supposed to be on *my* hook. I'm not supposed to be dangling from his.

"What do you want to know?" I ask.

"Start from the beginning. Give me the highlights."

"The beginning? All right." I huff out a laugh and settle into my seat. "I was born in Atlanta to the CEO of a major food conglomerate and a corporate lawyer. They met when my father's company was being investigated for fraud. My mother won his case. He proposed soon after." I leave out how the man's been whipped ever since. Or how my vision of true love looks like them. "I grew up doing beauty pageants and modeled as a teenager, then went to college at Georgetown for accounting. And then I . . . blew up on social media."

"Blew up?"

This is the actual beginning most people are interested in, but it's disingenuous to leave out the earlier parts, especially the wealth and privilege I come from. Nothing in my life would have been possible without it.

"I used to bake a lot in college," I explain. "It was a stress reliever. And I was *very* good at it." No use being humble, considering what I've accomplished. "So I would post my bakes and recipes online. I made little videos, really let my personality shine through—just had fun with it. I was known for my macarons."

It's slow, but I can see the recognition beginning to dawn. Oh, he knows who I am. He just didn't realize there was an actual person behind the name on the storefront.

"I got a lot of messages asking me when I was planning to open my own bakery," I go on. "It wasn't until my senior year that I started thinking about it seriously. I mean, a career in accounting sounded stable, but it sounded *boring*—unless I could work it into something I actually cared about. Like baking. My parents didn't love the idea, but my father bankrolled the flagship patisserie in DC, and that was it. In eight years, we've opened a hundred locations with more on the way."

Heavy silence follows my story, and Thomas searches my face like he's seeing me with new eyes.

"You're not just *Stella*," he finally says, and I swear there's a note of impressed awe in the words. "You're Stella *Margaux*."

"Guilty as charged."

"Huh." He leans back, elbow propped on the bar as he looks me over again, a grin spreading across his face. "How unexpected."

"About as unexpected as me meeting a race car driver." I take another sip of my drink, the liquor easing its way through me. "And I'm Stella Baldwin, actually," I amend. "Margaux is my middle name. I figured it sounded better for a macaron shop."

"It does have a nice ring to it."

"And macarons aren't my only venture." I don't know why I'm still speaking, but there's something about the way he's willing to sit here and soak in my every word that has me wanting to ramble on. "I have my fingers in a few pies."

His brow rises. "Literally?"

"Some days."

Another laugh breaks free from him.

"I have other bakeries," I explain, encouraged by his amusement. "My sweet tooth couldn't be contained with just macarons. I also have a few cafés and boutiques, but those are a pretty new venture."

"You're making me feel inadequate," he says, but there's no resentment behind the confession. "All I do is drive around a track for a living while you're out here taking over the world."

I drop my voice to a loud whisper. "And you're not even winning. I'm *much* more impressive."

When he laughs this time, he throws his head back, drawing my eyes down the line of his neck.

"You find me very funny, don't you?" He's been delighted by nearly everything I've said, no matter how dry or deprecating. With most people, I try to tone it down to keep from coming off as insulting, but I can't hold it back with him. More importantly, he seems to understand my humor, something Étienne hardly did.

Stop thinking about him. It's not like he's thinking about you.

Thomas shoots me a grin as he recovers. "What can I say?" he admits. "You're incredibly entertaining."

"I think you mean *honest*."

"I was trying to have some tact."

"Very English of you."

"Nice of you to notice."

"But you did call my ex a cunt," I point out, enjoying this back-and-forth far more than I should. "I think it's a little late for tact."

"And you all but invited me to fuck you, so I'd say we're on equal footing."

Heat blazes through me like a wildfire, settling somewhere in my lower belly as he stares me down. I have a name for that earlier feeling now—attraction. Maybe even desire. It's been so long since I've felt anything like it that the sensation is almost foreign. But this time, miraculously, only a faint brush of guilt joins it.

"As far as I remember," I say, trying not to let on to how breathless his casual comment has left me, "I was just giving you another option for a toast. It wasn't an invitation."

And it's true. This night isn't going to end with us in bed—or pressed up against a wall in a dark corner, or locked in a grody bathroom stall. Old Stella wasn't sleeping with everyone, but she was certainly (and happily) leading them on. That's all this is going to be.

He could get up and walk away now that he knows there's no chance of us hooking up. I wouldn't blame him for it either. Why waste his time hitting on me—if that's even what he's doing—if it's not going to go anywhere? I don't think he'll call me a bitch or a cocktease, like some other men might in this situation, but what do I know? This guy's a stranger I just happen to have a mutual connection with, and we've been thrown together in one of the strangest situations imaginable.

"Good to know," he says, like it's really that easy for him to accept the limit I've set. "I'm perfectly fine with just talking."

I snort, not buying it. "Oh, really? Am I that interesting?"

"Compared to our current company?" We both glance out at the rest of the high rollers' room just as Sydney climbs up onto one of the poker tables and throws a shower of plastic chips in the air with a joyous squeal. "I'm happy spending my night with you."

He's already looking at me when I turn my head back, his eyes like pools of dark water, threatening to drown anyone who dares to stare for too long. Even I'm tempted to take a dip.

My stomach churns again, stirring heat through me. I didn't expect to feel anything like this so soon after ending a relationship. It feels wrong and yet agonizingly right.

"Sweet words," I finally eke out, lifting my glass again in hopes that more whiskey will wash away whatever's simmering in my gut. Instead, it's like throwing gasoline on a flame.

I have to glance away, so I stare down at my lap. At some point, and I couldn't say when, I uncrossed my legs. Now we're fully facing each other, my knees parted just enough that one of his has slipped between them, while the other brackets my right leg, almost as if he's keeping me from bumping it against the bar. It's annoyingly considerate.

But it also means he can probably see up my dress. Not that I mind. Someone other than me might as well admire my designer lingerie, five hundred dollars' worth of chocolate-brown lace—but admiring is all he's going to be able to do.

Well . . . unless I let him do more.

Flustered by the intrusive thought, I hear myself say,

"Excuse me. I need to go powder my nose." And then I'm pushing his knee away and slipping off my barstool. I grab my clutch before hurriedly following signs for the restroom.

I pull out my phone the second I step into the dimly lit back hallway, and fire off a text to my best friend as I try to breathe deeply. I need to cool down and get a handle on whatever fucked-up hormones have me sweating, because this is *not* appropriate.

STELLA: There is a very hot man here and I'm trying not to act a fool. Tell me to get my shit together.

I wish she were here tonight, and she would have been if she hadn't broken her tibia five days ago while on a skiing trip in the Alps with her husband. While she's technically not related to Janelle, Daphne, and me by blood, she's still considered one of the Baldwin cousins since we all grew up together. More of our family photos have her in them than not.

Her reply pops up on my screen within seconds.

MIKA: Go fuck him

I guess that's what I get for asking her to convince me to do the right thing. Of my cousins, Janelle's the angel on my shoulder. Mika's the devil in a little red dress.

STELLA: That was NOT the answer I was looking for

MIKA: Why not??? You need to get laid, it's been too long. Pussy's probably got cobwebs all up in it at this point

Instead of replying, I call her.

"First of all, that was just rude," I scold when she answers after the third ring. "And second of all, I am *not* about to make any bad decisions tonight."

"Hooking up with a hot guy is not a bad decision," she counters without missing a beat. "Besides, he knows Ron, right? And don't we like Ron? Doesn't that mean this guy's essentially been vetted?"

We do like Ron. Mika and I put him through hell when he first started dating Janelle so we could be certain he wasn't an asshole who'd mistreat our girl. In the year they've been together, I don't know if I've ever seen a man—other than my father and Mika's husband—more hopelessly devoted to his partner. I'd be jealous if I weren't so hideously happy for her.

"He's a good guy," I concede. "But that doesn't automatically extend to the people he knows." And, as I've learned, Thomas isn't even close with him.

"You don't need a good guy to get your rocks off," she points out. "You're hooking up with him, not marrying—"

"Hey!" I interrupt. "Still sensitive about that topic, all right?"

She heaves a sigh. "I know, I know. But, babe, you and Frenchie just weren't meant to be. You need to put yourself back out there. He's certainly not wasting any time."

Her nickname for Étienne brings a hint of a smile to my lips. "I will eventually, but for now I'm trying to—" I cut myself short when her last sentence registers. "Wait, what do you mean he's not wasting any time?"

Silence crackles across the line. If there's one thing Mika never is, it's quiet.

"Mika, what did you mean?" I press.

"Stella, don't worry about it," she finally says, but from her tone I know she didn't mean to let that slip.

"Well, I *am* worried about it."

She groans, hesitant to tell me anything. "Look, I may have heard that he was spotted out with a woman last night and that they looked . . . cozy."

"Cozy?" I repeat, trying to keep the hysterical note out of my voice, but it's no use. "The fuck does that mean?"

"Stella . . ."

"Tell me."

"It means they were kissin' and cuddlin', all right?" she says bluntly. She's not doing it to hurt my feelings—she knows how much I appreciate honesty—but it still makes me wince.

I swallow past the growing lump in my throat. "And you trust the source it came from?"

"Well, the source was my own eyes, so . . ."

So Étienne really was out in the streets with someone else two weeks after leaving me at the fucking altar.

"You've *got* to be kidding me," I mumble, wanting to rub away the burn behind my eyes but knowing better than to ruin my mascara.

There's a strong chance he was cheating on me for at least part of the time we were together, especially toward the end, but I never had proof or anything more than my intuition. Hearing this, though . . . It makes me wonder what I might have been willfully oblivious to, all because I was so desperate to make it work.

I can't deal with this. Not here, not now. There's a pinching in my chest that always precedes a sob session, but I refuse to break down right now. Étienne stole so much from me already; I'm not about to let him steal more of my dignity by crying in the dark hallway of a casino.

"I'm really sorry, honey," Mika says, and I know she genuinely is. "But if not wanting to go out and have the time of your life has anything to do with loyalty to him, throw it out. He doesn't deserve it. It's time for you to go live your life without that dour French storm cloud hanging over you. C'est la vie, right?"

I pinch the bridge of my nose to ward off the tears, but I can't help the watery laugh that escapes me at her horrible attempt at a French accent. "Pretty sure you're not using that phrase correctly."

"Hey, you're the one who took lessons, not me."

It's a reminder of all the things I sunk into that relationship: French lessons so I could chat with his grandparents, missing store openings because he wanted me to constantly travel to Paris with him, all the nights I stayed out too late entertaining his business associates even though I had my own important meetings the next morning. I put a lot into keeping us together, only to be repaid with heartbreak and disrespect.

"I want you to be yourself again," Mika goes on when I don't say anything. "I want *my* Stella back."

I glance toward the doorway to the high rollers' room. "I was actually trying to bring her back tonight." If I thought Daphne's comments were enough to inspire Old Stella's return, then this news about Étienne has made me more determined to not hold back.

"Don't let me stop you," she says brightly. "I'm living vicariously through you right now. Kind of hard to get it on when you've got a cast halfway up your leg, though that hasn't put me off trying. Let's just say we've been getting creative with it."

"Good for you, babe." My eyes are drying, my smile returning. "Just don't break anything else."

"No promises. But hey, why are you wasting time talking to me? Go get that dick."

"There will be no dick getting tonight," I tell her firmly,

though I'm not sure who I'm trying to convince—her or myself. "But I *will* be flirting like my life depends on it."

She's right that I need to get myself out of this funk. It's okay to grieve, to sit and lick my wounds, but it's also okay to live my life however the hell I want. Who's going to stop me?

When we hang up, I swing by the bathroom to look at myself in the mirror and make sure my makeup is still perfect. I throw in a little pep talk for good measure.

"You're a fucking knockout," I tell my reflection as I zhuzh the roots of my silk press. "Total package. Brains *and* amazing tits."

It's the speech I know Mika would give me if she were here. For the rest of the night, I'm determined to cling to the devil on my shoulder. The angel's busy anyway.

Thomas is still sitting in the same place when I come back, his gaze tracking me as I approach. There's a part of me that expected him to be there, yet there's another part that's surprised he hasn't moved. He really didn't get up to find a different conversation? To find someone he can actually take to bed tonight?

"I think we're gearing up for the next event," he announces as I slip back onto my barstool, and I watch the waitresses attempting to herd people toward the elevators. "Want to be my buddy for this excursion? Something tells me this night is going to devolve into mayhem."

I don't think he's wrong about that. And considering he's been decent company so far, I wouldn't mind hanging out a little longer. He's making what started as a terrible night into something bearable. "I'll watch your back if you watch mine," I offer.

"Great, because I'm not sure I like how that lady over there is looking at me." He nods toward a woman a few feet away, sipping her vodka cran through a tiny straw as she shoots coquettish glances in his direction.

"That's Christine," I whisper like I'm sharing a dark secret. "You're right to be worried. She's on the hunt for her fourth husband. Number three disappeared under suspicious circumstances last year."

His eyebrows nearly shoot up into his hairline. "Seriously?"

"Nah, I've actually never seen that woman in my life." I hop off my barstool and offer him my hand. "Come on. Let's get the fuck out of here."

 **CHAPTER 5**

THOMAS

Nothing about tonight is going the way I expected. And that's a good thing.

I presumed this party was going to teeter somewhere between a bore and a nightmare, but right now, it's sitting on a completely different scale. All because of Stella.

She held on to my elbow during the journey from the high rollers' room back down to the casino floor, supposedly because of her shoes, which she proclaimed were *nothing short of a thousand-dollar death trap*, but I'm choosing to believe she just wanted an opportunity to feel me up. Now she's sitting next to me on the party bus, our shoulders and thighs pressed together thanks to the crowd pushing in from all sides. They were already a rowdy bunch, but after money won and lost and a handful more drinks in their systems, they're even worse.

We're jostled and tossed about as the bus lurches into motion. Almost everyone is cheering, ready for the next part of the night, and some of my earlier apprehension creeps back in now that we've left the safety and security of the casino.

"You're doing that British thing again," Stella shouts over the music.

I glance down at her, brow furrowing, but I'm tempted to laugh nonetheless. Some of the things she says . . . they truly come out of nowhere. But fuck if it doesn't get my mind off the thoughts that haunt me. "I'm sorry?"

"That." She lifts a finger to motion to my face before contorting her mouth into a confused mix between a pitying smile and a grimace. "That face is very 'my family is titled and I have a career that requires me to wear a powdered wig, but I swear I'm a man of the people.'" The statement is said in the worst attempt at an English accent I think I've ever heard. Like if Queen Elizabeth II grew up in Liverpool but was also somehow South African.

This time, I can't hold back a guffaw. "Are you serious? I literally told you I'm a Formula 1 driver."

"You didn't deny the title," she says, though she moves on before I can even try to do so. "Are you really having that awful a time, your highness?"

I hitch my chin higher to sell my forthcoming joke. "The proper address for me is 'my lord.'"

Her eyes go wide. "Are you seri—"

"I'm *kidding*," I interrupt, laughing as I bump her shoulder with mine. Americans. So gullible. "I don't have a title." My grandfather does, but she doesn't need to know that. "And no, I'm not having that awful a time."

"Maybe tell that to your face."

"Well then, maybe someone should explain to my face why the bride and groom are currently trying to consume each other five feet away from us."

I've been attempting to ignore it, to focus instead on the gorgeous woman beside me, but it's hard to block out the two people practically dry humping at the front of the bus.

Stella leans forward to peer around me.

"Now *you're* doing the British thing," I point out when she produces a grimacing smile. "But I guess it's nice to see just how in love they are."

"Nah, it's sickening," she confirms. "Still happy for them, though."

Something in her expression changes then, and her attention darts away from the entirely-too-happy couple. Instead, it settles on the woman who's just dropped into a seat across from us. Even with the motion of the bus, the woman's short hair doesn't move a centimeter.

Her eyes narrow as she takes in the two of us, as if she's not enjoying what she sees. When Stella suddenly throws her long legs across my knees like she's claiming me and smirks back at the woman, I start to understand what's going on here.

This is a game. And it probably has been all along, from the very second she laid eyes on me.

Stella sucks in a breath when I wrap my arm around her shoulders and pull her into my side. I get a hit of her perfume as I do. It's something sharp but sweet, like a citrus bloom off the coast of somewhere warm. Someplace I've been before and couldn't get enough of.

I inhale it again as I bring my lips down to her ear. "Was I just a challenge to you?" I murmur, glancing at the other woman for a split second before returning my gaze to Stella. "Part of whatever game you're playing?"

Her eyes swing up to mine, almost Bambi-like with their innocence, but she's grinning. "It's not exactly a game," she says, not upset that I've caught on. I think she's *proud* of me. "But would you be mad if I said you were part of it?"

"No," I admit. I knew she was prowling from the start; the reason for it doesn't matter. "I'm flattered you thought I was good enough to play along." I spare another look at the woman, who's frowning so deeply that I fear her face might get stuck that way. "Do you need more help with whatever it is you're trying to prove to that woman?"

"I wouldn't say no," Stella muses. "But just so you're aware, it wasn't about you specifically. I mainly wanted to show her that I could act like a 'nasty little slut' if I wanted to."

I blink, pulling back a little, though not letting her go. "Excuse me?"

"Her words, not mine," she reassures, reaching up to pat my cheek. She's clearly not going to explain past that. "But it's cute how that ruffled you."

"Not ruffled." After all, those words have left my lips before, though only in the bedroom and only when agreed upon. "Just surprised."

Her hand slips to my neck, fingers cool against my heated skin. "So . . . you still want to help me with proving that?"

I'm sure she can feel the way my pulse thuds at the base of my throat. That should be answer enough. I have questions, though. "That depends. Are you trying to prove it for real or just for appearances?"

Her touch stills, but her eyes stay locked on mine, searching for something, like maybe they hold the answer she's looking for. The truth is, *I* don't even know what answer I'm hoping for. But with each drink and every second I spend with her, I'm starting to think I want to invite a little trouble into my life. Besides, it would only be for tonight. I don't get the feeling she'd want more than that, and I'm not looking for it either.

"I haven't quite decided yet," she finally says.

I nod, free hand sliding over her thighs, skimming the feathered hem of her dress. I swear the woman across from us is about to explode with rage. "I can work with that."

Stella's brows rise, her eyes still not looking away. It's almost a staring contest at this point, the prequel to more challenges I'm sure are to come. "Yeah?"

"Yeah," I repeat, gently stroking her leg. She has the softest skin I've ever touched. If I were to slide my hand higher, would the rest of her be just as soft? "But you call the shots. You tell me how far we take this. You tell me to stop, I stop. No questions."

"What a gentleman," she drawls, reminding me of the women from earlier, and I have to wonder if she saw that interaction—if that's when she first set her sights on me. "But okay. I think you and I could have some fun tonight."

"We haven't already?"

Her grin tells me everything so far has only been a warm-up.

"Then I guess I'm in for—" I cut short when my phone buzzes in the pocket of my trousers. "One second," I tell Stella as I reluctantly pull my hand away from her thighs to grab it. When I see who's calling, I can't hold back an eye roll. It's like she knows when I'm paying attention to another woman.

Sending the call to voicemail, I move to put the device back in my pocket so I can return to my conversation with Stella. Before I can, it rings again, Figgy's name and picture—one that she programmed in my phone herself—reappearing. I decline it even faster this time.

"Someone you don't want to talk to?"

I glance at Stella, expecting her to be staring at the bubbly blonde who pops up on my screen once more, but she's looking at me. There's no judgment in her tone or her eyes, just calm curiosity.

So that's probably why I confess, "It's the girl my parents want me to marry."

She's surprised by my honesty, blinking rapidly a few times, but she's grinning sharply a split second later, like her choice to talk to me has really paid off. I'm fascinating after all.

"I'm guessing you're not interested in that," she surmises.

"No, not in the slightest." It's easy to admit this to someone who doesn't know me, who doesn't know Figgy or our history or our families. Or maybe it's just easy admitting things to Stella. Feels only fair after she confessed to her failed wedding. "She's never been my type."

Stella lifts her chin, neck on perfect display, tempting me to lean in and press my lips to the space where it meets her jaw. "What's your type, Thomas?"

You. "Not her."

Stella takes that in. I don't miss the way her eyes flick to my mouth, like she was imagining the same thing I was. She recovers better, back to looking up at me through her lashes as her fingers find the hair that brushes my collar, playfully twisting the strands. Not even the woman huffing loudly across the bus can get me to look away.

"I've told you my story," Stella says. "Time to tell me yours."

Mine isn't nearly as interesting, but I always reciprocate.

"Born and raised in London," I begin, phone in my hand still flashing with Figgy's face. "Middle child—one older brother, one older sister, and two younger sisters. Started kart racing when I was five because my brother was doing it and I wanted to be just like him. He eventually gave it up, went to university instead, but I stuck with it. I won championships in the UK and then around the world. Left school at fourteen. Moved to single-seaters and worked my way up through the Formulas." There's a hell of a lot more that happened over those years, but this is only supposed to be an overview. "Now here I am at the pinnacle of motorsport, driving for the team I was obsessed with as a kid."

She makes a thoughtful sound. "Living the dream, are you?"

What gets me is how she doesn't seem particularly impressed. Like all of this is routine. Like she's met far more accomplished people in her life. I wouldn't doubt that she has, and something about that—the lack of fawning, the acceptance of my story as completely normal—makes me like her even more.

But her question . . . Does she realize how loaded it is? Sure, five years in Formula 1 and a handful of wins under my belt should constitute *living the dream*. But is it, when you really look underneath it all? When I've never won a championship and likely never will? When I'm loathed by a broad majority? When my family is pushing for me to settle down so I can have something to focus on when *the dream* ultimately ends? An end that could come at any time in a sport like this?

"Not really, no," I hear myself say through the familiar spiral.

I don't mean to confess it. I'm all about honesty, but this . . . this isn't something I've even been completely honest with myself about yet. *Of course* I'm living the dream. It shouldn't even be a doubt in my mind.

Yet it is.

The question is in her expression before her lips can form the words. But she doesn't get a chance to ask it, because the bus comes to a hard stop that would have had her toppling to the floor if I hadn't grabbed her legs again.

"Thanks, Prince Charming," she chirps, shooting me a wink. It lightens the weight that's settled on my chest, the one that always comes when I start thinking a little too hard about my life and career.

I even welcome the distraction of Ron grabbing the microphone and announcing that we've arrived at our next stop, as if we couldn't already tell by the most aggressive braking I've ever experienced, even as a professional driver.

Stella taps my knuckles, prompting me to let her go so she can put her feet on the ground. I'm a little more reluctant to slip my arm from around her shoulders, but the lack of contact is brief, since she's quick to lift her lips to my ear and grab my hand.

"I won't abandon you, I promise," she murmurs. I can't see her smirk, but I can feel it. "Besides, the look on Daphne's face is just too good."

My eyes rise from our hands to the woman across from us who's just stood up. Her mouth is puckered like she's taken a hard suck on a lemon, hands fluttering over her white dress as she roughly brushes out nonexistent wrinkles in the fabric. I don't understand what her problem with Stella is, but she's not doing anything to endear herself to me.

And because sometimes I can't resist the urge to stir a little shit, I lift the back of Stella's hand to my mouth and press a lingering kiss to her skin.

"Shall we head inside, darling?" I ask, loud enough to be heard over the music—and by Daphne.

Delight flashes across Stella's face as I stand and help her up. Does the action force Daphne to take a stumbling step back to avoid getting trampled by Stella's stilettos? Perhaps. Do I care? Not in the slightest.

"You're going to have to tell me the whole story about what's going on with you and that woman," I murmur to Stella as she slips past me in the aisle, making me the buffer between her and Daphne.

She snickers and tosses her hair, the black silk curtain tumbling across her shoulders. I get another hit of her scent when she does, tart and fresh. It suits her perfectly. "All you need to know is that she's another one of my cousins and a judgmental monster," she whispers back. "And I'm pretty sure she sold the story about my wedding to the press."

"In that case, she's public enemy number one in my book."

Stella's laugh brushes over me like a caress. "Glad you're on my team."

Our linked fingers rest just above the lush curve of her ass as she leads me off the bus and through the doors of another hotel on the Strip. The familiar anxiety of being spotted creeps into my stomach, but it fades a little when Stella glances back at me, almost like she can sense my hesitation. Still, I'm tempted to let go of her hand; the last thing I need is to be publicly linked to anyone in the midst of the Lorenzo Castellucci drama. Stella doesn't deserve it either.

Thankfully, the raucous crowd surrounding us acts as a shield, and any photographers would have to work hard to spot us through it, so I hold tight to her as our party is herded through the expansive lobby.

As we walk, I press close to her, wanting to pick up our conversation again. "Why is your cousin so rude to you?" I ask as we turn down a wide, shop-lined corridor.

Stella easily keeps up with my long strides, even in those wild heels that make her nearly as tall as me. "Daphne's always been like that. One of those people who thinks if you don't live life exactly like her, you're doing it wrong. We've never gotten along, but Janelle keeps trying to convince me to give her a chance since we're family."

I almost snort. I know damn well blood can mean nothing, but I keep the comment to myself. "Janelle seems very kind," I say instead.

And Ron's a lucky man to have swung a woman like that, because the more I learn about her, the less I understand how he pulled it off. The guy I knew growing up was practically a bully—but then again, so was my older brother, and now he just ignores me. Maybe some people do change.

"She is," Stella confirms. "She's sweet and softhearted. Biggest romantic you'll ever meet. But she's a shark in the courtroom. If you ever need a defense attorney in Georgia, she's your woman." There's a pause before she hesitantly says, "Well, I . . . guess not anymore, considering she's moving to London with Ron after their honeymoon."

I can feel the dip in her mood, though she's quick to beam up at me again, trying to mask it. Underneath it all, she's not happy about Janelle giving up her career or moving to another country. Maybe both.

Or maybe it's about something else entirely. I won't pretend I know her—I met the woman barely two hours ago, even if being around her feels entirely too comfortable.

"Has she not already been living there?" I ask. I couldn't say why I'm curious, but Stella and Janelle's dynamic is unfamiliar to me. I have cousins, sure, but we barely know each other.

"She's been splitting her time between there and Atlanta," Stella explains. "And I live in DC, so it's not like we see each other all that often, but . . . it's going to be harder once she's permanently across an ocean."

"Planes exist," I point out, flashing her a cheeky smile as I bump her elbow, compelled to cheer her up for some reason.

This time, her grin is far more authentic. "*And* I'm rich enough to fly private." She then sobers some. "But I won't. Because I care about the environment."

"Wow, someone better get you the Nobel Prize."

"Thank you, I'm very deserving."

As I stifle a laugh, we're guided into a dimly lit restaurant. I keep my head down as we're led past tables of other patrons until we reach a private room. There's a crystal chandelier hanging low over a long table, which is outfitted with lavish place settings—and, unfortunately, place cards with names on them.

"Damn. Assigned seating," I mumble, spotting Stella's name at the end of the table, but mine is nowhere near it. "Think they'd notice if we switched around the cards?"

"Janelle absolutely would. She probably spent hours figuring out this seating plan." Stella lets out a soft huff of fond amusement, and then her eyes swing up to mine again. "Can you bear being separated from me for eight courses?"

I heave a sigh, reluctantly letting her hand slip from mine. "It'll be a struggle, but I'll try."

Her laugh draws eyes. Several sets of them linger, even from the men I know are married or in committed relationships, but I can't blame them.

It's unreal how beautiful she is. If she hadn't already told me she'd modeled in the past, I would have guessed as much. With legs that long and bone structure that perfect, it would have been a waste if she'd never been in front of a camera. Even now, the fact that she doesn't plaster her face across her storefronts around the world is a shame. This is a woman who deserves to be on billboards.

But a still photo couldn't capture what she's like in motion. It's the way her full lips pull into a smile, or how her nearly black irises catch the light in such a way that it makes me wonder if there are actual sparkles in them. And I can't deny that the way the silk of her dress clings to the curves of her hips when she moves just right has my trousers feeling a little tighter. She's a dream come to life.

"Looks like she's put me between those two," Stella says, either unaware of the handful of men still staring at her or choosing to ignore them. She nods to the footballers standing behind their chairs. "I think they're Ron's former teammates."

She's right, and my stomach sours over the idea of them being near her. It's uncalled-for and frankly ridiculous, considering I have absolutely no claim to her, but I'm dismayed nonetheless. I don't want Stella to move on to a different target—I was perfectly happy to see where being her chosen prey would lead. Even if it was just hours of conversation, even if all I got were a few stolen touches, it would have been better than anything else this night could have brought.

I can't help the sudden wave of possessiveness that crashes over me. Without thinking twice, I slip a hand behind her neck, my thumb brushing against her racing pulse. I want to press against it. Want to hear her gasp in surprise. Want to feel her give in to it.

As it is, I enjoy the way she tilts her head back, relaxing into my touch, waiting for me to explain the move. But I can't explain any of this. Not my actions or this desire to make her want to remember me.

"Don't forget about me in the meantime, yeah?" I murmur, resisting the urge to grip her a little tighter, to drag her to me. To taste that smirk on her lips.

"Oh, Thomas," she chides, but her dark eyes are wickedly alight. "You're unforgettable."

 **CHAPTER 6**

STELLA

I should be embarrassed to be this eager to get back to Thomas. But what can I say? The boy's fascinating.

I've been enjoying slowly unwrapping him, seeing what each new layer reveals. A Formula 1 driver who apparently feels like he's no longer living the dream, with a family breathing down his neck to get married? Fucking delicious. I don't even *need* to flirt with him. I just want to sit him down for an in-depth interview like I'm Oprah. Flirting's just an added bonus.

Moving on to the next event means we can get back to talking. Or maybe a little more than that. I didn't mind his hands on me while we were on the bus, and the way he gripped my neck before we sat down for dinner was . . . Well, it was hot. Panty-wettingly hot to be precise. Prince Charming, with his perfect hair and his polished words, clearly has a darker streak underneath the shiny exterior. Another layer to peel away.

Also, I'm verging on drunk. Each course has come with a wine pairing, and even though I haven't finished off any of the glasses, it's been a lot. I've only taken a few sips of this delicious dessert wine—why the hell wasn't I drinking *this* nectar of the gods while I was hiding out at home?—but I'm cutting myself off. I've got a pleasant buzz going, the kind where I can't keep the grin off my face or stop the heat in my belly from dipping lower every time Thomas and I lock eyes across the table.

Fuck, he's handsome.

Pretty boys, unfortunately, have always been my type, but Thomas is a little more rugged than Étienne. Sharper jaw. Thicker neck. A certain *something* radiating off him that has me nearly giggling. Did I ever feel like that with Étienne? I must have at some point, probably in the beginning . . . but for the life of me, I can't remember. I don't think I want to.

Mika was right. I owe him nothing. But I do owe it to myself to do whatever makes me happy after being miserable for weeks. Months. *Years*, even, if I'm willing to be truthful with myself. How did I ignore it for so long?

Don't go there, the little voice in the back of my head warns. So I won't. Instead, I'll focus on the pretty race car driver who's currently sitting too far away from me.

Thomas has relaxed some since the start of dinner. Like most of the men at the table, he's ditched his tuxedo jacket, and his bow tie is hanging loose around his neck. The moment he rolled his sleeves up to show off strong, veined forearms, I nearly choked on my wine. But I'm enjoying this version of him a little too much. I almost want the buttoned-up parliament-smiling Thomas back. The Victorian gentleman. That one was easier to control myself around.

Because this one? This isn't Prince Charming anymore. This is a rogue.

Heaven help my pussy full of cobwebs. My self-control needs to be Herculean once we leave here. And judging by the waiters clearing away plates and glasses, it's almost time to go.

Thomas is behind me the second I push back my chair,

offering a hand to help me stand. I take it without a second thought because, one, I'm already swaying. And two, I've kind of missed him touching me.

"That was *unbearable*," I groan as we step back and wait for the slightly drunker and slower-moving guests to finally budge. "Those guys were so boring. It's like all they knew how to talk about was soccer. Pardon me, *football*."

Thomas let go of my hand once I was standing, but our fingers brush again down by our sides. I don't know if it's accidental or on purpose. "At least you didn't get stuck between Rachel and Sydney," he mumbles in reply. "Now *that* was a nightmare."

"I thought you liked them?" He at least tolerated them earlier.

"I like you better." He pauses as the words settle like embers in my chest, but he doesn't seem to realize the effect they've had on me. "Also, Rachel kept stealing food from my plate, and Sydney moaned every time she took a bite. Loudly. It was all very rude."

I let out a less-than-flattering wheeze of a laugh, pressing a hand to my mouth to smother it, but Thomas grins down at me, apparently not minding the sound.

He's standing incredibly close. Close enough that I can see that his eyes are ringed by a darker shade of blue and his eyelashes are even longer than I originally thought. It's too intimate for a man I've essentially just met. And yet I find myself shifting toward him, leaning in, letting my shoulder rest against his. My body is inclined to believe we've known each other for ages. When his hand cups my hip, I get the sense that I'm not the only one who feels that way.

"Let's go!" cries a voice from the doors to the private room, and I glance away from Thomas to see Ron waving us out.

"Oh God," Thomas grumbles. "What fresh horror is next?"

"Strip club," I remind him, and there's that grimace again. "It's gonna be a *blast*."

Thankfully, our next stop is only a short walk away instead of another ride on the bus, and he keeps me pressed to his side for the journey. It's mostly for my benefit—these heels were definitely the wrong choice for a night of drinking, plus Daphne has once again made herself known with several loud huffs from behind us—but I'm convinced that he can't keep his hands off me. I shouldn't be so flattered, but goddamn, I'm going to bask in it while I can.

I know we've reached our destination when thudding bass vibrates through the air, and then two very large bouncers appear as we turn a corner.

"We're splitting up for this next endeavor!" Janelle calls from her place between the bouncers. She looks like a five-foot fairy princess next to them in her puff-sleeved dress. "Ladies, with me. Boys, you're with the groom."

Thomas's hand tightens on my hip before falling away, and my stomach drops. It's such a silly reaction, because this is what I wanted all along—separate parties for the bride and groom. But now that it's presented itself, it's no longer an appealing idea.

"See you on the other side," Thomas says regretfully.

I nod. "Unless you get smothered by a stripper's awesomely large bosom and don't make it out alive."

He considers the idea for a moment. "There are worse ways to go. Hope you enjoy your lap dance lessons."

"Can't wait to watch all these girls hump empty chairs."

"If you want, you can imagine it's me you're giving that lap dance to," he offers.

"Now I'm *really* not interested," I protest, but his smirk tells me he can see right through me.

An arm hooking around mine prevents me from saying a proper goodbye, because the next thing I know, I'm being dragged toward the now open doors of the club by Daphne.

"What the hell has gotten into you, Stella?" she hisses in my ear as we step past the bouncers. "Why are you acting like this?"

I have to stifle a gleeful giggle as I blink at her. "Like what?" I ask innocently.

Whatever she says next is lost to the music, which pours from speakers into the dark, vast space. We're up on a landing that encircles the outer edge of the room, with a bar on either side and a few more arched doorways like the one we just walked through. Three steps down is the main pit, where there are curved booths, standing tables with red velvet lamps on them, and wide leather armchairs. They're all placed to have a perfect vantage of the massive stage. A few gleaming poles extend up from it and disappear into the draped black fabric that hides the ceiling with its dips and folds.

As far as strip clubs go—and I've seen a handful in my time—this one is luxurious. Guess I should have expected as much from Janelle. Like Mika and me, girl's got expensive taste.

Daphne is still yapping in my ear, saying something about how I'm not being true to myself and how Janelle will be so disappointed with my behavior, but between the whiskey and the wine, I can't bring myself to pay her any mind. I'm warm and loose and determined to make the best of this time away from the distraction of boys.

I wrangle my arm free from her grip and take a few quick

steps to catch up with Janelle, who's leading us to one of the doorways on the left. Grabbing her hand, I link our fingers together, and swing them back and forth like we're a couple of kids.

"Hi, bride," I greet her. Other than hugging hello when I first stepped onto the party bus earlier, we haven't gotten a chance to spend time together tonight. "How you doin'?"

Janelle beams up at me, her big brown eyes a little glassy from whatever she's been drinking, but otherwise she's flawless. And she doesn't seem disappointed in me at all, so Daphne can go suck an egg.

"Oh, Stella," she says, and I'm starting to wonder if her eyes look that way because she's on the verge of happy tears. "I'm so glad you came."

I squeeze her hand tighter, emotion welling up in my throat. "I wanted to be here for you."

"I know," she reassures as we step through the doorway into a wide back hall decorated with tasteful black-and-white photos of models through the decades. "But you've been through so much lately, I would have understood."

Janelle is like a big sister to me. Our five-year age gap meant she went through nearly everything before me and passed down that knowledge. And everything she didn't—like marriage—we wanted to experience together, thus our closely scheduled weddings.

So much for that working out.

"Well, thanks for insisting I come along, even though your groom's friends are kind of boring," I tease, refusing to get lost in the ache in my chest.

Since we were planning our weddings at the same time, we agreed that we wouldn't make each other participate in our respective bridal parties. We were both just too busy, especially with our demanding careers on top of everything. It's why I wasn't involved in the organization of this combined bachelor-bachelorette night, or else I would have strongly advised against it. Then again, she may not have been *completely* off-base with the choice.

Janelle snickers. "I swear, the only thing most of them know how to talk about is soccer."

"I know! I was telling that to—" I cut short, not wanting to give away whatever I've sparked with Thomas. Even though she's a little drunk, she'll catch on to my interest. "To Daphne."

She brightens. "You guys talked?"

"You could say that."

"I'm so glad." Janelle tugs me closer. "I know you two haven't always seen eye to eye, but thank you for making an effort tonight. It means a lot."

I've yet to tell her my theory that Daphne was the one responsible for leaking the details about my wedding, and I'm certainly not about to spill it now, but one day I'll share my suspicions.

"Oh, yeah, of course," I say as we approach a woman in a black latex dress who's holding a clipboard and standing outside a closed door. "Definitely making an effort. Big effort. Huge."

Thankfully, Janelle's distracted by the woman in front of us, and I avoid anything more than a furrowed brow before she's smiling again. As they chat, I look behind me to find Daphne glowering in my direction. I give her a little finger wave with my free hand. She looks like she's tempted to say something, but a whoosh of air from a door opening has me turning back around.

The woman in the latex dress ushers us into the room with a grand wave of her arm, and Janelle tugs me in with a squeal.

It's a private suite, thankfully big enough to fit all twenty of us, with plenty of space to move about as everyone rushes in. There are a handful of white leather couches, a pole in the center of the room, and a small bar pressed against the wall that has flutes of champagne waiting for us.

Janelle drags me over to it and shoves a glass into my hands. "Down that. Right now."

"What? Why?"

"Believe me," she insists, taking two quick steps backward. "You're going to want it for what's next."

Well, I'm not about to challenge her on that, so I chug like a champ, grab another glass, and drop down on one of the couches next to Rachel.

"Do you have any idea what's—" I start to ask her, but I'm interrupted by the frog-croak-sounding first bars of the song blasting from the speakers.

Oh no. I know this song. It's a classic, albeit a slightly overplayed one, but Ginuwine's "Pony" means only one thing. My fears are confirmed when a shirtless, glistening Adonis of a man strolls through the door, followed by far too many of his equally attractive comrades.

"I know I said we were going to learn how to give lap dances," Janelle shouts over the chaos that's exploded all around us. "But I figured we should get them too!"

I'm in a *Magic Mike* hellscape, but Channing Tatum is nowhere to be found. Not to say that these men don't have impressive . . . features. But nothing about oil-slick abs and banana hammocks is doing it for me tonight. An Englishman in a tux who finds me funny and would rather talk than thrust his package in my face is, shockingly, more my speed right now.

When one of the strippers sets his sights on me, I shove my drink into Rachel's hands and then spring up from the couch, narrowly avoiding the man's touch. This dress is far too expensive for it to end up covered in baby oil and overpowering cologne.

"I'm gonna go find the bathroom," I shout to Janelle when she tries to push me back down. "Way too much wine at dinner! Don't want to accidentally pee on one of these guys, you know?"

It's a gross excuse, and I get a look of disgust, though she waves me off. "Hurry back!"

I will do no such thing, but I nod enthusiastically and then book it.

I wasn't lying to Janelle about having to pee, so I search for signs indicating where the bathrooms are. I spot one farther down the hall and start toward it, passing by another private suite on the way, and I can't resist the urge to peek around the ajar door. Lo and behold, I've found all the men from our party having their own experience with topless dancers. I'm searching for Thomas before I even register what I'm doing, more curious than I should be about how he's handling this turn of events.

I bite my lip to keep from cackling when I spot him. He's on one of the couches with his arms draped across the back, smiling in that powdered-wig way as a woman with the best boob job I've ever seen twerks in his lap. He's barely watching her masterful ass clapping, glancing down every so often as if to confirm that, yes, it's still happening, but otherwise he looks like he's just waiting for it to be over.

I don't stay long enough to see what he does next, scrambling down the hall before I pee my pants from laughing too hard. As it is, there are tears in my eyes, because of *course* he's the kind of man to politely accept a lap dance and then try to act like he isn't hating every second of it.

It's not like I would have faulted him for enjoying it, but it's even funnier to see him so out of place. What gets me is that he's a professional athlete—isn't this just a normal Friday night for his kind? It certainly seemed that way for most of the footballers in the room.

Whatever. His eccentricities shouldn't matter to me, but I can't deny that this has endeared him to me a little more. As much as I like the rogue I saw glimpses of, I've got a soft spot for the prince.

The bathroom is empty when I step inside, and I make quick work of ducking into a stall. When I'm done, I head to the sink to wash my hands, staring at my reflection in the mirror as I do. My mascara is a little smudged and my setting powder is working hard to hold back a glow, but I look good. I look . . . *alive*. I even look happy, if the tipsy grin is anything to go by.

I needed this night. I needed Daphne provoking me. I needed a man who laughed at all my jokes. I even needed a stripper in tiny briefs to try to dry hump me.

I needed to see that the outside world hasn't ended even though mine has imploded.

I finish washing my hands and dry them before grabbing my phone from my clutch. I fire off a text to Mika, updating her on the strippers and promising that I'll give her the full rundown over FaceTime once I'm back in my hotel room. After tucking it away again, I push my way out of the bathroom but stop short when the door to the men's room swings open across the hall.

Thomas steps out a moment later, a paper towel still in his hands as he finishes drying them. There's a flash of surprise in his eyes when he finds me standing there, but it quickly shifts to something pleased. His smile widens as he tosses the balled paper towel into the waste bin to his left, not even looking to see if he made the shot. But he did. Of course he did.

"Well," he says, gaze flicking appreciatively over me. "Fancy meeting you here."

"You stalking me now?" I raise a brow and tilt my head to the side, trying so hard to play it cool, but it's taking everything in me not to grin back at him. "Should I be worried?"

"As someone who's had a stalker before, I'd normally say you should be." He takes a step toward me, sliding his hands into his pockets. "But I'm not stalking you. Just lucky that we keep ending up in the same place."

"That's exactly what a stalker would say," I point out, but I'm closing the distance between us. "Is everyone else so boring that you had to seek me out?"

"Honestly?" We're practically in each other's personal space now. If I leaned in a little more, our chests would brush. "I guess I wasn't interested in having someone shake their ass in my face."

"Is *that* what Ron is doing in there?" I ask, eyes wide with false horror. When he laughs and that newly familiar thrill rushes through me, I let the act fall away. "Same, though. I know I talked a big game about loving Thunder from Down Under, but when they actually showed up, I bailed."

"Such a coward. Are you going to go back and try to be brave?"

"Absolutely the fuck not."

"Me neither."

"I'd love to leave," I admit, sparing a glance down the hall-way to make sure no one is about to come drag us back. "But I don't want to disappoint Janelle by ditching before the night is over."

She'd understand if I told her it was all too much too soon, but I'm determined to put myself as far out there as I can tolerate. Sticking around is part of that.

"I could get us a private room," Thomas offers, and as appealing as that sounds, especially with the way his voice pitches a little lower, I shake my head.

"I don't want to risk missing the others when they leave." Still, there's no way I'm going back to the girls and their boy toys. "Let's grab a booth on the main floor. We can watch whoever's onstage from a distance instead of having asses shaken directly in our faces."

The hand he puts on my hip to gently turn me in the right direction sends heat blooming across my body. There's a layer of fabric between his palm and my skin, and yet it feels searing, daring me to pull away. Instead, I place my own hand on top of his, keeping it there, and match him step for step as we make our way down the hall.

When we turn the corner and move through the archway to the main floor, Thomas's hand slips out from under mine, but just like I did earlier when he seemed almost disappointed that I'd stopped touching him, he grabs me again. This time, he holds on to my fingers and lifts them to shoulder level as he moves sideways down the steps, carefully ushering me down them like he's both helping me not trip and showing me off at the same time. There are seminude women on the stage not twenty feet from us, and yet his eyes are on me. It's such an ego stroke that I nearly shiver.

"Let's grab a spot over there," he says once we're on level ground, nodding to my right.

He keeps a loose grip on my fingers as he walks in front of me, only dropping them when we reach an empty table. The banquette around it is curved, allowing us to sit beside each other as we gaze out onto the club's bustling floor and the stage, drinking it all in before turning back to each other.

The lights are low, colorful strobes passing over us every so often, and I can't take my eyes off him. He's a true work of art.

"All right?" Thomas asks, smiling back at me, though there's a question in his eyes.

Right. Aimlessly staring at someone and not speaking isn't exactly normal behavior. "Fine," I answer, and cover up the reason for my silent admiration with a sly, "I was just thinking about how you never told me your type."

And it's true. He didn't. He left it at *not her* when that beautiful, bubbly woman called him repeatedly. Hopefully he's turned his phone off, because as nice as her picture made her look, I don't want to be interrupted. Especially not by someone he clearly has history with. Tonight's for new beginnings.

Thomas considers the question, eyes drifting to the stage where women with impressive core strength are defying gravity on poles. And yet when he looks back at me, I get the sense that he barely saw them.

"I like confident women," he says, then corrects it to, "*Over*-confident women. Cocky women. The ones who don't hold their tongues. Who know what they're worth and don't accept less. Who go after exactly what they want."

His hand is resting on the leather-upholstered bench in the small space between us, but I swear the side of it brushes my leg as he says the last words. I can't be sure, because I don't dare look down.

I heave a disappointed sigh, even though my heart is fluttering. "Shame. That doesn't sound like me at all."

The way his mouth quirks up a little more says he knows

I'm joking. He's right about this too. When I'm at my best, I'm the exact kind of woman he's describing. I know who I am, what I want, and how to get it. I don't doubt myself. I don't hesitate. I take my shots and I rarely miss.

But I'm *not* at my best currently. I'm struggling to find my footing. Struggling to make choices without second-guessing. I know I can get back to being the woman who owned any room she walked into, but right now, I'm not going to deny that I need a little external validation. And what do you know, there's a man in front of me willing to give me exactly that.

"Whatever you say," he murmurs. "But now that you know my type, I feel it's only fair you tell me yours."

If he really likes women who don't hold their tongues, then I'm not going to. I'm not fully sure what I'm looking for tonight, but I do know that I don't want it to end without him touching me again.

"I won't lie to you, Thomas," I say, just loud enough for him to hear me over the music. "Right now, my type is Formula 1 drivers with posh accents who are clearly resisting the urge to feel me up."

His gaze goes molten, some of that infectious humor fading away. "Is that an invitation?"

I shrug, delighting in the way his eyes follow the motion, sliding down my shoulder and back up again. I feel like a cat basking in the sun, soaking it in. "It's whatever you want it to be."

This time, I know I'm not imagining the way his fingertips brush back and forth against my thigh. "I don't play with consent. You either tell me enthusiastically what you want, or I do nothing." His fingers stop moving and I immediately long for the contact. "I think it's time for you to decide whether this is real or just for show, Stella."

He's done letting me toy with him, and I can't blame him. I've pushed us past the point of harmless flirting into something heavier. Something I find myself wanting to explore.

And honestly, he's the perfect person to explore with. I don't know this man and he doesn't know me. I'll see him at the wedding tomorrow, but after that, I'm sure we'll never interact again. This could be the perfect opportunity to start my journey back into the land of being single. Thomas can be my guide for tonight, my bridge to the other side, my palate cleanser to wash away the sour taste of Étienne.

I just have to be brave. I have to be the woman Thomas thinks I am—who I *know* I am underneath the hurt and heartbreak.

"Considering we no longer have an audience and I'm still here with you," I say, mind made up, "I think you have your answer." I shift so my leg presses against the side of his hand and my lips are at his ear. There's no mistaking my intentions now. "I want it to be real."

I watch the line of his throat as he swallows, unable to bring myself to see what's in his eyes, needing to hear it instead. "It's your turn to tell me what you want," I murmur once a beat passes without his answer. Only then do I look up. It's a relief to find him staring at my mouth.

"I want to kiss you." The confession is a deep rasp, and the tip of his tongue drags across his bottom lip before disappearing again. "Very badly."

That's all it takes for the little spark inside me to flare. "So do it."

Unfortunately, the words clear away some of the haze in his eyes, like it's exactly what he needed to hear to come back to his senses.

His smile is soft as he tucks a lock of hair behind my ear, fingers trailing down my neck until they rest on my shoulder.

"You're drunk." His thumb strokes my collarbone, like even though he's trying to shut this down, he can't move away. "We shouldn't."

It would sting more if he weren't fighting with himself, but even still, a thread of desperation weaves its way through my chest. I won't beg a man to want me—not anymore—but I'm not above pushing back.

"I'm not nearly drunk enough, believe me," I counter, lifting my chin. We're already so close, it wouldn't take much for either of us to reduce the gap to nothing. "You?"

"The same."

"Then what are you waiting for?"

"Someone could see."

I draw back a little, the blow landing hard. Does he not want to be seen with me? Am I a liability to his reputation?

What a useless question. Of course I am. I'm that woman who lost her shit for the whole internet to see. Not that he knows about that, but still. It makes sense that he wouldn't want to be associated with me. If I were him, I probably wouldn't want to be either.

God, I should have known better than to believe this could actually turn into something tonight. I might as well be tainted and he knows it.

"Does that bother you?" I challenge sharply.

His eyes soften when he realizes how I've taken his words, and he lifts a hand to cup the back of my neck, keeping me from going any farther. "Not for the reason you seem to be thinking. It's not about you."

The reassurance takes the edge off the hurt, but it still aches like an old bruise that's been pressed on. I cover it up with sarcasm. "Don't tell me you're a mind reader on top of being a driver."

"I can't expose all my talents, now, can I?" Before I can banter back, he says, low and quiet, "I'm just trying to protect you."

Something in my stomach tightens and drops dangerously between my legs. This appearance of the alpha male act shouldn't turn me on, but I'll be damned if I say it doesn't. "Protect me?" I scoff. "From what exactly?"

"Some of my fans are a little . . . intense," he explains, choosing his words carefully. "If they find out about this, they'll know everything about you in five seconds flat. I don't want you to face more scrutiny. You've been through enough."

It's so considerate that I almost want to slap him. I make do with sliding my palm up his thigh instead. If he wants bold, he'll get it.

"You're talking like you're a member of a boy band with rabid fangirls. Calm down, knockoff Harry Styles."

The hand on the back of my neck pulls me closer. It's a rough touch, almost a yank, but it's just shy of being too much. Either way, it sends a flood of heat to the apex of my thighs.

"Don't say I didn't warn you," he whispers, a hairsbreadth from my lips.

"Shut up and kiss me, Harry."

It's a ghost of a kiss when he finally closes the distance. A brushing of lips, up once, then down. Nothing more than a tease. I would pull back and scold him, tell him to kiss me like he fucking means it, but he's left me with nowhere to go. The hand on my neck is firm, and I suddenly realize that *I'm* the one being toyed with now. I'm the prey. And he's not going to let go until he's taken what he wants.

I'm close to whining in dismay, close to second-guessing what we're doing and the choices that led me here. But then his mouth finally settles against mine, and all my doubts go up in smoke.

If that first touch was just a taste, then this is the main course. I open for him when his tongue sweeps across my lower lip, but that's the last bit of control I'm allowed. Not that it matters, because the second his tongue presses against mine, I lose the ability to form a coherent thought.

There's nothing tentative about this kiss. It backs up his words and proves he's been thinking about this for a while. Something liquifies within me, like all the bullshit and anger and grief I've been holding on to are melting away. My whole body relaxes as the weight lifts, leaving Thomas to wind an arm around my waist to keep me from falling off the bench and into a puddle on the floor. His other hand slides from the back of my neck to cup my jaw, keeping my mouth to his, kissing me like he's tasting heaven. Like he's already addicted.

Good. He should be. If this is a game, then I'm the grand prize. He's lucky—not many have had the privilege of winning me over, and he's managed to do it in the span of a few hours.

But I'm the real winner here because, *fuck*, does this man know what he's doing. I can't remember the last time I was kissed like this, which is a shame considering I nearly married a man who hadn't made me feel this kind of way in years. Now, though? I swear my life force is returning, starting in all the places he's touching and climbing through my veins, reviving parts of me I feared might be dead.

I must be supremely deprived if something as innocent as a kiss is setting me on fire. Then again, maybe it's not so innocent, considering his hand has moved from my jaw to my throat, squeezing just enough that it has me breaking away with a gasp.

"Oh goddamn," I mumble as my eyes flutter back open. Somehow, my fingers have curled into his shirt, and I'm tempted to drag him back to keep this going.

He's already staring down at me, his hand lingering around my throat, but the pressure's gone. It's a possessive touch, one that has my thighs clenching, and boy oh boy—I like it a whole hell of a lot.

"Was that too much?" he asks, fingers trailing down to my collarbone and tracing the neckline of my dress. I recognize my own words thrown back at me.

I shake my head, struggling to respond as I blink my way out of the daze he's left me in. "Just enough."

The corner of his mouth quirks up; he's practically laughing at my struggle for composure, though he's enough of a gentleman not to bring it up. "I probably have lipstick all over my face now, don't I?"

The question gives me something to focus on other than the steady throbbing that's started between my legs. I clear my throat and scan his face. "Not a stitch."

"Really?"

"I do a lot of recipe testing," I explain, glad for the reprieve from the tension, though I'm sure it'll be brief. "I don't have time to keep reapplying lipstick after every bite. This shit doesn't budge." I drag my thumb across my bottom lip to prove my point, knowing the deep crimson isn't going anywhere.

Thomas's eyes once again drop to my mouth, following the movement. "Knowing that only makes me want to kiss you again."

I pout, settling back into my attitude, letting it wrap around me like a familiar embrace. I can't believe this man has me feeling more like myself than I have in a long while. Maybe some of the credit can go to the alcohol loosening me up, but I really do think it's mostly him. "Aren't you afraid of someone seeing?" I mock.

"At this point, Stella," he says, "I'd invite the whole world to watch."

He doesn't bother teasing this time—he dives straight in. This kiss is hot and searching, and there's something almost desperate about it. My pulse pounds, my blood rushes, and every nerve is flaming bright as I push myself closer to him. I'm the one addicted now, needing a deeper taste, so I palm his jaw to make sure he can't pull away before I get the fix I need.

He's more than willing to give it to me as he steals my breath. It escapes as a moan, and I'd be embarrassed by it if he didn't encourage the sound, tightening the arm around my waist and letting me taste the lingering champagne on his tongue. If we weren't in public, I would have crawled into his lap by now and wrapped my arms around his neck, unashamed and unabashed. I want to cling to the feeling of knowing I'm wanted, even if it's just sexually. Even if it's just for tonight. I needed this more than I knew. And as I'm slowly starting to realize, I need *more* of it.

It's him who breaks the kiss this time, turning his head so that my lips drop away. It shocks me out of my sudden and overwhelming desire, a cold reminder that we might not want the same things tonight. After all, he was quick to accept my earlier wishes to just talk, and he only said he wanted to kiss me. He could be done with me now.

"Not bad," I comment before he can say anything. I want to beat his rejection to the punch, because I can't bear to hear it.

I drop my hands back to his chest, which rises and falls just as rapidly as my own. The smirk on my face is forced, but I hope he can't tell. "I'd give that one a solid seven point five out of ten."

He blinks, his previously parted lips dipping into an offended frown. "Seven point five?" he questions in exaggerated offense, but there's a laugh he's hiding. "Come on. That's insulting."

"What?" I bat my lashes as I pull completely away, leaning back into my section of the booth and squeezing my thighs together to disperse the heaviness that's settled there. At least this way, I can keep my dignity by pretending I'm not disappointed that this is over. "It was nice and all. I just think you can do better."

He watches me carefully across the space I've put between us. "And I think you're lying. You liked that. A lot."

"Sure, maybe I'm lying." I glance around, looking for a waitress so we can order another round of drinks, something to help buoy the letdown. "But it's not like you can prove it."

When I glance back at him, there's a challenge I didn't expect lighting up his eyes. "Oh, I think I can."

I nearly jump when his hand lands on my knee. The feathers on the hem of my dress tickle me as his fingers drift higher, disturbing their careful placement.

"If I were to slip my hand under this pretty little dress," he murmurs, his lips against my ear, "what are the odds that I'd find you wet for me?"

Fire blazes down my spine at the sudden reversal, but I refuse to give in so easily. Not when this might be a game of his own. Gone are my days of trusting easily and taking men at face value. "Slim to none," I lie.

"Really?" The word is full of humorous disbelief. "Because I keep watching you press your thighs together like something's going on."

"Completely unrelated," I brush off, trying to force my muscles to relax, but all of me has gone taut under his attention. "This booth is uncomfortable."

"I have a better place for you to sit." His other hand pats his lap.

This is far from the rejection I was expecting. Although,

maybe it's only because, like me, he can't back down from a dare. Not that I meant it that way. My defense is to joke, to push the envelope before extracting myself from the situation and sauntering off to tend to my wounded ego in private.

But my usual methods and put-on nonchalance aren't fooling him, and I have no idea what to make of it.

I draw my head back a little, turning so I can look him in the eye. I'm being completely serious when I ask, "Do you actually want that? Or are you playing with me?"

He doesn't answer immediately. He merely stares me down as my stomach sinks and sinks and sinks, ready to hit the floor.

But it never does. Because Thomas hauls me into his lap with an arm around my waist, settling my back against his chest as I battle my surprise. The bulge in his tuxedo pants is solid under my ass, and I swear it only grows when I shift to get more comfortable.

"If you don't want this, then tell me," he says against my temple. "But I think you can feel exactly how much I want you."

His hands are heavy on my hips, anchoring me and yet light enough that I could move away if I wanted. Not that I would.

So I let my head fall back. Allow my body to melt into him. Press my cheek to his so he can feel my smile. "The feeling's mutual."

His right hand slides down from my hip to the top of my thigh, practically crushing the feathers there. "Then let me show you what I've been thinking about since dinner."

An eager shiver rolls down my spine. He feels it, I know he does. "Just don't damage my dress," I warn him. "It's expensive."

"I'll buy you a new one."

"It's couture." It's not.

Spitefully, he plucks off one of the feathers and flicks it to the floor. "Five new ones, then."

"Wealthy bastard."

"Says the woman wearing couture and thousand-dollar shoes."

"Six hundred," I correct, my breathing growing shallow as he spreads his legs apart, moving mine with them until cool air rushes up to meet the soaked lace covering my heated skin. "Got them on sale. Love a bargain."

"Don't tell me you're cheap," he chides, hand delving between my thighs but still far from where I desperately want it to be.

"I'm the most expensive woman you'll ever touch."

It's my turn to feel his smile against my cheek. "Now *that* I believe."

The table hides us from the waist down, the white tablecloth hopefully shielding the view straight up my skirt as his fingers finally reach the lace of my underwear. He dips one under the elastic, tracing the smooth skin there up and down, practically hypnotizing me with the motion.

"Tell me to stop," he whispers, but his teasing doesn't cease.

I shake my head. I'm struggling to form a single word as my pulse thuds heavily at my core. "No."

"No?" he presses, low and rough. "Are you sure?"

"If you stop," I tell him on a sharp inhale, "I might have to kill you."

He chuckles, not taking my threat seriously, even though I'm not remotely kidding. If he stops, I'll combust on the spot, and I'll take him down with me.

"We can't have that, can we?"

Another finger joins the first under the fabric, both slipping bit by torturous bit closer to where I desperately want him to touch. My heart races like I'm on mile twenty of a marathon. But it's the anticipation that makes it hard to breathe.

"Thomas," I beg, desperate for him to just *do it*, to just sink his fingers into me and stop with the torment. "I need—"

But my plea ends on a gasp when his touch drags down my slit, setting every nerve ending ablaze.

"You're soaked, Stella," he says, fingertips gliding up and down, letting my arousal coat them. "I knew you were lying. You want this as much as I do, don't you?"

My only answer is a breathless moan, no coherent words attached. It must tell him plenty, because he continues his torturous strokes, his touch moving farther inside with each motion until his thumb is pressing on my clit and his fingers are just barely dipping into my opening.

"Tell me how you like to be touched, sweetheart," he whispers against my ear, to which he gets a whine and a buck of my hips in response. "Come on, use your words."

A shudder rolls through my body as I fight to speak, turning my head enough so that I can meet his gaze. "You're a smart boy," I say. "Figure it out."

"Gladly."

In answer to my taunt, he doesn't go easy, sinking both fingers into me at the same time. I'm so wet that he barely meets any resistance as he pumps them in and out again, but there's just enough friction to make me shift my hips to seek out more. And—*there*. That spot. The one he hits when he curls up and presses harder against my clit, rubbing small, quick circles in tandem with the crooking touch.

It all has a hiss leaving my lips, pressure building low and hot and swift as my hands seek out something to hold on to, something to ground me as my world starts to shift on its axis. I grip his forearm, the one banded across my waist. It keeps me pinned to him—keeps me from moving too much and giving away what we're doing, even though I want to ride his hand like it's a bucking bronco.

"I'm guessing that's the spot," Thomas muses.

"The fuck do you think?" I pant.

"I'd say we can do even better."

I'm already dripping down his fingers, so I don't know what else he could possibly do to take this to another level. But he proves himself as he quickens the pace, and my inner walls clench with every flick and slide. I'm already close. It's not going to take much more to send me over the edge.

"You feel just as good as I thought you would." His lips brush my temple with an unexpected tenderness before drifting down to my ear, nipping at the lobe. "So tight and perfect. Fuck, I want that around my cock. I want to feel you squeezing me. Do you want that too, Stella?"

The words are enough to send me up and over the peak of pleasure, because *yes*—yes, I want that. I want this flaming high again and again and again, as many times as he's willing to give it to me. And I want to hear this buttoned-up man keep whispering these not-so-buttoned-up words, just for me.

The moan that tumbles from my lips is nothing short of filthy, my body shaking as the orgasm racks through me. I'd be curled over his arm if he hadn't pressed his hand to the center of my chest, forcing me back against him. My heart rages under his palm.

"*Fuck*," I exhale, my head hitting his shoulder when my neck decides it's too weak to hold it up. "You're a fast learner."

"I am. And there's plenty more I want you to teach me."

Once again, I can't give him more than an incoherent response as I float down from the hazy high, this one a cross between a sigh and a raspy giggle. "I have no objections."

"Then we should—"

He cuts short when someone walks in front of our table. His hand shifts back down my thigh, dragging my wetness with it and landing somewhere more appropriate, just as the person stops in front of us. I doubt they could see what he was doing under the table, but their presence is enough to snap me out of whatever spell I've been under.

I blink a few times before Rachel's face swims into focus. She doesn't look surprised to find us here—or find me sitting on Thomas's lap—but her pout tells me she's annoyed that she had to seek us out.

"Sydney threw up on a stripper and one of the groomsmen is crying uncontrollably because he misses his dog," she shouts over the music. "Janelle's too embarrassed to stay here any longer, so we're moving to the next spot. You guys coming?"

I finally notice the boisterous crowd of people winding their way through the club. It's a stark reminder of where we are and how we ditched the rest of the party to have a not-so-private one of our own.

Fucking hell, I literally let this man finger me under a table—*in public*—like we're horny high schoolers at prom. Old Stella was daring, sure, but she never would have done something like *that*. Whoever I'm becoming is bolder than her predecessor.

"Yeah, sure," I answer, still a little breathless. I consider sliding off of Thomas's lap, but he holds me in place. Right. He probably doesn't want Rachel to see his dramatically tented tuxedo pants. "Just, uh, give us a second. We'll catch up to you guys."

Rachel mumbles something before teetering off. Only then do I lean sideways and plop my ass on the bench next to Thomas, though my legs remain draped across his.

"So," I prompt without looking at him, my voice high as I attempt to process what we've just done—and how I desperately want to continue it. All my earlier rules, regulations, guidelines, and personal promises are out the window. My once-dormant libido is now screaming *I want to fuck this man*, and it will not be ignored. "Should we leave with them?"

I want him to say no. Want him to suggest we ditch them and go off on our own. I want him to sweep me out of here and murmur dirty things in my ear for the rest of the night, then slip out before the sun rises and look back fondly on our one night together for years to come.

"We probably should," he agrees. "Janelle and Ron might wonder where we went otherwise."

I have to fight to keep my face from falling; I'm so disappointed that it feels like a gut punch.

"Or," he goes on, "we could let them wonder and head to my room instead."

He says it so casually that my gaze snaps up to his face again, searching his expression to figure out if he's serious. His eyes hold a level of mischief I want to match, a knowing smile pulling up the corner of his mouth. It's obvious to him what my answer is going to be.

"All right," I say. "Let's have some fun, Prince Charming."

# CHAPTER 7

STELLA

I think I might be dying. Either that, or it's the hangover from hell.

My eyes aren't even open, and yet there's a pounding in my temples from the light seeping through my lids. My stomach churns painfully, still debating whether whatever I consumed in the past twelve hours is going to come up and out. And my feet ache so badly that there's no way I didn't do some serious running last night.

When I finally work up the nerve to face the day, I immediately notice I'm not alone. I'm lying next to Thomas in his rumpled bed, the white duvet bunched up under his head like a pillow. I couldn't say where the actual pillows are, but they're certainly not up here with us, unlike the assortment of take-out boxes, a half-empty bottle of Maker's 46, and a wilted bouquet of flowers. It's quite the array, but I'm too unwell to worry about it.

I don't even know why I'm still *here*. My entire plan last night was to hook up and then get the hell out of Dodge. Clearly the latter didn't happen, and another quick assessment of my body reveals that he definitely didn't stick his dick anywhere in me. I'm certain of that, because with what I felt through his pants at the strip club, there's no way I wouldn't be dealing with the aftermath today.

But if we didn't have sex, then why am I here when I should be back in my own hotel room with my cheek on a silk pillowcase?

My head throbs and spins, prompting me to close my eyes until I stop feeling like I'm on a rickety rowboat in the middle of the sea. I'm tempted to go back to sleep and pray I won't feel so spectacularly horrible in a few hours. And I would do it too, if this bed wasn't so damn uncomfortable. I'm betting that's what woke me in the first place.

I force my eyes open again to check if there's one of those take-out boxes underneath me, but as I feel around and pull out a bottle of Tabasco from under my hips, I find something stranger.

I'm wearing clothes. Like, my full outfit from last night— dress, underwear, even a bra if the irritation around my ribs is anything to go by. It's extremely odd because, one, I would *never* get into bed wearing my outside clothes. And two, you'd have to pay me a billion dollars to wear a bra for longer than strictly necessary, let alone sleep in one. Even if we did just get drunk and pass out here last night, there's no way I wouldn't have whipped that bad boy off the second we stepped inside his suite, whether we were going to have sex or not.

Thomas is also completely dressed. The tux is wrinkled beyond belief, sure, but every element of it is on him, including a very crooked bow tie. He wasn't even this put-together when we left dinner last night.

"What the fuck," I croak, loud enough that Thomas's eyelids flutter.

I'm too scared to move, still not sure if I'm going to puke, especially when he groans and flops over onto his back, causing the mattress to shake. It feels more like an earthquake than the slight tremor it actually is.

"I feel like hell," he mumbles, voice scratchy from sleep. I might find it sexy if I weren't too busy fighting to figure out what happened.

He lifts his hands to scrub at his face, bleary gaze finding me when he looks over a moment later. His eyes are unnaturally blue in the morning light, or maybe it's just because they're framed by red rims, but either way, they're beautiful. *He's* beautiful, even while hungover, with his hair sticking up in every direction and a light layer of scruff on his jaw.

When he smiles, my stomach flip-flops in a way I can't attribute to what I drank last night. It's easy and personal, the corners of his eyes crinkling just a little. But then he squints at me in confusion, eyes dragging up and down my body before looking at his own.

"Why are we dressed?" he asks.

I blow out a breath and lift a hand to swipe under my right eye, cringing when it comes away covered in mascara. "I was hoping you'd be able to tell me that."

I go to pull my other arm out from where I have it curled under my head, but something soft and sticky flops onto my face. If I had better control over my body, I might have screamed and batted it away. Right now, all I can do is grunt and slap haphazardly at my face, the scent of a sickly sweet bakery item assaulting my senses.

The offending thing lands between Thomas and me, leaving us staring at . . . a doughnut. If the chocolate streaks on my pinkie and middle finger are anything to go by, it was on my ring finger before falling off my hand.

This time it's Thomas's turn to say, "What the fuck."

I have so many questions that I'm not even sure where to start. Actually, no, I have so many that I don't want to ask any of them. I don't want the answers. Whatever happened is Last Night Stella's business. This Morning Stella doesn't want to know what led to her wearing a chocolate-iced doughnut, complete with rainbow sprinkles, like a ring.

"I'm not going to ask," I finally say when I look at Thomas, and he nods slowly, apparently feeling the same way.

Thankfully, my stomach has settled some, and I assess how the rest of me is holding up. My bladder is dangerously full, and I'm weirdly sticky in various places—gross—but those are things a trip to the bathroom and a long shower can fix. I'm just hoping that whatever's on me didn't get in my hair, because I do *not* have time to get it redone before the wedding.

Oh God, *the wedding*. A glance at the clock on the bedside table tells me it's only a little after eight a.m., which means I have a solid six hours to recover before I'm expected to be in Janelle's suite with a photographer up in our faces. I might have escaped being in the bridal party, but I still promised to be there for her today, and I plan to make good on that oath, even if I have to drag my half-dead ass to her. As long as my parents, my aunts, or any other family members going to the wedding don't hunt me down before then, I should be able to keep this drunken rendezvous my dirty little secret—especially if Thomas and I agree to never speak to each other again.

It takes an inhuman amount of strength to roll to the side of the bed, and I nearly cheer when I manage the slow trek to the bathroom. I do my best to clean myself up, making myself presentable enough to hopefully do a walk of shame back to my hotel without getting too many concerned looks. I'm not particularly optimistic, though.

Thomas has made it out of bed by the time I leave the bathroom, sitting in the green velvet wingback chair by the doors to the balcony and looking like he might pass out if he has to move any farther. His phone is in his hand, though he glances up when he hears me come in.

"I guess we should talk about what happened last night," he says, a little stiltedly, like this really isn't a conversation he wants to be having.

He's not the only one, especially since I can't even remember anything past leaving the strip club together. "Don't think there's much to talk about," I answer, scanning the floor for my clutch and shoes so I can get out like I should have hours ago.

"We . . . didn't have sex, right?" he asks, somehow even *more* awkward this time.

"Right," I confirm.

Couldn't tell him why, though, and it seems like he can't tell me either, but that's fine. I don't need to dwell on any of this, even if my blood flows a little hotter at the memory of his fingers sinking into me, wishing I could have had more. But that's not happening now that the time and opportunity—and liquid courage—have come and gone.

He nods. "Okay. I—Okay."

I'll leave him to process however he needs to because that is *not* my problem. The only thing I need to worry about is where the hell my phone is. I'm sure I have a million missed calls and texts, and I'm betting 90 percent of them are from Mika. As far as I know, I didn't make good on my promise to FaceTime her last night, so I won't be surprised if she thinks I'm dead in a ditch.

My back is to Thomas as I search the bedroom, picking up the duvet and moving take-out boxes, even squatting down to peer under the bed. It isn't until he inhales sharply that I look over, finding him frowning at his phone as he scrolls.

"I think I know why you had a doughnut on your finger."

I stand and slowly turn toward him, trying to keep the world from spinning. "You do?"

"Yeah." He holds up his phone for me to look at, expression shifting to something unreadable. "Apparently, I proposed to you with it."

I blink, digesting his words, but they still don't make sense even after a few beats. "Excuse me?"

He exhaustedly motions me closer. I have to squint at the screen once I'm standing in front of him to make out the blurry figures in the photo he's showing me, but . . . he wasn't kidding. There I am, proudly displaying the chocolate-iced doughnut on my left hand while Thomas beams up at me from down on one knee. We're both clearly shit-faced, and funnily enough, I look happier there than I did in any of my actual engagement photos.

I swallow hard, debating whether I should be freaked out that I don't remember any of this happening or amused since it's harmless enough.

"I know I'm a catch, but I didn't think you'd fall in love with me that quickly," I joke, trying to push down my rapidly growing discomfort. But this is as good a time as any to reestablish what this encounter was—or at least was meant to be. "I'm flattered, but I think we're better off leaving this as a one-night thing."

Fun as our conversations were—and as good as he is with his hands—I'm not in a position to get wrapped up in anything. I can't imagine he has time for it either as a professional athlete.

Thomas nods, turning his phone back around and swiping across the screen. "Absolutely, I know we both have—hmm."

I freeze, not liking that *hmm*. "What was that for?"

His parliament smile makes its first appearance this morning. "Well," he says lightly before clearing his throat and glancing back up at me. Something akin to panic is in his eyes. "It seems that last night we mutually decided we wanted *forever* instead of one night."

I'm standing so still that I'm not even breathing. "I'm going to need you to explain, Thomas."

Again, he turns his phone screen to me, and this time I grab it out of his hands. I have to see this up close to make sure his concern isn't misplaced. But the longer I stare, the less what I'm looking at makes sense.

"We got married," I hear myself say, even though I don't feel my lips form the words. "By Black Elvis."

"Yes." Thomas confirms what I didn't know was my worst fear, but it's now at the top of the *Shit That Scares Stella* list. "It would appear we did."

I keep staring at the snapshot of us standing at the front of a chapel, grinning at each other as we hold hands. A dark-skinned man in an Elvis costume—complete with a swoopy wig and sunglasses—next to us with a Bible in one hand and a guitar in the other.

My stomach is churning dangerously again. "This . . . this can't be real," I mumble, even though, logically, I understand this wasn't faked. "It's gotta be some sort of AI trash."

I swipe to the next photo, then the next, and the next. It's more of Thomas and me at the altar, us with our lips pressed together, me joyously waving a bouquet of flowers in the air. It's the same bouquet that's wilting on the bed.

Hand shaking, I tap on the screen, bringing up the details of the latest photo. According to the time stamp, it was taken fifteen minutes past midnight. Thomas and I left the strip club just after ten, which means there are at least two hours of mayhem unaccounted for between then and this photo being taken.

I force myself to stop and breathe, warding off the anxiety that's threatening to throw me into a full fetal-position panic attack.

"Okay, so it's real," I finally say, surprised by how level my voice sounds. "And it's not great. But it's not a legal marriage."

The relief that slides across Thomas's face is almost comical, but neither of us would dare laugh right now. "Are you sure?" he presses.

I nod as I hand his phone back. "Extremely. Don't forget that I've already been through this whole song and dance. For a marriage to be legal and valid, you have to get a marriage license before the ceremony. And considering we did this *way* past the working hours of any government agency that would issue a license, we definitely didn't get one."

His head falls back against the chair, a heavy breath escaping him. "Oh, thank *God*." I worry about the integrity of his neck with the way his head snaps up a moment later, eyes wide. "Not that—not that I don't think you'd make a wonderful wife, or that I'm pleased you've had another wedding go horribly awry, but—"

"Please stop," I interrupt, lifting my hands to rub my aching temples. "I know what you mean, and I agree."

This could have been disastrous for both of us. Honestly, it still might be if anyone else knows about it, legal marriage or not. Clearly there were witnesses—Black Elvis, whoever took those photos, and anyone else at the chapel—but I have to hope they're a discreet bunch who won't snitch on us to the press. If I thought the headlines before were bad . . . Fuck, I don't want to think about what these might be.

"I can't believe we did this," I go on, because what the *hell* possessed me to do something so ridiculous? All I wanted was to get railed. How did everything shift from sex to marriage?

"I guess we were inspired. And very drunk." He pauses, eyes drifting to the bed as he considers something. "I'm guessing that bottle of whiskey was the culprit."

A memory punches its way to the front of my mind when I look at the bed again, one of Thomas and me stumbling into his room, kissing desperately and tearing at clothes. If my shattered brain isn't lying to me, then I definitely ditched my dress and got to see his abs up close and personal after he shed his shirt. Oh God, I think I even *licked* them. But if I was already down on my knees, then why didn't it go any further than that?

The answer comes more as a feeling than a memory—disappointment. It didn't go further because neither of us had a condom.

Thomas must get hit with the realization as well, because a wash of color spreads across his cheekbones. "We went out to get condoms, didn't we?" He pauses, waiting for another thought to fully form. "And . . . tacos?"

He seems unsure about the last bit, but I'm suddenly not. "We eventually did. But before we went out, we called down to the concierge to see if they'd bring us condoms." I was half naked, after all, and Thomas was sporting an obscenely large hard-on. Not exactly a sight for public consumption. "And I was hungry, so we ordered food too. I wanted tacos, but *you* were the one who insisted on the whiskey." Despite that, I'm almost certain I dared him to do shots with me. *Shit.*

His expression is pinched, drawing something from the depths of his mind and ignoring my attempt to lay the blame at his feet. "I must have confused the concierge with my combination condom and taco request, because they sent extra *condiments* with the food."

Well, that would explain the container filled with a selection of salsas.

"So we ate, drank, got dressed, and went out to get condoms ourselves." Like the Hoover Dam opening, more details flood back, drop by horrific drop. "And the pharmacy just happened to be right next to—"

"A wedding chapel," he finishes for me, remembering it now too.

"A wedding chapel," I repeat on an exhale. Un-*fucking*-believable.

Regrettably, that's where my recollection of the night ends. I don't know what convinced us to go into the chapel, or what spurred him to propose, or what made me say yes.

"Do you have any idea where the doughnut plays into things?" I ask, hoping that might trigger something.

Thomas frowns as he ponders it. "Well, obviously, I couldn't get you a real ring on such short notice, and since you run so many bakeries, I guess I picked the one baked good with a hole in the middle."

"Huh. Creative."

I'm starting to slowly come down from my anxiety high, even though I don't have any more answers for us. I'm taking solace in the fact that the marriage isn't legal. We should be able to move on from this easily if we can clean up the other messes we made—and if no one else blabs about the trouble we got into.

"We should stop by the chapel at some point today or tomorrow and see if we can get everyone there to sign an NDA," I suggest, though I'm really just declaring what I plan to do to handle this. "I'll call my lawyers to see what they can do."

"Good idea," Thomas says. "If you need me to get my solicitor involved as well, just say the word."

I'm not unused to dealing with men as moneyed and powerful as I am, but it's always nice when they're willing to lend a helping hand instead of expecting me to figure everything out. "Thanks. My team should be able to handle it, though." That settled, I restart my search for my clutch and shoes. "Do you have any idea where my things are?"

"Maybe check the living room. You're wearing shoes in the photos, so I assume they made it back here."

I nearly gag at the idea of walking the Vegas streets barefoot, praying that even though I was hammered enough to marry a stranger, I still had enough wits about me not to do something so disgusting.

Leaving Thomas to recover on his own, I pad into the living room of the suite, taking in the destruction there. There's a box of a dozen doughnuts on the coffee table, but no signs of anything I actually need.

I'm on my hands and knees looking under the couch when Thomas calls out, "Stella darling?"

The endearment has me frowning. It's far too sweet and intimate for a one-night stand, even one I attempted to marry. But the more I turn it over in my head, the more it starts to grow on me. I mean, who doesn't want a hot Englishman calling them *darling*? I'm not immune.

"Yeah?" I shout back, squinting into the darkness to see if I can spot anything.

He comes around the corner a moment later and I sit back on my heels. He's wearing that damn grimace-adjacent smile again. "I need you to take a look at one more photo."

I huff in annoyance before I can stop myself. "If it's another one of me making a damn fool of myself, I don't want to see it."

"Not that," he reassures, but the cautiousness in his tone isn't soothing me any.

"Then *what*?"

He approaches me with the phone outstretched. I take it from him and scrutinize yet another blurry snapshot. This one is of us proudly holding up a piece of paper, Black Elvis beaming in the background. I don't even need to zoom in on the document, because with one glance, it's already too familiar to me.

No. *No.* There's no fucking way.

Thomas clears his throat and delivers the exact news I feared. "I think that's our marriage license."

CHAPTER 8

THOMAS

"Mother*fucker*."

Stella's drawn-out curse confirms my thoughts. As she shoves the phone back into my hands, the reality of our situation slams into me along with it.

We're married. Legally and officially *married*. And I have zero memory as to *how* or *why* it happened.

Motherfucker is absolutely right. I might even elect to go with something stronger, because we've just woken up in a nightmare. Or maybe even hell.

Stella paces the living room, still swearing, fury radiating off every inch of her. I always thought I was good at keeping my emotions under control, well trained by two sets of grandparents who believed in a stiff upper lip. But that idea of myself went to shit when the whole world heard my tirade against Lorenzo Castellucci, and it's going even further to shit now as I sit down hard on the edge of the couch, lifting a fist to my lips to keep from saying something I know will make Stella lose it more than she already is.

I take a deep breath, forcing myself not to let my anxiety

bleed into the air. Stella's panicking enough for the both of us, her chest heaving as she stalks back and forth in front of the coffee table. I need to be the rational one, because I'm getting the distinct feeling that—intelligent as she seems to be—she's not going to be smart about this.

"How the *fuck* did this happen?" she snarls, dark hair flying as she whirls on me.

Even in her wrinkled dress and smudged eyeliner, with pure fire in her gaze, she's a vision. I may not know how all of this came to be—how it went from just trying to get her into my bed to *marriage*—but there's no denying this is part of the *why*.

I'm well aware that's not what she wants to hear, though, so I keep my mouth shut.

"How did we even get a marriage license?" she presses. "All of this happened in the middle of the damn night!"

I nearly shrug, but I might be able to answer this one for us. I type a few things into the search bar of my phone, wincing when I see the result. "Apparently, the license bureau here stays open until midnight. I'm guessing we made it in right before closing."

Stella makes a strangled noise, hands lifting to clutch her head. If I don't want her to have a stroke, then I need to do something to walk her back from the edge.

"We're going to fix this," I say as evenly as I can manage, despite wanting to vomit from nerves myself. Or maybe it's the whiskey still sloshing around in my stomach. Either way, all of this has me feeling violently ill.

I can't be married. I just . . . *can't*. I've never even had a girl-friend, for Christ's sake. So how did I end up with a *wife*?

Fuck, this is a disaster. All I wanted was a night of no-strings sex with the hottest woman I've seen in ages—possibly ever. Instead, I ended up getting every string imaginable.

It's bad enough I've already ruined my reputation and jeopardized my career with one mistake—now I have another fuckup to add to the list. What are the McMorris team bosses going to think when all of this undoubtedly leaks? What will my sponsors think? Will I even *have* any sponsors once they find out I drunkenly married a stranger? What's to say they won't think I'm some irresponsible wanker who is more of a liability than an asset and finally kick me to the curb?

Yeah, I'm *definitely* going to be sick.

Stella tosses me a scathingly skeptical look at the suggestion this can be fixed, and I can't blame her. It sounded weak to my own ears. I have to do better. I need an actual solution.

"Look, we'll clean ourselves up and then go back to the chapel," I offer. That's got to be the best course of action here. "They have our license, right?" I wait until Stella nods haltingly before continuing. "In that case, we just have to find the officiant who performed the wedding before they send the license to be filed. We'll get it from them, destroy it, and be done."

It's the perfect solution, a way to prevent anything from becoming legally registered, something we can move on from without too much fallout. But Stella's frown isn't budging.

"I think it might be too late," she says. I'm sure her stomach is sinking with her words, just like mine is. "An organization like that probably mails those off first thing in the morning. They do dozens of weddings every day, and people are anxious to get their marriage certificates as soon as possible."

Shit. While there's a chance that they could still be sitting on our signed license, it's more likely they've already sent it back to be certified. Fucking America and their ridiculous laws that allow strangers to get married. This wouldn't have happened in England, but this is what I get for spending time in this anarchic former colony.

"We have to figure out how to get this annulled," she goes on, voice firm, like she's finally come to terms with it all and is willing to look at this logically. She got to this point faster than I thought she would. "Do you think anything is out in the media?"

There's a new shade of worry in her eyes as I admit, "I don't know."

"Well, *check*." She glances pointedly down at my mobile.

My stomach curdles, grip tightening on the device. "Are you really going to make me google myself?" I don't want to search my name and find more evidence of how much people all over the world loathe me, because I know that's going to pop up first. It always does.

"Desperate times," Stella says. "I'd do it myself but I have no idea where my phone even is."

Well, I certainly don't want *her* looking me up. I got through last night without her learning about my little rant, and I'd like to escape this situation without her discovering it.

"Fine, fine," I huff, clearing out the search bar again and reluctantly typing my name in.

I hesitate for a moment before hitting *enter* and hold my breath until the page loads. And—oh no.

I clear my throat and then swallow hard, trying to dislodge the lump that's settled there. "Okay, so don't panic," I say.

Stella makes another choked sound. "I would suggest not starting a sentence like that if you *don't* want me to panic."

She's right, but I really don't know how else to broach this. "There's no news about the wedding," I preface, but before she can consider sighing in relief, I go on. "There are, however, photos of us from the strip club."

A lot of photos, if the top few results are anything to go by. Some are of us innocently sitting beside each other and smiling. But most are of Stella in my lap, my hands on her body, her head thrown back, our lips locked—the money shots.

The articles only started hitting the media in the past ten minutes, which would explain why my phone isn't blowing up with calls and texts from my manager and PR team yet, but I'm sure they're on their way.

Stella's hesitant to take the phone from me so she can see for herself, and I realize then that it's not anger making her react like this. It's fear.

"*Fuck*," she exhales as she taps through everything. "You were right to be worried about this happening. I should have listened to you about being seen together."

It stings a little to hear that, but I'm the one who brought it up in the first place, so I have no right to be upset.

"At least no one can see where your hand is in these photos," Stella says, trying to be optimistic even though her voice is grim. "That's one good—oh." She shoves my phone back toward me. I hear it buzzing before I look down. "Figgy's calling you."

I almost make a sound of disgust, barely swallowing it back. The woman, determined to be the first at the scene of my crimes, must have a Google Alert set up for me, because she's always *right there* when something happens. I used to appreciate her uncanny ability to know when I was facing something big, good or bad, but there came a point when it started feeling . . . overbearing.

It's not a coincidence that it began around the time our families made it clear they wanted us together. The added pressure made me pull back from our friendship, but Figgy leaned in, trying to play the girlfriend role without having the title.

Seeing her name on my screen last night was a nuisance. This morning, it makes my shoulders sag with the weight of unmet expectations.

"You still ignoring her?" Stella asks when I don't immediately take the phone from her outstretched hand.

Very much so. "I'll talk to her later. I need to call my manager before this blows up into something bigger." I have to make sure I'm still going to have a spot in F1 after this. "You should do the same with your people."

If we get our teams on it now, maybe there's something they can do to tamp it down. I'm almost certain it'll be a lost cause, though. Once things like this hit the internet, there's no taking them back.

I finally take my phone from Stella when it stops buzzing, but it starts up again seconds later, Figgy's face filling the screen. I'm tempted to block her, just temporarily, so I can take a moment to *think* without her pushing into my brain. I've told her time and time again that I'm not looking to be anything more than friends. What is it going to take to convince her and my family that I mean it?

The answer hits me like a truck. I can practically *feel* the light bulb illuminating above my head. It glows brighter when it dawns on me that I could solve more than just this problem in one fell swoop.

"Actually," I say, dragging out the word as the idea swirls and forms. "I don't think we need to worry about this."

Stella gapes at me before spluttering, "*Excuse* me?"

I sound absolutely unhinged. Mad as a hatter. Like I've completely lost the plot. But if I'm going to go for it, I might as well hit full send.

"I think we should just leave all of this alone." I take a breath and then go in for the kill. "We shouldn't get an annulment. Not yet, at least."

I take in her wide eyes and parted lips, her horror palpable. "Are you fucking with me right now?"

"Hear me out . . ." Before I say more, I motion for her to sit on the couch, but she's not budging. Okay. Well. If she passes out after she listens to what I'm about to suggest, I'll do my best to catch her on the way down. "Obviously something made us want to get married, right?"

"It would be great if we could remember what it was," Stella snaps, folding her arms across her chest.

"Well, I think I know what my motivations were." I take her in from head to toe, still gorgeous despite the circumstances. "I mean, first of all, you're stunningly beautiful and incredibly accomplished. You're a catch, Stella. Undoubtedly."

She points an accusatory finger at me, calling out my game, even if I've done nothing but speak the truth. "Flattery is always appreciated but will *not* get you anywhere right now."

"Understood." I almost snort, though I make myself plow on instead. "Second of all . . . do you remember me telling you how my parents want me to marry Figgy?"

It takes a beat, but Stella puts my clues together and scoffs. "What, you thought that if *we* got married, they would stop pushing you toward her?"

I nod, because *yes*, I'm almost positive that's what I was thinking last night. "Look, my family cares more about the illusion of me settling down than me actually doing it," I explain. "If I showed up with a wife, especially one as perfect as you, the hounding would end, and Figgy could finally move on and find her own happiness elsewhere."

Plus, if I showed up with a wife, maybe—just maybe—it might be something to endear me to some of the people who've taken to hating me. But if I admit that all of this was one big mistake instead and leave a woman who's already been jilted once . . . Well, I wouldn't blame anyone for loathing me more.

Stella's squinting, like she's trying to judge whether this is a strong enough reason for me to have proposed to her. Her silence lasts so long that sweat beads on my forehead. I'm about to get shot down—hard.

"I could see you married to a woman named Figgy," she finally says.

It's so matter-of-fact and unexpected that I have to run my tongue over my teeth to stifle my amusement, knowing she won't appreciate it in a moment like this. But she's so unintentionally funny that I can't help it. I don't even mind that her jokes are almost always at my expense.

"I'd rather *not* be married to a woman named Figgy," I say as solemnly as I can. "Which is likely why I chose to marry you instead."

She gives a disbelieving laugh this time, shaking her head. "Okay, sure. If that was your reasoning, then what the hell was mine?"

I try to think back to any of the conversations we'd had at that point in the night, but it's all jumbled and incoherent. I have to come up with *something*, though, or else she's going to walk out of this room and take my chances of fixing my Figgy and F1 problems with her.

"You said you wanted to show your ex you could move on," I lie, though something niggles at the back of my mind that tells me it's not too far off from the truth. "You wanted him to see how easily you could find someone else." I pause, desperate to come up with more reasons why she'd want this, because I can't imagine simple spite would be enough. "You also mentioned that your board members would prefer to work with a married woman instead of a single one. That being married would show that you could really commit to something."

I know I'm pulling that reason straight out of my ass, but it *could* be real. I've seen it happen before. My eldest sister was always passed over for opportunities at our family's company until she showed our father she could "settle down" and "be serious," even though she was the most qualified candidate for the roles. Maybe Stella doesn't have the same problem, considering she's the big boss, but the way her expression darkens tells me I might have hit a nerve.

"Staying together could be good for us both," I urge, careful to keep my voice low and soothing. "We could just think of it as a business arrangement. It doesn't have to be forever—just long enough for the heat to pass and for us to fix our problems."

Stella stays quiet. Dare I say it, but I think she's actually considering my offer. If I could just—

"This is a terrible idea," she says forcefully a moment later, dashing my hopes. "If we stay married, people are going to think I was cheating on my fiancé the whole time!"

It's a very fair point, considering that breakup happened only a couple of weeks ago. Most people don't move on to their next committed relationship so quickly, unless something shady was already going on.

There's a twisting in my chest telling me to drop this. My life is too much of a mess to drag Stella into it anyway, and she isn't even aware of how bad it is. She doesn't deserve to be led unknowingly into the disaster.

Besides, maybe going our separate ways could still be a good thing. Maybe this drama will distract everyone from what I said about Lorenzo. As it stands, our wild night out is already replacing the previous headlines. Sure, it's once again not a great look for me, but I'd rather it be news about this mess— followed by the reveal of my quickie wedding and annulment, if we can't keep it secret—than me wishing death upon someone.

But as my phone continues to buzz, Figgy's picture reappearing, I can't help but try one last time.

"There are worse things for people to think," I push. "This could just be one of those *when you know, you know* situations."

The look I get this time is pure disgust. "You can't be serious."

"Okay, yeah," I concede, sighing. "I don't love that either."

Eventually, her disgust fades and steely determination returns. "Even if we *did* stay married, we don't have a prenup," she points out. "That could make things messy in the end. I have no interest in that."

"We could do a postnup," I suggest, though I never thought any woman I married would be worried about that. Between my personal wealth and my family's, *I* should be the one who's concerned. "Simply agree that our assets stay our own." I take another breath, prepared to press one last time. "I really do think we can make this work, Stella."

I'm watching the cracks appear in her armor, my words seeping through and reaching her heart. She's considering it, teetering between giving in and shutting it down. What's it going to take to get her on my side?

Unfortunately, before I can offer up anything else, she shakes her head and steps back, arms tightening around herself.

"No, I can't do this," she blurts, looking anywhere but at me. "Everything last night . . . That's not actually who I am, Thomas. I don't roll with the punches, and I definitely don't take up men I barely know on offers to stay married."

I sag in disappointment, but I'm not going to push her any further. She's given me an answer, a firm no. All I can do now is respect it.

"Okay," I say, putting my hands up to show I'm done. "It

doesn't look like anything about the wedding has hit the media, so that's good. We can get our publicists and PR teams in touch, and they can handle everything from here on out. Let's get through today and then reassess tomorrow, all right?"

Some of Stella's defensiveness slips away as she drops her arms back to her sides. "I can do that. Today's about Janelle and Ron, not us."

Right. The wedding we're *actually* here for.

I point toward the console across the room that has the TV atop it. "Your bag is behind the television, by the way. And your shoes are under the chair."

I get a quick nod in thanks before she's off to collect her things. With her heels on, we're back to being nearly eye to eye when she approaches again, clearly ready to get out of here without too much more chatter.

"We'll figure this out," I reassure, holding her gaze. "I promise."

She sighs, resigned to our fate. "This was supposed to be easy. Just one night."

"And now you're stuck with me." When I find myself on the receiving end of her glare, I tack on, "Legally. And temporarily."

There's an awkward beat, neither of us sure what to do next. Is she just supposed to . . . go? Feels kind of wrong considering our circumstances and conversations, but I guess that's the next course of action after what was supposed to be a one-night stand.

"I'd kiss you goodbye if it didn't taste like a small animal died in my mouth," I tell her.

I wish I could take back the words as soon as I say them. Could I *be* any more embarrassing? Yet, somehow, Stella looks briefly amused by the comment before she forces it away with a frown.

"Disgusting," she admonishes. "But . . . same."

It drags a laugh out of me as I walk her to the door of the suite. She pauses and turns back to me when we're standing on separate sides of the threshold.

"I'll go call my people." She glances at her phone, which she slipped out of her bag, grimacing when she sees whatever's on the screen. When she looks back at me, I don't miss the determination in her gaze. She wants this handled, and fast. "See you at the wedding?"

"See you there."

I wait in the doorway until she disappears down the hall, then slump back inside as I unlock my phone, tapping on my manager's name before Figgy can call me again.

"I know you're not going to want to hear this," I tell him on a sigh when he answers. "But I seem to have found myself with another PR problem . . ."

# CHAPTER 9

STELLA

There's an old saying that goes *Man plans, and God laughs*. For example, it was always in my plans to show up to Janelle's wedding as a married woman. And what do you know? That's exactly what's happening.

Except I'm not married to the man I thought I was going to spend the rest of my life with. No, I'm married to a complete fucking stranger. But hey, I'm married! And the cackling I keep hearing must be God.

At this point, I've done all I can to get a handle on everything. I've called my lawyers, set my PR team on high alert, and frantically googled *quickest way to get an annulment in Nevada*. None of it has made me feel better about my less-than-stellar life choices, but it's time to compartmentalize and be there for Janelle on her big day.

The bridal suite is awash with excitement when I step inside. Aunt Caroline, Janelle's mother, hugs me tight and gushes over how beautiful I look. I'm still sweating out whiskey, but I've managed to clean up well, and I accept her compliment with a smile.

"Where's our bride?" I ask.

Aunt Caroline nods to the balcony with a wry smile. "Said she needed a minute to catch her breath, but to send you out the second you got here."

I skirt my way around the room to get to the balcony door, nodding and waving to bridesmaids with a brightness I don't feel. The fakeness falls away when I slide the door shut behind me and draw in a breath of the crisp air outside.

"About time you got here," Janelle comments from where she's sitting in lotus pose on a yoga mat. She squints, taking me in as I lower myself down next to her. "What's wrong?"

Well, that didn't take her long to spot. "Nothing's wrong," I say, forcing a lightness into my voice. "Just a little hungover, that's all."

"You're *a lot* hungover," she counters. "But that's not the problem."

Goddamn this girl and how well she knows me. "Seriously, I'm fine."

"One more chance to tell me the truth," she singsongs as she adjusts the tie of her white silk robe. "Or else I'm gonna tell my mama that you disappeared last night and probably got into some trouble."

Who will, in turn, tell *my* mama. And if that happens, I can expect to receive endless disapproving looks for the rest of my life. Worse still, if she and my dad discover I got hitched . . . Oh God, I'll be in such deep shit that I'll never find my way out. That news leaking absolutely *cannot* happen—at least not until I figure out a way to gently break it to them.

"Fine," I grumble. "I disappeared with Thomas and got into *a lot* of trouble."

Janelle's face lights up like the Fourth of July. "Okay, now! Looks like Stella got her groove back!"

I did, for a little while at least. Then it all went to shit.

"I was hoping you were with him," she goes on. "He's hot as hell. Great for a one-night fling, which is exactly what you needed."

I flinch, and my anxiety has me wondering if it's possible for your stomach to rip its way out of your body. My cousin, unfortunately, doesn't miss my reaction, and I'm not quick enough to try to hide it.

"Something's definitely up," she says, humor gone. "Spill it, Stella."

I shake my head, my throat tightening around the things I want to tell her. She and I don't typically keep secrets from each other. "We can talk another time," I make myself say. "This day is about you, not me."

"Get outta here with that mess." She drops the yoga pose and turns all the way toward me. "I want to know what's going on. You're worrying me."

The full force of her attention has me ready to spill, just like it always has. She looks ridiculous with her hair up in rollers, her makeup almost done except for lashes and lipstick, but none of that can disguise the intensity of her stare.

"I did something bad, Elle," I eventually mumble.

She doesn't blink. "Did you shoot a man in Reno just to watch him die?"

"Right state, wrong city," I volley back, but her deadpan joke has my shoulders loosening a little. Nothing I say will faze her past some surprise at first. "And no. Not murder. A different *M* word."

She perks up. "'Manslaughter'?"

"You're such a lawyer." I shake my head, gearing up to confess. "Not manslaughter. Try . . . 'marriage.'"

Her eyes lock on mine, and a series of emotions flash

through them. Surprise, as expected, comes first. With a blink, it's replaced by acceptance. And then, horrifyingly, it's pure, unadulterated glee.

"You married Thomas Maxwell-fucking-*Brown* last night," she says so loudly I'd be surprised if the whole Vegas Strip hasn't heard her.

I violently shush her, hands flying up to cover her mouth before I think better of it, not wanting to ruin her makeup. Instead, they flutter dramatically around her face. "Keep your voice down," I hiss. "I don't need the whole world finding out about this. No one else knows yet."

"This is *so* good," she gushes, drawing her knees up to her chest so she can kick her feet in the air. "I knew y'all hit it off, but not so well that you felt compelled to marry the man!"

"I didn't know either." I pinch the bridge of my nose to ease the lingering throb of my headache. "It was a drunken mistake."

Her grin is far too wide. "Hey, at least we'll have the same anniversary."

"I am *not* staying married to him."

My vehemence turns her amusement down a few notches. "Oh, honey." She slips her arm through mine, tugging me closer. "Tell me everything."

So I do. I let it pour out, getting choked up when I mention Mika's news about Étienne and laughing when I describe Thomas's impressive switch-up from polite smiler to dirty talker. By the time I'm done sharing this morning's awkward conversation, Aunt Caroline is seconds from dragging us back inside because we've been out here for so long.

"Janelle, get your behind in here and let this poor woman finish your hair," she complains. "You're never too old for me to bend you over my knee, remember that. I don't care that it's your wedding day."

"I bet you wanted Thomas to bend you over his knee," Janelle says out of the corner of her mouth, just for me to hear, as she springs to her feet.

I nearly choke as I struggle to stand as well. When Aunt Caroline ducks back inside, Janelle turns to me one last time.

"We're not done talking about this." It's not a promise but a threat. "Once I say 'I do,' you're going to tell me what you plan to do about this."

I'm almost too afraid to make plans at this point, but I have my lawyer looking into how quickly—and quietly—I can get this marriage annulled.

"Who knows," she goes on breezily as she starts for the door. "Maybe Thomas will end up being a better husband than Étienne ever could have been."

"I told you, I'm *not* staying married to him."

But my words are lost to the wind as she steps back inside.

▗▚▗▚▗▚

If I have to field another pitying glance or mock-sympathetic *How are you . . . really?* from one more wedding guest, I'm going to scream.

I've never been more thankful for my parents, who intervened after the dozenth attempt to mine me for juicy details about Étienne and what I did to make him leave me so dramatically. Dad gently guided the husband of the couple off with generic chatter about golf while Mom gave the wife a loud backhanded compliment about her dress.

It gave me a chance to escape the people milling around in the receiving area of the church, and I slipped into the sunshiny flower-draped nave instead. On the bride's side, I slid down the pew until I was as far away from anyone else as possible, then pulled out my phone to watch the countdown timer for when I could open Instagram next.

Things are . . . bad. So bad that I've had to set screen time limits for myself to prevent any doomscrolling. All the news I've gotten so far about the situation has come from my publicist, lawyer, and assistant, each of their texts and calls limited to only the most pertinent information. The last thing I need is to have a meltdown in the middle of Janelle's big day because I stumbled on something that set me off.

Only in the past hour have I been identified as the "mystery woman" on Thomas's lap. I might be offended by how long it took everyone to figure out it was me if I weren't sick over it instead, but I guess that's what happens when you're objectively less famous than the man you were spotted with. And had he been less famous, I'm sure this wouldn't be as big a deal as it's blowing up to be.

It could be worse, though. There's still no news of our marriage, and getting caught with a race car driver is certainly better than being spotted with an athlete from a more well-known sport in the good old US of A. It would be game over if he was a Super Bowl–winning quarterback or an all-time points scorer of an NBA team. But a Formula 1 driver? Sorry to my good man, but in the grand scheme of sports, he's not at the top of the charts.

Still, I just want to know what people are saying about me. It's silly, and I *know* I shouldn't care. I never really did in the past, because unless it affected my company, I figured people's opinions of me were none of my business. But again, Étienne's betrayal has shifted something in my mind that suddenly has me desperate to be in the know.

The countdown finally hits zero and I tap on the app,

opening it up as quickly as my fingers can manage. I only have two minutes before it will lock me out again, and I'm going to make the most of those 120 seconds.

"'Get your grubby little hands off my man, you chocolate bitch,'" I read quietly to myself, frowning at the latest comment in my Instagram notifications. The racial undertone isn't great, but hey, at least they said my hands were little.

I scroll, desperately searching for a comment with more substance, but a gentle touch on my shoulder has me glancing up.

"I think it's time to put the phone down, love."

Thomas stares at me with a knowing smile, like he's well aware of what I've been up to. He's wearing a beautifully tailored three-piece suit in dove gray, and it pains me to admit that he looks spectacular in it, possibly even better than he did in the tux last night.

He's back to being clean-shaven, with his hair perfectly swept back, and the whiff I get of his cologne has me breathing deeper. If he's still feeling rough, like I am, I'd never be able to tell.

I scowl in return as he drops down next to me on the pew. "Shouldn't you be sitting on the groom's side? Somewhere far away from me?"

He points toward the aisle, and I follow his finger to a sign that reads CHOOSE A SEAT, NOT A SIDE. "According to that, I can sit wherever I want."

Damn Janelle and her quaint tastes. "I'm not sure we should be seen together."

I swear there's a flash of something wary in his eyes, but it disappears when he blinks, and I convince myself that I imagined it.

"We've already been seen together," he points out. "What's

one more instance? Promise to keep my hands to myself this time."

I see his point. It's not like there's anyone else here I want to talk to, and he's a good buffer for avoiding more stilted inquiries into how I'm doing. Not to mention a good distraction from checking my phone—which I am now once again locked out of.

I slink lower in my seat and glance at him from the corner of my eye. "How are you holding up?"

"Not great," he says cheerfully. "I am *so* wickedly hungover that I doubt I'll be able to legally drive a car by this time next week."

A wheezing laugh escapes me before I can stop it. "I feel the same way."

"Bit more of a problem for me, considering that's my entire job."

"Should have thought of that before ordering that bottle of whiskey, now, shouldn't you?"

"Live and learn, I suppose."

We fall into silence as a handful of people sit in front of us. The ceremony's due to start in about ten minutes, and knowing Janelle, the procession will begin on the dot.

"Can I ask you something?" Thomas says quietly after a couple of minutes.

I nod, and he turns so that our knees press together. It's reminiscent of our time sitting together at the bar.

"I understand having the stag party here," he begins, "but why the wedding? Should I expect Elvis to show up here like he did at ours?"

I don't love the reminder that Janelle isn't the first person from our family to get married this weekend, so I focus on his other question. "This is where Janelle and Ron met," I explain.

"We were here for a concert that weekend, and Ron was celebrating his soccer retirement. We saw him with his friends at some restaurant, surrounded by a bunch of those *Happy Retirement* balloons, and my sweet, nosy cousin couldn't help but go over and ask what he did for work where he could retire before thirty-five."

Thomas chuckles and shakes his head, like nothing about what I've shared surprises him any. "That means you've met my brother already."

My eyebrows shoot up. "Are you serious?"

"Yep. He was there that night."

"Huh. Small world." I narrow my eyes at him. "But if he was there, wouldn't you have known that's how Janelle and Ron met?"

His lips part to answer before he stops himself, pressing them into a firm line instead. It's a long beat before he speaks. "My brother and I . . . don't really talk much."

Like last night, I'm intrigued by the dynamics of his life and relationships. Whatever's there is just begging to be dug into.

But it won't be by me, because on Monday morning I'm going back to clean up the broken pieces of my life in DC, with Thomas nothing but a distant memory. My lawyer is going to figure out how to get the annulment on the grounds that we were both drunk out of our minds—whatever the legal term for that is. Those pictures may be forever, but this marriage doesn't have to be.

So I keep my mouth shut and don't press for more. The silence between us this time is tense and awkward. He's moved his leg away, leaving me surprisingly cold. I refuse to read into it and keep my gaze trained ahead, watching the church fill up and letting out a relieved breath when my parents choose to sit up front with my grandmother and Aunt Caroline. As the string quartet that's been quietly playing in the background picks up in volume, I finally relax a little, glad for the distraction of the ceremony starting.

A dapper tuxedoed Ron appears up front with the minister, practically bouncing on his toes in excitement. By the time the bridesmaids and groomsmen finish making their way down the aisle, he looks like he's about ready to bolt. But unlike Étienne, he's not looking to run out of the church, but straight toward the vision in white tulle standing just inside the doors.

I climb to my feet with everyone else, eyes drawn to Janelle. She's glowing, practically levitating as her father escorts her down the rose petal–covered path, and my vision swims with tears at the sight of her. She deserves this happily ever after, one that I had the privilege of watching blossom from the very start. One that I can't wait to watch grow and bloom even further.

"Are you crying?"

Thomas's whispered words have my eyes cutting from Janelle to him. "Shut up." I swipe underneath my eyes. To be honest, I'm about five seconds from blubbering like a baby.

The next thing I know, he's holding up his silk pocket square to me. "Here."

I shake my head. "I'll get mascara all over it."

He pushes it closer to my hand. "I can buy another."

I hesitate before taking it and mumbling my thanks as I dab at my eyes. By the time my vision clears again, Janelle and Ron are together at the altar, smiling at each other like there's no one else in the room. I hate to keep thinking about him, but in the brief moments we were up there together, Étienne certainly didn't look at me like that. But . . . I don't think I looked at him that way either. All I felt in the moment was sheer relief that we'd made it, that our wedding was finally happening and that we'd be able to settle into our lives together with no more stress.

That everything would be okay once we walked out of the church together.

But instead, he walked out without me.

A rumble of laughter has my attention snapping back. I must have missed some joke Ron made in his vows, and I force a delayed chuckle. I want to be present in this moment, to be as joyful as I'm capable of feeling, because Janelle deserves nothing less. But damn if my chest isn't aching.

Down by my side, Thomas's hand brushes mine. I don't have time to draw my fingers away before he's hooking his pinkie around mine and holding tight. I glance over at him, confused, but he's staring at Janelle and Ron, paying me no mind.

So I turn my attention back too and leave our hands linked in this little way. Because, as much as I don't want to admit it, I think I need this. I need this grounding. The reminder that I'm not standing in this mess alone.

I may be moving on from this man by the end of the weekend, but I'm glad to have him right now.

▚▚▚▚▚

Thank God for assigned seating and bless the DJ for wanting to get the party started ASAP, because this reception is exactly what I needed.

Janelle was kind enough to move my seat from a table of young couples to the one with our grandparents and other older folks, people who are more than willing to glare and loudly shoo away anyone determined to talk to me. It also helps that most of them have no idea how to use the internet past logging into Facebook, so my newest online shitstorm hasn't reached them yet. Maybe this is the crowd I need to hang with from now on.

I have to admit, I'm not having the worst time. The country club venue a few miles from downtown is beautiful, dinner was delicious, and the DJ is spinning all the cookout classics, including a few tracks that have members of Ron's family looking more than a little flustered. They've been extremely accepting of Janelle into their family otherwise, so I'm writing off the clutched pearls as a little culture shock.

Most importantly, the bride's enjoying herself. After planting a kiss on her new husband's cheek, she bops her way toward where I've taken up residence in the middle of the floor, our grandmother my dance partner. If there's one thing I've learned tonight, it's that Grandma can throw ass with the best of them.

"Surprised you're not dancing with Thomas," Janelle says as she bumps her hip against mine. "He keeps looking at you."

I roll my eyes and bump her back before excusing us from Grandma, who wastes no time hustling into line for the next song. She almost slapped the life out of me while doing the Wobble, so I make sure Janelle and I are a safe distance away for "Candy," because that woman is absolutely planning to touch the floor. I don't want to be in the danger zone for it.

"He can look all he wants," I tell Janelle as we ease into the steps. I don't know how she's managing it in a ball gown. "I'll talk to him tomorrow once our lawyers are on it."

"So you're going ahead with the annulment?"

"Of course." I shoot her a look as I lean and shoulder-shimmy. "It was a mistake, one that I plan to remedy as soon as possible. I've got other shit to worry about."

"Yeah, all right, I get it."

Based on her tone, it seems like she *doesn't* get it, and it has my frown deepening.

"What, you want me to stay married to him?" I scoff. "Elle, I don't even know the guy."

"You can get to know him," she says innocently.

I could. But I'm sure once he gets to know *me*—once he sees the mess I am—I can't imagine he'd want to stay.

"And just think about how you can rub this in Étienne's face," she goes on.

"Right, because spite is the best decision-maker."

"Maybe not usually, but what he did to you was—" She cuts short to gather what she wants to say. "I just want you to live again, Stella. Because whoever you've become, whoever he turned you into . . . that's not someone I recognize."

Janelle's words hit me so hard that I can't believe I manage to keep dancing, albeit a little half-assed. It's muscle memory, I guess. And muscle memory is what I've fallen back on when it comes to my entire life lately. I've been going through the motions, doing exactly what was expected of me, only to realize I was doing it without thought. Without feeling. Without passion.

Last night, though . . . That was nothing but passion and impulse and sheer fucking delight. *That* was being alive.

Mika essentially said she wanted the same thing for me that Janelle is saying now. I knew I'd retreated in on myself some, but I didn't think anyone had really noticed or hated the change. I thought that was just what growing up looked like. Doesn't everyone pushing thirty calm down and settle in for the ride of adulthood ahead?

The answer to that is standing right beside me in her wedding dress, tipsy again after a hectic bachelorette party. With her law degree and successful career. With her love for going out every Friday night just to dance and drink martinis. Who married a sweetheart British footballer because she was bold enough to approach him first. If that's what your thirties can look like, then why have I been so adamant about suppressing the parts of myself that I love?

But staying married to a stranger is one step too far.

"I'm getting back to my old self," I tell her. "I don't need a man to do that."

"No, you don't," she agrees. "But there's nothing wrong with a little help."

The next dance step has me turning my back to her and my ensuing shoulder shimmy is far less enthusiastic than the ones before. Not even Grandma's loud laughter can shake the unsettled energy from my chest. And it only compounds when someone moves in front of me, forcing me slightly out of line.

"Stella," Thomas says, low enough that I barely hear him over the music and merriment. "We need to talk."

I glance away from him, shifting so that I can keep on beat even though he's in my way. "I'm trying to dance here, Thomas."

"It's important."

"So is the Electric Slide."

He grabs my elbow firmly, though not anywhere near enough to hurt, but it makes me look up at him, taking in the concern written across his annoyingly handsome face.

"The news is out." He takes a breath, then confirms the worst, even though deep down I already know. "The world knows we're married."

# CHAPTER 10

THOMAS

My wife is furious.

She'd be even more upset to know that I'm referring to her as *my wife* in my head. Even my stomach churns at the idea. But that's what she is, whether we like it or not. And it would appear Stella's still leaning toward the *not* option.

"How did it get out?" she fumes, stilettos clicking against the tiled floor as she paces. I'm learning this is her stress response—angrily stomping and somehow looking sexy while doing it. "Who leaked it?"

We've tucked ourselves away in a small back room in the reception venue, a space that was likely meant for newly wedded couples to escape the chaos of their big day and have a moment alone. The irony is certainly not lost on me.

"It was an anonymous source, according to the articles I've seen so far," I answer from my spot on the small sofa.

Between my own quick googling and the overload of links my assistant has sent me—which tipped me off in the first place—I've figured out that the person who sold the story has to have been at our wedding. The pictures that accompanied the articles weren't the exact ones I found on my camera roll, but they're close. Like whoever took them on my phone immediately pulled out their own and snapped more.

"But they were at the chapel with us," Stella pushes. "Our *photographer.*" She spits the last word like it's poison.

"They were. But that could have been anyone. Another couple getting hitched, an employee, some random person who followed us inside . . . It's impossible to know."

She lifts her phone, scrolling before reading aloud, "'According to the source, the couple proclaimed they were "ecstatic" to be getting married, even though the bride swapped around the groom's hyphenated surname in her vows before correcting herself in a fit of giggles. Baldwin was set to marry French businessman Étienne Beauchamp just over two weeks ago, but the wedding was called off at the last second. The source says they were "shocked" to see Baldwin move on so quickly but that they wished the new couple well.'" Stella looks over at me, her brow scrunched. "'They were shocked.' Doesn't that sound like it's someone who knows me?"

I shrug, not having gleaned that from the quote. "Anyone who heard about your other wedding would probably say the same. It *is* kind of shocking."

I've put my foot in my mouth and her glare confirms it.

"But that doesn't matter," I follow up quickly. It's time to change the subject. "Tell me how you want to handle this and I'll follow your lead."

Stella makes to answer, but the phone buzzing in her hand distracts her. "Sorry, I need to take this," she mumbles before turning her back to me and answering.

"You're *married*?" a woman screeches, loud enough for me to hear without the call even on speaker. "What the *fuck*, Stella?"

Stella desperately tries to lower the volume as she shuffles toward the corner. It doesn't do much.

"Why am I reading about this on TMZ instead of you telling me?" the woman demands. "Is this for real?"

"Lower your voice, Mika," Stella hisses, and I sadly can't hear the rest of the conversation from there.

This Mika person is barely giving Stella the chance to get a word in edgewise, though. There are plenty of cut-off sentences and stressed reassurances that she'll tell Mika everything when she can. By the time she hangs up, she's dazed and unsteady on her feet.

"Things are . . . not good," she says, pressing a hand to the wall to stabilize herself. "My best friend says she found out about the wedding from one of the upper-level staff members at my company, which means . . ." She takes a deep, shuddering breath. "Which means that *everyone* at my company is likely to find out soon, including my shareholders."

I don't know the ins and outs of her business, but it's sounding like this is going to cause a problem. "What percentage of the company do you own?" I ask warily. If her board of directors can get rid of her, then *not good* is a vast understatement.

"Fifty-one percent," she says. "So they can't oust me. But they can make my life hell if they don't believe in my leadership abilities."

I won't say I know too much about business, but I know enough from growing up around my family's hospitality company to understand this could be career-ruining if her board decides to jump ship.

"It's just a silly accidental marriage," I try to reassure. "You were at a hen do. Crazier things have happened on those. I'm sure they can forgive you that little lapse in judgment."

She snorts humorlessly. "I think they're going to focus

entirely on the *lapse in judgment* part. This shows that I'm irresponsible. That I can't be trusted. And . . ." She trails off, taking a moment to wet her deep crimson lips. "This isn't the first misstep I've had lately. I didn't tell you the whole story of what happened after my ex left me." She lets out a humorless laugh. "I'm surprised you haven't seen the video yet, honestly."

"I haven't looked you up," I confess, which is a bit silly to not have done at this point. "It felt like an invasion of privacy."

But now I'm wishing I had because *what* video is she talking about?

She blows out a breath and looks back down at her phone, tapping at the screen, then hands the device to me. "Press *play*."

The cover photo of the video is of a drunk Stella staring into the camera, a nearly overflowing glass of red wine in her hand. From what I can see, she's fully dressed—or at least the black rollneck sweater gives that illusion—so that rules out one of the horrible ideas that popped to mind. Plus, it's only a minute long, which I hope means she wasn't able to pack too much into it.

I press *play*. There are a few seconds of silence—so far, so good—before Stella leans in to the camera, nearly spilling wine as she does. And then she starts talking.

"Oh," I exhale, eyes wide, as I take in her ranting. "This video is . . ."

The real-life Stella groans as the one on-screen tells the world that love is *a made-up, steaming pile of bullshit*, and that men are *dick-waving sadists* who get off on making women love them, only to leave in the end. At least, that's the gist of it. Her speech has a few more-colorful words than that.

I watch the rest of the video in silence. It ends with an emphatic "*And fuck the French! All y'all suck. And macarons aren't even good!*"

"Well," I announce as I attempt to gather my thoughts, silence ringing through the room. "That wasn't great. But it isn't as bad as you made it seem." And it's true. I've seen worse. I've *done* worse. "I think the most incriminating part is you saying macarons aren't good. You built a business around them."

"I know!" she laments, dropping onto the sofa with me. "It's a bad look all around."

"Drunkenly screaming about how love isn't real and men suck isn't so terrible. I mean, you weren't wrong about either."

She slides me a look from the corner of her eye. "You'd really put your whole gender down like that? I can't believe I'm married to a misandrist."

I shrug, ignoring her sarcasm because I'm serious. "I've just seen enough shitty men do shitty things."

It's clear she wants to question that, but she pushes on with her other crimes. "What about the love part? You don't believe in it?"

"I've never been in it. What would I know?"

Again, I see curiosity spark in her gaze even as she tosses another query. "What about me hating the French?"

"Can't blame you there either. They're kind of universally hated."

She elbows me, scowling. "They're not bad people, and I shouldn't have said that just because I hate *one* Frenchman."

"Whatever you say."

She huffs and leans against the cushions, head falling back dejectedly. "But this is why I've tried to be on my best behavior lately. Us getting drunkenly married is the cherry on top of all the bullshit I've been involved in."

It's a hat trick of less-than-great things, though nothing she can't recover from. "You're going to be okay, Stella."

"Maybe," she mumbles. "But people finding out about the

annulment is going to be another blow. Our marriage was irresponsible enough, but separating immediately after? That's just admitting I massively fucked up."

The hope that sparks in my chest shouldn't be there. She's already given me her answer about not wanting to stay married, and I'm determined to respect it. She said *no*, not *convince me*.

But is it considered trying to convince her if it really could help the mess she's in?

"What if you reconsidered my previous offer?" I ask before I can think better of it. "To stay married."

Her head lifts slowly, eyes cautious as she stares at me. When she doesn't say anything, I push on, even though my brain is screaming at me to shut up.

"Things were different when this wasn't public yet," I rush to explain. "The news coming out has changed the situation. Like you said, it's going to look worse if we go forward with the annulment now. So . . . what if we stay married and ride this out together? Would that help you?"

Is it shady to frame it so that my offer is more about her than me? Absolutely. But I *do* want to help her, and that flicker of hope is refusing to be extinguished.

Yet there's a growing rock of guilt along with it, because my own indiscretions haven't been revealed. Does she know what I've done? How hated I am?

"Have you looked me up?" I blurt before she can answer.

She blinks, thrown by the change in direction, then shakes her head. "No. I told myself I didn't want to know more about you than I already did if we were getting an annulment. A clean break."

Well. That's problematic, but she deserves to make an informed decision. I can't keep this from her.

I pull my phone out of my pocket. "I also have an incriminating video I'd like to show you."

Stella looks at me like she can't believe her luck. "Oh no."

"Oh yes." I tap at the screen, then reluctantly hand it to her. "Behold, my own personal nightmare."

I stare at the ceiling as my furious recorded voice rings out through the room. As much as I want to gauge Stella's reaction, I don't want to see her horror.

"He could have fucking killed me!"

There's the crack of my helmet hitting the concrete, heard even over the scream of wheel guns and cars passing in the pit lane. I'm standing in the back of the McMorris garage, barely visible behind a partition leading to where the engineers are set up. When I first saw the video, I couldn't believe I'd missed someone filming me, because there's no hiding in those back hallways. I should have seen someone there.

There are a few seconds of silence as the team principal tries to calm me down, speaking quietly. Then: *"Oh, don't give me that. Castellucci knew* exactly *what he was doing. He does that shit on purpose and enjoys it!"*

There's more of my ranting—very similar to Stella's, actually—but the worst is still to come.

"Fuck him," I spit as my tirade starts drawing to a close. *"If he keeps driving like that, he's going to get himself killed too. And you know what? I hope he does! I hope he dies. I hope the rest of us never have to worry about him again. He deserves the worst. Let the trash take itself out."*

There's more background noise before the video cuts, but hearing the horrible things I said all over again has me nauseated. I was angry and hurting—literally, because I'd just pried myself out of my ruined car after Lorenzo forced me into the barriers—and lashing out. I didn't mean any of it. But whoever filmed this either didn't realize it or wanted to make me look as awful as possible.

I force myself to glance over at Stella when she presses my phone back into my hand. Shockingly, she doesn't look as upset as I expected.

"That wasn't cute," she says. "But unless that guy actually died, this isn't terrible. I mean, he nearly killed *you*. I'd be pissed off too."

I swallow hard and rub my jaw, eyes darting away.

"Oh shit," she blurts, rocking forward so that I can't avoid her gaze. "Did he actually die? Did you kill him? Oh my God, did I marry a *murderer*?"

"Jesus, no!" I drop my hand again, heat creeping up my neck and into my cheeks. "I didn't have anything to do with it, but he—" I cut short as guilt burns through me. "He ended up having a terrible accident about a month after I said all of that. He lived, but now he's paralyzed and everyone hates me because someone leaked this video of me behaving like an absolute twat."

Stella leans back again and grimaces. "Okay, that's not as bad as you killing him, but that's still bad," she amends. "And you don't know who posted this?"

I shake my head. "I'm still trying to figure it out. I have a hard time believing anyone from the team would do this with all the NDAs we've signed. It was a huge risk to take."

"Someone there must really hate you."

That stings. I've always thought of myself as being well-liked, especially within the McMorris team. I spent two years with them as a junior driver before they bumped me up to being their test and reserve driver. Then, the next season, I was in one of the race seats, partnering—and often outpacing—their veteran driver. I've only signed multiyear contracts with them in the five years I've been in F1, and I'm hoping to re-sign for a few

more years come the end of next season when my current contract is up. The money I bring to the team with my personal
sponsorships doesn't hurt either.

But this video has thrown a wrench in that plan, even
though our team principal and CEO have assured me it hasn't
changed the way they feel about me. They could be lying
straight to my face. And they probably are, considering several
sponsors have reached out to express their concerns about my
behavior. But no one has dropped me or the team yet, and I
won't know anything about my future at McMorris until that
new contract comes across my agent's desk.

More than anything, though, I wish I knew *who* hates me
this much.

"That's my drama," I finish. "I understand if this makes you
want to run away from me screaming."

Stella's nose wrinkles. "I don't run. I'm a Pilates girl."

I'm in no mood to laugh, and yet her quip has a surprised
huff leaving my lips.

She shifts to face me, tucking one long leg underneath her.
The bronze silk of her dress pulls around her hips. My eyes are
drawn to the dramatic curve, even though I know this isn't the
time to admire her, but it's hard not to when she looks like a
goddess. I nearly tripped when I spotted her in the church earlier, because somehow, she was more beautiful in the daylight
than in dim club lighting. Even this morning, hungover with
smudged makeup, she was gorgeous. But Stella all done up? I
don't know how anyone could keep their eyes off her.

"Look," she says, leveling me with a stare. "It's clear we're
both in less-than-ideal circumstances, with no room to judge
each other. But do you really think staying married and making people think this wasn't some drunken mistake is going to
fix anything? Or that they'd even buy it?"

"Yes. I absolutely do." I sound more confident than I feel, but I really think this could ease the uncomfortable situation we're in. "It won't be hard for people to buy. We can have our PR teams play up how hurt and abandoned you felt by your ex-fiancé and how I swept in at just the right moment."

Stella snorts. "Wow, you really are Prince Charming," she drawls, sarcasm dripping from every word. But there's an upward tilt to her lips that's far more genuine.

I hold her gaze and hope she can see how serious I am. "This will benefit us both. It'll get Figgy and my parents off my back, and maybe it'll even make me look better to my team."

"And my board of directors won't think I'm a damn fool who got married and divorced in the span of forty-eight hours," Stella adds, and I can see the wheels turning in her head. "You might be right about this, Thomas."

I know I am, but I certainly won't say that. Stella has to come to her own conclusions without me pushing her into it.

"Anything else incriminating I need to know before I say yes?" she asks.

My heart leaps. "Not that I can think of, no."

She makes a vague sound, then looks back down at her own phone, quickly typing something in and scrolling. I frown and shift closer so I can see what she's doing.

"Are you googling me?"

Stella doesn't acknowledge me, unabashedly reading. "Gotta know what I'm getting myself into." Her brow knits, then she glances at me. "You're a Libra?"

I feel like I should be offended. "What's wrong with that?"

"Nothing! I'm a Leo. We're . . . actually pretty compatible."

I let out a breath. Last thing I need is the stars deciding we're not a good match. Not that I believe in any of that stuff, but if she does, then I need to start doing my research.

Stella locks her phone again and bites her lip, a hint of apprehension in her eyes. "How long would we do this for? I mean, obviously we're not going to stay married for the rest of our lives. This is a temporary, mutually beneficial arrangement."

Spoken like a true businesswoman. But she's right that this can't last for long. We both deserve the chance to find and date other people we might have a connection with, even if there *is* a spark of . . . *something* between us. I'm under no impression that Stella is my forever person—despite reciting vows that said as much—and she clearly feels the same.

"We can do it for as long as we think it's helping us," I suggest. "And when one or both of us are ready for it to end, we'll talk it over and set a divorce date."

"We should stay married for at least a year," she declares, and she must take my surprise for alarm because she quickly follows it up with, "Just on paper. If we decide we're sick of each other sooner than that, then we'll quietly separate and do our own things until time's up. But divorcing any earlier than that won't look good."

She has a point. And who knows if we'll have accomplished what we want by then anyway.

"That's reasonable," I agree. "So . . . does that mean you're in? You want to do this?"

Her gaze drops to her lap as she considers. This is quite possibly the most absurd thing I've ever done, and I'm sure she feels the same.

Yet her eyes find mine again a moment later, and the determined glint in them tells me her answer before her lips form the words.

"I'm in," she says. "Let's stay married."

# CHAPTER 11

STELLA

Agreeing to stay married to Thomas is one thing. Actually following through with it is another, especially when members of my family are on the other side of the door.

We need to get out of here as quickly as possible before anyone corners or questions us. Thomas and I aren't done talking—there are a thousand things we need to hash out before we can move forward with this plan—but this isn't the right venue for it. I'm about to suggest we go back to my hotel when the door bangs open and we're both left blinking at a cloud of tulle.

Janelle shoves herself inside the room. "You two are in deep trouble," she announces. "Not only are you stealing my spotlight, Stella, but your parents are freaking out. They want to talk to you." Then she jerks her chin at Thomas. "And him."

"*Fuuuck.*" I drag the word out on an exhale, eyes sliding closed to shut out the world for a heavy second. "I'm so sorry, Elle. I hope I didn't ruin your day."

The scratch and shuffle of fabric floats through the air, getting me to look over at Janelle again, but she's already in front of me, attempting to squeeze herself into the tiny space between Thomas and me on the couch.

"No apologies," she says, grabbing my hand and holding tight. "You didn't mean for any of this to happen. Is there anything I can do to help? I know you've got lawyers of your own, but do you need me to find you someone local to get started on the annulment? You probably don't want to put that off now that the news is out."

I lock eyes with Thomas over Janelle's head, icy panic spreading through my veins. How the hell am I supposed to answer her question? Do I tell her the truth—that we're staying married but it's a sham? Or do I lie and tell her to start looking? Neither seems like a good option, and judging from the way Thomas is British-grimacing right now, he's leaving the choice up to me.

"Actually," I start cautiously, still staring at Thomas and hoping he'll give me a sign if I take my answer too far, "we've decided to stay married for now."

Janelle jerks away like I've slapped her, eyes wide. "That's a big departure from your attitude earlier."

The cold panic shifts to hot embarrassment when one of Thomas's eyebrows rises questioningly. He knows I've been adamant about getting us out of this situation, so it shouldn't be a surprise that I told Janelle our story and how I felt.

"Yeah, well, we decided it could be for the best." I clear my throat and force myself to look at her instead of Thomas. "Can we talk more about this tomorrow? I need to get out of here before my parents find me."

Her lips twist to the side. "I don't know if you'll be able to leave without talking to them. They're on the warpath."

I bite my tongue to keep from swearing again, because *great*. Just great! I might be able to avoid the finer details in this conversation about what's going on, but there will be no avoiding it with my parents. They're going to make sure all the information comes out *now*.

Plus, this isn't the way I wanted Thomas to meet them—if he ever had to at all. Logically, I know it has to happen eventually, because not meeting your partner's loving and supportive parents is a massive red flag. But introducing my real-but-actually-fake husband to them is the last thing I want to do.

And then there's the whole issue of *how* I'm going to introduce him. It's too much of a risk to let them in on the truth of the situation lest they accidentally let something slip and ruin the charade, but that means I'm going to have to lie. And that somehow feels even worse.

"Then we'll just have to face them," Thomas says, and my eyes snap back up to him.

"You cannot be for real."

"I'm very much for real." He pushes some of Janelle's tulle off his lap, and I hate myself for once again noticing how large his hands are, especially when he stands and offers one to help me up. "Let's do this and get out of here."

I scoff and burrow into the sofa. "I'd rather stay in this room all night than face them."

"I can carry you out if it's going to come to that."

"Ooh, like a real bride!" Janelle squeals.

I glare at her. "Don't you start."

But I'm reminded of how easily he lifted me into his lap last night, and the warmth of mortification I've been feeling shifts into a different kind of heat. He could absolutely carry me out of here if he wanted. And I'd let him.

"Ugh, fine!" I shove up from the sofa before my brain can make an unwise decision. "Let's get this over with. How do you want to explain this situation?"

"Like I said yesterday, we can stick as close to the truth as possible. We hit it off recently and decided to get married."

I roll my eyes. He's a fool to think anyone who knows us well is going to believe that half-assed story. "We need actual *details*. Like dates and a timeline and—"

The door swinging open cuts me off. And then I'm staring at my mom and dad.

"Estelle Margaux," Mom thunders as she strides into the room, and I know by the names she's used that I'm in big, big trouble. "What in the *world* is going on?"

Dad is a half step behind her, ready to back her up if necessary. He knows she's got this handled, though. She always does.

I try to answer, but everything I want to say gets stuck in my throat, leaving me opening and closing my mouth like a fish. It's Janelle who breaks the silence with the rustle of her giant skirt as she picks it up.

"That's my cue to leave," she announces, marching to the door. "Love y'all. No murders allowed on my wedding day."

When she's gone, the door clicking closed behind her, there's nothing left for me to do except swallow hard and say, "I'm not sure where to start."

"You can start with how you're apparently *married* and how your father and I had to find out through the grapevine instead of you telling us yourself."

"So, about that . . ." I wet my lips, searching for the right answer. "It wasn't—I didn't—"

"I'm so sorry about the confusion, Mrs. Baldwin," Thomas cuts in as I flounder. "Our nuptials happened a bit suddenly, and we didn't want to take any attention away from Janelle and Ron today. We also didn't expect the news to leak the way it did. Stella certainly wanted to tell you both as soon as possible."

Mom's sharp gaze snaps to Thomas, who's moved up beside me. "And who exactly are you?" she asks, voice so chilly that I shiver.

He offers her an easy smile and his hand to shake. "Thomas Maxwell-Brown. It's a pleasure to finally meet you."

"*Finally?*" Mom repeats, ignoring his outstretched hand. "Considering my daughter has never mentioned you, I can't imagine you've been waiting *that* long."

Thomas's hand drops, confidence shaken. Can't even blame him since that's Mom's specialty. "I—well—"

I snap out of my daze as he fights for a reply. We can't both be flailing here. "We've known each other for ages," I blurt. I'm not sure where the lie comes from, but now that it's out, I can't stop. "We met the same night that Janelle met Ron. He was there too. Isn't that right, Tommy?"

Thomas shoots me an incredulous look, and I swear I see him mouth *Tommy?* before he clears his throat and shifts his tight smile back to my parents. "That's right," he corroborates. "We've kept in contact ever since." He stops, thinking for a moment before his eyes widen. "As friends, of course. I knew she was in a relationship. I never—I never interfered with that."

I'm burning up as I nod along. "Yep, just friends! But then when everything with Étienne exploded, Thomas was kind enough to reach out to see how I was doing." I glance up at him, hoping he can read the panic in my eyes and pick up this awful improv where I've left off.

"Mm-hmm." The sound is incriminatingly high-pitched. "I wanted to make sure she was okay, especially after that little video of hers went viral."

I let out a laugh that's more of a groan, hating him for bringing that up. "He's such a good guy," I gush, grabbing his hand and squeezing hard. I'm vindicated when I feel him wince. "We decided to meet up in Vegas right before Janelle's bachelorette party and realized just how much we clicked. It kind of felt like fate."

Mom stares at us, bewildered. She's the one fighting for words now, because there's simply *no way* she believes anything we've just said. And despite her sparkling career in the court-room, she seems lost as to what to ask us next.

"And that led to you two getting hitched?" Dad asks for them both, squinting as he struggles to piece it all together. "Se-riously?"

"There was also alcohol involved," Thomas says apologeti-cally.

I want to kick him for admitting that. Then again, how else could we explain such a rash decision? The world is well aware that I don't make the best choices while drinking, and my par-ents know it too. Their intelligent, levelheaded daughter wouldn't pull a stunt like this without some sort of influence.

"Our feelings for each other are very real, though," Thomas continues before I can butt in with another explanation. "This wedding was rushed, yes, and certainly an on-the-fly decision, but I have no regrets."

My desire to inflict harm on him wanes with how genuine he sounds. I know it's an act, but it's a good one, and judging by the way Dad's face softens, Thomas is on the right track. Well, with one of my parents at least.

"Not a single regret?" Mom has found her voice, and it's dripping with doubt. "You don't regret that you've never met us? Or that Stella kept you a secret for all this time? Or that you've rushed into this binding contract with a woman who's just had her life turned upside down by a man and is clearly still trying to heal from that?"

"Mom," I snap, but Thomas's thumb brushing the inside of

my wrist distracts me from following it up with anything too harsh. "I wasn't some unwilling participant, so don't make it out like he's taking advantage of me. I'm sorry I didn't talk to you guys about it beforehand, and I'm sorry that you found out like this, but we're married, and that's that."

She throws her hands up with a scoff, whirling to face my father. "Is this girl for real?" she asks him. "Are we just supposed to accept this?"

Dad is solemn as he stares down at his wife. "I think we all need to take some time to process what's going on. We can discuss this more when everyone's calmer."

Mom makes another sound of distaste, but she knows he's right. She turns back to Thomas and me, expression flickering between confusion and hurt.

"We're flying back to Atlanta in the morning," she says tightly. "Will we see you there for Thanksgiving?"

I nod. I'll be there, at least. Who knows about the man standing next to me, though, because anything could happen in the next twelve days.

"Good. We'll talk more then."

With that, she turns on her heel and strides out of the room as quickly as she came in.

Dad's slower, coming over to kiss my forehead and shake Thomas's hand—a bit too firmly, but at least he makes the effort—before backing away.

"Call us if you need anything," he says, and then he's gone too.

I stare at the empty doorway, praying I'll suddenly wake up and realize all of this was just a bad dream. But when that doesn't happen, I whirl on Thomas and yank my hand out of his.

"That was so bad," I hiss. "This is never going to work!"

He's paler than he was earlier, but there's a deluded determination written across his face. "It will," he urges. "That was just a little stumble."

"A *stumble*? I almost made it sound like I was cheating on Étienne, and you admitted we were drunk!"

"It wasn't my finest moment," he admits. "But really, were they going to believe anything else?"

I groan and throw my head back because no, they wouldn't have, and I hate that it's the only part of the truth we can share with them. Maybe I should have told them the whole wedding was a mistake and how we're trying to make the best of a bad situation. There's still time. I could chase after them and confess it all.

But when I look at Thomas again, I know we went with our best option. At least we have a story to tell the world now.

"I need to get out of here," I mumble. "I want to go to bed and leave this shitty day behind."

"Then let's go." He gathers my things and passes them over before putting a guiding hand to my shoulder. "I'll tell my driver to meet us at the back exit."

I should thank him for getting us out of here as stealthily as possible, but my throat is too tight to force more words out. Still, I hope the weak smile I flash after we slip into the back seat of the sedan says more than I currently can. When he returns it, the vise grip around my esophagus eases some.

We're both too lost in our own thoughts for the silence to be awkward, though I know we're going to have to speak to each other soon enough. We have at least a thirty-minute drive ahead of us, plenty of time to get the basics of our plan down as we head back into the heart of Las Vegas, but I'm still struggling for words ten minutes in.

"Your name's Estelle?"

I glance over, relieved that he's kicked off this conversation but also wincing at the reminder of my mother's tirade.

"I was named after my great-grandmother," I explain. "But my parents always call me Stella. Unless, of course, I'm in trouble, as you just saw."

He nods like he's filing that information away. "Guess it's a good thing I know your full name now. Probably something a husband should know about his wife."

I give a scratchy, surprised laugh. "Oh, honey, that's not all. I don't know if you're ready for my government name."

"Try me." He crosses his arms over his chest in challenge, smirking. "I'm not sure much can beat Thomas Phillip Henry Arthur Maxwell-Brown."

"Oh yeah? Try Estelle Margaux Wilhelmina Tyrrell Baldwin."

He lets out a low, impressed whistle. "It sounds like we're a match made in heaven. Have you considered taking my last name? Maybe triple hyphenating?"

I don't want to smile, because the situation we're in is nothing short of a nightmare, but his dry jokes have my lips involuntarily twitching upward. "I already have trouble fitting my name on forms, so I'll pass."

"That's understandable." He pauses, his tone a little less light when he speaks again. "We need to know everything about each other if this is going to be believable."

I swallow hard, torn over whether we're making a huge mistake. Will we actually fool people into thinking we're a real couple? Maybe the general public will fall for it, but what about the people who know us? His family, my family, Figgy, my board of directors . . . Are we just asking to fail miserably?

"Guess we should start with the basics." I bite my lip as it hits me just how little I know about this man. "I don't even know how old you are. I'm choosing to believe you're at least old enough to legally drink in this country."

I'm once again falling back on humor to keep from shoving my head between my knees so I can stave off the mounting panic. He looks young, but not *that* young. If I had to guess, I would say he's probably my age. Factor in how his parents are pushing him to get married—something that typically doesn't happen for men until they're in their thirties, the bastards—and maybe I'll be pleasantly surprised when he reveals he's older than me.

Thomas laughs. "I just turned twenty-six."

I swear the car shudders to a stop even though we're smoothly moving through traffic. "Twenty-six?" I repeat, and it's followed by an involuntarily low, keening groan that makes me glad there's a divider between us and the driver. "Oh *God*. I'm older than you!"

He looks at me like that's hard to believe. "Seriously? How old are *you*?"

I should take his disbelief as a compliment, but I'm already preparing to undo my seat belt so I can bend over and ward off the spinning. "Twenty-eight! I'm a cougar!"

"Sweetheart, it's two years," he says, scoffing at my dramatics. "Calm down."

"*Calm down?* Do you understand how frowned-upon it is for the woman to be the older party in a hetero relationship?"

Étienne pretended he didn't hate that I was only nine months younger than him, as if the fact that we were literal peers and I wasn't some fresh-faced ingenue was a problem in the crowds he ran in. It was obvious, though, especially since on my birthday and for the three months a year when we were the same age, he acted like saying the number we shared was blasphemy.

"My mother is six years older than my father," Thomas reveals. "And as a grown man, I don't give a fuck if a woman I'm attracted to is older than me."

I blink, almost compelled to clutch my nonexistent pearls at his bluntness. He's right that it shouldn't matter, though. We're both consenting adults, and the stigma shouldn't exist, but it's something I have to get over thanks to Étienne's influence.

"Okay, fine," I concede. "Let's just . . . move on from that." I take a breath as I figure out what to ask next. Most of this is going to be information that would come up organically over the course of dating someone, but this is about to be a crash course. "Speaking of parents, tell me about yours."

"Hopefully they won't ambush you like yours did to me," he says wryly. "Iris, my mum, is an artist, which is just a nice way of saying she's a rich woman with too much time on her hands. Phillip, my father, inherited our family's hospitality company and is technically the one in charge, even though my eldest sister runs most of the day-to-day operations and my brother is the face they present to everyone."

Before everything went to shit last night, he mentioned that he was the middle child of five. I'm going to have to learn about them soon enough, but first I want to know more about the family business.

"When you say your family runs a hospitality company," I preface, "what exactly does that mean?"

"We're in hotels."

It's a vague, to-the-point answer, and I wait for him to elaborate, but I get nothing else. "As in, your products are in hotels?" I prompt.

Thomas shifts in his seat. "No, as in, we . . . own hotels."

"You *own* hotels?"

"A chain of them," he says quickly, looking back to me

almost apologetically. "A large luxury chain. A.P. Maxwell International, if you've heard of it."

"Oh." My breath catches as recognition hits. "I've definitely heard of it." I was supposed to honeymoon in one of their opulent Maldives resorts. "So you're *rich* rich."

He fidgets a little more, and there it is, that parliament smile. "We're comfortable, yes."

That's wealthy people talk for *we're fucking swimming in it.* "And to think I was the one worried about a prenup," I muse. "You better hope I don't come for half of everything you have in the divorce."

Even in the dim illumination from the streetlights streaking by, I swear he goes paler. "I suppose we should get that postnup drawn up soon."

"Mm-hmm. Better call your solicitor in the morning and hope I don't disappear in the night."

I can practically see him making himself a mental note, and I stifle a snicker, delighting in toying with him. But then the worry clears from his face and he angles himself toward me, his eyes falling to my hands in my lap.

"I need to get you a ring."

I look down at my left hand, still not quite used to seeing it bare. Embarrassingly, I have a slight tan line from where my last engagement ring used to sit. I guess I wouldn't mind having a new one to cover it up. But something about slipping another ring onto my finger when I just managed to take off the last one has my stomach in knots.

"I'll leave that up to you," I tell him, not wanting to think about the ring sitting in a drawer in the home I was supposed to share with Étienne. "Just get me whatever and something for yourself that matches."

He seems thrown by my request, eyes flicking over me. He probably can't believe the woman wearing hand-picked jewels and a designer gown wouldn't care about a ring she'll have to wear with every outfit. But this isn't a real marriage, and even if I hate what he picks out, I'll only have to tolerate it for a year. Why get invested when I'm just going to give it back? I've already made that mistake once.

Eventually, he nods and moves us on to the next topic. "When do we want to go public as a couple?"

"Haven't we already?" I ask dryly.

"Against our will. I meant more along the lines of when do *we* want to announce to the world that we're together?"

I bite the inside of my cheek, some of that dizzy anxiety returning. "I don't know. Do you have any ideas?"

"Remember when I told you I have to be here for work?" He flashes me a crooked smile, but I do recall that detail. "We could make our debut at the Grand Prix. Would you be up for that?"

Ah yes, that's right, I'm married to a Formula 1 driver. I don't know exactly what a grand prix entails, but I get the feeling it's a big televised deal.

"It does seem like the perfect opportunity," I say, contemplating the idea, but it also sounds like an opportunity for things to go terribly wrong and the whole world to witness it.

"We don't have to," Thomas says, sensing my hesitation. "There's still time to back out of this."

There is, and I could. My parents wouldn't like finding out that I lied to them, but I'd be able to tell the truth. They're the least of my worries, though. My board of directors and my tattered reputation have to take precedence here. And I wouldn't hate rubbing my new relationship in Étienne's face either . . .

I glance away from Thomas, not wanting the understanding in his eyes to sway my decision. The heavily tinted windows make the night appear darker than it is, but there's no disguising the neon glow of the Las Vegas lights drawing closer. I might have made a mistake in this city, one that would be nice to leave here, but it's going to follow me no matter what I do. I might as well use it to my advantage. And if it helps Thomas in the process, then it's an added bonus. My good deed for the year.

I turn back to him. "Fuck that," I declare. "I'm in this. For better or worse, your highness."

But it definitely won't be *till death* that we part.

# CHAPTER 12

THOMAS

"Your parents are shitting themselves."

My best mate's voice carries through my hotel room as I set my phone down on the bedside table. I don't doubt that my parents are currently panicking over the breaking news, but I wouldn't know for certain, considering I blocked their numbers—along with Figgy's and my siblings'.

Joshua, however, was saved from a similar fate because he knew I'd call him when I was ready to unload. It's how our friendship has worked since we met in primary school, with me bottling everything up and him simply waiting for the moment when the cap pops off.

"I'll call them soon and explain everything." I kick off my shoes before pulling at the knot of my tie. "Or at least the parts of it that I can."

Not that Stella and I have had time to discuss what parts that will entail. I invited her up so we could talk more, but she insisted we could do that tomorrow, then practically threw herself out of the car when we pulled up to her hotel. I called Joshua immediately after and confessed everything.

Considering Janelle knows the truth about us, Stella can't be upset that I've told someone in my circle. Sure, Joshua's not blood related—I, sadly, am not Nigerian—but he's unquestionably my family.

"You're *really* going to go through with this?" Joshua asks for what must be the dozenth time. "It's pretty dramatic."

"It's a fucking movie plot!" his wife calls out in the background. Obviously, I couldn't have told Joshua anything without Amara knowing it as well. "I can't wait to see how this one ends!"

"It ends with us happily divorced in a year," I say, a little louder so she can hear me. "And yes, I know it's ridiculous, but you have to admit it's a genius way to make the best of a bad situation."

Joshua heaves a sigh that says more than enough on its own, but he still follows it up with, "I can think of far better ways to handle a situation like this."

"Yeah? Do any of them involve getting my parents and Figgy off my back while making me look like a kindly family man to the public? A public that, mind you, thinks I'm some hateful, death-wishing monster?"

His silence gives me my answer.

"Exactly," I say as I toss my tie aside and unbutton my waistcoat, shrugging out of it and my jacket. "It'll be worth it to finally have some peace. Plus, this helps Stella out too. It's a win for both of us."

"I'm not saying it's a terrible plan," Joshua hedges, even though he might as well be saying as much. "But you're acting like this is going to be so simple. Do you actually think people will believe this is a real relationship? Or that this woman will keep her word and not screw you over somehow?"

His concerns aren't misplaced, and I share them for the

most part, but I'm bristling anyway. "We're going to have a postnuptial agreement drawn up and go about this carefully. I'm not completely mad."

There's a loud snort from Amara, and I know Joshua is shooting her a glare to quietly defend me. But I get her doubts. I haven't made the best decisions in the past, and as my other and longest-standing best friend, she's been witness to many of my less-than-clever moments. Case in point: trying to adopt a pack of feral cats when I was five; snowboarding blindfolded at eleven; breaking into my grandfather's wine cellar to steal a bottle that turned out to be centuries old at fourteen; and "accidentally" setting part of my ancestral home on fire on my seventeenth birthday. She was there trying to talk me out of it all while simultaneously egging me on.

I wouldn't say I'm reckless, but I don't always think things all the way through. It's why Joshua is my voice of reason, gently pulling me back from the edge, and Amara is . . . Well, Amara's there to pat me on the shoulder after I've jumped off the cliff and say, "I told you so."

"While I don't love the fact that you got drunkenly married to a stranger," she says, "I have to admit . . . you could have done a lot worse than Stella Margaux. Her macarons are to *die* for. Ooh, can you ask her when she plans to open a shop in London? I don't want to have to fly to Paris every time I need a fix."

"Amara, come on," Joshua scolds. "Let's get back on topic."

"What?" she shoots back. "That's his wife now! He should know all about her career and aspirations . . . which hopefully include opening a location five minutes from our flat."

I may not care much about the macaron shop part of it all, but Amara's right. Stella is my wife—and there's a lot I need to learn about her if any of this is going to work.

⊽⊽⊽⊽⊽⊽

There's a knock at nine a.m. sharp.

Padding out of the bathroom with a towel in hand to dry my hair, I open the door to Stella and step back so she can enter. She messaged late last night to say she'd be over in the morning to keep talking, but she's staring at me like she's surprised to find me here.

"Good morning." The greeting is cautious as her eyes flick to my bare chest. When they rise again, I swear I see a spark of attraction there, but I'm distracted when she lifts a cardboard drink tray in front of her face. "I brought the beverage of your people: tea."

"Oh." I don't know how to break it to her that I'm actually a flat-white man. I have a feeling she'd have a field day with that combination of words. "Thank you, that was very kind."

She snorts and shoves the tray into my chest. "I'm just kidding, they're both quadruple-shot lattes." She skirts around me and steps into the suite, careful not to let any parts of us brush. "I have a feeling we're going to need the caffeine."

She strides toward the living room, leaving me surrounded by her sweet scent. I should probably feel ashamed of how my eyes travel down her back to her swaying hips, but her ass looks too good in that slinky chocolate-brown skirt. She's paired it with a cream-colored jumper, and even though she's covered from knees to neck, it clings to her figure in all the right places.

It's a perfectly professional outfit. I bet she wears this to her office on a regular basis. But that doesn't stop me from wanting to reach out and bunch the skirt around her hips so I can see exactly what's underneath.

I still can't wrap my head around the fact that we didn't

have sex. It's where everything was headed, and yet we somehow got so distracted that we passed out with all our clothes on after reciting binding marriage vows.

Now that she's my wife, though . . . Well, maybe we'll get to consummate that union soon. It's what we both wanted in the first place. We're just going to get to it a little later than planned.

Closing the suite door, I stop by the bedroom to ditch my towel and grab a T-shirt, then join her in the living room. She's already set up at the small dining table by the floor-to-ceiling windows, sorting through the expensive leather handbag she had slung over her shoulder. I set the lattes down in front of her before tugging on my shirt. When my head pops out, I find her staring at me—or, really, at my abs. I can't resist flexing before tugging the shirt over them, breaking her concentration. She blinks once, then again, before her flustered gaze finds mine.

"Sorry to cut the show short," I tease as I drop into a chair across from her. "Figured we didn't want to waste any time."

She clears her throat and shakes out her hair, forcing a coolness back into her expression. The woman across from me is different from the one I met Friday night. That one was hunting, looking to take me down and add me to her trophy case. This is a businesswoman who's in no mood to entertain my jokes.

"No, we don't," she agrees. "We have a lot to discuss, including ground rules for this relationship."

My brow shoots up. "Ground rules? You're certainly taking this seriously."

"Considering it's my reputation and livelihood on the line, I'd say I am, yeah."

I offer an apologetic smile. It would be nice if I could stop fucking up. "Understood. Well." I spread my hands, offering up the floor of discussion to her. "Let's get started. What are your rules?"

She wets her lips, and my eyes drop to them, lingering just a moment too long to be an innocent glance. Based on the way a corner of her mouth ticks up, she's noticed. That's fine. We're on even ground with our admiration of each other.

"Rule one," she begins grandly. "No secrets. We tell each other everything, no matter how big or small. This won't work if we're hiding anything from each other. I don't want to be caught out if I'm asked something about you that I should know the answer to."

That's reasonable, and it's not like I have anything to hide. Most of my life is out there for anyone to find. "As long as we can agree that certain details stay between us," I add. "I'm sure we both have things that need to remain confidential."

She nods. "We'll make that clear up front."

Works for me. Might be nice to have someone else to dump all the stuff going on in my life on other than Joshua and Amara.

I motion for Stella to continue.

"Rule two: This is an equal partnership." She levels me with a hardened stare, as if she expects me to reject that. "Neither one of us should have to give up or give more than the other. Our respective careers are important and obviously come before anything, but one isn't more important."

I shrug. Don't see why that needs to be a rule. It's common sense. "Okay, got it."

Stella stares at me for a beat, like she can't believe I'm agreeing so easily. Or maybe she thinks I'm going along with whatever she wants just to get through this now and ignore it later. I'm not and I won't, but I guess she doesn't know that.

"Great," she says slowly. "I only have one more rule."

Again, I eagerly await her next sensible mandate. It'll probably be something along the lines of *let's keep our bank accounts separate* or *let's split spending holidays evenly between our families*.

"Number three: No sex."

I freeze, and then I'm metaphorically stumbling, leaning back in my chair as the words hit. "Excuse me?"

"We're obviously attracted to each other," she goes on, like she expected this reaction. She's stated an undeniable fact considering how she's been eyeing me and how I can't get the idea of bending her over this table and finishing what we started the other night out of my head. "But I don't want to make this more complicated when we eventually walk away from each other."

"And you think sex would do that?" I push, trying not to sound like an entitled prick who expects his wife to sleep with him. But . . . I *did* expect that, especially since wanting to fuck each other got us into this in the first place. "Could we have a no-strings situation?"

She shakes her head. "Better safe than sorry. And to add on to that, we should keep all physical intimacy—like touching and kissing—for PDA purposes only. It's exclusively for selling our relationship to others."

Someone's knocked the air right out of my lungs. Was I really that wrong to think this arrangement would be more along the lines of *friends with benefits* instead of *wife I only get to touch when other people are watching*?

"Are you planning to be celibate the entire time we're together?" I challenge. Because this is going to be a *year* of our lives.

She clenches her jaw before relaxing again. "Not necessarily."

"So you're going to *cheat* on me?" I sound outraged because I *am*. This relationship might not be real to us, but it's supposed to be to nearly everyone else in the world. Pursuing someone else would ruin that image and put everything at risk. She can't be serious. She can't want to make us look *worse*.

It's Stella's turn to lean back, eyes widening and full lips turning down. "It's not cheating if we're not really together. And you'd also be allowed to do whatever or whoever you wanted, as long as you kept it on the down-low."

"Are you having a fucking laugh?"

It seems like she's literally about to laugh, because the way her face pinches tells me she's trying not to crack. "You are *so* British," she finally says.

I throw my hands up.

"Okay, okay!" She holds her own hands out in front of her, stopping me from shoving away from the table. "We can put that part on the back burner for now and reassess later, but I really do think the no sex rule is for the best."

I force myself to blow out a breath and see where she's coming from. I'm able to separate sex from feelings, but maybe it's harder for her, and maybe she doesn't want to risk it after just getting out of a relationship. I can understand that. And I can respect it.

But fuck, it's going to be a long, complicated year.

"Fine," I grit out. "No sex. And if we do want to seek out other people, we talk about it first."

She nods enthusiastically, glad to have me on board. "Exactly. It's all about communication."

I say nothing as she toys with her stack of delicate gold necklaces, though before either of us can break the tense silence, her phone buzzes on the table. I catch a glimpse of a calendar notification among dozens of other banners on the screen. My wife is clearly a busy, much-in-demand woman.

"We should merge our calendars," I suggest, because

otherwise, I don't know how I'll keep up with her schedule on top of mine.

She looks up from the screen, grimacing. "Oh Jesus, we really are married."

That drags a laugh out of me, and Stella's shoulders lower from where they've been practically jammed up to her ears. "A true family unit."

She gags dramatically as she grabs her coffee cup, though it's clearly to hide a smile, and I spot a hint of it as she goes to take a sip.

"Anyway," she says after lowering the cup again. "Now that I've gotten my rules out there, do you have anything you want to add?"

"I think you covered it all." More than I would have, at least. "Now what do we do?"

I'm more than happy to let her take the lead on all of this, and judging from how she brightens, she's pleased with it too. But I'm less happy when she pulls out a sheet of paper from her purse with the headline "100 Questions to Ask Your Future Spouse." Feels a little late for that considering we're already married, but I guess we skipped a few important steps. Or a hundred.

Stella levels me with a determined stare. "It's time to get to know each other."

▝▝▝▝▝▝

If I never have to talk about myself again, it'll be too soon. Unfortunately, it's media day—the one day during race week when we sit down for interviews with the press and make social media content for our teams—and that's essentially all I'm expected to do for the next several hours.

Stella's version of *getting to know each other* consisted of me

answering hard-hitting questions like *What's your love language?*
and *How do you react to stressful situations?* for several hours
straight. A lot of my answers were along the lines of *Am I supposed to know what that is?* and clueless shrugging until she got so
fed up that she claimed she had a work call she desperately had
to take. Considering it was a Sunday, I was almost certain she
made it up to get away from me.

We didn't see each other on Monday. I had to meet with my
assistant, manager, and performance coach, who'd all just arrived in town, in order to start prepping for the week ahead.
Stella was busy putting out her own work fires remotely, including talking to her board, which was all made harder by being
stuck in Vegas with me. She could have flown back to DC, but
I can't imagine that would have been convenient. So far, I don't
think we're doing justice to rule two.

Tuesday was more of the same, but we managed to squeeze
in a call to update each other, rule one in action. I told her how
my assistant nearly cried laughing when I told her the news of
our marriage. In return, she shared that her own assistant sent
her a list of the best divorce lawyers in Nevada. Are we off to
the best start convincing people our relationship is genuine?
Not so much.

Despite that, I spent hours picking out a ring for Stella. If no
one believes our words, maybe they'll be persuaded by an over-
size diamond on her finger.

"I still can't believe you're married."

Glancing up from the bowl of fruit I'm trying to choke
down before heading off to the drivers' press conference, I find
my teammate sitting across from me, slowly shaking his head.

"I thought we were going to be bachelors together forever,"
he bemoans, loud enough that I'm sure everyone else in the

McMorris hospitality motorhome can hear. "How could you betray me like this?"

Arlo Wood is a twenty-year-old racing wunderkind, known for his backwards caps, gold chains, and a streaming career that he somehow has time for outside of Formula 1. McMorris signed the Mancunian two years ago, and he's been hot on my trail in the points ever since. He's an asshole, but the endearing kind—the little brother I never had. Most of the time, though, I wish he would shut his yapping little mouth.

"Unlike you, I don't have a reputation as a teen heartthrob to uphold," I reply, pushing my bowl away and checking my watch. I have ten minutes before I need to walk over to the interview room. Ten minutes until I have to stare down a bunch of reporters who hate me. I wish I could have swapped with Arlo, but we're forced to take turns, and he did the press conference last race.

Arlo bats his lashes. He has the kind of big brown eyes that remind me of a baby cow, all wide and innocent, even though he's anything but. "Now you're just another old married man," he says woefully before brightening. "Didn't take you for the kind to get married in Vegas, though. Maybe you're not as dull as I thought."

I stifle a smile. "Piss off. I'm perfectly fun."

"Says the posh arsehole wearing his shirt buttoned all the way up to his chin."

I look down at my McMorris-branded collared shirt. "What's so wrong with that?"

Arlo groans. "If you have to ask . . ."

Before I can retort, McMorris's reserve driver drops down at our table and slaps hands with Arlo in greeting. As usual, Finley Clarke ignores me and launches into a conversation with

Arlo about some internet thing that I'm completely oblivious to, leaving me to watch the former F2 teammates get on like a house on fire.

McMorris brought them both in at the same time, though only one got the desired position as a lead driver for the team alongside me. It's no secret that Finley desperately wants my seat—every reserve driver wants a chance to be part of the main show, not the backup whose role exists to take our place if we're ever unable to compete.

He'll have to keep waiting, because I have no plans to leave. And let's be honest, it's definitely *my* seat he wants so he and Arlo can go back to being teammates. I'm the person standing in the way of his hopes and dreams.

And I'll keep standing there, because one of McMorris's biggest sponsors is A.P. Maxwell International, the logo for which is displayed proudly under the team badge on my shirt. I bring in way too much money for them to replace me with someone who would bring in less. But if they could find someone on my monetary level . . . Well, my seat wouldn't be safe.

Neither of the boys notices when I stand from the table. A quick wave to my press officer at a table across the room gets her to join me by the door. She briefs me on what will likely be asked in today's driver press conference—how I'm feeling going into the penultimate race of the season, if I think McMorris can take third in the Constructors' Championship over D'Ambrosi, and so on. She's hesitant when she mentions that they'll probably focus on my impromptu wedding, but I already know it's coming. Sometimes the off-track drama is way more entertaining than what's happening on it.

And we're both proved right when Steven Watters, our interviewer, homes in on me first, even though there are four far more interesting drivers sitting next to me on the couch.

"Thomas, all the paddock can talk about are the photos that came out over the weekend of your wedding right here in Las Vegas," Steven says, practically salivating since he knows he's the first to ask me about it. "What made you want to get married right before such an important race? As we all know, Mc-Morris is trailing D'Ambrosi in the points and has a chance to pull ahead in the Constructors' Championship. Has the wedding been a distraction?"

I try to ignore the camera flashes and the way the reporters in the audience are a little too eager to hear what I have to say.

Well, Steven, I wish I could tell him. *I was shit-faced, and a very accomplished woman with a beautiful, filthy mouth seduced me. The last thing I was thinking about was my job.*

Instead, I lift my microphone and say, "Stella and I figured there was no use in waiting. We wanted to get married as soon as possible, and with our crazy schedules—she's a very successful business owner, you know—we thought there was no better time or place than right here in Las Vegas." I flash my most charming smile to the crowd. "If anything, having our wedding so quickly has allowed me to focus exclusively on this weekend and what's at stake."

Steven obviously wants to press for details, but he's cut off by Dev Anderson grabbing Reid Coleman's hand and declaring that he'd also like to announce their marriage.

"We may race for different teams," Dev says, grinning so widely that I'm amazed it fits on his face. "But our love is real."

Reid rolls his eyes and removes his hand from Dev's clutches, though he doesn't seem particularly upset. We're all used to Dev's antics. He's gotten a little more insufferable now that he's moved from one of the worst teams on the grid to one of the best—if not *the* best—but at least he's entertaining. The Mascort team is lucky to have him filling in for their number one driver, Zaid Yousef, while he recovers from the broken wrists he sustained in the Singapore crash.

"I don't think your girlfriend would appreciate you saying that," Reid remarks before turning his attention back to Steven. "Can we talk about racing now, please?"

Steven goes red in the face and clears his throat. "Right. Yes. Of course. As I mentioned, Reid, McMorris and D'Ambrosi are nearly neck and neck in the points. Do you think D'Ambrosi will be able to pull further ahead after this weekend?"

Reid, dressed in head-to-toe D'Ambrosi red, doesn't glance my way as he answers. "We have a strong car that should perform well on this track. There's a good chance we'll be able to expand our lead, but we do have a rookie on our team who's still learning the car. It certainly makes things tougher."

What he's not saying is that the man who's supposed to be in that other D'Ambrosi car, Lorenzo Castellucci, will likely never drive again. And even though I had nothing to do with that crash, my harsh words hang over every mention of Lorenzo like a storm cloud. What's worse, though, is that Reid hasn't spoken to me directly since. It seems the Scuderia D'Ambrosi protocol is to shun me.

But that's fine. This is the first time since Singapore that the first question asked of me wasn't something related to Lorenzo or my rant. My wedding and whirlwind romance are the new hot topic.

And if talking about Stella is the key to getting the heat off me, then I'll brag about my wife in every conversation from now until the day we part.

 CHAPTER 13

STELLA

I'll be honest, if anyone had asked me if I knew the difference between Formula 1 and NASCAR before this week, I would have said no. But I was a straight-A student in school, and I'm hideously competitive on top of that, so I've done nothing but study up over the past few days in the moments between meetings and conference calls. I might as well be part of the pit crew at this point.

But no YouTube video or Wikipedia page could have prepared me for actually being at a race.

Vegas is *probably* not the best choice for my first to attend. For starters, the race is on a Saturday night instead of a Sunday—which, apparently, is not the norm—and as Thomas warned me, this is a grand prix on steroids.

I'm seeing that firsthand as we slowly pull into a cordoned-off parking area, having driven no more than a single mile per hour as Thomas fought through traffic to get here. Between the flashing neon lights, the crowds snapping photos, and the general chaos, I'm doubting my decision to make this our first public outing. Maybe I should have come for media day or for the practice sessions, when things would have been so much calmer, but we decided race day would be the most significant time to debut our relationship.

The new ring on my left hand is just loose enough that I can spin it around my finger, a nervous tic I've picked up in the short time since Thomas slid it on.

"I think Cartier suits you a little better than Krispy Kreme," he joked as we both stared down at the diamond glinting in the light of my hotel room. "But I can get you another doughnut if you'd like."

"I prefer diamonds," I answered, unable to tear my eyes away from the ring.

Even now, as I twist it around and around, I'm still thrown by how much more I like it than the one Étienne got for me. The solitaire diamond on this one is just as big as the other, but the band is slim and gold, compared to the thick, gem-studded platinum one of my first ring. *It's bold and flashy, just like you*, Étienne declared when he pushed the slightly-too-tight thing on my finger. I almost laughed when Thomas said nearly the exact opposite.

"I hope it's not too much," he fretted. "I know you said you didn't care what I got, but I figured you'd want something classic. Nothing too gaudy. And with a gold band because all the jewelry I've seen you wear is gold."

It's wild that a man I met just over a week ago knows my taste better than the one I was with for five years—that he's paid enough attention to notice such a small detail as my jewelry choices.

"Just enough," I choked out.

We've only spoken a few words since we left my room. I'm tempted to crack some half-assed jokes to ease the tension, but nothing is coming to me. I roll my lips between my teeth and watch as Thomas eases the low-slung McMorris sports car into a parking space, turning the wheel with the heel of his palm like it's nothing. And I suppose it is to a man who's about to go race at stomach-dropping speeds.

There are already a few photographers milling around the car, taking pictures of us through the tinted windows. Part of me wants to turn to Thomas and demand he drive me back to the hotel, though thankfully there's a braver part that has me swiping my tongue over my teeth to make sure there's no lipstick on them and then hauling myself out of the passenger seat. My grin is brighter than the camera flashes.

Internally, though, I'm a quivering, shaking mess. I'm sure Thomas can feel it, especially when I slide my hand into his.

A look of shock passes over his face at the contact. "Jesus," he breathes out, "your fingers are *freezing*."

I nearly rip away from him, his words reminding me of Étienne in the worst way possible at the worst moment possible. I'd rather be the one to pull back this time instead of being rejected, especially in front of all these cameras. But before I can, Thomas presses my hand to his chest, keeping his on top of mine to warm it. His gold wedding band shimmers under the lights.

"We've got to get you some gloves," he comments, more to himself than to me. "I should have brought some, I'm sorry. Didn't realize how chilly it was going to be tonight."

He stares down at me, checking to make sure I'm okay, but I'm too surprised by his actions to reply. He must not believe I'm fine, because he gives me a reassuring smile next, then closes the small gap between us to speak into my ear.

"Just breathe," he says, and I draw in a deep breath at his prompting, inhaling his clean scent along with the cool night air. "I'll be right beside you."

His words take the edge off, and I don't drag my feet when he guides me toward the paddock's security checkpoint. We both nod and smile to the staff there as we tap our passes against the checkpoint sensors. The fact that I even have a VIP pass on a lanyard draped around my neck makes me want to laugh, because who the hell would have thought I'd end up here?

I'm no stranger to red carpets or high-profile events, but this isn't just *some event*, despite the handful of celebrities I've already spotted. I'm here to support my husband—*God*, that's still wild to say—at his job. My role today is doting wife, the kind who keeps her mouth shut and smiles and sticks to the sidelines . . . or whatever the motorsport equivalent of the sidelines is.

Thomas and I agreed that we'd walk in together so we could be seen by photographers and fans, but after that I'd slink away to the McMorris hospitality suite. Which is fine with me, because as we make our way into the chaos of the paddock, I'm realizing this is . . . a lot. It's loud and crowded and there are so many things happening at once that I don't even know where to look. But there are plenty of eyes on us.

"Everyone is watching you," I murmur from the corner of my mouth, keeping a practiced but pleasant smile on my face.

Thomas gives a slight shrug, like all of this mayhem is perfectly normal. "You get used to it."

I'm skeptical. "Really?"

"Well, you learn to ignore it," he corrects, lifting a hand and grinning broadly at someone on the other side of the busy pathway. "And you learn how to deal. It's part of the game."

I thought I was playing the game already, but clearly not. This is a whole different level.

He greets everyone we pass, from fans with paddock passes to members of rival teams. He jokingly salutes a few people wearing hideous red-white-and-blue uniforms and good-naturedly slaps Dev Anderson's shoulder. He even stops to take a picture with a gaggle of children who can't be more than eight years old and should be in bed by now. For supposedly being hated, he's faring pretty well around here as far as I can tell.

But that changes when a group of people in head-to-toe red uniforms walks by us, and all Thomas gets when he attempts to offer them a smile are cold silence and disgusted glances.

"Let me guess," I murmur. "That's the Scuderia D'Ambrosi crew?"

I already know it is, just like I've known a lot of the faces and team colors so far—I've done my research. But Thomas's sigh and his slumping shoulders tell me more about the situation than any website or article ever could.

"They don't *all* hate me," he tries to reassure, though he's clearly saying it more for his benefit than mine. "Reid Coleman, their other driver, knows I didn't mean what I said. Although, he's not talking to me at the moment either, so I can't really say for certain that he hasn't been convinced to hate me."

I file that detail away. It might not ever be relevant, but it's probably good to know the dynamics between him and the other drivers.

"Have you tried making nice with the guy you talked shit about?" I ask, clinging a little tighter to him as we pass by a group of people with their phones raised, recording every move we make.

Thomas shakes his head. "I apologized and explained myself after the video came out, and he laughed in my face. I haven't been able to get in contact with him since the crash, though. I don't think any of the drivers have. And no one from D'Ambrosi will even acknowledge me, as you just saw, so I can't ask them anything. I just want to know how he's doing."

There's a new forced quality to Thomas's smile. He's not happy with the situation, and I wouldn't be surprised if guilt was eating away at him. He probably hates himself more than anyone else out there ever could, and the gut punch I get thinking about that makes me almost stumble.

"Is there anything I can do?"

A dip of surprise appears between his brows before clearing away. "No, I don't think so. But I appreciate the offer."

I nod, trying to brainstorm how I might be able to help, though I'm pulled out of my thoughts when he slowly draws me to a halt in front of a set of stairs leading to McMorris's hospitality motorhome, the team name lit up in green neon lights.

"Unless you want a garage tour, this is where we part ways," he says, and I slip my hand from his, my heart rate ticking up.

But instead of bidding me adieu and leaving me to fend for myself, Thomas turns toward me and cups my shoulders, waiting for my answer. I glance across the paddock toward the back end of the team garages, noting the team members flowing in and out. A tour means being introduced to everyone working in there, so that's a big *no thank you*.

"I'd rather go hide now, if that's okay," I reply, strangely comforted by the contact of his hands on me. He's had them in places far less appropriate, and yet this has me melting a little bit.

Maybe he's just doing it for the cameras. Or maybe he's just a touchy-feely kind of guy who doesn't think twice about this stuff. Whatever it is, I'm thankful for it.

"Perfectly acceptable. I'll get my assistant to take you up to the suite." He glances around, frowning as he looks for some-one. "She said she'd meet us here, but—oh shit."

I jump when a woman practically materializes out of thin air beside us. The brunette can't be taller than five feet, but she has the energy of a six-foot-six linebacker.

"You're late," she snaps at him, eyes narrowed. "You were supposed to be here half an hour ago."

She's speaking English, but it takes me an extra beat to comprehend the words in her thick Irish accent. Despite her tone, which I'd never allow anyone who worked for *me* to use, this must be his assistant.

I should apologize since I'm the reason he's late. He would have been here sooner if he didn't have to worry about sliding a ring onto my finger. But before I can speak, Thomas shifts so his arm is around my shoulders and I'm tucked into his side.

"Sorry, Maeve." He doesn't sound sorry at all. "Stella and I got a little caught up. Lost track of time."

Emerald eyes flick to me before returning their venom to Thomas. "What you're not going to do is place any blame on your beautiful wife. I already know you can't tell time."

I'm both flattered and taken aback. And yet Thomas looks perfectly content with her ribbing, his smile genuine as he peers down at her. Jesus, I think he *likes* it. No wonder he understands my humor.

"No one tell the watch brand that sponsors the team," he says cheerily. "Anyway, I should run. Would you mind escorting Stella up to the suite and getting her settled?"

Maeve scowls. "She's a perfectly capable woman, Thomas. Don't act like she's some child who needs her hand held."

"I'm not—"

"But yes, Stella," she continues on, turning to me. There's a sparkle in her eyes that tells me this is the typical dynamic be-tween them, and she enjoys it as much as he does. "I'd be happy to take you up. I'll give you a moment with your husband to wish him luck. He's going to need it."

With a little wave, she saunters off, and I glance up at Thomas in near disbelief. "Well, she's . . . something."

He nods. "I'm sure you'll get along fine. She also thinks the English are a bunch of twats."

"I never said that."

"You're American, it's ingrained in your DNA."

I snort, and it gains me a glimpse of satisfaction on Thom-as's face, as if making me laugh is his new favorite thing.

I'm acutely aware of his arm around me, the heat of his body seeping into mine. Last Friday night's shenanigans flicker on the edges of my memory—the soft press of his mouth over mine, his broad palm under my dress, his sturdy chest to my back, our hearts racing in tandem. It was all so reckless, and yet the flashback has me wrapping my arm around his waist in re-turn, not fighting the desire to hold him closer. I'd be breaking my own rules if we weren't in public. If he questions me, I'll give that as an excuse, even if my reasoning is simply that I crave the comfort the contact brings. It doesn't have to be more than that, does it?

Thomas must be able to read my mind, or maybe my thoughts are just written on my face, because his gaze drops to my lips. In my black pumps, I'm once again not much shorter than him. It's the perfect distance for a kiss. For me to tilt my chin up a little and for him to dip his head. So easy. Too easy.

A camera flash has me blinking, snapping me out of thoughts that were quickly growing dangerous. I start to turn my head to see where it came from—and to give myself some much-needed distance from my husband—but Thomas's fingers on my jaw stop me.

His eyes are darker in the paddock's floodlights but no less blue. Still easy to sink into. To drown in.

"Should we give our onlookers a show?" he asks softly.

The ground is unsteady beneath me as his mouth lifts in a knowing smile. I'm struggling to find my footing, desperate to grasp the upper hand again. One look shouldn't be enough to practically knock me on my ass. *I* should be doing that to *him*.

"Are you asking me for a good luck kiss, Thomas?" I finally volley back, batting my lashes. Really, though, it's to clear away the hearts that have descended over my vision.

"Mm, I think I need it," he says, tugging me against him until our chests are flush.

It's bold as hell, far more than I was expecting from Mr. Buttoned-Up while sober. We do have a show to put on, though, and there are plenty of cameras catching this, but it doesn't feel as fake as it should.

"I'm adding *no flirting* to our list of rules," I muse as his hand moves to cup the back of my neck.

"Come on, Stella. Where's the fun in that?"

His mouth is on mine before I can answer, stealing away my words and my breath. Compared to our past kisses, this is chaste. It's even tender. There's no brush of tongues or biting of lips. Nothing fierce or commanding about it. This is the quick, casual touch that a couple in love would share without a second thought. It's the exact thing we need in this moment. It's us saying, *Of course we're the real deal, can't you see?*

Or at least that's what it's meant to be until I make the mistake of curling my fingers into his shirt as he starts to draw away. I don't mean to do it. I think. Okay, maybe I do mean to, but this is just so *nice* that I don't want it to be over so soon. Is that such a crime?

And clearly Thomas doesn't mind, because he draws me closer and kisses me again like it's his absolute pleasure.

But it's over almost as fast as it happened, our lips parting slowly. I know I need to bring back my practiced smile and act like that kind of kiss is something we share on a regular basis, but I'm blinking up at him like my whole world's been rocked. All over an innocent kiss. I'm losing it.

I clear my throat and release his shirt from my grasp, focusing my attention on smoothing out the wrinkles I made. Doting wife, am I right?

"That should be enough luck to get you on the podium," I quip, amazed I can even find my voice.

"I think that's enough to get me the win."

I glance up at the laugh in his voice to find him grinning down at me, that same slightly dazed sheen in his eyes that I know is still in mine too.

"Now, now, don't get ahead of yourself." I pat his chest again. Not that I need to, since his shirt is smooth. It's just . . . *damn*, this man is built. "Go win me a trophy. Any size will do."

"I bet you wouldn't say that about most things."

I snort and cover my face in an attempt to smother it, but Thomas reaches up to pull my hand away, revealing the smile I'm trying to hide.

"Whatever my wife wants, my wife gets," he says before pressing a kiss to my knuckles like a true fairy-tale prince. "See you after the race."

My head is full of clouds as we step away from each other. I somehow make it over to where Maeve is standing, ignoring how she's rocking back on her heels with her hands clutched in front of her, fully smug. She's kind enough not to bring up what

she's witnessed, instead instructing me to follow her a little farther down the paddock to get to the entrance of the suites that
sit above the team garages.

I know I shouldn't, but I glance over my shoulder to see if I
can still spot Thomas. A jolt of giddiness passes through my
chest when I find him standing with a group of fans, the grin
that I inspired lingering as he scrawls his autograph on items.
It's so endearing that I'm mirroring that same gooberish look,
waiting to see how long it takes to disappear from his face—
which means I'm not watching where I'm going.

I might have thought Maeve had linebacker energy, but
turns out I'm the actual one. The woman I run smack into
stumbles back like she's hit a brick wall, and I have to dart out
a hand to keep her from landing hard on the concrete. Her curtain of dark curls flies into her face, leaving me staring down at
a faceless figure in red. Fucking great. I've nearly wiped a
D'Ambrosi employee off the face of the planet. Thomas and I
are two for two when it comes to making these people hate us.
It's like we were made for each other.

I force that thought away and check the woman over for
damage, but she seems to be fine, thank goodness.

"Are you okay?" I ask, still clutching her shoulder as she
uses her other arm to flip her hair back into its rightful place.
"I'm so sorry about that."

Her light brown cheeks are flushed, but she doesn't seem
upset that I've almost killed her. "No, I'm sorry," she rushes to
say, eyes about level with my chest. She's the same height as
Maeve, and with the two of them flanking me, I'm starting to
feel like a giant. "I was too busy taking pictures and I wasn't
watching where I was—"

She finally looks up at me, the words dying on her lips
with a small squeak. Her eyes go wide and her jaw hangs

open in a way that would be unflattering if she wasn't so fucking cute.

"Holy shit," she breathes out, gazing at me like she's just found the love of her life. "You're Stella Margaux."

I don't get recognized all that often, but it happens. And I'm sure it's going to happen more now that my viral rant will haunt the internet for the rest of eternity. Maybe that's where she recognizes me from, though I doubt she'd be vibrating with excitement over meeting someone who acted a whole fool for the world to see.

"I was the last time I checked," I say with a smile, praying she's not about to bring up the video.

Her face brightens even more, like a full ray of sunshine beaming through the paddock. She even has dimples in both cheeks.

"I can't believe you're here," she gushes, hands clutching together around the phone she was likely taking pictures with. "I'm a *huge* fan. I'm really trying not to freak out right now."

I'd say she's doing a decent job, considering she hasn't tried to barrel me down with a hug or started crying, which I saw Dev Anderson dealing with as we walked in. I'm not on that level of fame anyway, though she's gazing at me as if I am.

"Congrats on your wedding, by the way," she goes on. "When I saw you'd married Thomas, I told my boyfriend I hoped we'd see you in the paddock."

I take my hand off her shoulder and use it to jokingly frame my face. "Here I am." It's always a little strange when someone knows all about me when I don't even know their name. I glance down at her uniform again, searching for a topic change. "You work for D'Ambrosi?"

That snaps her out of the fangirl haze. "I'm Reid Coleman's social media manager," she explains before sticking her hand out to me. Her handshake is surprisingly firm. "Willow Williams."

"So nice to meet you, Willow."

And it is. It's always nice to meet a fan of my businesses and products. But instead of basking in it and taking comfort that my recent scandals haven't put everyone off me, I'm focusing on her job—or really, who she works for.

Reid Coleman. Didn't Thomas say Reid wasn't speaking to him? If anyone's going to know anything about Lorenzo Castellucci and his condition, it would probably be his teammate.

Thomas might have told me there wasn't anything I could do to help, but I think the key to doing so has just crashed into my life.

"Hey," I say, hand back on her shoulder. "If you have time, I'd love to sit and chat . . ."

 **CHAPTER 14**

THOMAS

There's a certain peace in sitting on the starting grid.

It's just me, the rumble of the engine, and the press of my fingers around the steering wheel. No distractions. No thoughts other than making it off the line. The calm before the chaos.

It's a slow breath in, eyes locked on the five red lights above me, and an exhale as they all go out.

I'm out of my P5 grid box and wheel to wheel with two drivers ahead of me in a blink. It's an excellent start, proof of my experience, the reliability of a McMorris-designed car, and my confidence in a team I know so well after five seasons together. This is all second nature now.

I'm P3 as we follow the racing line of the first corner. Dev's leading, with Reid hot on his rear wing, but I'm more concerned with keeping the two cars I passed behind me. There's a flash of navy and neon yellow in my mirror before I spot the Specter Energy car beside me, trying to edge me out as we barrel down the Las Vegas Strip. Their straight-line speed is lightning fast, which should mean I'm about to concede one of the places I've gained. But I brake late into the next turn, giving me the advantage even though I take it wider than I would have liked. I'm quick back on the throttle too, pulling away as he pushes through my dirty air. There's still not much of a gap between us, but it's something.

I get a reprieve as the two behind me have their own battle, giving me the chance to pull away and push.

"Nice job," my race engineer comments over the radio. He's never effusive with his praise, so this might as well be him screaming from the rooftops. "Arlo lost a few places at the start. He's down in P11."

I almost sigh. My teammate started seventh, and the strategy for this race was to have him help defend my higher P5 grid placement. That's out the window now that we're running eight places apart. He'll be lucky if he can make his way up the grid to finish in the top ten—to actually get our team some much-needed points in the Constructors' Championship.

So this is all on me. Fantastic.

To make up for that deficit, I'm going to have to fight for my life to keep P3. And God, is it a task. Between keeping the Specter Energy driver off my ass after two different safety cars bunch up the pack and then repeatedly trying to catch Reid, I'm driving hard. Possibly harder than I have all season.

It's not that I was complacent before, but . . . maybe I was. I know I wasn't giving my all in the months and weeks before the Singapore crash that took out the three front-runners in the Drivers' Championship. It was maybe 90 percent of what I was truly capable of, because what was the point of giving more when it wouldn't have gotten me more? With them and their teammates almost always ahead of me, the best I could usually finish was seventh. The best of the rest.

Zaid Yousef of Mascort and Axel Bergmüller of Specter Energy were the only ones who had any chances of winning the

Drivers' Championship anyway—the title every driver competes for individually. Lorenzo was a dark horse, trading off with Reid for third place. But with them out of the running and their teams dealing with the chaos of getting other drivers in those seats, it's given the rest of the pack a chance to catch up.

Especially me. I still have no chance of winning the championship, but in the last five races, I've made it onto the podium three times. If I can hold on, I'll make it a fourth. This might never happen again with Zaid and Axel set to return next season.

I ask my engineer where the other D'Ambrosi car is and do the quick maths of figuring out the points their team would earn if these were the places we all finished in. Grimacing against the padding of my helmet, I realize that they'd still be ahead of McMorris in the Constructors' rankings. I need Arlo to prove why this team signed him and make it up to ninth at the very least.

The laps are grueling, and I'm thankful for the cooler-than-usual night. The bright neon lights of the buildings that stretch up and around us are nothing more than a blur as I pass them. By the time there are only fifteen laps to go, Reid is in my sights. I could take second—if I can get my quickly degrading tires to last.

"What's the gap to Coleman?" I ask. It comes out as a demand.

Judging from his pause, I already know my engineer is going to dissuade me from trying to catch the D'Ambrosi driver. "Keep the pace," he instructs. "Our focus is on the cars behind."

Of course it is. But I'm hungry tonight. I want more than a third-place riser.

Stella flashes through my mind then, her words on a loop.

So you're a loser, she teases again and again. She was joking, playing down the fact that she was impressed, but she wasn't wrong. Anything other than first is a loss. I know I won't be taking the top spot tonight, but one step down . . . that's something.

I take a breath and push.

In three laps, I'm on him, much to my engineer's dismay. Reid defends hard, leaving me to nearly clip his rear tires as I try twice to overtake. It's not the cleanest racing, I'll admit it, but that want, that desire, can make you do unwise things.

Unfortunately, my tires seem to be on my engineer's side, and I'm forced to fall back again when the battle proves to be too much. He might as well say *I told you so* the next time he comes on the radio.

No one can see me sulking behind my helmet at least. It's tough to want something that's just within reach but not be able to grasp it. And it's even tougher when I'm forced to watch Reid challenge Dev a couple of laps later and overtake the race leader.

The move up means more points for D'Ambrosi. It means McMorris's chances of landing third in the Constructors' Championship are dwindling.

It means even though I'll be holding a third-place trophy on the podium, I'm still a loser.

▰▰▰▰▰

I'm being booed. Loudly. *Very* loudly.

It's practically drowning out the announcer introducing me to the podium. I've always appreciated the passion of the Scuderia's devotees, but right now it would be nice if they could tone it down a little. Limited as my knowledge of Italian is, I can certainly make out their shouts of *asshole* and *idiot* and—my personal favorite—*ugly fucker.* I can't deny the truth of the first two, but the last one? Inherently untrue.

They didn't like me before tonight, and they like me even less after the moves I pulled on Reid. But at least their darling boy proved he's a damn good driver.

The saving grace of this onslaught of hate is that there's only one race left this season. One more opportunity to be publicly abhorred, and then I can escape it all over the winter break.

The boos start to dwindle when Dev steps out and waves to the crowd, the cheers drowning out the hostility. And as Reid finally climbs up onto his first-place riser, there are only screams and chants and shouted declarations of love.

The American national anthem plays for Reid's win—still such a wild thing to hear—followed by the Italian one for Scuderia D'Ambrosi, and then the champagne sprays. I congratulate both drivers again, and while Reid has been gracious enough to offer me a few half smiles and quick moments of eye contact, he's careful to keep Dev in the middle of our celebrations.

And speaking of the other American up on the podium, Dev could have won this race, just like he could have won the last three in Austin, Mexico, and Brazil. Instead, the same thing that happened tonight happened then—Reid overtook him at some point and won.

To most, this wouldn't look suspicious. After all, Reid's an incredible driver and has been at D'Ambrosi for years, while Dev's still adjusting to driving a new car and getting to know how Mascort operates. It's amazing enough that Dev's achieved a string of second-place finishes after being chosen to sub in for Zaid Yousef with seven races left in the season. It's not easy to switch to a completely different car after driving for the same terrible team for years. Mistakes can and will be made.

But I know just how good a driver Dev is. He, Reid, Axel,

and I were all F1 rookies in the same season, and he beat us all for the title of Rookie of the Year. He consistently scored points at Argonaut, his old team, even though their car was reminiscent of a tractor. He even managed to *win* a race this season in that hunk of carbon fiber. We shouldn't expect anything less from him than win after win now that he's driving a car that's a hundred times better. He's capable of it.

This race has cemented something for me, though—Dev and Reid are conspiring. Because after all the points Reid has racked up lately, if he wins the last race of the season next week in Abu Dhabi, he'll win the Drivers' Championship by the narrowest margin.

I know better than to voice my suspicions, but the whispers are already there without me adding to them.

After the podium celebrations are over, I make my way back to my driver's room to decompress for a few minutes before I'm expected at the postrace press conference with Dev and Reid. I greet and thank McMorris team members as I pass through the garage, hugging and slapping the shoulders of the people who have been amazing all season. But I pull up short when Finley Clarke steps into my path, grinning. Not sure what our reserve driver is so happy about—he never cares if I end up on the podium—but he's gleeful tonight.

He claps a hand on my shoulder, though it's a bit of a reach for him since he's barely five foot six and I'm six-one. "Not a bad drive," he commends. "Maybe it'll convince the bosses to keep you around."

I squint at him. The hell is that supposed to mean? My contract isn't up for another year, which means they'd have to pay me a pretty huge sum of money to get me to leave early. After that, who knows what could happen, but he's acting like I'm already out of a seat.

"Thanks," I say slowly, waiting for him to remove his hand before I walk on.

I don't get far, though. I'm stopped by the impact of some-one throwing themselves into my arms, their own going around my neck. Stella's scent hits me even harder, the sweetness of citrus wrapping itself around me and holding tight.

"For our onlookers," she murmurs against my ear. "They're going to eat this up."

Her lips against my skin and the press of her body have me short-circuiting, thrown back into the memory of our first night together, having thoughts that aren't remotely appropriate for our current setting. Like how soft her inner thighs are, or how her ass felt grinding in my lap, seeking more friction as she moved with my fingers inside her. Even our kiss earlier, whole-some as it was, sneaks into my mind, because that was still a taste of Stella. And every little sample I get makes me wish I could have more. I just want to *know*. Maybe then I could get this out of my system and move on.

She pulls back before I can return the embrace. It's probably for the best. She doesn't need to feel what she inspires in me.

Even in her signature heels, Stella is practically bouncing on the balls of her feet. She's shed her leather jacket, leaving her arms and shoulders bare, the thin straps of her black silk dress crisscrossing over them, and—fucking hell, she's definitely not wearing a bra. It's made extra obvious with every excited move she makes up and down.

"That was *fun*," she says, eyes bright and smile wide, like she's just discovered the delicious high of a new drug. "Who would have thought watching cars go fast would be so enter-taining?"

I force myself to put a hand to her back to guide her to the rear of the garage, her skin smooth and warm under my palm. "I'm guessing that means you're a fan now."

"You could say that," she teases. "There was something sexy about watching you drive like that." She pauses, eyes cutting to me. "I mean the plural *you*. All of you. All the drivers. All y'all, as my people say."

I huff a laugh at her backtracking. Even with her rules, she can't help flirting with me. I'm no better since I'm happy to entertain it. I like her banter and the way we play off each other. More than anything, I like how easy it feels.

"I don't feel particularly sexy after sweating for nearly two hours," I say as we step out of the garage.

Stella's eyes are on me again, flicking up and down. My hair's damp and wrecked from my helmet, plus running my fingers through it a million times afterward, and there's nothing flattering about the postrace exhaustion on my face.

"You make the look work for you." She clears her throat, eyes forward again as we cross over to the McMorris motorhome. "Anyway. I . . . may have done something."

"Done something?" I ask cautiously, then follow it up with, "Good or bad?"

"Good, I hope," she says. "I met Reid Coleman's social media manager, Willow Williams. Turns out she's a big fan of mine. We had a really great chat, actually. And . . . I found out from her that Reid has been in contact with his ex-teammate."

I almost stumble, pulling up short outside the doors to the motorhome. It's not because of her revelation that Reid and Lorenzo have been talking—that's not particularly surprising—but that she took the time to find it out in the first place. "Seriously?"

Stella nods, engagement ring glinting under the lights as she sweeps her hair over her shoulder. "Seriously. And not only is she working for a driver, but she's dating one too. Girl's living the dream."

"You do realize you're married to a driver, correct?"

She drops her voice so as not to be overheard by anyone. "Accidentally and temporarily," she points out, then returns to a normal volume. "I asked her to see if Reid might talk to you, which will hopefully lead to you speaking with Lorenzo. Maybe then you can clear the air and get an update on how he's really doing. No promises that'll happen, but she's got some sway with Reid."

Something is working its way through my chest, twisting and squirming, wrapping around my heart. "You did that for me?"

She shrugs like it's no big deal, but this is massive, especially for someone who hasn't known me long enough to understand how much this has been hanging over me. "Figured I might as well try."

"Thank you," I say. And I really, truly mean it. "I appreciate that."

I open the door to the hospitality motorhome for her and guide her back to my driver's room. It's a small space, but there's enough room for a love seat, a massage table, and a shelving unit. Stella wastes no time hoisting herself up on the table, hands tucked under her mostly bare thighs as she hooks one ankle behind the other.

"So," she prompts, breaking our silence and forcing me out of my swimming thoughts. "What happens now?"

There are about a thousand ways I could answer that question, but I go with the most obvious and immediate. "I have to go do more interviews and a race debrief with the team." I check my watch. It's far past midnight. "You must be exhausted.

If you want to head to bed, we can talk more in the morning before I have to fly out for the next race."

"And where's that one?"

"Abu Dhabi." I grab a towel off the shelf and scrub it over my face. "It's the last of the season, then I have a few more work commitments before I get about a month break."

Her lip catches between her teeth before releasing. "Then I think this is going to be where we part for a while."

I'm surprised by the note of disappointment in her tone and its echo behind my ribs. We haven't spent much time together over the past week, but I've adjusted to our check-ins. It'll be odd to be on the opposite side of the world from her.

"Right." I have to clear my throat to keep the word from getting stuck there. "You have your company to get back to."

"I mostly work remotely," she explains with a rueful smile, "but I need to go check in on things after being away. And then it's Thanksgiving on Thursday, so I'm going to be with my family."

It all makes perfect sense, yet my stomach dips with each addition that will expand our separation. "So you won't be at that race."

She shakes her head. "Not unless I hop on a flight first thing the next day."

I take a second to gauge whether she might be up for that, but quickly shut down that line of thinking. Yes, I want us to parade our fake marriage around, and I want to spend more time with her, though not at the expense of her missing out on being with people she loves. "I won't ask you to do that. Being seen together tonight should tide the masses over for a bit."

"What about after that?" she asks, and it's a relief to know I'm not the only one concerned about how everything is up in the air. "Where will you be?"

"London mostly. You?"

"DC."

An ocean apart. An eight-hour flight, sure, but it's not an easy commute. Plus, with the commitments I have in the UK following the end of the season, I wouldn't get back to the States until mid-December. And we still haven't figured out whose family we're going to spend the holidays with, or how we're going to present a united front to my parents, or when Stella and Figgy will meet . . .

A million questions and logistical nightmares swirl in my head. And then there's the little fact that I'm . . . going to miss her. Which is probably the reason I end up blurting, "Come to London with me."

Stella leans back at my outburst, brow dipping in the center. "Excuse me?"

"Let's make it look like we're a real couple." My momentum is building, fueled by an anxious energy to make this fake marriage work for us. For her to never be too far away for too long. "Come to London. Move in with me. Be my real pretend wife who's by my side."

Stella's staring at me like I've lost every single one of my marbles. But that's okay. I can make her come around, I know it. I convinced her to stay married to me, so there's no reason I can't pull this off too.

"We can consider it a flatshare," I push on. "I have a bunch of bedrooms. And I'm always back and forth to McMorris HQ at Silverstone, so I'm hardly there anyway. You'd practically have the place to yourself."

"Thomas," she says slowly, and I know she's trying to figure out a way to let me down easy, but I can't let this opportunity slip away.

"You said you work remotely, right? You can be anywhere

in the world. So why not London? If you need to go back to DC at any point, you can absolutely use my family's jet. I'd make sure it was always available for you." I take a breath, stopping myself from rambling further. But that still might not be enough. I need more to convince her to stay with me. "Besides, won't Janelle be living there soon?"

There it is—there's the spark in her eyes I was waiting for. Clearly I'm not enough of a draw (understandable), but Janelle? She's my key to everything.

"My whole life is in DC," she tries to reason, a waver of doubt passing over her face. "I can't just up and leave."

She doesn't fully believe what she's saying. Yes, her job is there, and I'm sure she has a network of friends in the city she'd miss if she left. But there's an ex-fiancé there too and what's certainly a mountain of memories and regrets she wants to move on from.

"You could have a fresh start in London," I offer gently, not daring to push too hard. "You could make some new connections—business or otherwise. Maybe open another Stella Margaux's. Or hell, start a brand-new chain of whatever you want. The European market is ripe for it, and it would be so much easier to explore it from that side of the pond. I'll help you as much as I can."

Her full bottom lip is back between her teeth, biting down as she thinks, and my eyes drop to her mouth. I might be ashamed of where my mind has gone if I didn't already know this attraction was achingly mutual. She's the one who pulled me in for that second kiss, after all.

"Fine," she finally blurts, surprising herself judging by the way her eyes go wide. "I'll move to London."

I'm too busy resisting the urge to kiss her to register her words at first. But then they hit me, sending my heart into overdrive and making me want to kiss her even *more*. "Are you serious?"

Stella nods. The move's a little hesitant, sure, but there's a smile edging onto her lips. "I'm serious."

I break into a grin of my own, not bothering to hold it back, because this is perfect.

My wife's moving in. And I'm going to do everything to make her want to call it home.

# CHAPTER 15

STELLA

"This place gives me the fucking creeps."

Glancing up from the dry ingredients I'm sifting together, I shoot Mika a look. She's sitting on the other side of the marble island, ass planted on a barstool with her casted leg propped up on two more. She's a haughty queen overseeing her domain—except this is my house and my kitchen she's in.

"That's because it's empty," I explain. "Most houses feel that way when there's hardly any furniture."

And this place will never hold more than what's already here. This is the house Étienne and I were supposed to live in together after our wedding—a six-thousand-square-foot fully remodeled colonial-style build in Alexandria, Virginia. I was the one who pushed for the suburbs instead of the city, a calmer location to raise our future children instead of smack-dab in the city. Our penthouse in Dupont Circle was beautiful and located a stone's throw away from several of my businesses, but it wasn't where I saw myself staying forever.

I started moving my things in here the day the contractor said it was safe to occupy. But Étienne dragged his feet. I see now why he did. Back then, though, I wrote it off as being attached to the place where we'd made so many great memories together.

How wrong I was. Now I'm stuck with a house that will never feel like home.

"Nah, it just has bad vibes." Mika shakes her head. "Shitty house juju."

"Then I guess it's a good thing I won't be here much."

She grins wickedly at the reminder that I'll be moving in with Thomas in less than two weeks, but it only makes my stomach twist. I'm picking up my entire life and shipping it across an ocean to live with a man I've spent practically zero time with.

"Have you told anyone you're moving yet?" she asks.

I grab the bowl of egg whites I've already separated, slowly adding them to the almond flour mixture. I'm back to recipe testing today, working on Stella Margaux's summer menu. "My board knows. They're supportive of my desire to expand our reach in Europe." And thankfully, they were also supportive of my impromptu wedding, if a little surprised. "I'm going to set up an office in London and put together a team." I raise a questioning brow in her direction. "You want in?"

Mika is the marketing director for Stella Margaux's North American Division. Some might scream favoritism, but her talent is part of the reason we're so successful. I only hire the best.

She snorts. "I love you, and I want to be close to you and Janelle, but no. Reason number one." She points accusingly at her cast. "I'm in this for a few more weeks, and hobbling around a new city sounds miserable. And two, I can't ask Vaughn to just up and leave. He may be a househusband, but I don't want to disrupt his life like that."

I understand, and it was a reach to ask, but I had to see if I could keep my other best friend with me. "Promise you'll come visit?"

"Oh, honey, you couldn't keep me away if you tried." She shoots me a wink before pushing a little jar of pink food coloring my way. "So the board knows you're going. What about your parents?"

My lips twist into a grimace. "I was planning to tell them at Thanksgiving."

"Girl." The word is a warning. "You've got to give them more heads-up than that."

"They'll have a few days to process before I leave." I unscrew the cap on the food coloring jar and add a tiny scoop to my mixer's bowl. "Besides, I'm a grown woman. I can do what I damn well please."

"A grown woman who's scared of disappointing her parents."

The truth is a pinch in my chest. It's ignorable enough, even though it comes with a lingering sting. But it's about more than just disappointing my parents—it's about disappointing *anyone*. I've been handed so much in my life, all because of the success that those who came before me achieved, and I refuse to sit back and let their wins carry me through life. Raising the bar is my only option to show that while, yes, I've been given so much, I'm worthy of carrying the torch. Worthy of the success I've found myself.

"Whatever," I brush off, not as casual as I hoped to sound. "It'll be fine."

She gives a noncommittal murmur before letting the silence hang, the whir of the mixer the only sound. I know what she's about to ask next before her mouth even opens.

"Have you spoken to him yet?"

She doesn't have to specify which *him*. Her cautious tone says it's Étienne.

I shake my head, keeping my eyes down. "He hasn't tried to get in contact, and I haven't called him either."

I thought he would say something after news of my Vegas wedding leaked, but it's been radio silence. We'll have to speak soon enough to decide what we're going to do with our properties and other shared possessions. But the fact that he hasn't sent me a text or a letter or even sicced his lawyers on me? It's fucking crushing that he could cut me out of his life so easily after so many years together.

"You should talk to him before you leave for London."

I scoff. "If he wants something, he can reach out. He's the one who left, not me."

Mika blows out a disappointed breath, but she doesn't push. I'm being stubborn, yeah, but can anyone really blame me? That man didn't just break my heart, he fully humiliated me. And while I definitely did my part in adding insult to injury, he's the one who blew up our relationship. He can be the one to initiate the cleanup process.

"All right," she concedes. "Just let me know if you need any help handling that when the time comes. I can be your DC liaison for anything face-to-face if you don't want to make the trek back from London."

Despite the mood shift, I have to smile at Mika's commitment to being my ride-or-die. If I asked her to, she'd hunt down Étienne and make his life miserable. The only reason she hasn't yet is because of the broken leg and her dedication to keeping me sane. She can't do that if she ends up in prison.

"Thanks," I say as I turn off the mixer. "But first, you've got to help me get through Thanksgiving."

Mika's cackle echoes through the empty house. "Hope you're ready to get eaten alive."

CIA interrogators have nothing on Black aunties who insist on being in your business.

I don't know how I'm related to half the women who descended on me the second I stepped into my parents' Atlanta-suburb mansion, and yet I've been asked questions I wouldn't feel comfortable answering even if Mika or Janelle posed them.

Speaking of those traitors, neither one has come to rescue me yet despite the frantic texts I keep shooting off. Not even Ron came over, even though I know he spotted me in the living room when he passed by the doorway a few minutes ago.

"It's a good thing he's handsome," one of my great-aunts quips, a gnarled hand lifting her cane to point at me. "You can't be having babies with no ugly man. Our genes are strong, but they only go so far."

"I liked the other one better," says another woman, who stares down her nose at me. "At least he was cultured. This man looks like he thinks the world begins and ends with England."

"Give the girl a break," an auntie in pink and green cuts in. I'm almost relieved that someone is coming to my defense until I see her wicked grin. "The dick must be spectacular if she married him that fast. Ain't that right, Stella?"

There's a mix of cackles, scoldings, and invocations of the Lord that make me want to groan and scrub my hands over my face. I know that'll just give them more to gossip about, so I settle for sending another GET YOUR ASS OUT HERE text to Mika. Again, I'm left on read.

I'm dragged back down to the couch two more times when I try to get up, but my third attempt at escape is successful when

I announce that I absolutely *have* to go check on the status of the desserts. No one here would dare stand in the way of the sweet potato pie's fate.

The hallway offers a reprieve from the aunts, though their laughter and raucous commentary continue to float through the air. But my peace doesn't last long, because Daphne rounds the corner, bouncing her adorable toddler on her hip.

"Stella," she greets brightly, like it's a pleasure to see me leaning against the wall and looking miserable. "I was wondering when you were going to show up." She makes a big display of glancing around the hallway, searching for someone else. "Your husband didn't want to join us?"

She asks it so innocently, but I can hear the glee in the question, as if Thomas's absence is an indicator of a relationship on the rocks. Or worse—that it's not a real relationship at all.

"He's working," I say, smiling at her daughter instead of giving Daphne more attention. "The Formula 1 schedule stops for no one, not even newlyweds."

The baby grins back at me, and the sight succeeds in mitigating the blood pressure spike Daphne's arrival inspired. The kid is precious, with her chubby cheeks and cherub curls, and I swear there's a pang in my ovaries when she lifts her little fingers and waves, making me almost wish I hadn't canceled the appointment to get my IUD removed a few months ago. I'd done it at Étienne's urging, after he changed his mind about wanting to start our family right after we got married. Instead, he asked if we could wait a year, to let it be just us for a while. I reluctantly agreed.

Now kids won't be in my future for at least another year anyway, one more wrench thrown in my life plan. If the past month has taught me anything, it's that I might as well wing it all.

"Newlyweds," she repeats. "I had no idea you were interested in him for more than one night."

She says it teasingly, like we're both in on a joke, but even though I force out a laugh, I know she's judging me hard.

"In fact, I had no idea you knew him before the bachelorette party." Daphne cocks her head to the side, eyes searching my face. "When did you two meet?"

I'm careful to keep my expression schooled into something neutral and pleasant. Nothing that betrays the way my heart rate has skyrocketed and how my armpits have gone suddenly damp under my cashmere sweater.

Thomas and I haven't decided on an official story yet, but I can't deviate too far from what I told my parents in case Daphne seeks them out to verify the details. As far as I know, the general public doesn't know our "love story" past the little things Thomas has mentioned in a handful of interviews, so at least I have that going for me. But this woman is sharp as hell.

"We actually met the same night that Janelle met Ron," I answer with a *wow, what a wild coincidence, am I right?* kind of tone. "Vegas is such a lucky place."

I don't dare give her any more details, lest she poke holes in the story. But that doesn't seem to matter, because she's already raising a skeptical eyebrow.

"Really?" she challenges. "Because Janelle never mentioned that you knew Ron's best friend's brother."

"Why would she mention it?" I fight to keep my voice light. "Thomas and I were just casual acquaintances then. Besides, she has plenty of friends that I've never heard of before. Is she supposed to know all of mine?"

"Just a little strange that it wouldn't ever come up, don't you think?"

"Not really," I reply cheerily before making a silly face at her daughter, earning me a delightful little baby giggle.

Daphne shifts so that I'm forced to stare at her instead of the toddler, and . . . Wait, why does she look worried?

She swallows before wetting her lips, as if she's fighting to find the right words. "Stella, I just—"

But she's cut short by rushed footsteps careening into the hallway, and we glance over to find Janelle hustling toward us with an apron clutched in her outstretched hand.

"You better get in the kitchen before Grandma decides she's on pie duty," Janelle warns as she shoves the apron at me. "It'll be your fault if any of them have soggy bottoms."

Desperate as the dessert situation seems, I find myself glancing over at Daphne again, curious about her concern and wanting her to finish her sentence. But upon second look, the crease between her brows is gone and her breezy smile has returned, widening further when her daughter loudly repeats, "Soggy bottoms!"

"That's right, baby," Janelle coos. Then she refocuses on me, a plea in her eyes. "Can you take care of it?"

I sigh and take the apron. "Yeah, of course."

"Thank you," she gushes, backing away. "Just be warned, it's chaos in the kitchen. And I think your mom wants to talk to you."

She's gone before I can protest, disappearing around the corner as quickly as she came. I hesitate before turning to Daphne again, hoping to return to our conversation, but she's already headed for the living room. Her daughter gives me a bright wave before they step through the doorway. I'm tempted to rush after them, but knowing my mother wants to speak— and wanting to avoid all the aunts—keeps me from doing so.

With a groan, I stride after Janelle. I'm in enough trouble with my mother. Putting off this conversation won't get me back in her good graces.

But when I get to the kitchen, there's too much happening for us to talk besides shouting to each other to pass the butter and asking if anything needs more seasoning. Just as I think I've escaped the fate of having a chat until after dinner, Mom crooks her finger, motioning for me to follow her out of the kitchen. Damn it.

As the others start bringing platters and bowls out to the dining room, I brush past and sulk my way to Mom's office. She doesn't see clients at home often, but the space is set up to facilitate it, making me feel like I'm sitting down for a deposition.

She takes a seat in the cushy leather chair behind her massive oak desk while I take one of the two smaller wingbacks in front of it, crossing my legs and trying not to shrink in on myself. I've never been afraid of her, but I've always been . . . intimidated. She's a no-nonsense woman, and it carried over into her parenting style.

"Did your assistant get that list of divorce lawyers I sent over?" she asks without preamble. No *How are you doing, honey?* No *How's married life treating you?* I didn't expect there to be, but it would have been nice.

And of course she's the one who drew up the list, though my assistant failed to mention that in the email. "She did," I answer. "Thanks for that, but I won't be needing it."

Mom's lips turn down at the corners. "You're really going to stay married to that man?"

Her comment has me bristling. I understand she doesn't know Thomas and she's well aware that I've stumbled into this marriage, but the dismissal of him and our relationship—fake as it is—hurts. She thinks I've made a terrible decision, one that she's determined to rectify, despite me telling her multiple times now that I don't want or need her help.

"*That man* has a name, you know," I say, trying to keep the annoyance out of my voice. "And yes, we're staying married, because that's what two people who want to be together do."

Her scoff is loud and harsh, though the way she cringes a little as it echoes through the room tells me she didn't mean to let it out. Either way, it stings like a slap.

"We both know that marriage was a mistake," she says, gentler this time, but her disbelief continues to shine through. "This was a drunken Vegas wedding to a man you claim you know. Maybe you *do* know him—maybe you weren't lying to me about meeting him when Janelle met Ron. But my gut is telling me that you did something you regret and now you're trying to cover it all up."

Her gut's not wrong, and mine is churning hard enough that I'm worried the truth is going to come up and out, splattering all over her desk.

"This is all very real, Mom."

She stares me down, either searching for signs of deception or waiting for me to break and tell the truth. It's a look that has worked on plenty of people in the past, myself included, but today I stay strong.

Eventually, she sighs and glances away, realizing she's not going to get what she wants out of me. "I'm just . . . I'm disappointed in you, Stella."

A crack opens up in my chest. Her words seep into it, burning and biting the entire way down.

"I understand you're hurting from what Étienne did," she pushes on, dark eyes finding me again. "And I know you have that wild streak—I swear it's been there since the day you were born. But the daughter I raised knows better than to let it run her life, and yet you went ahead and got yourself into a mess." She leans forward, forearms on the smooth wood, her gaze imploring. "Let me help you. We can clean up this mess together and you can move on with your life. Please, Stella. I don't want to see you doing this to yourself."

I'm wavering, the chasm in my chest filling now with the love I know she has for me, even though she has a hell of a way of showing it. I could so easily collapse into her arms and confess everything, then sit back and let her fix it all in that calm, efficient way of hers. She's offering it up on a silver platter, waiting for me to take it. Waiting for me to admit that I need her help because I'm incapable of fixing this on my own.

But I'm not. I'm perfectly capable of handling this in the way that I see fit. To be quite fucking honest, the fact that she thinks I can't is infuriating.

I don't need Mommy to coddle me. I don't need her cleaning up after me like I'm a child. I've already got a plan in place that helps not only me but Thomas too, which has given me an opportunity to start fresh in a new city.

She views everything I've done as a misstep. And she's not wrong—none of this was meant to happen, and it's put me on a different path than I expected. But I'm viewing my actions as stepping stones instead. They're taking me to the life I want to be living right now. That I *need* to be living.

"I appreciate the offer," I say calmly, even with fire ripping through my veins. "But I've got this handled." Before she can say anything else, I push back my chair and then stand, smiling tightly across the desk. "Let's go eat before the food gets cold."

I catch a glimpse of her astonishment, but I don't dwell on it. I just stride back out into the hall, though I don't turn in the direction of the dining room, where the rest of our family is laughing and chattering, blessedly oblivious to our conversation.

My purse sits on the narrow table in the foyer, where I was forced to drop it when the aunts cornered me. I grab it without a second thought and pull my phone from my pocket. After tapping the screen to life, I navigate to my contacts and then listen to it ring.

"Maeve?" I ask when a woman's groggy voice greets me. "Hi, it's Stella. Listen, sorry to wake you, but do you think you can get me a paddock pass in the next sixteen hours?"

# CHAPTER 16

THOMAS

It may be nearly December, but the weather in Abu Dhabi didn't get the message.

I'm dripping sweat as I push through my last flying lap in qualifying, gritting my teeth and praying it's enough to put me in front of my teammate on the starting grid tomorrow. I wouldn't normally be so pressed to outqualify Arlo or to prove I'm the superior driver in our pairing, but our reserve driver's words from the last race linger in my head.

I still don't know what Finley meant with his cryptic congratulations. Isn't my seat safe for the rest of my contract? Isn't there enough money behind me to keep me around even if my performance is lacking? Not that it is, considering I've at least placed on the podium this season, unlike Arlo.

Thankfully, my final lap time is enough to slot me into P5, behind Dev, Reid, one of the Specter Energy drivers, and Dev's Mascort teammate Otto Kivinen. It'll be a tough fight to move up tomorrow, but I'm ready.

I push the thought away as I guide the car to parc fermé. After hauling myself out, I make my way over to an awaiting

FIA official to be weighed, slapping hands with Dev and congratulating him on yet another pole position as I go. Reid is out of reach before I can commend him as well.

I head toward the McMorris garage as they leave to do top-three interviews. Thankfully there's no Finley waiting for me this time, just a swarm of mechanics and engineers and—

Stella.

My wife lingers at the back of the slowly thinning crowd, like she's trying to stay carefully out of the way, but there's no missing her. She stands out as if there's a spotlight beaming down on her, and I blink a few times to make sure I'm not imagining things. But when she lifts a hand to wave at me, grinning widely, I know she's more than just a dream.

My helmet, HANS device, and balaclava are off and gone before I realize what I'm doing. Apologies to the poor soul I likely shoved them at, but I'm too shocked to care much.

My feet automatically carry me over, stopping right before I run into her. The watchful eyes around us have me grabbing her hand and pressing it to my chest, just over my thudding heart. Though, really, I think I've done it because I want her to feel my genuine reaction to her presence.

"You're here," I say, rather unnecessarily, but they're the only words I can form.

I'm just . . . I'm happy to see her. Happier than I thought I would be, especially with all the chaos we've brought into each other's lives. I still haven't spoken with my parents, allowing my assistant and my friends to act as my go-betweens, using the excuse that I need to focus on the end of the season. It's a lie, and we all know it, but I'm not ready to face them. I figured I needed more time with Stella, for us to get to know each other, before I could confidently confront them.

And now she's here.

Somehow, Stella's grin brightens. Her nearly black irises reflect my own mooning smile. "I am."

"I didn't think you were coming." I'm struck with a wave of guilt when I remember why she wasn't planning to be here. "Aren't you supposed to be with your family for the holiday?"

"I had more than enough time with them," she casually dismisses, though there's a tiny waver in her expression before she's back to beaming. "And I'd rather be here watching you stick it on the third row." With her free hand, she gives my shoulder a congratulatory punch. It's not a very spousal move, but hopefully anyone watching will put it down to that just being her personality instead of questioning our relationship. "You had me on the edge of my seat. I almost thought you weren't going to make it out of Q2. Kivinen should have gotten a penalty for impeding you like that."

He should have, since I was forced to swerve around his slower car and missed the apex of the next corner. Thankfully, I recovered without too much drama or time lost. "Sheer luck I made it, honestly," I answer.

But I'm hung up on the fact that she's gone from knowing nothing about F1 to being this well versed in a mere two weeks. And not just that, but she's done it during such a tumultuous time, when she definitely had more important things to focus on. God, it's impressive, and she's done it all for me. For us.

My breath catches when Stella leans in closer. "Don't do that," she whispers.

If there are any cameras around, I hope they're snapping away, because I'm sure I look like a man fully obsessed with his wife. "Do what?"

"Write off your talent. That wasn't luck. That was skill."

I didn't think I was writing anything off, but her reminder is refreshing. She's right. I've worked hard for it to be this way.

I'm about to tell her exactly that—and then possibly tell her how much I'd like to pull her into a private corner—when a hand clamps down on my shoulder and shakes me excitedly.

"Nice fucking job, mate!" Arlo shouts over the noise of the garage.

I have to hand it to the kid, I don't think I've ever had a teammate cheer for my success this much. Maybe it's because neither of us has been in the running for titles or glory. Might as well cheer each other on in that case. Someone's got to get points for the team.

I thank him and ask where he's starting tomorrow, but my question is ignored because Arlo's full attention is on Stella.

He grins up at her, all bright white teeth and excessive charm. He's shown me the web pages dedicated to him, and there's no denying he's a fan favorite among the younger demographic. I can't blame them, because he looks like he should be the lead singer of a boy band. If anyone's the knockoff Harry Styles here, it's him.

"This the wife?" Arlo asks me, even though he's staring at Stella. "I get why you married her so fast. You'd be a fool to risk someone else swooping in before you could lock that down."

That shocks a loud laugh out of Stella, whose hand presses harder against my chest, as if she's silently asking, *Can you believe this kid?*

Unfortunately, I can absolutely believe him, because this is classic Arlo Wood. Cheeky fucker extraordinaire.

"Bless your heart," Stella says, that American drawl coming out strong. It's so saccharine that it's borderline condescending. "Bet the girls are lining up around the block to have a go at you."

I have to bite down on the inside of my cheek to keep from smirking at the way her eyes flick over him. I'd call Arlo out on his comment if I thought Stella wanted me to, but she's got this handled. Watching her draw herself up a little taller has me tempted to step completely aside to let her have a go at him.

I don't, though, because he's interrupted a moment with her that I didn't want interrupted, especially since it will have to end soon.

"Don't you need to be getting to the media pen, Arlo?" I cut in, heading off whatever he was about to say.

For a moment, I swear he's going to ignore me and carry on flirting with Stella, but he must see the insistence in my eyes and puts his hands up instead.

"I'm gone," he announces, unzipped race suit fluttering around his hips as he steps back. "Let the grown-ups have their romantic moment. You better join me soon, though."

He winks at Stella before sauntering off, my half-hearted glare on his back. Again, she laughs, drawing my attention, and my annoyance floods away at the sparkle in her eyes.

I want to stick around and talk to her, especially about her upcoming move to London on Monday, but I really do need to head over for the same media circus I sent Arlo off to. "I'm sorry, I have to go do interviews and then I have the team debrief. But I'll be back as soon as I—"

She cuts me off with a shake of her head. "Go do what you need to and don't worry about me. I'm the one who surprised you at your job. If you did the same to me, I wouldn't hesitate to ignore you."

She's teasing about that last part, but I know she's serious about the rest of it. She wants and expects me to focus on what I'm here to do. I appreciate that push.

"We can talk later," I offer, but she's already scrunching her nose at the idea.

"I'm jet-lagged as hell, so I'm going to bed. Come find me

whenever you have time tomorrow. Maeve knows where I'll be."

Speaking of my assistant, she and I need to have a chat about keeping secrets, since clearly she was the one who organized Stella coming here. Then again, it wasn't exactly an unwelcome surprise.

"See you tomorrow, Prince Charming," Stella murmurs, closing the distance between us to press a warm, lingering kiss to my cheek. "And tell Arlo he better watch his damn mouth the next time he talks to me or else McMorris is going to need to find a new number two driver."

Turns out I don't have to wait long to see Stella the next day, considering we're hotel room neighbors.

"I don't know how Maeve pulled this off," I say when Stella opens her door, "but I think she deserves a raise for it."

She snickers and steps back to let me into the room, where I spot breakfast for two set up on a table by the floor-to-ceiling windows, certainly Maeve's doing once again.

"She may not be your biggest fan, but she seems fond of us together," Stella comments. "Does she know all of this is fake?"

I shake my head and move to the table, pulling out Stella's chair. She's not yet dressed for the day, considering she's wearing what looks like a camel-colored cashmere tracksuit, but she makes it look sexy. How does this woman manage to make *trackies* look good?

Once she's settled, I go to sit across from her. "I told Maeve our lie," I answer. "Not sure she believes it, though. And I had to amend it a bit from what you told your parents. She knows I wasn't in Vegas when Ron and my brother were, so we couldn't have met then."

Stella's expression falls like a brick, which makes my stomach dip along with it.

"Shit," she whispers, fingers lifting to her lips. "I messed that up, didn't I?"

I swear the tips of her ears and the bridge of her nose have gone red, the only places where I can see her blush. She's upset with herself, mortified even, to a degree that I don't quite understand. It's not wonderful to have several versions of our lie out there, sure, but it doesn't warrant this reaction.

I offer her an easy shake of my head and a gentle smile. "Nothing we can't handle," I reassure.

But Stella just stares at me, expression unchanged, like she's waiting for something else. If she's expecting me to burst out in a fit of anger, she's sorely mistaken. The longer I stare, though . . . I really do think she's waiting for me to blow up.

I don't know what else to do except push on. Try to make her feel a little better about what's a minor mistake. "As luck would have it, I was actually in DC for a few days not long after that trip," I say, picking up my fork and knife. "So our timeline of knowing each other doesn't have to change much."

It's another beat before Stella nods, dropping her hand from her mouth and clearing her throat. "Interesting to think our paths could have crossed before the wedding," she says. There's a slight tremor in her voice, but she's fighting to get it level. "What were you there for?"

I look away to let her finish composing herself and slice into my omelet. "I support this initiative that Zaid Yousef runs to get more girls and marginalized kids worldwide into STEM and motorsport. He was hosting an event there and I was the special guest." I take a bite and chew for a moment before tacking on, "There's actually a gala to raise money for the charity coming up in London soon, if you'd like to go as my date."

Stella snorts. "I think being your wife automatically qualifies me to be your date, no?"

"I'd never want to presume. But . . . you'll go with me?"

"Of course I will. I *live* for a gala." She pauses to spear a strawberry on her fork as I grin, pleased that she's willing to join me. "Or any excuse to wear a gown, honestly. If I wasn't a baker, I'd want to be in fashion."

I perk up at that. "You'll get along great with my second-youngest sister, then. She has her own line."

"Shut up." Stella leans forward, engrossed. "How have you not told me this sooner?"

"We haven't exactly had much time to discuss our families and their careers. Been a little too busy figuring out each other's first."

She thoughtfully chews her strawberry. "True. But I guess that's going to be important soon. When do you want me to meet your family?"

It takes effort not to grimace at her question, considering I've been putting off talking to them for weeks. "Let's give you a few days to settle in first, then I'll release the demons on you."

An unease settles over Stella's features, prompting me to blurt, "That's a joke, I swear. They're not that bad." Well, most of the time.

Her dark eyes remain guarded. "What if your family doesn't like me?"

The question isn't self-conscious. It's more like she's trying to steel herself for the inevitability of it. Of course, there's the minor chance that one of my siblings or either of my parents might irrationally dislike her, but I really doubt it. Dad loves anyone with business acumen. Mum will appreciate Stella's culinary creativity. Edith will be cold and aloof, just like always, and Andrew won't care one way or another since the only people he pays attention to are his wife and Ron. As for Geneva and Calais . . . well, I should probably warn Stella to brace herself for how obsessed they'll be with her, but where's the fun in that?

"I can promise you right now," I say, "they're going to love you."

Stella's eyes flick over me, likely taking in my pale skin and ridiculously posh bearing. I know I come from a certain echelon that has been notoriously unkind to people who look like her, and I don't blame her for worrying. "You sure about that?"

"Absolutely certain," I confirm, but I won't go into any more detail. "Now eat up. It's race day."

I'm waiting for the lights to go out.

This is the last time I'll be on the starting grid this season—the last time I'll sit in this particular car. It's served me well, all things considered, even though I wish it could have landed me a little higher in the Drivers' Championship. If I can gain a place and cross the line in P4 today, I'll finish sixth in the standings, just ahead of Lorenzo Castellucci. My haters will have more ammunition, unfortunately, since I'll have outranked their favorite, but it's an accomplishment I'm damn proud of. And who knows, maybe next year McMorris will produce a car that will let me challenge Zaid Yousef and Axel Bergmüller—once they return—plus all the other drivers who finished in front of me.

A man can dream, can't he?

I'm hot off the line when the five lights go dark, my reaction time so good that I immediately have to cut to the inside to avoid tagging the Specter Energy car's rear wheels. He's smart enough to head me off into the first turn, though, forcing me to fall back and scrap with Otto Kivinen.

Otto takes the outside line, nearly squeezing me off-track as he moves inward, but I keep on, gritting my teeth as I slot in behind him. Thankfully, it's only a brief annoyance. The slipstream I pick up in the straight makes it all worth it, the reduced drag allowing me to gain speed and close him off in the next corner.

And what do you know—I'm in fourth.

From there, it's not a particularly interesting race. As the laps go by, there's enough of a gap between the drivers in front of and behind me that not much can happen. Even my pit stops—both perfectly timed and executed—don't get me more than a fresh set of rubber. It's not mind-numbingly boring like some races can be, but I certainly don't have to use as much brainpower as a circuit like Monaco requires or push particularly hard.

Yet there's no place else I'd rather be.

Maybe I was wrong to tell Stella I wasn't living the dream. No, I'm not winning. And no, I don't have a championship title in sight. I probably never will. The truth is, most drivers will never win a championship, let alone win a grand prix. I'm lucky that I've at least done the latter a few times.

But even without dozens of wins or a title under my belt, I don't want to give up this life. I don't want to lay it all down and walk away. I want to be here, under these lights, in front of these crowds, and on these circuits for as long as I can. They'll have to drag me away kicking and screaming, because I'm not leaving willingly.

On lap forty-five, my engineer updates me on driver positions. At the front, Reid and Dev have been battling, and there have been plenty of switch-ups behind too, including Arlo making his way up from P10 to P7. It's a great improvement, but unfortunately, the second D'Ambrosi driver—a rookie who's been trying his best to keep up with the expectations set by the man he replaced—is ahead of him by more than five seconds.

With Reid now in first and his teammate in sixth, McMorris's chances of beating D'Ambrosi in the Constructors' Championship are out the window. It's a shame, but sometimes that's just how seasons go. It's amazing we even came that close. Next season, though . . . we're coming for that third-place spot at the very least.

When the checkered flag waves, I take care to thank the entire team over the radio, including all the people back at the factory. And then, cheeky as it is, I say, "And, Stella, if you're listening, thank you for taking a gamble on me. You've brought me more luck than I could have ever hoped for."

Even if she's not tuned in to our team radio, there's no way the broadcasters will resist airing it, and undoubtedly the public will eat it up too. It's a little nod to our Vegas wedding and a heartfelt shout-out to my wife—how could anyone resist that? It might not endear me to everyone, but maybe it'll take the edge off some of the general hate. And I really do want Stella to know how much I appreciate her giving our faux marriage a chance.

I also tack on my congratulations to Reid on winning his first Drivers' Championship. It's mind-blowing that he's pulled it off, and I'm still certain *something* has gone on behind the scenes to make it happen. But a win is a win, and it's exciting to see someone other than Zaid or Axel walk away with the trophy for the first time in years.

In parc fermé, I climb out of the car and go through the usual end-of-race procedures before heading back to the

McMorris garage. I'm greeted with hugs and handshakes and high fives, relief palpable now that the season is over. We're all ready for a break—from this world, from one another, and from the stress of keeping an elite team running. Of course, not everyone will get extended time off, or even have their holiday begin now. I'm almost certain the engineers never rest, and Arlo, for instance, will have to stay a few more days for all the mandatory postseason testing.

Me, though? I'm out of here the second my race debrief and all my media duties are over. Perks of being the senior driver on the team.

But truthfully, the work never stops. I'll still be in the gym nearly every day, spending plenty of time in my home race simulator, and I'll be back at our Silverstone headquarters before I know it. And as much as I'm desperate for a break, I'm not particularly mad about the prospect of going back to work in a few weeks.

To my delight, Stella is once again waiting for me at the back of the garage, a green headset draped around her neck. From the way she's beaming, I know she heard my radio message.

Her arms are around my waist a moment later, our chests pressed together. Her heels are a smidge shorter tonight, though no less dangerous than usual, forcing her to tilt her head back a little farther. The long line of her neck has me tempted to press my lips to the very top of the column. I don't resist the urge.

Her giggle vibrates against my lips, and I don't even care if no one's watching. This is just for me.

"You are so fucking *good*," Stella gushes as I pull back, her hands cupping my jaw. "I take back everything I ever said about you being a loser."

I grin down at her. "I mean, technically, I *am* a loser. I didn't come close to winning the championship."

"If that was losing, then I'd watch you do it anytime. That was a damn good drive."

Her joy is infectious, flooding my body. I thought I was happy before, but hearing her praise . . . I don't have a name for the emotion rushing through my bloodstream. Whatever it is, I like it more than I should.

"Thank you," I say, pressing my cheek farther into one of her palms. "Glad to have survived the season. Glad we *all* did."

Some of us may not have come out of it unscathed, mentally or physically, but we're still alive. In a season like this one, that's all we could have asked for.

I clear my throat to dislodge the heaviness threatening to settle there. "Anyway," I say. "I have a few more things to wrap up, but I'll see you in the morning for our flight out. You ready to go home?"

There's a flicker in her eyes at the word *home*, and I fear I've said the wrong thing. I don't know how else to phrase it, though. *Ready to go back to my place?* No, too full of innuendo. *Ready to be married but completely platonic housemates?* Christ, that's worse.

But then the flicker passes, a smile blooms across her face, and—fuck. *Fuck.* I'm not sure if living together is a good idea anymore.

Because keeping my hands off my wife is going to be next to impossible.

 **CHAPTER 17**

STELLA

London is wet. Dreary. Hideously cold. Just plain nasty. And I'm thrilled to be here.

This is far from my first visit, but my face was still glued to the window as the plane descended, admiring the gray-green scenery. Even in the back seat of the sedan Thomas hustled me into, I was paying more attention to the (less-than-thrilling) views of the congested M4 than anything he was saying.

But now that we're easing our way into Kensington, the reality of our situation starts pressing down on me.

"Is my stuff already here?" I ask Thomas.

The look he gives me says he's already talked about this, but he graciously repeats himself. "Yes, everything your assistant sent over arrived yesterday. The staff hasn't unpacked anything, but if you want them to, just tell me and I'll pass along the message."

I'm curious as to what kind of staff he has. Maids, chefs, maybe even a full-on butler? He seems the type to ring a little bell and call for a man named Alfred.

I don't get a chance to ask, because the sedan comes to a smooth stop in front of a row of attached houses. Each one has a slightly different exterior, but they're all architecturally stunning—and expensive. I'm betting every house on this street costs at least a cool £10 million. Even the tiny front gardens and winter-barren landscaping can't hide the wealth that lives here.

"Home sweet home," Thomas says as the driver opens my door, a cold blast of air stinging my cheeks.

Home. I don't know if I really *have* one anymore, but this is at least where I'll be living. When Thomas asked if I was ready to go home, the idea excited me, warmth blooming in my chest at the thought of having a safe place to land after surviving so much chaos. But now that I'm here, it feels like just another house, four new walls that won't bring me the comfort that my apartment with Étienne did.

Looking back, I can certainly complain about the ugly parts of our relationship, but there were beautiful times too, especially there. All the nights we stayed up too late watching his favorite shitty horror movies, cuddled up on the couch he hated but that he insisted we buy because I liked it. All the bakes I made, which he'd take into his office the next day, returning with praise for me from his employees. Or the time when our faucet broke and sprayed water all over the kitchen and he put on an Édith Piaf album and slow-danced with the mop as I laughed from my dry spot up on the counter.

It wasn't all bad, and that apartment got to see the best of it. It's what, in my lowest moments, I want to return to.

But I'll never have that back, no matter how much I yearn for the solace of that place and the memories made there. So fuck it. I might as well start over and make the best of what's been offered to me.

And I've been offered something *very* nice.

Thomas escorts me through the wrought iron gate that separates the sidewalk from the front garden and up the narrow path to the white stone building. There's a bay window to the right of the front door, and I catch a glimpse inside before he turns the knob of the gleaming black door. It looks a lot like the lobby of a hip luxury hotel with low-slung velvet couches and oil paintings in heavy bronze frames. It's far more contemporary than I was expecting from Prince Charming's classic—okay, let's be honest: old-fashioned—vibe.

When the door swings open, I'm met with a wider foyer than I expected, and I consider ducking back outside to make sure we haven't suddenly been transported somewhere else.

"This is way bigger than I thought it would be," I say as I glance around, taking in the herringbone-carpeted staircase and the black-and-white gallery wall leading to the second floor. "It looked so narrow from outside."

Thomas rubs the back of his neck, a sheepish smile on his face. "That's because it's actually three buildings put together. We kept the facades of the individual houses but knocked down the interior walls."

I was wrong. This isn't a £10 million house, it's £30 million at the very least.

I glance around appreciatively, leaning past him to take in the room that branches off to the left. "Didn't realize racing paid so well."

"Sometimes it does."

It's another vague answer, like when he told me his family was in hotels and was reluctant to elaborate. I shoot him a wry look. "But it didn't pay for this, did it?"

"Not completely," he admits. Eager to change the subject,

he extends an arm, motioning past the staircase to the house beyond. "Shall I give you the full tour?"

I drop my purse on the sideboard and kick off my shoes. "Lead the way."

We start at the back, where there's a beautiful sunroom off the kitchen. "Doesn't actually get much sun," he says dryly.

I take my time in the kitchen, peeking in the aggressively large stainless-steel fridge and running my fingers over the stove's eight burners. There's a wall-mounted double oven and top-of-the-line equipment that I'd bet good money he's never touched a day in his life. In fact, some of it is so new that there's still plastic wrapped around the cords.

Maybe it's because he doesn't spend much time here, considering he's busy traveling around the world, but wouldn't his chefs have removed that by now? Unless . . . unless it's not his chefs' equipment.

I don't have to look closely to see the stand mixer is the same brand I use for small-batch testing and cooking at home. Same with the handheld appliances lined up perfectly on the marble countertops. They're even the same color that I prefer— a shade of café au lait that's available only by custom order. But those aren't mine sitting there. No, mine are beat to hell from use. These are fresh out of the box.

There's no way he bought them just for me. To have gone through all the trouble of not just purchasing them, but in the exact specifications I love. Absolutely not.

But . . . did he?

We're moving on with our tour before I can work up the nerve to ask. There's an impressive gym in the basement, with mirrors lining the walls and every weight and cardio machine a gym rat could want. There's even a Pilates reformer machine in the corner. The thought of him sliding around on it has me covering up a laugh with a cough.

Our next stop when we go back upstairs is a space I wasn't expecting, but I give an impressed click of my tongue when he swings the door open.

"And *this* is my trophy room," he announces with a grand gesture.

I stare at the rows and rows of sparkling trophies, plaques, medals, and even helmets that I'm guessing were specially made for past races. If this is anything to go on, man's been winning *a lot* in his life.

"Damn," I murmur, impressed. "I need to get one of these for myself."

"We can share," he says easily. "I'll make room for you."

I snort, backing out of the room again, but there's a flutter in my chest at the idea of him wanting to display my accomplishments next to his. The simple idea of him making room for me in his life.

Remember, this is temporary. It's not even real.

The voice in the back of my head is right. I shouldn't get caught up in his sweet words, as heartwarming as they are.

"Okay, time to show me to my room," I urge, gently shooing him back toward the foyer and the staircase.

I do my best not to stare at his ass as he leads us upstairs, but I'm only human, and *damn* he has a nice one. To distract myself, I peruse the photos hanging on the wall as we pass them. It's mostly an array of him and his family over the years, with a couple of friends thrown in. I stop when I spot a vaguely familiar face, still recognizable even though she's a few years younger in this snap than the one I've already seen.

I tap Thomas's back, then point to a photo of the smiling

blonde when he stops and glances at me. "Is this Miss She's Not My Type?"

His eyes follow my finger, lips pursing slightly. "That's the one."

"She's beautiful." I don't say it because I feel threatened or inferior to her, but because it's the truth and I'm not about to deny it. She's a stunner with big green eyes, a wide toothy smile, and the kind of wavy hair that takes a hell of a lot of hot tools to achieve, even though it looks effortless. Truthfully, she and Thomas would make a gorgeous couple, but knowing that she's not his type and that he's never been interested changes the dynamic. "Is she actually in love with you? Because I don't want to go out of our way to hurt her."

He stares down at me from his vantage point on a higher step, considering my question. I appreciate that he's thoughtful about it. Men who only care for and respect the women they're attracted to are the kind I prefer to stay far away from, and his answer will decide whether I need to pull up that list of divorce lawyers my mother sent over.

"She may think she's in love with me," he finally says, and there's an honest note in his voice that almost reads as sorrowful, "but she only loves the idea of me. What I represent. Not me as an actual person."

There's something crushing to that response that resonates in my chest. It's a combination of my own hurts, my ability to relate, and his pain from being viewed that way. It makes me want to grab his hand and hold tight.

But that's against my own rules, so I keep my fingers curled at my sides, ignoring the urge.

When I don't say anything else, Thomas turns and keeps going. The second floor is a soothing space, all soft neutrals and plush cream-colored carpet. He mentioned having several bedrooms, and I'm assuming there are a few in each wing of the house, with the room straight across from the landing acting as an office-slash-library.

"I had your things placed in the east wing's primary suite. I hope that's okay."

I glance down the hallway, then back to him. "Where's your bedroom?"

"The west wing. I figured you'd want plenty of privacy in case you . . ." He trails off before clearing his throat, a hint of pink tingeing his cheeks. "In case you have visitors."

Right, it's my own get-away-with-cheating rule by another name. I don't have any plans to utilize it, but I'm not the only one with the option, and I don't want to hear *his* potential visitors either. This benefits us both.

"That's fine," I say, pushing away the strangely stomach-turning idea of him with someone else. "You probably won't want to hear all of my work calls anyway. I've been told I get a little passionate when it comes to new macaron flavors for the menu."

Thomas huffs a laugh. "I think I'd actually like to hear that."

He can say that now, but he'll regret it when I'm ranting on the phone at ten p.m., thanks to the time difference between here and America's East Coast. I'm about to tell him as much when I spot a shadow over his shoulder and almost bolt down the stairs before I realize it's Maeve coming out of the office.

Thomas is less lucky, letting out a small, horrified sound as his assistant appears at his side.

"Jesus *Christ*," he breathes out, taking a half step away from her. "How did you get here before us? Weren't you on a later flight?"

"Witches can teleport," she answers, so serious that I almost believe her. "And be glad I got here first, because I intercepted Edith on your doorstep earlier."

The mention of his older sister has the sweet blush on Thomas's cheeks fading. "What did she want?"

"You and Stella are expected at the Cotswolds house tomorrow afternoon. You'll be staying a few days with the family."

"It's a Tuesday," he protests. "Doesn't everyone have jobs to get to?"

"Well, you don't have anything in your diary until Friday, and the entire world obviously revolves around your schedule, so no." Maeve's attention shifts to me. She's far less snarky when she speaks again. "If there's work you need to do while you're away, I can have the house staff set up an office."

I shake my head. "That won't be necessary. I'm off for the rest of the week."

And now I'm glad I am, because meeting Thomas's family this soon was *not* what I was expecting. It sounds like I'm about to be thrown straight into the vipers' nest.

Maeve nods, then looks back to Thomas. "Be warned, your mum's new hobby is bartending. She's apparently getting really into it. Loves a porn star martini these days."

He grimaces, full-on pained this time, the parliament smile not enough to express his disdain. "I hope I never have to hear her say those words."

"I'll keep you in my thoughts." Maeve claps her hands. "Right, I'm off. Just wanted to make sure you were warned, Thomas, and that you have everything you need, Stella. Did you see all those fancy gadgets he made me order for you? Literally had me call up your people to find out all your favorite—"

"She's fine, Maeve, thank you," Thomas interrupts brusquely, shooing Maeve toward the staircase. "And if there's anything she needs, I'll get it for her."

I blink before my gaze swings up to him, though he's pointedly not looking at me. A flush once again dots his cheekbones.

Huh. So I was right. It *was* all for me.

His assistant flashes me a bright smile as she's herded down the steps. "You have my number, Stella. I'll be here in a snap of my fingers if you need me."

Witch powers or not, I do believe she's capable of it. "Thank you, Maeve. Appreciate it."

It isn't until she disappears downstairs and the front door slams shut that Thomas blows out a heavy breath. Running a hand through his hair, he turns his attention back to me.

"I'm sorry," he says regretfully. "I wanted to give you some time to settle in before I brought you to them."

I wanted that too, but it is what it is. And I guess it's better we know early on if this is going to work before we sink more time and effort into this marriage project.

"Probably smart to get it out of the way. We've definitely got to get our stories straight, though." I'm about to suggest we order some food and interrogate each other for a few hours, but I'm forced to cover a yawn instead. My ass has been thoroughly kicked after being in three time zones over five days. I don't know how this man does it week after week.

A concerned crease appears between his eyebrows. "You should get some rest. We've got about a two-hour drive to the house tomorrow. We can talk then."

We really shouldn't waste time, but I'm so worn out that I wouldn't retain anything he told me anyway. "Yeah, okay." I hook my thumb over my shoulder in the direction of the east wing. "Guess we'll go to our separate corners now. If you hear me up wandering in the middle of the night because my body can't figure out what time zone it's in, mind your business."

He laughs, full chested and unguarded, and the sound chases away my exhaustion for a blissful moment. "I promise to ignore you."

"Smart man. Good night, Thomas."

I'm left staring back at a slightly crooked grin, a tenderness in his eyes that touches me a little too much. "Sweet dreams, Stella."

◆◆◆◆◆◆

"Okay, you win. A full English breakfast is . . ." I heave a dramatic sigh. "Not that bad."

Thomas points his fork at me triumphantly, a mushroom threatening to fly off it. "I *told* you! How dare you say that beans don't belong on the plate. Blasphemy."

I shake my head and take another bite of sausage to disguise my smile. "Look, where I come from, beans like this are not a breakfast food," I point out after chewing. "You've got to understand why I had my doubts."

I didn't expect to be proved wrong so quickly, though. After sleeping like the dead, I woke this morning to the smell of bacon frying and let my nose lead me down to the kitchen. To my surprise, it wasn't a hired chef at the stove, but my fake husband himself, wearing a truly hideous Union Jack apron that I've already sworn to replace before I have to do any recipe testing here.

Truth be told, I didn't think cooking would be on his list of talents, but I don't mind the discovery one bit. Mainly because, for once, I don't have to lift a finger. With Étienne, I did all the cooking, with him claiming it was because he didn't know how—and refusing to learn.

Thomas put his hands on my silk robe–covered shoulders and sat me down at the island, then placed a coffee, an orange juice, and a glass of water in front of me before flourishing the steaming plate of food. Upon seeing it, I blanched at half its contents. And yet Thomas cajoled me into taking a few bites, promising I'd change my mind. I had to confess he was right.

"Ah, my American wife," he says fondly before popping the mushroom in his mouth. "You have so much to learn about my beautiful culture."

I roll my eyes, but his terrible jokes and the simple act of cooking me breakfast—and a good one at that—have my heart tumbling. Or maybe it's just palpitations from the third cup of coffee he's already poured me, never letting my mug go empty.

I've nearly cleared my plate when his phone chimes on the counter. "We should head out soon," he says after glancing at the screen. "Do you need any help packing?"

"No, I've got it." I pause, reconsidering. "Actually, is there, like . . . any sort of dress code I need to be following?"

It's such a ridiculous question to ask. It's not like this is the first significant other's family I've met, but I don't know how these upper-class English families function. I'm half expecting to stumble upon a scene from *Downton Abbey* or *Bridgerton*.

Thomas considers, tongue running across his lower lip. "Well, it's winter, so you don't have to worry about packing your tennis whites," he says, "though you may want to bring your riding gear. You do own breeches, yes? Oh, and I'd suggest an evening gown or two for Mother's white-tie dinners. They're always spectacles."

My stomach drops straight to the floor. "Are you—"

"Stella, I'm kidding," he interrupts, a laugh in his voice as he grabs my hand. "I swear, it's nothing like that. Wear whatever you'd usually wear. You always look amazing anyway."

I'm scowling, but the compliment warms me. "Respectfully, fuck you, your highness."

"As long as it's respectful." He shoots me a grin before drawing his hand back and standing. "Go get ready. Is there anything you need?"

He's already asked me that question at least a dozen times in the half hour we've been having breakfast, and I once again shake my head. "I'm fine. I have everything I could possibly need and more."

Seriously. Last night, when I went to shower before bed, I found what was essentially a fully stocked pharmacy under the sink, along with every hair tool and expensive skin care product I could have ever wanted. I didn't even have to pull out my own silk pillowcases from my bag—there were some already on the bed. I even double-checked that they weren't mine, peeking in one of my suitcases to see if someone had unpacked my things for me, but no. They'd been graciously supplied by my host.

"I just want to make sure you're comfortable here," he says. "This is your home too."

He's so earnest, I can't doubt that he means it. He's looking out for me in all the ways I haven't had from a man in . . . too long.

I hop down from my barstool. "Give me twenty minutes and I'll be ready to go."

"No rush. I know you have to go through your selection of evening gowns."

His banter may be awful, but it still has me snickering as I leave the kitchen, grudgingly thankful for his rich-white-man humor. Never thought I'd see the day.

Closer to a half hour later, I'm in the passenger seat of a boxy SUV that would look more at home in the countryside than in the city. Considering that's where we're headed, I guess it's the perfect choice.

The streets are narrow and the car is wide, but he navigates down to the high street with ease. I watch the shops and restaurants and people as we pass by, trying to commit as much of it to memory as possible. Like Thomas keeps saying to me, this is my home now, so I'll do my best to learn it and make it feel that way.

It isn't until we've been on the motorway for a few minutes with nothing much to look at that the silence starts to feel awkward. Thomas must sense it too because he says, "You can put on some music, if you'd like."

We said we'd use this journey to talk, but we need an icebreaker first. I hit the button for the radio, letting the station it was already on pour through the speakers. To my delight, it's tuned to a top pop hits channel, and just as the host stops speaking, one of my favorite songs comes on. This has to be an omen, a sign of good things to come. Or at least I'm taking it as one, because the idea of meeting his family has me nervous as shit and I'm desperate for something to take the edge off.

I'm two notes into humming along when Thomas groans.

"I cannot *stand* Ed Sheeran," he complains, taking one hand off the wheel to grab his phone from the center console. He tosses it gently in my lap. "Put on one of my playlists. Passcode is seven-zero-four-five."

The Ed Sheeran slander is a topic we'll have to address at a different time, because I'm too thrown by him offering up his passcode so easily to dwell on my offense. That's a sign of trust if I've ever seen one. That, or the man has nothing to hide.

I type in the code and the screen unlocks. "Those numbers have any particular meaning?" I ask as I tap on his music app.

Thomas hesitates, hands drifting around the steering wheel,

like he's not sure he wants to admit it to me. "My racing number is seventy," he finally confesses. "And . . . Zaid Yousef's is forty-five."

My head snaps up, eyes wide in delight. "Oh my God," I say, laughing as I take in the color creeping up his neck. "Are you a *fanboy*?"

"Can you fault me?" he shoots back, but I have to respect that he's not denying it. "Man's a legend. He was winning titles before F1 was even a gleam in my eye. Besides, this has been my passcode since I was a teenager, and I've been too lazy to memorize something else."

"You're adorable," I coo, and I get to watch the color spread to his cheeks before I look back down at his phone. But as I scroll through his playlists, my humor fades into disbelief. "Are you logged into your own account?"

I feel more than see the glance he shoots me. "Yeah, why?"

"Because your music taste is all Afrobeats and hip-hop."

He shrugs when I lift my eyes again. "Yeah, I like it."

Okay, who kidnapped my pure English rose and replaced him with . . . this?

"I had a lot of West African mates growing up," he elaborates when all I can do is stare at him. "I inherited their taste in music."

Somehow, this explains so much about him and yet I'm still so surprised. "Are you still friends with them?"

He nods. "Our group survived primary school and all my racing years. You'll definitely get to meet Joshua and Amara at some point. Oh, and just a heads-up, Amara's already in love with you."

I guess it's a good sign that he wants to introduce me to his friends, though I'm worried that if our lives get too intertwined, it will be difficult to extricate ourselves. We're barely three weeks into this sham—hell, it's not even December yet. What are things going to look like in three months, let alone a year from now?

Then again, I spent five years with Étienne and all we really have left to split are our houses and one joint bank account. We barely had any mutual friends—his friends were his and mine were mine—and all his family was in France, with zero interest in coming to visit us in the States. As far as separations go, ours has been straightforward, minus the emotional entanglements on my end.

So maybe I shouldn't ask, all for the sake of keeping my distance, but I do anyway. "Tell me more about your friends? Especially Amara. She sounds like my kind of woman."

░░░░░░

Two hours later, I know my husband a little better, relaxed in the knowledge that I probably won't mess anything up with his family. Also, we're firmly in the middle of fucking nowhere.

We're on a road that looks like it was meant for horses and carriages and certainly not modern-day SUVs. There are sheep to my left and fields of some sort of grain to my right. And I, a city girl, am out of my element—especially when we turn down another narrow lane and trundle toward an honest-to-God manor.

Thomas turns into the circular drive, winds around a decorative fountain, and comes to a stop in front of the beautiful stone home. It's not Downton Abbey levels of large, but it's certainly bigger than any house I've ever owned, covered in twisting vines of dormant wisteria and dark green ivy. I almost expect two lines of staff to come bursting out the tall wooden doors, but it looks like we're on our own when it comes to escorting ourselves in.

Even from the outside, there's an antique opulence to the building. And when I follow Thomas into the front hall, taking in the tapestries on the walls and the hand-carved furniture, I can't do much more than stare open-mouthed at it all.

I am a rich woman—there's no other way around it. But this? This is *wealth*. Old, terrifying wealth.

"All right?" Thomas asks me, and I press my lips closed again, though I'm sure he's already seen me slack-jawed.

"Yep," I eke out. "Great. So great."

He snickers and takes my weekender bag from my hand, giving me the opportunity to turn and take in the high ceilings and exposed wood beams. "It's a lot, I know. Promise, this is the least-modern room in the house, though. And before you ask, *yes*, we have running water. There's even a pool in the back garden. It's heated if you want to take a dip while we're here."

I didn't think to pack a swimsuit, but now I'm not convinced that Thomas was joking about breeches and evening gowns.

As I admire it all, he strides over to one of the arched doorways and calls out to see if anyone's home. After a few seconds of waiting and no response, he sighs and sets our bags down.

"Looks like no one's here yet." He glances at the expensive watch on his wrist before looking back over at me, brows raised. "You want a tour in the meantime?"

I sure do, because when else am I going to wander a sixteenth-century English manor? "Absolutely. But first, can you guide me to one of those bathrooms with running water that you claim to have?"

Thomas laughs and points to the archway straight ahead. "Go down that hall and turn right. It will be the first door on your left."

I thank him and hurry off, bladder full from all the beverages he served me at breakfast. Thankfully, his directions are easy to follow, and I emerge relieved a few minutes later, eager to start our tour before anyone else shows up. Our conversation flowed in the car, even if most of it was spent with him telling me about his friends and the history of this place, and I wouldn't mind picking it back up.

"I hope you're ready to give the tour of your life," I say as I turn the corner back into the front hall.

And then I walk straight into Figgy.

# CHAPTER 18

THOMAS

Apparently, my family isn't here yet, but Felicity-Anne Peregrine is.

I've barely finished stuttering hello to her, surprised by her sudden appearance—seriously, where the hell did she come from?—when Stella comes back around the corner. She stops short to keep from running into Figgy, then takes a quick half step back.

"Oh my God, sorry!" Stella blurts. "I'm just determined to mow everyone down lately."

I have no idea what she's on about, but there's no time to ask, because my wife and the woman I've been expected to marry for practically my whole life are now face-to-face with each other—and they couldn't be more different.

Stella, brown-skinned and leggy, wearing a cashmere dress belted at the waist and her dangerous stilettos. Figgy, flaxen-haired and petite, dressed in the Cotswolds uniform of jeans, boots, and a Barbour jacket. But it's not just in appearance where they deviate. My wife is no-nonsense and sharp edged, all sly humor and twinkling eyes. And my old friend turned unwanted admirer is . . . well, none of those things. She has the softness of a woman who was handed everything at birth and has never strived for more, content in her status, knowing it would never be challenged as long as she followed the path set out for her by marrying well and carrying on the legacy.

But a challenge has appeared in the form of Stella, and I have no idea what that's going to bring out in her.

My stomach twists into something vaguely pretzel shaped and sinks. This is *not* how I envisioned their first meeting going. I had hoped for more time to prepare Stella and to maybe have a chat with Figgy to once again explain that she and I were never going to happen. I didn't want either of them thrown into the arena with no preparation. Yet here we are.

"You're fine, don't worry," Figgy says on a laugh, light and lyrical. It's the exact opposite of Stella's rumbling chuckle. "At least we're all still standing."

Well, I might not be for much longer.

Figgy moves next to me, standing so close that her arm brushes mine as she lifts a hand to extend to Stella. "It's so lovely to have you here," she says. The statement is warmly welcoming, as if she's the lady of the manor greeting a guest. "It's about time Thomas brought his wife home to visit. I'm Figgy, an old family friend."

I'm glad that's the explanation of our relationship—or lack thereof—that she went with. The woman is tactful, I have to give her that. And Stella is a practiced businesswoman, so the smile and handshake she offers Figgy in return are perfectly polite, even downright friendly.

"It's wonderful to meet you. Thomas has told me so much about you."

"All good things, I hope," Figgy chirps as she drops Stella's hand—and wraps her arm around mine. When I dare to glance at her, she's beaming up at me. "Unfortunately, he knows all my secrets and embarrassing stories. Guess that's what happens when you grow up together."

I shouldn't be surprised Figgy's breaking out the possessive behavior, but I didn't think she'd lay it on this thick so quickly. Thankfully, Stella's unbothered by the woman clinging to me like a koala, smiling fondly at us both.

"I bet you have such good stories about this guy," she says, smile shifting into a conspiratorial smirk, like they're already best friends. "Could we maybe sit and chat over a mimosa? I'm going to need *all* the dirt on him, and you're the best source."

My attention ping-pongs between the women, not missing the way Figgy's expression flickers with confusion for a moment before she's back to cheery. Stella's offer has clearly taken her aback, not having expected such an affable proposal.

"Oh, I'd love to," Figgy says, though I can sense the *but* coming. "But I only popped round to drop my things for the week. I'm actually off for a facial in town with the *best* aesthetician. If you want me to book you an appointment, I absolutely can. Those long-haul flights make you look so rough."

The sly insult has my eyes flaring wide. Stella could call her out on it, but Figgy phrased it in such a way that she could laugh it off and say she included herself in that *you*, the world traveler that she is, and then Stella would come out as the loser in that battle.

"I might actually take you up on that," Stella says, much to my surprise. I doubt she missed the slight, but she's so perfectly composed that I can't be sure. "I could use a self-care day. Thomas has kept me so busy lately, what with following him around the world, that I've barely had a moment to myself." At that, she shoots me a wink, and it's oh so clear she has the upper hand. "But I can't complain."

Again, Figgy's expression wavers, this time with what I swear is outrage, but then she's laughing. To her credit, it doesn't even sound forced. "I bet not." With that, she detaches herself from me and tosses her hair over her shoulder before giving us a little finger wave. "See you!"

Stella waves back, but I can't do much more than watch her stride toward the doors.

"Oh, she's *fun*," Stella says brightly when Figgy's gone. "I won't go so far as to say she hates me, but we certainly aren't going to be friends."

It takes a few more beats before I get my wits about me, wincing when I realize I left her to fend completely for herself. "I'm so sorry. I had no idea she was going to be here. No one told me."

Stella waves off my apology. "It's fine. I wasn't expecting to meet her before your family, but I knew it would happen eventually. Like I said, better to get it out of the way."

"You're stronger than me." I search her face for any signs of distress or discomfort. I find nothing, though that doesn't mean she's not feeling either. "But are you sure you're okay? You've had a lot thrown at you in the past twenty-four hours, with more to come."

"Thomas." She catches my gaze, forcing me to hold it. "I'm fine. But if I need a break, I'll tell you, okay?"

"Okay." It won't stop me from checking in on her, but I'll acquiesce for now. "So do you think we'll be able to fool Figgy into thinking we're the real deal?"

"Oh, honey, she's already on the defensive." Stella grins and pats my cheek. "That's a good start, though I don't think she's going to let go of you easily."

I knew that was going to be the case, but I hoped Stella

might have a different read on things. My mind whirls, contemplating more ways we can convince Figgy it's time to let me go. This will all be for nothing if we can't.

As if she can tell I'm getting lost in my head, Stella grabs my hand and tugs me toward one of the archways. "Now that we're alone . . . how about that tour you promised me? I'd love to see how the point-zero-zero-one percent lives."

After taking Stella on a tour that left her out of breath and swearing to add more cardio to her fitness routine, we've retreated to our separate bedrooms to settle in and rest.

She seemed relieved when I told her we wouldn't have to share a room, and I know no one will make a fuss about us staying apart for two reasons. One, because propriety suggests that we have our own bedrooms until my parents officially approve of our union. And two, because nearly every couple in this family sleeps apart since they can't stand their spouse.

Unfortunately, Stella and I are down the hall from each other, since Figgy already claimed her usual room next to mine.

"Do you need anything?" I double-checked before we went our separate ways. Mostly, it was to buy more time with her.

"I'm *fine*," she reassured. "And thank you for everything you've done so far. I can't believe you stocked your house with all of my favorites."

I told her it wasn't a problem, because it wasn't. All it took was a couple of phone calls to her people, and then I relayed messages to my own. But what I really wanted to say was *Why wouldn't I do it?* It's merely good hosting etiquette. (Thank you for that lesson, Mum.) And besides, is it so bad that I liked doing it for her? That I like watching the way her face lights up, even if she doesn't realize it, at every detail she notices? That alone would make me want to give her everything.

In the few hours we've been apart, I've been busy thinking of more things I can do to keep her happy while she's in the UK with me. The list so far is typed haphazardly in my phone's notes app, consisting of things like *hire estate agent to find suitable property for a London Stella Margaux's location* and *keep house stocked with almond flour.* It's a work in progress.

I'm about to write down another idea when a text from Geneva appears. It's a quick message to let me know she and the rest of the family will be arriving in time for dinner, followed up by And I mean the whole family. Edith's bringing her entire brood and Andrew's trotting out his wife. If she goes into labor here, I am NOT sticking around.

It's time to warn Stella, then. Poor thing is going to have to face everyone tonight, and I have to pray she's ready for it. That we both are.

She calls for me to come in when I knock on her shut door, but I stop in my tracks after taking one step inside.

She's lying on her stomach across the bed in just a towel that barely clears the generous curve of her ass. Her long legs glow and glisten, bent at the knee and crossed at the ankle, feet in the air. Her laptop is open in front of her, a half-typed email on the screen, but I'm certainly not interested in what she's been writing.

Fuck, this woman is sexier than sin. And I'm somehow expected to keep my hands off her.

"Sorry," she says sheepishly, drawing my gaze up from her legs to take in her crooked smile. "I know I said I was taking the week off, but I seem to have slipped and fallen into my inbox. I did have a bath in that fantastic tub, though. Couldn't resist."

My mouth is almost too dry to form words, but I somehow say, "Just wanted to tell you that my family's on their way. We'll be having dinner together."

At that, her smile takes on a pained quality, laptop forgotten as she sits up. The motion draws my eyes down to the swell of her breasts peeking out above the edge of the towel. It would be so easy for the fabric to come untucked, to slip down, to show me more of her . . .

"Oh boy," she exhales, dragging me out of the thoughts I shouldn't be having. She's made it abundantly clear where she stands on us having a physical relationship, and even fantasizing feels out of bounds. "You think we're going to pass their tests?"

As I consider the question, she gets up from bed and pads over to the wardrobe, where she's unpacked and hung up her outfits.

"I've got to hope." I step forward when she's about to push past a classic black dress, putting my hand on top of hers. "Wear that one."

She glances back at me, eyes finding mine for one heated second. There's no way she can't tell what I'm thinking or even feel it radiating off me. And I'm sure I feel it in return in the way her gaze flicks over me.

She drops her hand before either of us can make a mistake. "Black dress it is."

The breathless words betray her outward composure. She's just as affected as I am. It's both a comfort and a torture; knowing we both want *something* to happen is difficult to reconcile with the fact that we shouldn't let it.

"Now get out so I can get dressed," she demands, shooing me toward the door.

"Come on, I'm your husband," I cajole with a grin. "Don't you want my help doing up the zipper?"

"I'm afraid it will never get zipped if you stay. Now *out*."

The door shuts in my face before I can process her words. When I do, I fear she might have been right.

"Do we have to wait for someone to announce our grand entrance or can we just go in?"

Stella's whispered question as we approach the dining room has me stifling a snicker. I don't know where she's getting all these ideas of how things work around here. Maybe she needs to lay off the Jane Austen.

"No announcement necessary." I offer my elbow to her. "You ready?"

Stella blows out a breath and rolls her shoulders a few times before sliding her hand into the crook of my arm. She's like an athlete preparing for the biggest competition of her life. In a way, I guess this is all a game, so I won't begrudge her the preparations.

"Okay, let's do this."

Voices rumble from the other side of the broad oak doors as we approach. The clink of glasses and a few laughs tell me Mum must be bartending already. All I can hope is that everyone stays *happy* drunk instead of *let's lay out all our family drama in front of company* drunk. It's happened a few too many times to count, and Stella doesn't need to face that this early into our marriage.

Everyone is milling around the vast room when we step in. Edith's spawn rip and race past the long table and the sideboard where Mum is wielding a cocktail shaker with concerning gusto. Andrew stands off to her side, gloomily sipping an espresso martini as he eyes his heavily pregnant wife sitting at the table, who in turn is watching my mother with longing in her eyes as another drink is poured.

Dad is chatting with Edith's husband, who nods a little too enthusiastically at everything the man says, a habit of his ever since Dad announced his plans to retire in the next five years— as if his suck-up act will get Dad to name Edith CEO. Edith herself is having an animated conversation on the phone, pacing circles in the corner and throwing a disgruntled hand up every so often. Business, undoubtedly. Even with Dad still technically running A.P. Maxwell International, she's the one keeping everything afloat.

Calais is the first to notice our entrance, elbowing Geneva in the ribs. They aren't twins, just barely two years apart, but they look and act more alike than the rest of us. Calais is wearing one of her own designs tonight, likely something from the new collection that I was forced to see as I sat front row at her last show. It's bright and floral and would look more at home on a beach in Florida than in England in winter. By contrast, Geneva's lime-green puff-sleeved dress is tame. As a model, she's worn far worse, but it's still an eyesore by my standards.

"Thomas!" Calais exclaims, spreading her arms wide as she approaches. Her grin is nothing short of devilish. "And Stella Margaux! Welcome, welcome!"

I notice the last person in the room when her head whips toward us, having previously been half-hidden behind Mum. Figgy's eyes go from wide to narrowed to perfectly angelic in the time it takes me to blink, her face lighting up when she notices me looking. I swallow back a groan, praying I haven't just given her the wrong idea.

As Calais comes over to pat my cheek a little too hard and then exchange double air kisses with Stella, gushing over her outfit choice, Mum swans over with two espresso martinis in hand.

"My newest daughter-in-law!" she greets, and I swear there are tears in her eyes. Based on how she's beaming, they're happy tears. "Oh, darling, it's so wonderful to finally meet you. Thomas has kept us at such an arm's length, but I've been *dying* to get you here."

Mum then shoves one martini at me and another at Stella, motioning for us to drink up. I take a sip, wincing at the burn of straight vodka with a splash of coffee liqueur. Before Stella can even take a swig of hers, she's being herded away from me by Mum, Calais, and Geneva. I make to follow, but Figgy slides into my path.

"Is Stella enjoying herself?" she asks. "She seemed a little intimidated when she first walked in."

It's such a lie that I almost let loose a guffaw. She must be saying this to make herself feel better, because Stella couldn't have held her head any higher.

"She's loving it," I answer, sparing a glance in Stella's direction to make sure she's all right. From what I can see, she's already charming my mother, smile wide and eyes sparkling. "I'm going to take her on a tour of the area tomorrow, show her all the Cotswolds has to offer."

Figgy, to her credit, doesn't let her easy demeanor fade. "Just don't take her to all our secret places," she teases. "Not that I think she'd want to hang out with Mr. Duggan's sheep. She seems a little high-maintenance for that."

Again, I don't miss the dig. Just because Figgy doesn't mind traipsing through sheep shit and climbing trees to watch the sunset like we used to do as teenagers, doesn't mean she's better than Stella—it just means they're different people.

Figgy's always been a little pushy, but these underhanded comments are new. Is this her last-ditch effort to see if I would ever choose her? Because if it is, it's failing—miserably.

I don't want to be unkind, despite how low she's stooping. "I promise those will stay just for us."

Her mask finally slips, betraying her underlying anxiety. "Really?" she presses. "Because with how you've been avoiding me, I have to wonder if we're even still friends."

I soften a little. "Of course we are, Fig." We've known each other a long, long time, and I'm not trying to completely throw away the friendship we've built, even if she seems desperate to do so for a chance at a romantic relationship. "But that's all we're ever going to be, okay? I need you to understand that."

"Thomas," she pleads, clutching at my arm. "Come on. Everyone knows this marriage of yours isn't real. She's just some woman you married while drunk in Las Vegas, and now you're trying to figure out a way to cover that up." Her grip tightens, nails digging into my skin. "You don't have to lie to me."

My heart pounds so hard that I swear everyone in the room can hear it. No one else has called me out this bluntly so far, though I know plenty of people have been thinking it. It makes sense Figgy would have her doubts, but she's not buying this at all.

The hope written across her face has me sick to my stomach. She truly thinks she still has a shot—that all she'd have to do is get Stella out of the picture and we could ride off together. I don't know how else to get it through her head that it's never going to happen.

"Even if I were lying to you," I grit out, pulling my arm

from her grasp, "it wouldn't change the fact that I'm married and I respect the vows I made to the woman you seem so intent on insulting. That's my *wife*, Figgy, whether you like it or not."

Her lips part in surprise, hand falling back to her side, and for one awful moment I think she might cry. But then she narrows her eyes and says, "I'm going to tell your parents this is a sham marriage. That you're trying to fool everyone and failing miserably at it. What would they think of that?"

The last question is a taunt. What *would* they think? My eyes dart to Stella and my mother laughing together. To Calais and Geneva giving each other the look that I know means *Oh, we like her.* Even Evil Edith is watching Stella curiously from the corner of her eye. My family has already opened their arms to her, even if they have their own misgivings about how the marriage came to be.

Besides, in a world like ours, reputation means more than the truth. Stella and I can't back out now that we've declared to the world that we're together. And I know my family will stand behind the lies for as long as they benefit the Maxwell-Brown name, whether they like my wife or not.

"Do whatever the fuck you want," I snap, then, a little too loudly I say, "Would you mind moving your stuff out of the room next to mine?" The question draws eyes to us, but I don't care. I'm burning from the inside out, furious thanks to her petty threats. "I'd prefer to have Stella closer to me."

Before she can reply, Andrew calls out, "Wait, you and your wife aren't in the same room?" When I look over, he squints at me. "Why not?"

I'm already heated, but my face somehow grows hotter at being questioned. "We have enough bedrooms in this bloody house that everyone could have two of their own," I huff. "Is it so wrong to have our own space?"

He scoffs, and even my younger sisters snicker, but they all know if Mum or Dad had decided automatically that they disliked Stella, we'd be on opposite sides of the house.

"You're newlyweds, Thomas," he drawls, swirling the dregs of his espresso martini. "You'll be sneaking into each other's rooms to fuck anyway."

"Andrew!" Mum scolds, turning to slap his arm before giving me an exasperated but apologetic glance. She then turns to Stella. "I'm so sorry for my eldest son's behavior, but we'll have your things moved into Thomas's room. No need to sleep separately." She snaps her fingers at the staff member lingering by the doors, and the woman nods before rushing off.

As Mum turns back to her bartending setup, Stella and I lock eyes across the room, the same thing written on her face that I'm sure is written across mine.

Oh shit.

Looks like I'll be sleeping with my wife tonight.

 **CHAPTER 19**

STELLA

"So . . . I guess we're roommates now."

I stare at my bags in the corner of Thomas's bedroom. I've been too afraid to look at him since dinner ended, not sure what I'd find on his face. Annoyance at having to share his space with me? Eagerness at the idea of being in bed together? Hopefully not disgust, but I can't rule it out.

"I guess we are," he says, and I finally let my eyes swing up to him.

I don't find any of the things I was considering. Instead, I see a knowing smile, like we should have expected this to happen all along and he's not remotely mad about it.

I think that might be the worst of them all. Because this . . . *this* I don't know how to handle.

"How do you think dinner went?" he asks, shutting the door behind us and moving toward the dresser.

We didn't talk on the way up to his—*our*—bedroom, lest anyone in the family overhear, so I guess it's time for the debrief. But other than being bombarded for hours with questions about my life, my businesses, and my marriage, dinner was a breeze.

It's exhausting, but I'm fantastic at putting on a show. My superpower is being able to talk to anyone, to lean in and make them feel like they're the only person in the room worth giving my attention to. I can humor and empathize with even the sourest of grapes. In this case, that would be Edith, whose dour attitude, gray shift dress, and tight ponytail made me wonder if she's ever had fun in her life. But she cracked a smile when I was asked to tell the story of how I built my macaron empire, almost as if she were proud of me for pulling it off.

Calais and Geneva were easy sells too, fashion being our common ground. And Thomas's mother, Iris, practically held my hand all through dinner and made me more drinks whenever mine got low. Guess I know where Thomas gets it from now.

Andrew and Thomas's dad were harder to bring over to my side. The latter came around after I offhandedly mentioned my company's profit margin last year. But Andrew . . . I don't know. There was something about him I didn't care for. Plus, every time he looked at Thomas, I swore resentment thrummed through the air.

And then there was Figgy and the constant fight for my husband's attention. I might have found her interjections into the conversation and the anecdotes about their long, storied friendship amusing if I didn't know she was trying to steal my man.

My man. Oh God. That's not—I shouldn't be—thinking of Thomas that way; while technically correct, that shouldn't be allowed to go through my head.

"It went really well," I answer, forcing the thought away.

"Your mother's in love with me. Even Edith warmed up by the end."

It might have had something to do with the ten thousand espresso martinis Iris shook up. Those would make anyone friendly. I've had just enough that I'm loose and a little lightheaded now, but not enough to be drunk. Considering what happened between Thomas and me the last time we were shitfaced, it's probably a good thing.

"I did see Edith smiling." Thomas finishes taking off his cuff links and places them carefully on top of the dresser. "Shocking, considering I didn't think her face could do that."

I playfully roll my eyes at him as I move toward my bags. "She's not *that* bad. Terrifying, yeah, but definitely a shrewd businesswoman."

"Which is exactly why she's on track to take over the family company. Dad's planning to retire in the next few years, so she's gearing up for it."

Impressive, but from what I saw tonight, not unexpected. While Andrew mostly sat back and sulked, Edith wrangled four kids, took at least six business calls, and filled in all the blanks whenever her father faltered for an answer.

"Good for her," I commend as I kneel down to gather my nighttime skin care products from my bag. "She seems like the perfect person for the job."

Before I stand, I spare a glance over at Thomas, and I nearly drop the lotions and potions cradled in my arms at the sight that greets me. He's unbuttoned his white dress shirt down to his stomach, pausing to untuck the rest of the material from his navy slacks before finishing the job—and giving me an unobstructed view of his defined abs and the top of his V-cut hips. And it's . . . it's quite the sight.

We haven't discussed how rooming together is going to

work, let alone sleeping in the same (thankfully giant) bed, but Thomas clearly doesn't think that undressing in front of each other is off-limits. As I stumble to my feet, he shrugs out of his shirt and hangs it carefully in the wardrobe, leaving me staring at his rippling back muscles this time.

Okay, I have to say it: My husband is hot. Appallingly so, considering our promise that we'd keep our hands off each other in private. It wasn't so difficult a task when I was fully sober and he was fully clothed, but now that we're neither of those things, my belly is swirling with desire and I'm *very* afraid I might break a rule tonight.

Shaking myself out of it, I mumble to Thomas that I'm headed to the bathroom to get ready for bed.

"Oh, I'll come brush my teeth," he says, following me into the white-tiled space.

He's either an oblivious fool or is trying to taunt me with those beautiful muscles on display. But I don't stop him as we approach the double sinks, with him taking the left and me on the right. He's seen me hungover and half-dead, so I don't mind taking my makeup off in front of him, but standing together in the quiet is more than I can take.

"Hey, what were you and Figgy talking about before dinner?" I ask as he searches for his toothbrush in his toiletry bag. "I mean, if you don't mind me asking. It seemed kind of . . . heated."

He heaves a sigh and ceases his searching for a moment, meeting my gaze through the mirror. "Well, I was totally wrong about her believing our marriage is real."

My blood runs cold for a horrible moment. The whole reason he wanted to stay married was to get her off his back—if that hasn't worked, what skin does he have left in the game? She'll keep pushing if she doesn't see me as a threat. Our entire reason for him to want to be with me has completely gone up in smoke.

But *I* still need *him*. Loath as I am to admit it, my reputation is still on the line, and splitting up so soon would only send it spiraling farther down. We haven't even been together for a full month yet; what will my future look like if he says he wants an annulment and we fuck off to separate corners of the world?

"Do you want to end this?" I blurt.

Thomas blinks at me in horror. "Absolutely not," he says with a vehemence that has me drawing back.

"Damn, all right, just asking."

"I'm sorry, I—" He cuts short and reaches out to touch my elbow, driving his apology home with a light squeeze. "Just because Figgy doesn't believe us now doesn't mean she won't finally get the message and move on. I want us to stay together. I want to make this work."

What strikes me first is that these are the exact words I wanted to hear from Étienne once upon a time. The words I *thought* he would say upon realizing he'd made the worst mistake of his life and came crawling back to me.

I understand this context is completely different, and yet it's still so affirming to hear—Thomas wants me, at least in this small way. He's not pushing me aside. He's not leaving me.

"Okay," I say, because that's all I can push past the growing lump in my throat.

It's another long moment before he drops his hand, but he doesn't immediately look away, searching my face for something. He must find what he wants when I force myself to smile. Only then does he return to looking for his toothbrush and I start in on step one of my skin care routine.

He's done before I even reach step two of ten, gently touching my arm again before leaving the bathroom, shutting the door behind him to give me some privacy. I slump a hip against the sink and take a breath to ground myself.

Figgy not believing we're married for the right reasons isn't *great*, but Thomas is right—if we stick this out, she'll hopefully get fed up and move on. And considering his mother is my newest fan, I can't imagine she and Thomas's father will keep pushing Figgy toward him. Everything is going to be *fine*. No one's stealing my husband.

I finish the rest of my routine and change into my pajamas—champagne-hued silk shorts and a camisole. Might have been a mistake, though, because the second I step into the bedroom, I shiver as my feet hit the hardwood. I could have sworn it wasn't this cold when I first walked in, but maybe that was the effect of hiking up two staircases and the liquor warming me up.

I know for certain my sartorial choice is a mistake when Thomas looks over. He's sitting on the edge of the bed, down to only his black boxer briefs now, and if I felt a pull toward him when he was just shirtless, Thomas in nothing but his underwear is . . . Yeah, it's going to be a problem. *He's* a problem. Why couldn't I have married someone slightly less attractive who I wouldn't have such a hard time keeping my hands off of?

When his eyes dip from my face to somewhere lower, I don't have to guess what he's staring at. I can feel how hard my nipples are, pointing loud and proud through the thin material. It's mostly because I'm freezing, but also because—

No. *Nope.* Not even going to acknowledge it. Not gonna think about it. And I'm certainly not going to give any value to the pressure that's growing between my thighs.

Refusing to think about *any* of it, including the way he's looking at me like I'm a whole damn meal, I march over to the opposite side of the bed and pull back the covers. Again, the pillowcases are silk and they're not the ones I brought with me. Either everyone in this family knows the merit of sleeping on them, or this is just another thing Thomas has done for me. If it's the latter, then my ass is definitely in trouble, because acts of service are my weakness, and he keeps throwing them at me like grenades.

Even though I'm curious, I don't ask. I simply slide under the covers, tie my hair up with my silk scrunchie, and pray it'll still look good in the morning, because I am not about to let this man see me with a bonnet on. We may be married, but we sure as hell aren't on that level yet.

The bed is thankfully an oversized king, the kind where you could roll over twice and still not make contact with your bed-mate. I barely feel it when Thomas climbs in on his side.

"Well, good night," I tell him, reaching over to turn off the lamp on my bedside table. "We'll try again with Figgy tomorrow. Maybe if we stare lovingly into each other's eyes over breakfast and call each other the most disgusting pet names we can think of she'll believe us."

Thomas snorts as he turns off his lamp, plunging the room into darkness. "I'll start brainstorming. Good night, sugar muffin."

"Night, baby cakes."

I force myself to stop smiling and shut my eyes, to turn over onto my side with my back to him. Jet lag is still riding me hard, so falling asleep shouldn't be difficult. Or at least it wouldn't be if I didn't feel like I was slowly being turned into an ice cube. Seriously, did someone turn down the heat in our room specifically?

I spend twenty minutes shivering before I finally flop over onto my back, fed up. I'm about to push back the duvet and search my suitcase for a sweater when Thomas asks, "You all right?"

I squint over in the darkness, guilty that I might have woken him, but I'm not about to lie. "This old-ass house is freezing," I say through clenched teeth. "Are there more blankets somewhere?"

I can't completely make out his features, though I can see him shake his head. "Probably not in here. I run hot, so I don't usually ask the staff to keep any extras in the chest." And then he says, a little lower, "Come closer. I'll keep you warm."

For a terribly weak moment, I consider it. I even inch a little closer before I halt. "*No*," I snap, mostly for my own benefit. "No cuddling. Rule number five."

"I thought we only had three rules."

"I added *no flirting* as number four."

He chuckles, a rumble that vibrates straight up my legs to their apex. "We've broken that about a million times already. Shall we just make *no cuddling* a rule and break it too?"

"Oh, don't be a smart—"

Heated skin meets mine before I can finish the insult. I almost feel bad when my toes brush his calf, but even though he lets out a shocked hiss of air between his teeth at their temperature, he doesn't pull away. He just hauls me closer, tucking himself around me.

"Crikey, you really are freezing," he mumbles against my hair. His arm is locked across my waist, hand tucked under my rib cage, just an inch or two below the curve of my breast.

"Please never say *crikey* again in my presence," I exhale, but *fuck*, he does run hot and it's glorious.

"No promises."

Despite the position, I relax as the heat of his body seeps

into mine, loosening my muscles and easing the goose bumps on my skin. My nipples, the traitors, are still hard as rocks. Unsurprising, considering the press of his body against mine is delicious, and I'm not talking about him being a sentient heating pad.

Staring at Thomas and his marble-statue body is one thing. Feeling it up close and personal is another. He's all smooth skin and rough palms, hard muscles and soft touches. He even slips his knee between mine, every inch of my back pressing against every inch of his front. The sensation sends me straight back to the night at the strip club, sitting in his lap, his fingers gliding up my thigh and sinking into my wetness. The way he sent me over the edge of pleasure with such little effort. How easily he could do it again—and how I know I'd let him.

"Stop fidgeting."

The grumbled words against the top of my head have me stilling, not even realizing I was moving. "I wasn't," I huff, grateful he can't see my face and the embarrassment written across it, because okay, yeah, maybe I *was* moving a little to alleviate the growing ache.

"You were." His hand moves down from underneath my ribs to grip my hip. It sends a bolt of lightning through me, igniting the fuel that was already coursing down to my center. "You were grinding back against me. Keep it up, and you're going to start something we can't finish."

I inhale sharply. Mild-mannered Thomas has disappeared again and the gruff one is back, the one I only seem to get in private.

Maybe it's the lingering liquor in my system, or maybe it's my hormones running wild thanks to having a man pressed up against me like this for the first time in ages, but I murmur, "I mean, maybe we could."

I don't quite regret the words when they're out, even though Thomas tenses for a moment before slowly relaxing again. "You're the one who made the rules, Stella."

It's certainly not an enthusiastic *yes* or even a *we could give it a try*, and yet the way he breathes the words against my ear feels like an invitation. The way he tilts his hips up, letting me feel exactly what my movements have inspired, is another gentle nudge in that direction. But he's still allowing me to make the choice.

"We could amend them," I propose. My heart races as I slide my hand over his and keep going until I reach his body, then drift across the waistband of his underwear. "I owe you for what you did for me at the strip club . . ."

He doesn't stop me as I slip my fingers under the elastic. His muscles go taut as I move lower, almost to his—

"You don't owe me anything." The sentence is pained as he gently grasps my wrist. The rejection stings until he confesses, "Besides, if you do that, I might fall in love with you, which is *not* allowed."

I laugh at his weak attempt at a joke, turning my cheek into the pillow to stifle it, but it's no use. "I'm sorry. I'll keep my hands to myself."

He returns his arm to my waist. "Yes, I'd say that's a good idea." As if he can't help it, he presses a kiss to the spot just under my ear, and it makes me shiver in delight. "Now go to sleep."

"I will when your dick stops poking into my ass," I shoot back, which earns me a swat on said ass. I gasp and lift my head to look at him in shock, trying to hide my amusement. "Did you just *spank* me?"

"That was nothing more than a love tap. You'll know when I spank you."

Forget needing his body heat, I'm suddenly hotter than a raging inferno. "Don't threaten me with a good time."

"Go to *sleep*."

"Fine, fine."

I tamp down on my libido and attempt to settle in for the night. But after another five minutes, sleep continues to evade me. Thomas's breathing hasn't evened out either.

"I can't sleep," I whisper into the darkness.

"It's all those bloody espresso martinis," he grumbles, burying his face in my neck for a moment before dragging us both over onto our backs. "She should have made porn stars."

"Bet you never thought you'd say that about your own mother." I roll toward him, pressing my luck and throwing my leg over his, mostly because I don't want to lose my heat source.

"God, truly." He wraps an arm around my shoulders, thumb sweeping absently back and forth over my skin. "Talk until we get tired? Keep getting to know each other?"

"Oh, I'm feeling very well acquainted with certain parts of you right now."

He heaves a sigh. "You're a menace."

"So I've been told."

He's quiet for a beat, thinking. "Tell me something no one else knows."

That's deeper than anything we've touched on so far. We've focused on the stuff we might be quizzed on in public but nothing that would help us truly know each other. I think we've been avoiding it, lest we like what we find.

I think back to the drive here, about his playlists and the friends who inspired his tastes. But it's what he asked me to turn off that influences my answer.

"I unironically like Ed Sheeran," I say. It wouldn't sound like much of a confession to a lot of people, certainly not something to be embarrassed by, but my friends would never let me live it down. And considering Thomas's disdain for the guy, this might as well be me divulging my deepest, darkest secret. "He's been my most played artist for seven years running."

Thomas groans, squeezing his eyes shut. "Jesus *Christ*. Take it back."

"What's so wrong with Ed Sheeran?" I accuse, pushing up on my elbow to stare down at him. "He's a nice redheaded man who makes catchy music!"

Thomas presses his palm to my back, keeping me from pulling too far away. "Look, I've got nothing against the man himself. And maybe his music's not so bad, but I just . . . can't listen to it."

I scoff. "Why? Did something traumatic happen to you while one of his songs was playing?"

He grows silent again. Oh shit, *did* something traumatic happen?

"One time, I was stuck in the Dublin airport after my flight was delayed, and I swear all they played was every Ed Sheeran album on shuffle," he explains after a long moment, sounding like a man who survived a battle. "I thought I was in hell. You would have loved it."

I slap his chest. "You made it sound like you witnessed a gruesome murder while 'Galway Girl' played in the background."

"Oh, I forgot to mention that I had the onset of food poisoning too," he goes on. "I was fighting for my life, trying not to be sick all over the place, and then as I'm rushing to the toilets all I saw were those Kerrygold butter ads. They were *everywhere*." He shudders, haunted. "Now every time I hear one of his songs, I think of butter and then immediately want to vomit."

I really shouldn't laugh. I do my best to fight it. But the

image of him on hands and knees in an airport bathroom with the pop star crooning ominously in the background has me near tears as I bury my head in his shoulder, my body shaking with silent laughter.

Thomas, bless him, pats my back and waits me out until I can breathe normally again. "So if I ever ask you to turn off one of his songs," he says, "you know why."

"I'll keep that in mind." I swipe under my eyes, cheeks aching from smiling. "Wow. Okay. Your turn. Tell me something no one else knows."

He cuts me a look. "I just did."

"That doesn't count, it was an offshoot of mine."

His lips part to protest again, but he seems to think better of it. Instead, he glances away, staring up at the ceiling for a few long seconds before his gaze lands back on me.

"Certain people already know this, but I feel like you should know too . . . I've never been in a relationship before. This is my first."

I almost snort and call him out on the lie, but something stops me. Instead, I lift my head and squint at him, searching his expression for any hint that he's joking. He has a good poker face, and he's fooled me here and there before, but . . . he looks completely serious.

"You're shitting me."

He shakes his head. "I swear to God."

"Really?" I press, sitting all the way up and letting his hand fall to my hip. "*Never?* Not even when you were younger?"

"I mean, I've dated people. But it's never been anything that had an official title or required monogamy."

I keep staring at him, waiting for the other shoe to drop, but all he does is stare back at me with a wry half smile. He's not lying.

"I was *not* expecting that." I pause again, the reality of it hitting me. "I can't believe you jumped straight into having a wife."

"Definitely skipped a couple of steps. So if I do something wrong, just know it's from my lack of experience."

"You've been doing an excellent job so far," I commend with a pat on his shoulder. "Much better than my ex."

I meant the last bit as a joke, but it tastes bitter on my tongue and comes out the same way. It's like throwing a wet blanket over our conversation, suffocating our levity, and we're left with an awful silence as Thomas digests what I've said. *Fuck.* Why did I have to go and ruin a good thing by bringing up my ex? Who in their right mind does that while in bed with someone else?

"I have kind of a weird question for you," Thomas hedges, distracting me from the spiral. "When we were having breakfast together before the race in Abu Dhabi, you acted like you expected me to be mad at you over the lie about how we met. Why is that?"

I blink, embarrassment making way for confusion. I didn't expect him to remember that moment. Honestly, I barely remember it, but my gut twists at the reminder. I consider lying or denying it, but with how truthful he's been with me so far, I owe it to him to do the same. "Because Étienne—my ex-fiancé—would have been furious."

At least, he would have been at first. With him, there was a need for immediate drama, an exclamation of *Ah putain*, and then a few overly enthusiastic hand gestures before settling and sighing and grudgingly telling me it would all work out. With Thomas, I was expecting the same. That immediate frustration, that guilt trip, all before the reassurance that everything would be okay. But like him skipping straight to having a wife without ever having a girlfriend, Thomas went straight to reassurances.

"I guess I was bracing for that kind of reaction," I finish.

Thomas frowns and his grip on my hip tightens a fraction. Possessive, almost. "He doesn't seem like a very nice man."

"He was," I correct, but I have to add a caveat the longer I consider it. "When he wanted to be."

"Tell me more about him?" Thomas pauses, then backtracks, shaking his head. "No, I mean . . . tell me more about who you were when you were with him."

He isn't wrong to ask about Étienne, because knowing him is important in understanding the person I became when we were together.

I take a breath. "Étienne held all the power in our relationship. It wasn't always like that, but some men just . . . They take it away from you so slowly that you barely notice."

We met when I was freshly twenty-three, struggling under the weight of running my own company and finding my place in the world. He was less than a year older and yet he had his life together in a way that I didn't. And I loved that. I loved his loud confidence, the guidance he offered me, the way he held my hand through tough moments.

"He ran a tech company that he started as a teenager, backed by his family," I continue, remembering how impressed I'd been by that, by how similar our stories were, and yet he'd found so much more success than me in the same amount of time. "It was thriving when we met and I was . . . in awe, I guess. I saw his wins and somehow thought he knew better than me—in business, in life, just overall. And he had a way of reinforcing it with the comments he would make—but it was always subtle. Always phrased in ways that made it seem like he was helping me when he was really trying to put me down."

I see now that they were delicate ways of taking control, of making me put him on an ever-growing pedestal and relying on him for direction. I'll admit that I *was* a little much at the beginning—loud and proud and certain I knew what I was doing, even when I didn't—so his influence felt like maturity. It didn't feel like someone dimming my light or molding me into what they wanted. It felt like an expectation I was supposed to meet, especially when it was joined by his praise.

And that was the best part. To have his full, beaming pride. To know I'd done a good job in his eyes, that I'd made him happy. That I was doing things *right*.

What I didn't know was that his pride in me meant nothing. That the little digs would add up and the praise was to make me want to do what he liked while pushing everything else aside. None of it actually benefited me. More often than not, he was the one who profited off it. My success made *him* look better. My blossoming status brought *him* attention. And the support I gave him yet rarely received in return only made *him* the shining star in our relationship.

I was essentially . . . gone. Sucked into his orbit, revolving around him, and spat out years later with no explanation.

"I made myself small so he could feel bigger," I finally say when I realize I've been silent, lost in the memory. "He didn't like when I stole the spotlight. So I stopped giving it a reason to shine on me."

Thomas's hand rubs small circles on my hip, comforting me without interrupting.

"I'm still working on that. And I'm already doing a hell of a lot better. But it's going to take time."

He makes a soft sound of acknowledgment, soaking in my confession. It's a long moment before he asks, "Is there a reason you stayed with Étienne for so long?"

I pull away from his touch, taken aback by the question. It's one I haven't allowed myself to consider yet, and hearing it posed now—while lacking judgment, just tinged with curiosity—has me bristling.

"Can we talk about something else? These are questions you can ask me once we've been together a full month." Again, I mean it as a lighthearted joke, but it comes out all wrong, leaving Thomas frowning.

"I'm asking because I want to know you," he explains gently. "I'd like to see the full picture."

"Do you really need to know me? It's not like any of this is real," I snap, then soften when I hear how harsh it sounds. "I don't want to get into it tonight, okay? Can we try to go to sleep now?"

I expect him to push me to open up and share the things that haunt the back of my mind. And I think I would. I think I'd spill it all, let him take it on, let him share the burden with me, even if I'm not ready to admit some of these things to myself.

But Thomas doesn't push. He doesn't ask me another question or grumble about my inability to let him in. He simply grabs the hand resting in my lap and tugs gently until I'm lying next to him once more. It's entirely too tender, too much for what we're supposed to be, and yet I don't stop him when he curls an arm around me to keep me close. It's a loose embrace. It's exactly enough.

"It's only supposed to get colder overnight," he murmurs. "But I promise to keep you warm."

I know better than to believe men when they make promises. But tonight, I close my eyes and let myself believe him. Just this once.

# CHAPTER 20

THOMAS

The other side of the bed is empty when I wake.

Judging by the sound of the shower running, Stella hasn't gone far, but my stomach twists with disappointment nonetheless. It's silly. Absolutely ridiculous. And yet I find myself wishing she would have stayed a little longer.

Last night was like a red-flagged race. Our conversation was going well, headed somewhere important, before she hit a wall and shut it down. Maybe I was wrong to ask about her ex, but he played a role in shaping her into who she is today. There are moments, these brief but beautiful sparks, when I see exactly who she was before he came in and wreaked havoc on her life. The woman I met in Vegas, *that's* the Stella I thought I was going to get 24-7. Instead, I'm left with only a glimpse of her before the gates she's built swing shut and I'm left standing on the outside.

I don't want to be on the outside anymore. I want to know the woman I married. Whether that's a good idea remains to be seen, but I'm too curious to stop.

Stella emerges from the bathroom in a cloud of steam a few

minutes later, wearing nothing more than a black lace bra and matching panties. If her pajamas last night had me staring too hard, then it's a miracle now that my eyes stay in my head.

"Shit, I thought you'd still be asleep," she says when she spots me sitting up in bed. "I forgot my robe out here."

She doesn't try to cover herself or yell at me to shield my eyes as she pads over to the closet, grabbing her silk robe and shrugging into it. She's got to know I'm watching her every move, but she doesn't seem to care, so remarkably confident in her body that she could be fully naked and still act the same way. Between that, the lingerie, and how goddamn perfect every inch of her body is, my cock is aching, nearly rock-hard in record time. Thank God I haven't thrown off the duvet yet, or she'd be getting more than an eyeful.

I'm kicking myself for not letting her touch me last night. Instead, my outrageous desire to respect her rules won out over everything. It's probably for the best, but *still*. I can't get the fantasy of her hand stroking over me out of my head. Of pressing her onto her back and pushing between her soft thighs, hearing her sounds of pleasure panted in my ear.

It's a feat to pull myself back into the present when I realize Stella's talking to me as she belts her robe with a flourish, asking what the plans for breakfast are.

I clear my throat, dislodging what I really want to say to her, something along the lines of *I don't give a fuck about breakfast. Come back to bed and let me finish what you started.*

"Breakfast is at eight," I tell her instead. It comes out scratchy and low. "It'll be the whole family again, just to warn you."

"As long as I don't have to eat beans, I'm fine with whatever."

I snicker and drag a hand through my hair. I don't miss the way her eyes trace the line of my biceps or the way her teeth scrape across her full bottom lip, so quick I'd miss it if I weren't already watching her closely. It would be so much easier if this attraction were one-sided, but no—we're both suffering through this mutual mess of keeping our hands to ourselves for the sake of the greater good.

But I'm about ready to tell the greater good to go fuck itself so I can rip those lace panties off her.

"The chef will make you whatever you'd like," I say as I try to discreetly adjust myself under the covers. "Are you done in the bathroom? I'll get ready once you are."

She nods, the topknot perched on her head quivering with the motion. Even like this, with her hair tied up and skin glistening with whatever she's smoothed over it, she's the most beautiful woman I've ever seen.

And if I didn't know it before, I certainly do now—I'm in trouble if I can't find something to hate about my wife.

Stella and I are the last ones down to breakfast, even though we're perfectly on time. Which means everyone else got here early—absolutely unheard-of in this family—and *that* means something is up.

I glance at each face around the table as I escort Stella in and pull out her chair. Geneva smirks as we sit down, as if she's in on the secret, while Edith and Calais keep themselves busy on their phones. Andrew and his wife look like they couldn't care less about what's going on. Figgy, however . . . Well, she may be staring at the empty plate in front of her, but her shoulders are tense and her lips are pressed into a firm line. Huh.

Thankfully no one makes a fuss about our arrival. Mum smiles at Stella from across the table, practically vibrating with excitement—another warning sign. Dad sits to her left at the head, jaw set as he looks between us, and unease creeps up my neck when his gaze moves to Mum. We're about to be ambushed.

I'm proven right when Mum claps her hands to get everyone's attention. "Now that we're all here," she says as she glances around, "I want to make an announcement."

Under the table, Stella's hand lands on my thigh and squeezes. Despite the positioning, it's not a sexy touch—it's more of a *What the fuck is happening here and do I need to be worried?* kind of thing. I catch her eye and give a small shrug. I'm as clueless as she is. But I get the feeling I'm not going to like what's about to come out of Mum's mouth next.

"Thomas," she says, and I slide my hand over Stella's, keeping it there and squeezing back. "Your father and I were so upset we weren't invited to your wedding. That should have been a full family affair. It was incredibly disappointing to hear about it secondhand, to say the least."

I should have known that was coming. She planned both Edith's and Andrew's weddings, pushing the respective brides out of the way each time to do exactly what she wanted. At least Stella and I avoided that fate by eloping.

Or so I thought.

"And that's why we've decided to have another wedding for you here!"

I freeze. Stella freezes. The only sounds in the room are of Edith's children playing with their toy cars in the corner and Geneva's snickering. I bet she was the first one Mum told about her plans, considering my youngest sister is her favorite. Calais looks like she's trying to tamp down her excitement for our sake, though I'm sure she's already been asked if she'll design Stella's dress. Andrew, Edith, and their spouses don't look shocked to hear any of this news either. Even Figgy doesn't seem surprised.

We're really the last to know.

Mum waits for our reactions, but Stella's parted lips and wide, unblinking eyes tell me she's too stunned to speak. If she could form words, I already know they'd be along the lines of *You've got to be fucking kidding me, lady.*

I search for something to say that won't hurt my mother's feelings or set off Dad. I can only grit out, "When?"

Mum's delighted by the question. "Well, we're on quite the tight timeline if we want to do it before your season starts, but we were thinking mid-February. Maybe around Valentine's?"

Stella's nails press through the fabric of my trousers and dig into my skin.

"Why not wait until the summer break?" I ask, trying not to shut her down completely. If we were a real couple who'd married on a whim without our families present, we'd want to have a celebration with them, right? "The weather will be better."

And it will buy Stella and me more time to build our lie and convince them *not* to have what's sure to be a massive, multimillion-pound wedding. We don't need more eyes on our relationship if we're going to be divorced by the end of next year.

"Nonsense, there's no reason to wait." Mum waves a hand, dismissing the idea, before looking to Stella. "I'll handle everything, dear. All I need are your measurements for your wedding dress—Calais will be designing it, of course—and a list of your color preferences."

Stella nods over and over again, processing as quickly as she can. "That sounds amazing, Iris," she eventually replies.

There's a breathless note to her voice that I recognize more as panic than excitement. "I'll leave it all in your capable hands."

"Then that's settled." Mum claps again, bringing an end to the ambush. "Let's have a wedding!"

▞▞▞▞▞▞

"We *cannot* let her do this."

Stella and I are tucked away in a hallway corner, debriefing after breakfast and that hit from my mother. I get where Stella's coming from with her hissed refusal, but I don't think we can shut this idea down now that everything is in motion, especially not with Mum at the helm.

"Look, we can let my mother plan, but we don't have to go through with it," I offer, keeping my voice low so we're not overheard if anyone comes out of the dining room. "Maybe the wedding can be our new divorce deadline."

Stella's eyes go wide. "We said we'd try for a year. That would barely be *three months*. It would look terrible for us both."

She's right, and I can't deny that. "I don't know, maybe I could initiate the divorce and blame it on wanting to focus exclusively on racing?" I swear a flash of hurt slides across her face at the suggestion. But it's gone as quickly as it came, her mouth once again set in a grim line. "But obviously I don't want it to look like you're being left again."

"How kind," she drawls. "Would that give you enough time to make sure Figgy lays off, though? I get the sense she's in this for the long haul."

"We'll just have to put on a hell of a show until then."

"I don't know if—" She cuts short, and I'm about to ask what's wrong when I hear footsteps.

My back is to whoever's coming down the hall, but I move closer to Stella anyway, crowding her farther into the corner.

Her shoulders hit the wood paneling with a gentle *thud*, a sharp inhale passing between her lips. The sound distracts me for a moment, sending less-than-pure thoughts through my mind as I slip an arm around her waist, my other hand sinking into the hair at the nape of her neck.

To anyone looking on, we're sharing an intimate moment. And to be honest, up close and personal with Stella, it feels exactly as it looks.

She doesn't miss a beat, bringing her hands up to my chest and curling her fingers into my button-down. The motion tugs me closer, and I've got to wonder if this is an act or if she's making up for what we missed out on last night. I don't mind it either way, because the press of her body is blissful.

I dip my head, lips close to her ear, and ask, "Can you see who's coming?"

Stella must have short-circuited, because the first sound I get from her is a soft whimper. It's another second before she gives me an actual answer, breathy as it is. "No. Maybe one of your siblings?"

It could be. Or it could be Figgy, the exact person we want to convince that all of this is real. My mother doesn't need any help on that front, but everyone else? It wouldn't hurt.

I let my lips drift down to Stella's neck, pressing a kiss to the spot right under her ear that made her shiver last night. I get the same reaction now, her body swaying into mine like her knees have gone weak, and I have to smile. She can make up new rules and regulations, but her body tells me everything her words won't.

I do it again, scraping my teeth over her skin, and this time I get the softest moan that sends blood rushing to my cock. I jacked off in the shower—*twice*—this morning after seeing her in those barely there panties, and I'm certain there will be another shower session in my future if this is how my wife is going to keep affecting me.

If we could just have one night, one time together to cut this aching tension, maybe we could—

Someone clears their throat behind me. A woman. Figgy.

Reluctantly, I lift my head and glance back at her.

"Your father wants to see you," she announces. Her expression is unreadable, but her words are just this side of cold. "He's waiting with Edith and Andrew in his office."

I frown, fingers drifting out of Stella's hair to rest on her shoulder. If my older siblings are there too, then it must have something to do with the company.

"I'll be as quick as I can," I murmur to Stella.

She nods and smooths out the wrinkles she created in my shirt. "Do what you need to. Don't worry about me."

With one last squeeze of her waist, I force myself to step back and follow Figgy down the hall. There's no need for the escort, but when she looks up at me, eyes blazing, I know it's so she can interrogate me.

"You're really going to keep up this charade?" she snaps.

I don't rise to her bait. "I'm going to keep being affectionate with my wife, yes."

Figgy scoffs. "Come on, Thomas. This can't be what you actually want. A big wedding planned by your mother? That's been your nightmare since we were kids."

The reminder of how well she knows me stings. It doesn't matter that I have a very public job and my face is plastered on billboards around the world, I've always liked my privacy. I like keeping my circle small. I don't need strangers prying into my life, and that's the only thing a spectacle of a wedding would bring.

Figgy knows I don't want that. Surely Mum does too, so why would she—

"Did you tell my mother you think this is all fake?" I demand, the pieces suddenly fitting together. "Is that why she's pushing this huge wedding on us? To make us prove our relationship is real?"

Figgy's eyes dart away, but her chin stays defiantly lifted. "I said I would do it."

"Unbelievable." I huff a humorless laugh. "Well, I hope you enjoy my wedding. If you're lucky, my mother won't rope you into helping plan it."

I watch her go pale, but I don't feel more than a twinge of guilt over the idea. "Thomas . . ." she says softly. "I just—"

"Save it, Figgy." We've reached my father's office, but either way, I'm done with the conversation. "It didn't need to be like this."

I step inside before she can say anything else.

My father's already seated behind his desk, with Edith in one of the chairs across from him while Andrew stands by the window. I shut the door behind me, pushing aside my brewing anger with Figgy, then take a seat next to Edith.

Whatever I've missed must have been the equivalent of a bomb dropping, because when I glance at my sister, she's slack-jawed and barely breathing. My attention shifts to Andrew, whose arms are folded tightly over his chest, but there's triumph in the set of his shoulders.

"What's going on?" I dare to ask.

Our father inhales deeply as he laces his fingers on the desktop. "As you know, Thomas, I'll be retiring soon. I was just discussing A.P. Maxwell's succession plan for when that happens at the end of next year. I figured since we were all together, now was the best time to make my intentions known to everyone."

The timeline has me leaning back in my seat, surprised. Last I heard, he was planning to stay on as CEO for a few more years. This is a massive shift.

"Edith will remain as COO," he continues. "And Andrew will become our CEO."

That explains the mood in the room. I could have sworn Edith was going to take over the show. It's not that my brother is incompetent, but Edith is just . . . better at everything. The idea of her having to report to him is positively laughable.

No one here's laughing, though.

"Congratulations," I say to Andrew, but it's an empty commendation. He knows I don't think he deserves it.

As if he can tell, Dad rises from his seat and goes to stand beside Andrew, patting him twice on the back like a child who's just won a football match. Guess someone has to be happy for him, because it certainly won't be me or Edith.

Andrew straightens, arms dropping to his sides. He even puffs out his chest. "I'll be making some changes when I take over," he says, but I don't understand why he's directing it at me.

I nod, my smile pacifying. "As is your right."

"And one of those changes is that A.P. Maxwell International will no longer be a sponsor of the McMorris Formula 1 Team."

I stare at my brother, unsure I've heard him correctly. There's no way I could have. There's no way he would take this away from me.

Without that sponsorship, without that *money*, I'm not worth much in the world of Formula 1. In fact, some people might go so far as to call me a pay driver. And while I'm *very* good at what I do, I'm still not the best of the best. On my own, with just my talent and smaller sponsors behind me, I might not be enough to warrant one of the twenty coveted spots on the grid. I know that. And Andrew knows it too, because he tried to get there with the same resources, only to fail. It was my talent that got me through to my first F1 season—but is it enough to keep me there five years in?

My heart stops dead for a second before restarting. "Excuse me?"

I need him to repeat himself. He has to look me dead in my fucking eyes and say that again so that I know without a doubt he's doing this to me.

"Our resources are better spent elsewhere," he explains, but none of this is making *sense*. "We're not seeing the return on our investment that we hoped when it came to our backing of the team. I'm sure you understand. And besides, Thomas, it's not a good look for us to be sponsoring a driver who wishes death upon his opponents. I mean, come on. You screwed yourself there."

There's a ringing in my ears that starts quietly and builds. It's shrill and screaming, drowning out everything else Andrew's saying. My eyes drift to Edith, taking in the hard set to her eyes. She knows what this means for me. She knows what I've just lost, and I can see the same in her.

We've both had our futures ruined in one fell swoop.

My father comes over and puts his hand on my shoulder, meant to soothe, but it's another weight pushing me down. "You're a great driver, Thomas. They may want to keep you even without our backing."

I already know they won't. I already know exactly who's coming for my seat.

And I already know this is where my dreams end.

# CHAPTER 21

STELLA

"I'm making you a dress and that's that."

I put my hands up, not about to argue with Calais's offer to design a dress for me to wear to Zaid Yousef's upcoming gala. It's on top of the wedding gown she's creating—one that I won't be wearing if Thomas and I officially split up before then—but she seems more than happy to have the extra work.

We've been talking fashion and the woes of running our own businesses ever since Figgy dragged Thomas away. Calais strolled around the corner a moment later, then looped her arm through mine and escorted me to one of the many sitting rooms to chat with her and Geneva.

"We're the leftover siblings," she said, flipping her honey-brown hair over her shoulder. "The ones our father doesn't give a single shit about because we're not interested in hotels."

For being only twenty-three, she has a shockingly level head on her shoulders. To be running her own fashion line at such a young age is admirable, and I see a little of myself in her. She's the same age I was when Stella Margaux's really took off, which serves to remind me how far I've come. One hundred stores opened, millions of macarons sold, and next week I'm set to start working on plans for our long-awaited London location.

I have to thank Thomas for that last one. Without him asking me to move here, I don't think I would have thought much about branching into the European market, aside from our two stores in Paris. North America has kept me busy enough, but it's time to dream bigger.

Speaking of the man, I catch sight of him striding past the wide archway of the sitting room. His jaw is tight and his hands are balled into fists at his sides; there's a tension to him that I haven't seen before.

Something's wrong.

"Thomas?" I call out, hoping he'll hear me and stop, but he doesn't even slow. I flash an apologetic smile at Calais before pushing up from the settee. "Sorry, excuse me a second."

Hustling into the hallway, I make it in time to see him disappear around the corner. He's lucky I'm a champion at running in heels, because I catch up to him a few seconds later, grabbing his elbow to get him to stop.

His head whips around to me, furious until he sees who's stopped him. When our eyes lock, the set to his jaw softens but the anxious crease between his brows remains.

"What's going on?" I ask, keeping my hand on his arm. "Are you okay?"

"I'm—" He cuts off before he can say *fine* like I expect, lips pressing into a firm line as he considers what he wants to actually tell me. "I just . . . I got some news."

I frown. "I'm guessing it wasn't good news."

The exhalation that leaves his lips is probably meant to be a laugh but it's more of a pained grunt. "You could say that."

I don't want to push him to tell me what's going on. He

didn't make me last night, and I want to return the favor now. But whatever Thomas sees on my face as he searches it must make him want to share.

"Dad announced the company's going to Andrew when he retires next year."

I won't pretend I know much about their family dynamics, but based on what I've observed in the past twelve hours, this seems like an unexpected move. "I really thought it would be Edith," I admit.

"Me too. And I guess I was either banking on it being her or my father staying on for a few more years."

"Why?"

Thomas takes a deep breath, steeling himself for whatever he's about to say. "Because with Andrew at the helm, A.P. Maxwell International will no longer be a sponsor of the Mc-Morris Formula 1 Team."

Again, I'm no expert, but just from a business standpoint, this doesn't sound good. "I'm sure that'll be a blow to the team."

"Stella." He puts his hands on my shoulders and dips his head so we're eye to eye. There's a plea in them for me to understand. "My place at McMorris hinges on that sponsorship money. Without it, there's a chance I'm no longer on the team."

I freeze. "Wait, *what*?"

At my outburst, he holds me tighter. "Formula 1—honestly, racing in general—is all about money when it comes down to it. Teams want drivers who not only perform well but pull in as much revenue as possible. You have to be fucking spectacular to come into the sport without heavy financial backing, and it's especially important if you want to *stay* there."

"You have other sponsors, don't you?" I press.

He nods. "I do. But none as big as my family. And with my

behavior lately, if they jump ship, more are sure to do the same. That's the biggest problem here—if they leave me too, then I definitely won't have a seat."

Shit. Thomas and I may still be in the process of learning about each other, but I know enough—have *seen* enough—to know he wants to stay in this sport. That he's worthy of staying. To think he might lose his place at McMorris because his family will no longer back him is a massive blow, one that gut punches me when the magnitude of this announcement finally settles.

In the time it takes for me to think of something to say, Thomas is already letting go of me and dragging a hand through his hair, his motions agitated. "Our *reserve driver* somehow knew before me," he says as he paces a few steps away, then turns and does it again. "I think he knew I wasn't going to get my contract renewed because of this. It's been in the works for a while and yet *no one fucking told me*."

Anything I could have said dies in my throat. There's nothing I can do to make this better and it kills me. He doesn't deserve this—to have his dream snatched away because of a decision out of his control. Maybe he could talk to his brother and get him to change his mind. But unfortunately, I get the sense they don't have that kind of relationship.

"I have one more season and then it's over," he goes on, so pained that I can feel it in my chest. "This wasn't how it was supposed to end."

"It doesn't have to be the end," I blurt. I take two quick steps forward to block his pacing, putting my hands on his chest. "Maybe you can convince Andrew to keep sponsoring the team. Or, hell, maybe you can convince them to keep you just based on your talent alone. Look at how much better you're doing compared to Arlo."

Another huff escapes him, but this one has a darkly sardonic edge to it. "I wish it were all that easy."

I drop my hands when he shifts to move just out of reach. The rejection stings, but I push it down. This isn't about me. I've already had my world rocked by the loss of the future I thought I would have. It's Thomas's turn to face that horrible reality now, and all I can do is stand by and be there if he decides he needs me.

"I'm going for a drive," he mumbles, glancing in the direction of the front hall. "Need to clear my head."

I nod. I'd need some time alone to process such massive news too—which is exactly why I locked myself away for two weeks and drank a ridiculous amount of wine.

But then he surprises me by asking, "Want to take a ride with me?"

I can't resist the hand he holds out to me. So I don't. I slide my palm into his and let him lead me out to the front of the house.

My heels sink into the gravel as we walk to his SUV. Even torn up, his manners are still impeccable; he opens my door, helps me put my seat belt on, and even makes sure the hem of my dress is safely tucked inside the vehicle before closing the door again. We don't speak as he climbs in next to me and turns over the engine, letting it rumble for a few seconds before he shifts into drive and navigates us onto the narrow country road.

The quiet is heavy. It's not my place to break it no matter how oppressive it feels or how tempted I am to pester him with questions. I don't even care where he's driving us.

For now, I keep my eyes locked on the sights out the window, on the trees and the farmland and softly rolling hills. It really is beautiful out here, so different from the endless concrete of the cities I've spent my life in. I imagine it would be peaceful to live here full-time. I'm almost tempted to pull up a real estate website and see what's available around here. Would Thomas mind me being neighbors with his family even after our divorce?

I might ask if I didn't want to be the first to break the silence, but my head snaps in his direction when music starts to softly play.

"If I throw up," he says over the opening bars of Ed Sheeran's debut album, "I'm blaming you."

I fight a grin, a bubbling warmth flooding my chest. "Is this a bad time to tell you my pockets are full of Kerrygold?"

Thomas lets out a loud laugh that seems to surprise him, but it has his shoulders relaxing a fraction. "You're never going to let me live that down, are you?"

"Hey, you're the one who made the mistake of telling me your deepest, darkest secret."

"I hope I can trust you never to share that with anyone."

"I think our wedding vows cover embarrassing stories, so you're safe."

The corners of his lips pull up a little more. When he reaches over to grab my hand, I let him take it, lacing our fingers and not thinking twice. It feels right. It's the comfort we both need.

"I'm sorry." He glances my way, eyes softer now, before returning his attention to the road. "I didn't mean to unload on you. You didn't sign up for that."

"Again, pretty sure I did by agreeing to marry you," I point out. "And while we're married, I'll be here to listen to all your rants." I pause. "Mostly because I love being in people's business. It's my only flaw."

He gives a soft chuckle this time and the sound has me desperate to hear more. There's something about making him laugh, especially in a moment like this, that feels like it's my purpose. We may have made a mess for ourselves, but maybe we stepped into each other's lives at the exact right moment.

"My nosy wife." It's a fond—if not vaguely insulting—endearment, but it still makes my heart skip a little beat. "Anything in particular you want to know?"

I strain against my seat belt so he can see me better in his periphery. "Well, if you're giving me carte blanche . . ." I wait until he nods before settling back and continuing. "You told me once that you and Andrew aren't that close. Why is that?"

His fingers tighten for a second and I consider telling him, *Never mind, you don't have to answer.* But when his grip relaxes, thumb brushing over mine, I keep quiet.

"I think I also told you how everything my brother did, I wanted to do it too," he says after a few long seconds. "He was the first in our family to get into karting, the one who made me want to start. My father was thrilled to have both of his sons involved in motorsport, but Andrew wasn't as welcoming of me getting into it. He wasn't happy when Dad started focusing more on me."

I may not have any siblings but I've heard horror stories of rivalries from others. With the way this tale is starting, I think I know where it's headed. "You said he stopped racing to go to university instead. Was that the whole truth?"

Thomas's parliament smile makes an appearance at my question. "Not completely," he admits. "He stopped because our father decided to throw all his money and attention behind my career. I was only twelve at the time, but I guess he knew I had the potential to go far. Andrew, on the other hand, wasn't performing as well. Dad gave Andrew an ultimatum: He could keep racing without our family's support or go to university and have a guaranteed spot at the company after graduation. We all know what he chose."

And now, if the conclusions I'm jumping to are correct, Andrew is getting his little brother back for stealing his dream.

"And your father's fine with Andrew pulling the sponsorship?" I ask in near disbelief. "Seriously?"

Thomas blows out a breath. "I brought it upon myself with the Castellucci situation. If I hadn't said those things . . . maybe this would be different. But I see where they're coming from when they say they don't want me representing the company."

I watch the fight practically drain from his body. It's like he's just *resigning* himself to all of this, like he really thinks it's over.

"No, fuck that," I hear myself say before my brain can catch up. "We can't let them use that as an excuse."

"We?"

Of *course* that's what he questions. "Yes, your highness, *we*. This is a group project now. We're going to clear your name and make sure you keep that sponsorship."

Thomas scoffs. "That's a reach, Stella."

It probably is, but I'm up for the challenge. "I already said I was going to get Reid to talk to you, but we're going to get you straight to Lorenzo Castellucci. He's our key to getting your reputation back on track."

Thomas stays quiet, but it doesn't matter. The wheels are turning so loudly in my head that it would drown him out anyway.

My gaze darts back out the window. A few minutes ago, I was loving the calm pace of life out here, but now I'm ready to be back in the thick of the city. Back to the chaos I thrive in.

"Can we go home?" I ask, turning back to him. "Do we have to stay out here any longer?"

The word *home* slips out accidentally. I meant *go back to London*, or somewhere other than that manor full of people conspiring against him—against us.

But Thomas doesn't seem to mind the phrasing. He gives my hand one last squeeze, then lets go in favor of putting both of his back on the wheel. He's hanging a U-turn a second later, gunning it back toward the house.

"How fast can you pack?" he asks.

"Ten minutes, tops."

"Perfect." The soft smile he shoots me has my heart lifting to dangerous heights. "Let's go home, love."

# CHAPTER 22

THOMAS

It's wild to think this could be the last year I set foot in the Mc-Morris factory—and wilder still that I can't talk to anyone about it.

My manager has instructed me to keep quiet and let him do his job. While he's out hunting for new sponsorship deals and stealthily feeling out whether any teams will have seat openings after next season, I have to be at HQ finishing up my post-season duties and acting like everything's fine and dandy.

Today, I'm back at Silverstone after a day spent with Stella in London, recovering from the aftermath of the Cotswolds trip. I've done my season debrief with the team, filmed social media bits to get us through the winter, and had my last session on the simulator before we retire this season's car. The next time I'm here, it will be to test our setup for next season, but I have a monthlong break before then.

It's dark out when I head down to the building's lobby, passing by classic McMorris F1 cars from bygone years. This has been my home for so long; four of my cars from previous seasons sit in front of the walls of glass, a reminder of each year I've spent with them so far. The fifth will join them soon.

To think I may not return . . . it's a thought I need to hurry up and come to terms with, or at least stop dwelling on. Truth is, I don't know for certain that they'll get rid of me. Maybe I've proved myself valuable enough to keep, even without the A.P. Maxwell International sponsorship.

But I'm not getting younger, and fresh talent is knocking at the door every day, as Arlo Wood and Finley Clarke are keen to remind me.

"Tommy boy!"

I exhale and stop at the voice calling after me, turning to find Arlo hustling up. He's got his cap on backward and is wearing a jacket that won't keep him warm in the December cold, but he looks every part the hip heartthrob.

"Aren't you sick of me?" I ask as I button up my coat. "We've been together for a whole season and you still want to talk?"

"Just getting my last dose in before you're gone for the winter." He grins and rocks back on his heels. "You going to Zaid's gala?"

The event is in a week, the day after the FIA's annual prize-giving gala, which neither Arlo nor I have to attend because we weren't in the top three finishers of the Drivers' Championship and McMorris didn't come close to winning the Constructors' Championship. Zaid came in second, with Axel Bergmüller in third, but after the Singapore crash and their injuries, it's still up in the air whether either one will be at the prize-giving in Baku. Like Lorenzo, Axel hasn't been seen publicly since the crash, but he's at least put out a few press statements saying he'll be racing again next season.

"I'll be there," I answer. "Are you going?"

Arlo nods, but I don't hear anything he says next, because I'm distracted by my phone buzzing with a text from Stella.

STELLA: What time will you be home tonight?

"Sorry, one sec," I mumble to Arlo as I start to type.

THOMAS: No later than 10. You okay?

STELLA: Perfectly fine. Just don't be surprised if you walk in and it looks like everything in the kitchen exploded.

THOMAS: Do I need to be worried?

STELLA: Of course not. I'm a professional, baby.

"That your wife?"

I lift my head at Arlo's question, then wipe away the grin that's somehow appeared on my face. "How'd you know?"

He smirks. "Because you've got fuckin' hearts in your eyes, mate. Hope a woman makes me look like that one day."

I snort. "We both know it will be several women, Arlo."

"We can only hope." After shooting me a wink, he shoulders his way around me and heads for the automatic doors to the car park. "See you at the party next week, old man."

I watch him go, his words pinballing through my head as I grip my phone in my pocket. *Hearts in my eyes?* Seriously? He couldn't be further from the truth.

I'll admit that I'm very attracted to Stella, and have been from the first second I spotted her, so maybe that's what he saw.

But it's not much more than that—physical attraction. There are thousands of women out there I could say the exact same thing about.

Except . . . I can't deny that Stella is a cut above the rest. And, well, our trip might have changed things a little. The way she handled herself with Figgy and my family, plus how she was once again so willing to step up and help me, even when a solution seemed so far out of reach, had me looking at her in a completely different light.

Maybe it's been building since we agreed to stay married. Kind of hard to avoid an emotional connection when you're forced to get to know someone, especially when that person is fascinating. And hilarious. And intelligent, and kind, and so wickedly sharp, with a smile to match.

It's hard not to like someone when they're everything you could ever ask for.

The realization hits me hard, like a blow straight to the gut.

Ah shit.

I think I'm falling for my wife.

▰▰▰▰▰

It's nearly ten p.m. when I push through the front door, the scent of vanilla and sugar hitting me like a sweet slap.

"Stella?" I call out, dropping my things before heading to the kitchen where I assume she's baking. I'll be disappointed if it's just a scented candle.

Thankfully, there's food to be found when I round the corner. As one might expect from Stella Margaux, there are macarons on nearly every surface, but they're joined by cupcakes, several varieties of cookies, and what I'm guessing are three different types of frosting. It's a sugar lover's paradise, and I'm so glad it's the offseason so I can actually taste all of this and not have to explain it to my dietician tomorrow.

"Wow," I exhale as Stella turns off a mixer. "It's like my own personal episode of *Bake Off* in here."

She shoots me a grin over her shoulder, an adorable smudge of flour across her cheek. "And I didn't have a breakdown while making any of it either."

I believe that based on the glow emanating from her. This is her happy place. She's surrounded by the sweetest treats, her ideas coming to life in her hands. Somehow, I can't imagine her doing anything else.

"I'm sorry for the mess," she says. I appreciate that she doesn't sound apologetic in the slightest. "Once I have a commercial kitchen, I'll be out of your hair. Thanks for sending me that estate agent's number, by the way. I've set up a few viewings."

I pull out one of the stools at the island, sitting down and moving a plate of unassembled macarons out of the way. "I like having you here," I admit. "It's been nice having someone to come home to."

Has it only been a day of that? Yes. But was it a delight yesterday to hear her upstairs on a conference call, a reminder that I'm no longer alone in this ridiculously large house? Also yes.

Stella snickers and returns to the batter bowl, taking it off the mixer stand a moment later. "Sounds like you should have gotten a dog ages ago."

Smiling, I shake my head and grab a macaron off one of the many plates. I can't say I know much about them, but these look perfect. And so does Stella—who's wearing my Union Jack apron, which she swore she was going to hide when she saw me in it this morning. The sight has something glitching in my brain, the rule-abiding part of it shutting down.

I push up from my seat and approach her from behind. She startles when I wrap an arm loosely around her shoulders, my forearm banded across her collarbones, her back pressed to my chest. I hold up the macaron in my other hand. "What flavor is this?" I murmur next to her ear.

"Thomas." The warning coincides with her tilting her head back in invitation, even if she doesn't mean it to be. "You're breaking several rules right now."

"Can I not give my wife a hug?"

"Fake wife," she takes care to remind me, but I feel the way her heart rate picks up.

"Fine. Answer my question and I'll let you go."

Stella huffs and looks down at the macaron, quickly answering, "Blood orange and vanilla cream. I'm working on our summer menu for next year."

I nod and let my arm slip from around her, though I swear her shoulder follows my fingertips as they drift away.

"Don't go far," she blurts as I take a step back. "I need you to whip some cream for me."

"Is that a euphemism for something?"

"You wish." She then points to a bowl with cream in it, a whisk next to it. "I'd put it in the stand mixer, but I don't have any clean attachments at the moment." We both glance at the dirty dishes in and next to the sink. "Get that to soft peaks for me."

"Okay, that is *definitely* a euphemism."

Stella laughs and it's like music. A song I'd put on repeat for the rest of my life.

After shoving the macaron in my mouth, I pick up the whisk and get to work. I don't know what the hell soft peaks are, but I'm sure she'll tell me when it happens.

"What do you think of that flavor?" she asks, coming over

and leaning a hip against the counter next to me. "Remind you of summertime?"

No, it doesn't remind me of summer. It reminds me of just a minute ago, with my lips by her ear and inhaling her sweet citrus scent. It reminds me of dark Vegas clubs, of sweaty hugs after a race, of burying my face in her neck while in bed together because I simply couldn't go another moment without feeling her skin against mine.

I swallow hard. "It's my new favorite."

Stella smiles and I swear I feel it deep in my chest. "Then that's settled. It's going on the menu."

She turns away and goes back to whatever she was working on before. But even as I keep whisking, I can't take my eyes off her. Seeing her in her element is exhilarating. Is this how she felt watching me on-track? If it is, I get her postrace reactions now.

"Hey, Stella?"

She glances over at me again, brow raised, expression so bright.

"Even when you find a new space to bake," I say, "I still want you to do some of it here."

Her smile turns teasing. "You just don't want to miss out on being my taste tester."

That's not even remotely it, but I still nod. "You caught me."

When she laughs again, I let it seep into me, savoring the champagne fizz of it through my veins.

Yeah. It's not even a question anymore. I've gone and fallen for my wife.

# CHAPTER 23

STELLA

"You're so lucky you moved to London with only a couple of suitcases. If I have to unpack another box, I'm gonna scream."

I snicker at Janelle's complaint as I sweep setting powder under my eyes. Her call is keeping me company while I get ready for the day, and I'm relieved we're finally in the same time zone. Trying to coordinate with a five-hour difference at play has been tough. Poor Mika will probably keep getting accidental four a.m. phone calls from me.

"Once you're settled in, you've got to come over for dinner," I suggest. "I'll make all your favorites."

"God, yes, please. I told Ron I was craving biscuits and gravy and the man looked at me like he just discovered he'd married a serial killer."

"I had the same reaction when Thomas told me his favorite dessert was something called *spotted dick*."

By the time Janelle recovers from cackling, I'm done with my makeup and out of the bathroom. "How's living together going?" she asks. "You haven't shown up on my doorstep yet, so I'm assuming things are good?"

"Honestly?" I pause, considering her question as I move to the dresser, where my ring sits waiting for me in a little ceramic dish. "It's going really well. He's so easy to be around."

It's been nearly two weeks since I moved in, and barring that trip to his family's house, things have been smooth sailing. Dare I say it, things have been nice. *Really* nice. Concerningly so, because the last thing I need is to develop a crush on my husband. Which I . . . think I might already have.

Oh God. Don't go there. We're not ready to admit that.

Even as busy as we both are, we've made time to have dinner together every night. We've been on walking tours of the neighborhood and wandered Kensington Gardens together. Hell, he even vetted the Pilates studio down the road to make sure they had the type of classes I told him I liked—and then he bought a membership for me. It was so thoughtful that I nearly teared up when he handed me the studio's brochure. How embarrassing.

It's amazing that he's even been able to do all of that with or for me. He's been slammed, going to meetings with his manager, filming commercials for his remaining sponsors, and wrapping up other postseason business. He'll be free from F1 obligations after Zaid's gala tomorrow night and I'm curious to see what it'll look like for us when he has free time. I won't have any, considering my schedule is chaos until Christmas, which is barely two weeks away. The holiday season is our busiest and there will be plenty of fires I'll have to put out—possibly literally.

"And have you decided if you're going through with the second wedding?"

I blow out a breath as I pick up my ring, watching it sparkle under the lights. "Not yet," I answer honestly. "Thomas and I need to talk more about it."

We seem to be operating under the impression that it'll happen. I sent my measurements to Calais and told Iris I'm a big fan of warm neutral colors, so whatever happens now is out of my hands.

Janelle giggles. I can practically imagine her twirling a curl around her finger. "Can't wait until you call me to say you finally let that man dick you down six ways to—"

"I'm going now," I interrupt loudly, not about to entertain that thought—mostly because I've already been entertaining it nearly every night while alone in my room. "Call you again soon."

"Hopefully after you've gotten that great British—"

"Good*bye*, Janelle."

I punch the button to end the call before she can finish that terrible pun, then slide my ring on with more force than necessary. Last thing I needed was a reminder of the sexual tension between Thomas and me—and my hand in the dark.

"Sounds like Janelle is supportive of our second wedding."

I whip around at Thomas's voice coming from the doorway to my bedroom, not having realized that my door was open or that he was even upstairs. Oh God, the call was on speaker . . .

"How much of that did you hear?" I hedge, face ablaze. I've never been so glad for the dark brown of my skin.

"Enough," he says, smirking, though it's just a twist away from being a full-blown grin. "I think there was something about my great British—"

"*Nope*," I interrupt, striding forward to push him out of my room. "You're going to forget you heard a single word of that conversation."

Thomas laughs and walks backward as I press at his chest. His solid, strong, absolutely perfect—

Ah *fuck*. I've been a horny mess ever since our night spent cuddling for warmth, and that doesn't seem to be waning any. But the kindness and attention he's shown me since then have only served to turn me into a simpering mess. I already knew we had a physical connection, but I've discovered that I actually like the guy as a person.

It's a complication I don't need if we're going to have a clean break, whether that's in two months or by the end of next year. We can be friendly, sure, but I don't need this veering any further into *I have a crush on my husband* territory.

I stop when Thomas does, though it takes a beat before I pull my hands away, not above feeling him up. He doesn't mind it, if the glimmer in his eyes means anything.

"I came to see what's on your schedule for today," he says. "Busy one?"

I nod and check my watch. "I have about ten minutes before I need to leave for my first property viewing." I glance up, a question coming to my lips before I can think better of asking. "Do you want to come with me? I could use a local's opinion on the neighborhoods." When my brain finally catches up, I quickly add on, "I know you've probably got a lot to do, so it's fine if you can't."

The few beats he takes to consider it feel like the longest of my life and I regret asking. Of course he's too busy to go property hunting with me, what was I thinking?

"I'll reorganize a few things and tag along."

My face is somehow hotter than it was before. "Thomas, you don't have to."

"I know I don't have to," he says. "I want to."

He's so casual about it, as if it's really nothing for him to reschedule his entire day so he can come with me. Such a simple thing and yet it alters my brain chemistry, shooting off those pesky attachment hormones. "Okay," I choke out.

His smile wrecks my insides, but it gets worse when he holds out a hand to me. "Come downstairs, I have something for you."

Sliding my hand into his is a mistake for my emotional stability but great for keeping me physically steady in my heels. Even when we reach the bottom of the staircase, his fingers stay wrapped around mine, guiding me along behind him until we're in the kitchen. His broad back blocks my line of sight, so it isn't until he steps out of the way that I see what's sitting on the island.

An open box of a dozen chocolate-iced doughnuts greets me, a single candle shoved into the one in the center. I stand still and watch as Thomas flicks open a silver lighter and then holds the flame to the candle, drawing back once it's lit. He then turns to me, eyes creasing at the corners with his smile.

"Happy one-month anniversary."

I press my lips together to fight against the delighted laugh that threatens to bubble up and out because this man is *ridiculous*.

"If you're planning to make me wear one of those as a ring again," I say once I'm convinced I can keep my voice level instead of squealing like an excited schoolgirl, "I'm leaving you."

"I'd actually prefer if we could eat these, if you don't mind."

"Then I *guess* we can stay together."

I approach him and the box, knees wobbly, and then bend to blow out the candle. I grab one of the doughnuts, the chocolate sticking to my fingers, and offer it up to him. But instead of taking it from me, Thomas leans down and bites into it, his eyes not leaving mine as he does. It's so sexy that I might need to go back upstairs and change my now-incriminatingly-damp panties.

He licks his lips and stands up straight again, leaving me to practically shove the rest of the doughnut in my mouth to keep from asking if he wants to spend the day eating these in between rounds of mind-blowing sex.

Thankfully, Thomas breaks me out of the spell by announcing that we should probably head out if we don't want to be late for the first viewing. I go to wash the sugar off my fingers, letting the cold water from the tap cool me down. I don't need to be thinking about Thomas putting his mouth on me like he did that doughnut while we're looking at industrial ovens.

I shouldn't have invited him to come with me. Because I'm not going to be able to stop thinking about my husband—and all the things we could have done by now if it weren't for all my rules.

░░░░░

After surviving a full day spent with Thomas on Friday, Saturday brings Zaid Yousef's gala. And I've got to hand it to Calais—the woman makes a damn good dress.

As I slip into the gown she designed, I make a mental note to hire her for all my couture needs in the future, even once Thomas and I go our separate ways. Although, if this silk column dress with the most beautifully draped neckline and thigh-high slit is a taste of what I can expect for my wedding, I might want to go through with the whole spectacle just for a chance to wear it. What's a church aisle if not a runway by another name?

I'm buzzing for tonight. Partially because it's an excuse to get dressed up and drink champagne while contributing to a good cause. The other part is because I get to see Willow Williams tonight—and I've got my fingers crossed that she'll have come through on her promise to get Reid to speak to Thomas.

We've been texting back and forth recently, mostly me

sending her photos of my bakes and running flavor ideas past her after I discovered she's familiar with our entire menu. In addition to being a superfan of mine, she's an incredibly cool person, and she's even given me some advice about being in a relationship with an F1 driver. It's strange to belong to this mini WAG club, but it's growing on me. Certainly helps that Willow's sweeter than everything I've ever baked.

"Stella darling?" Thomas calls from the hallway. "You nearly ready?"

"Almost!"

I'm standing in front of the full-length mirror, debating which shoes to wear, when there's a knock on the doorframe. I glance over, prepared to tell him that I need another five minutes, but the words die on my lips as I take him in.

As expected, he's in a tux, and I already know from past experience that I'm a sucker for him dressed like that. But tonight, he somehow looks even better than he did in Vegas. How is that possible? It's the same damn man. Same ocean-blue eyes perfect for drowning in. Same chestnut-brown hair, expertly swept back except for an errant tendril that brushes his forehead. And same broad chest and narrow hips and big hands that can do absolutely wicked things.

Maybe it's because you like him for more than just his looks now? the little voice in the back of my head suggests.

I tell it to shut the fuck up.

I want to stamp my foot and whine because it's not fair how alluring he is dressed like this. Honestly, if they need a new James Bond, he should be it. Then again, not sure I'd trust a man who commonly says *sod it* and *crikey* to have a license to kill.

As I admire him, he's doing the same to me, eyes drinking in every inch from head to toe. I've swept my hair up into a chic twist, leaving a few strands out to frame my face, and I've gone full glam with my makeup. The dress is the true star of the show, the silk skimming my body in all the right places and leaving just enough to the imagination, but it's undeniably provocative every time the fabric ripples back to expose up to the top of my thigh. I look good, but I feel even better.

"Wow," Thomas breathes out, still unabashedly staring. "You look . . ."

I arch an eyebrow to prompt him into finishing the sentence. I don't need his compliments, but I want them. I want his praise and his adoration and anything he's willing to give, all because I want to give the same back to him. It lingers on the tip of my tongue, threatening to spill out in waves of *I might just be the luckiest woman in the world to have you on my arm* and *Sometimes it scares me how much I love your smile.*

"You look . . ." He trails off again, pausing to take a breath that practically shudders through him. "There are no words for how stunning you are, Stella. It's a bloody privilege to even lay eyes on you."

He sounds so achingly genuine that it steals the oxygen from my lungs. Something is shifting between us and it's getting dangerous. I didn't expect to feel anything like this so soon after my world was turned upside down. I thought it would be years before my cracked heart could beat again. But it's limping back to life, giving a *thump* here and there to remind me it's not dead. That with the right touch, the right electric shock, it can thrive.

I just don't know if I'm brave enough to offer it up to be healed. What if it gets shattered all over again?

"If I'm getting compliments that good, then the woman who marries you for real is going to be so lucky," I say to remind us both that this can't be anything more, but the words taste like ash in my mouth. I look down at myself again, needing to break our connection before I do something silly like drag him to me and press my lips to his. Instead, I smooth my hands over my hips. "You sure the color is okay? I feel like I've been overdoing it on the white lately."

He shakes his head, snapping out of whatever daze he was in. "It's perfect. Besides, we're still newlyweds. Take advantage of it for as long as you can."

"And we have another wedding coming up." I dare to look back over at him. "Have you found a way to get us out of that yet?"

"Haven't really been trying," he admits. "But I'm starting to think we should let it happen. Really cement our relationship to people. Plus, any excuse for a party, right?"

He might be right. This can be our classy do-over to prove to everyone how serious we are. Surely Figgy can't continue to harass him after she watches us recite our vows. And it's not like I have to plan, organize, or pay for anything, so I should be on board for those reasons alone. I don't have much left to protest.

Except the little fact that this isn't feeling so fake these days.

I shake the thought away, pointing to the three pairs of shoes sitting in front of the mirror so I can change the topic. "Help me pick. Which ones go best with the dress?"

I already know which ones I'm wearing—the heeled sandal with pearl-embellished straps—and I don't expect Thomas to have enough knowledge of fashion to make the right choice. Shockingly, he picks up the ones I want, then motions for me to sit on the bed.

I do as I'm instructed, expecting him to hand the shoes over so I can put them on, but he's kneeling in front of me a moment later. A shiver races down my spine as his hand curls around my ankle to lift my foot, then slides the shoe onto it. The buckle on the ankle strap is fickle, but he manages it with ease before repeating the process on the other side.

I'm not breathing when he looks up, a pleased smile on his lips from completing his task. Seeing him on his knees is hot enough, but that tiny act has a wildfire blazing a path straight through me.

"Ready to go convince more people we're madly in love?" he asks.

My answer comes out as a shaky exhale. "Absolutely."

Because right now, that doesn't seem like a very hard task.

▰▰▰▰▰

Thomas's hands haven't left my body since we stepped out of the car to walk the red carpet.

Right now, one lingers on my hip, keeping me tucked into his side as we wander the ballroom and greet all the people he knows, from drivers past and present to politicians and humanitarians to celebrities I try not to gawk at as he proudly introduces me as his wife. Before that, our fingers were interlocked as he guided me up the marble steps into the venue, making sure my heels didn't catch in the hem of my gown. I can't wait to discover where his touch ends up next.

I take a gulp of champagne to wash the thought away, glad for the brief reprieve from people approaching us. I'm scanning the room for anyone I know, and while there are a few vaguely familiar faces from the circles I run in, I still don't see the one I'm looking for.

I try not to be too disappointed that I haven't spotted Willow yet, but Reid Coleman is circulating on the other side of the room, and I'm desperate for him and Thomas to talk. Willow promised she'd be the facilitator of that tonight, and I'm not about to drag Thomas over and simply hope for the best. No, we need our sweet-talking mutual friend to make sure this goes smoothly.

"Would you like to dance?"

Thomas's question gets me to glance up, distracted from my searching. "You know how?"

He huffs a laugh. "Sweetheart, I grew up going to galas like this. I learned how to waltz about five minutes after I learned to walk."

"Well, now you're going to have to prove it."

I down the rest of my champagne before letting Thomas sweep me through the crowd and onto the dance floor. True to his word, he does know how to dance, and he's gentlemanly enough to keep his hands in all the proper places, except for a slip here and there when his palm finds my lower back.

"People are watching us," he murmurs in my ear as we turn around the floor again.

I stare over his shoulder into the crowd. He's right, there are plenty of eyes—and a few cameras—on us. "Unsurprising," I say breezily. "We're hot as hell. I'd be offended if they weren't looking."

His chest rumbles against mine as he chuckles. "I'm trying not to get jealous over all the men staring at you."

Jealousy has no place in our current relationship, and yet a wave of giddiness crashes through me. "I mean, my ass *does* look fantastic in this dress, so no wonder they can't keep their eyes off me."

In response, Thomas's hand slips lower on my back. "You'd think they'd have the decency not to ogle another man's wife."

"Maybe you should kiss me," I tease, feeling nearly as bold

as I did the night we met. "Show them you're the one who gets to take me home tonight."

"I could."

It's a vague answer, one that trails off as if he's not really considering it. God, I shouldn't have said it, shouldn't have suggested it in such a flirty way, but we *did* agree that we'd save things like that for the public. Who cares how I've said it? It's all still fake. For show.

"But?" I press, needing to know what's stopping him. "It's just a little PDA."

Thomas looks down at me, our faces close enough that it would be so easy to bring our lips together. "That's the problem."

We share a breath, a beat of silence. A second where I swear we're the only ones in the room.

"When I kiss you again, Stella," he murmurs, "it's not going to be for show."

My heart stops. I'm not sure if we're dancing anymore. I don't know anything except the depths of his eyes, the truth that lies in them. He means every word of what he's said.

And if I'm honest with myself, I want the same. I want a moment of real, of genuine, of the trouble I told myself to avoid to keep myself safe.

My lips part, but I don't know what I'm about to say—that I want this? That it's a bad idea? I need more time to *think* before I do something I can't take back.

So it's probably a good thing that someone clears their throat from beside us and saves me from making the choice.

Head snapping to the right, I find Willow standing there with a sheepish smile. Her hands are clasped in front of her stomach like she's nervous to have intruded, but there's a determination in her eyes that I can't ignore.

"Willow!" I exclaim in surprise, dropping my hand from Thomas's and taking an unsteady step back. "I didn't know you were here yet."

"I'm really sorry to interrupt," she says. "But, Thomas . . . Reid wants to talk to you."

# CHAPTER 24

THOMAS

Reid Coleman isn't thrilled to see me. I can't blame him.

We're in one of the venue's back rooms, allowing us some privacy for our chat, though the man looks like he might bolt any second. Still, he offers me a weak smile, which I'm taking as a good sign.

"Congrats again on the championship," I say to ease us into the conversation. I fear it would be bad manners to simply blurt, *Can you please put me in contact with your teammate so we can clear the goddamn air?*

He drags a hand through his golden hair, smile twisting into something more authentic, even though it doesn't quite reach his eyes. "Thanks. Still can't believe it."

Me neither, considering how he managed to win it. But I like the guy, so I won't question what, if anything, has been going on behind the scenes. I've got enough of my own drama to worry about.

"I'm sure it felt a little more real with that trophy in your hands last night," I joke, knowing he had to attend the prize-giving gala. Such is the life of a champion—not that I would know.

I'm relieved when he chuckles, even if it's slightly forced. This is awkward, we both know it, but what makes it worse is that it didn't used to be like this.

We used to joke about the joy and trauma of coming into F1 at the same time, trying to find our footing not just in the highest echelon of motorsport but at teams with long legacies and even longer lists of championships. Dev and Axel were rookies with us too, but their situations weren't quite the same. They went to teams that had either never won a Constructors' Championship—like Dev and Argonaut Racing—or that were just finding their footing—like Axel and Specter Energy. They didn't have the pressure of historic teams and fan bases weighing down on them like we did.

Of course, Reid and Dev were always closer, just on the basis of them being American and growing up in the same karting circuits. But Reid and I? We had our own thing. And it all went straight to shit when his teammate nearly killed me.

Personally, I don't think Reid blames me for what I said about Lorenzo Castellucci. How could he, when his own teammate pushed him off-track, brake-checked him, and ignored team orders that favored Reid dozens of times? If I were Reid, everyone would have known how much I loathed the man.

But I guess that's why Reid's still sitting pretty at D'Ambrosi while I'm hated by every single one of their fans and possibly going to be out of a job. He kept his mouth shut. I didn't.

"How's Lorenzo doing?" I force myself to ask.

Reid sighs softly. "He's . . . coming to terms with what happened."

That's not the encouraging answer I wanted to hear, but then again, what did I expect? "Have you seen him?"

"When I left Abu Dhabi, I went to visit him at the rehab center." Reid's gaze skims the floor before lifting back to mine. "He's keen on keeping a low profile at the moment."

"Do you think you could convince him to see me?" I hedge. "Or, hell, just take a call? I really need to speak with him."

Reid is quiet for so long that I know I'm going to get shot down. But I *have* to make this happen. Even if our chat doesn't lead to Lorenzo publicly announcing that he doesn't hate or blame me for anything, I still need to clear the air, face-to-face. Selfishly, I need to know there are no hard feelings. And I need to know that, even if he's not right now, he's going to be okay one day—whatever that looks like for him.

"I've already asked," Reid finally admits.

My brow shoots up. "Excuse me?"

"I don't have an answer yet," he quickly tacks on, "which is why I didn't want to tell you anything, so don't get your hopes up. But I did ask if he'd be open to speaking with you when I went to visit."

"How did you know I—"

"Your wife got Willow to hound me about it." This time, I get a wry smile. "They're both very insistent women. And if Dev has taught me anything, it's to never piss off your social media manager."

He's not wrong about any of it. What hits me harder, though, is that Stella managed to pull off exactly what she said she would. She has me here talking with Reid and even got him to reach out to Lorenzo on my behalf, two things I haven't been able to do myself. Not even my manager, with all his connections, could get me in touch with anyone. But Stella did it.

"You're lucky to have someone fighting for you like that," Reid continues when I can't find my voice. "I honestly thought you'd lost your mind when I heard you'd gotten married in Vegas, but you landed yourself a good one."

There's no doubt about that. Even if it was all by mistake, even if it was drunken lust guiding us, I chose the perfect person.

"I really did," I say, not fighting a smile. "Stella's . . . amazing. I need to thank her for setting all of this up." I would run to her now if I didn't need to chat more with Reid, to make sure everything's okay with us too.

But he can see I'm itching to leave, because he nods to the door. "Go get your girl. We can talk again before the break's over."

"You're done following the D'Ambrosi protocol of shunning me then?"

He lets loose a grin that solidifies his golden boy moniker. "I guess I could break the rules."

I'll believe it when my phone rings, but for now, we're on steady enough ground that I don't feel bad when I slap his shoulder in goodbye and then stride out of the room.

Finding Stella when I return to the ballroom isn't a challenge, only because there's a crowd around her. She's sucked in a group of people and is regaling them with some tale that has her motioning with her champagne glass, and they can't take their eyes off her. Neither can I as I slip past bodies and make my way toward her. My hand settles on her elbow, drawing her confused gaze away from her audience. When she realizes it's me, her face lights up so brightly that I have to blink to keep from staring at her in a daze.

"Come with me."

She wastes no time turning her wide smile on her hangers-on and excusing herself from the conversation.

"So?" she prompts, clinging to my arm as I guide her through the crowd. "How did it go?"

"Reid asked Lorenzo to speak with me," I rush to answer. "No guarantee that he will, but this is a start."

Stella makes a sound of excitement and tugs me closer. "He'll talk to you, I know it. We're going to clear your name."

There's that *we* again. I love the sound of it from her lips, but there's really no *we* here—this has been all her. With her insistence and her inability to take no for an answer when it comes to helping me. My own family is content to leave me to rot, but Stella? She's been ready to help since practically day dot.

I take her to the room Reid and I were just in, though there's no sign of him now. Good. I need this moment alone with her.

"Is there anything else I can do to help?" she asks, slipping her arm out of my grasp and staring up at me expectantly.

"Not right now. I just wanted to thank you."

"For what?" she teases. "Annoying the shit out of Willow, who in turn annoyed the shit out of Reid?"

"For making this happen. For taking a chance on me."

Stella's expression softens from wide-eyed joy to tender amusement. "Oh, Thomas. Did you really think I'd let my own husband suffer? You know I like you better when you're smiling."

I lift a brow, almost glad she's not taking me completely seriously. If she did, I fear I might confess something that neither of us is ready to admit—that we like each other more than just on a surface level of attraction or mere friendship. "Oh, you mean *that British thing* I do with my face?"

"What can I say? It's grown on me."

"Well, your grating American accent has grown on me."

She gasps and slaps my chest, and even though she's faking

offense, there's no hiding the laugh behind her words. "You never said it was grating!"

Because it isn't. It never has been. I could listen to her talk about anything and everything for hours on end. She could read me every page in the dictionary and I'd be content to sit and drink it in, as long as it came from her.

I close my fingers around her wrist before she can pull back. "To be fair, it's a very sexy kind of grating."

"Are you flirting with me?" she jokingly chides, looking up at me through her lashes. "Does my terrible accent get you going?"

I could answer that verbally. I *should* answer, because it's an easy *fucking absolutely*. But instead I wrap an arm around Stella's waist and haul her against me. Then I dip my head until my lips find hers. *That's* my answer.

If she's surprised by the move, I don't feel it. She leans in without hesitation, opening for me when I sweep my tongue over her bottom lip, inviting me in. Has she been thinking about it as much as I have? Because I've been hungering for this. Desperate for the chance to taste her again. She's just as sweet as I remember.

This feels like we've picked up exactly where we left off in that Las Vegas strip club, before everything was put on hold for wedding vows and crisis control. And this time, I want to see it through. I want to see where it could have led. What a night together could have been like.

I just have to be so damn careful not to let the twinge of affection I feel for her get in the way.

Her mouth is pouty when I draw back, and it takes a second before her eyes flutter open. We're still so close that we're trading breaths, but I have no plans to move away.

"You just broke the rules," she taunts, winded, and the

threat has no edge. "Although, I guess you warned me that you would."

I chuckle, my hands moving down from her waist to grip her hips. "What consequences am I going to face?"

"No consequences. That was . . ." She sucks in a breath, then lets it out on a shaky exhale. "Honestly, it was fucking fantastic."

She can say that, but I'm getting a different message from her body language. She's gone tense under my touch, her shoulders rounding, and although she isn't pulling away yet, I can feel it about to happen.

"I sense a *but* coming," I hedge, and my stomach falls inch by inch as Stella steps back.

"We can't do that again, Thomas." It's a quiet sentence, said with the kind of resignation that tells me she's already thought about this too much.

I sigh and lift a hand to rub the back of my neck, my skin burning as her rejection settles in. "I know."

And I really do. I know the rules and why we have them. I know I shouldn't be breaking them and tempting her to throw them away. It's shitty and selfish of me, but how can I be expected to not want another taste of the woman I've been trying to get my hands on since the first night we met?

"We've been lax about things," she goes on. "We're introducing complications we don't need. I'm guilty of it too, so don't put all the blame on yourself."

I deserve to, though. Sure, she's done her fair share of flirting, but I've done nothing but encourage it. Because I wanted it. I still want it.

But this conversation is the death blow to that easy dynamic. And that's completely my fault.

"I get it," I make myself say. I even force a smile, one I hope

comes off as casual. "We'll be more careful moving forward."
Then, just to drive the knife further into my own gut, I hold a
hand out for her to shake. "Friends?"

Something crosses Stella's face that I can't decipher, but it's
replaced by an easy smile that would seem almost natural if I
hadn't already seen the real thing so many times.

She takes my hand in hers and squeezes. "Friends."

It's the only word I don't want to hear her say.

# CHAPTER 25

STELLA

I've made everything weird, and I could slap myself for it.

I know it was the right decision to put the brakes on things between Thomas and me last night, but it's built a wall between us that's entirely too high. After the gala, we walked away from each other once we got home, barely saying *good night* before retreating to our separate wings, like we were suddenly strangers again. I thought declaring our friendship—and our intentions to keep it that way—would ease the tension and make this fake marriage simpler to navigate, but nope. All I've done is add another complication while trying to prevent one.

I knew from the second his lips touched mine that I was going to be in deep trouble if I didn't reinforce the rules—the kind of trouble that would make divorcing him one day emotionally messy. Worst of all, it made me question if I'd even *want* to leave. It was such a sudden, unbidden thought that it nearly had me running from the room, yet I somehow kept my feet planted. I even *explained* myself while my heart threatened to choke me, trying its best to stop the logical words from coming out.

But I had to do it, for my own sake. Because I can't run the risk of getting attached to another man I've come to care about, just to have him leave me behind. Or worse, turn me into a version of myself that I no longer recognize. I barely made it out alive the first time; I don't think I would survive a second.

Thomas is pouring two mugs of coffee when I shuffle into the kitchen. He's bright-eyed and fresh-faced, even though I know he had just as much champagne as I did last night. In comparison, I'm squinting against the faint sunlight coming in through the windows and I haven't bothered to take my bonnet off yet. Hard to believe that not long ago I refused to let him see me in it, but hey, we're officially *friends*. No point in hiding any aspect of myself from a man who's going to be nothing more than that.

That's exactly what you want, Stella. Stop being bitter and start being smart.

"It's not fair that you wake up looking like a Disney prince," I mumble as he hands me my favorite of the two mugs.

His laugh breaks some of the lingering awkwardness, and I relax as I stir cream and sugar into my coffee.

"That might be the nicest thing you've ever said to me." He plucks the spoon from my hand and uses it in his own mug. "How are you feeling today? Up for more exploring?"

It's comforting that he's trying to get us back to the way we were before the kiss. He's not holding my choices against me . . . which only makes me like him more.

I take a gulp of my coffee, scalding my tongue, but at least it burns away the yearning. "I'm meeting Janelle for brunch," I answer. Then, not wanting him to think I'm pushing him away, I blurt, "Maybe after?"

He nods and leans against the counter. "Yeah, absolutely.

My schedule's empty until I start training again after the new year."

"Must be nice." I sigh, all the work I need to do pressing at the edge of my thoughts. "It's going to be hell for me until Christmas, but I'll get a break between then and the first week of January."

"Speaking of Christmas," he prompts, "do you have any plans? Did you want to go home?"

I grimace, reminded of the last chat I had with my mother. We haven't spoken since Thanksgiving other than a few check-in texts, mostly her making sure I'm still alive. "Is it bad if I say not really?"

Thomas shakes his head. "I have no interest in spending Christmas with my family this year either. Not after what Andrew and my father pulled."

Can't blame him there. "And I'm sure your mother would hound us about the wedding anyway. Probably best if we avoid them and do our own thing."

It'll be my first holiday season in five years without Étienne, so things are already going to be strange. Might as well shake it up more by not going home and spending it with my pretend husband. Besides, it wouldn't take much to make it better than last Christmas when Étienne took me to visit his family.

I spent the entire holiday excluded from conversations or straight-up laughed at every time I attempted to speak French. He pacified me by saying it was all in good fun, that I really wasn't missing out on much, and he promised we wouldn't have to visit again for years. I could handle a few days of that, couldn't I?

"What do you want for Christmas, anyway?" Thomas asks, drawing me out of my thoughts.

I shrug and take another sip. "Nothing I can think of." I can buy everything I want, so who needs gifts?

"Wrong answer," he shoots back. "What do you want for Christmas, Stella?"

"For you to let me drink my coffee in peace."

"No chance. Try again."

I groan, knowing he's not going to give up. "I don't know . . . Maybe a vacation? An actual one with sun and warmth, where I can turn my phone off and not have to worry about work for a while."

He nods, considering. "You know, Joshua and Amara are going to the Maldives for the holidays. We could tag along with them."

His suggestion gets a quick and emphatic "Absolutely the fuck not" before I can even think to temper my response.

Thomas's brow shoots up, and I know I'm going to have to explain.

I grimace. "I was supposed to go there on my honeymoon."

Understanding passes over his face. "I see." The conversation lulls for a moment before he says, "You don't talk about Étienne much."

I don't, and every time he's come up I've changed the subject. I want to say it's because I'm not ready or that I'm still processing the trauma, but it's neither of those things. I just don't want to be judged.

"Because there's no need," I brush off.

But Thomas decides to press on the bruise. "Why not?"

He does it in such a gentle way, but it still hurts. I consider lying, but I don't see the point. He did say he wanted to know me, so . . . fine. I'll finally answer the question I avoided that night in the Cotswolds. Maybe it will scare him off enough that neither of us will have to worry about anything complicating our divorce plans.

"Because I feel stupid for staying as long as I did," I tell him, and as much as the words scratch my throat as they come out, there's a freedom in saying them aloud. "For overlooking everything that was wrong in our relationship."

Thomas is quiet again, simply staring at me, but there's no hint of the judgment I feared in his eyes. Again, he's so tender when he questions, "Why do you feel that way?"

I take a breath, daring myself to be completely honest—to let my worst parts be seen. "Because, deep down, I knew he didn't want to be with me far before our wedding day. And I still stayed."

Now that I've admitted it, I swear a dam has burst somewhere in my mind, letting all of my guilt and grief and *hate* for myself surge up and over. I have to get it out before it eats me alive or I do something unwise—like drink another bottle of wine and record my drunken rantings for the world to see. Thomas is about to be in the middle of the tsunami whether he wants to be or not.

"I stayed because it was easier than leaving." The words come out in a rushed exhale, some version of a sad laugh. "I thought things being *good enough* meant they were *good*. I mean, better the devil you know than the one you don't, right? And then when he left on our wedding day, I thought—"

I cut short, running out of breath, and the inhale I take shudders through my body. But Thomas doesn't try to interrupt or stop me or do anything except reach out to steady my trembling hand, keeping me from spilling hot coffee over my skin.

"I thought he would come back," I finally admit—to Thomas, to myself, for the first time to anyone, anywhere. "I waited for him to come back. Even though he literally said to me *I just don't want to be with you, Stella*, I waited. I sat in a back office of the church for hours, just hoping he'd change his mind and realize he'd made a mistake."

This time, I do laugh, because it's fucking comical how foolish I was to think that would happen.

"But he didn't come back. My parents took me to my house—the house Étienne and I had bought together that he *still* hadn't moved his things into—and I kept waiting. I stayed there for a few days, then went to the apartment we'd been living in together, but he wasn't there either. In fact, all of his stuff was gone."

I don't think Thomas realizes that he's squeezing my hand, but the pressure is soothing, even if the flash of anger in his eyes isn't. I have to look away before I can speak again.

"The rant that got me into so much trouble?" I remind him. "That's what happened when I got back to the house and started drinking, as if that would help me forget how pathetic I was for waiting on something that would never happen." I shake my head, still sick with myself over it. "You know, sometimes I think I'm still waiting for him to come back. To tell me he made a mistake. To take me back."

Thomas's grip tightens just a little more.

"And now you know the full story," I finish with a halfhearted shrug and an even weaker attempt at a smile. "Bet that's not what you were expecting to hear."

When I stop speaking, the silence is thick, and I can feel Thomas's gaze on me, though I still don't dare to look up until he murmurs, "Oh, Stella."

I pull my hand out of his grasp, somehow not spilling the coffee, but I can't take the sympathy in his voice or the way his eyes have gone achingly soft. It's not pity written across his face, which I'm thankful for, but whatever this is—this look of understanding and what almost comes off as anger on my behalf—is somehow so much worse.

"I need to go get dressed," I choke out, setting my mug down on the counter and dipping my head again so he can't see my embarrassment up close and personal. "Don't want to be late. See you for dinner later?"

"Stella, hold on," he calls, reaching for me.

But I'm already leaving the kitchen, determined to forget this conversation ever happened.

〰〰〰

"I'm such a fuckup."

Janelle eyes me over the edge of her glass, the mimosa not even touching her lips yet. "Let a girl have a sip of her drink before we start with the self-hate, damn."

I sigh and rest my elbows on the table. "Sorry. Go ahead and down half of that, then I'll get into it."

She does as she's instructed, then daintily dabs at her lips with her napkin. "Proceed."

I waste no time unloading, catching her up on everything that's happened since we last spoke—like the kiss at the gala and the following friendship conversation, culminating in my minor breakdown this morning. I'm interrupted once by our server coming over to take our orders, and I don't finish my story until our meals are being placed in front of us.

"I—wow," Janelle stammers. She slowly picks up her cutlery, looking like she's struggling to find the right words, either to comfort me or to tell me that I've been a complete and utter asshole over the past twenty-four hours. "Can I say something I don't think you're going to like?"

Should have known it was going to be the second option.

"Go for it," I grumble, picking up my fork and stabbing at my eggs.

"Number one—"

"Oh *God*, it's a whole list?"

"Number one," she repeats. "I understand why you made the rules you did, but they're ruining your life."

"What's that supposed to mean?"

"It means you're preventing yourself from being happy." She slices into her eggs Benedict with perfect precision. "You could be getting your rocks off with a nice man who seems like he's *very* willing to give you all the orgasms you could want."

My face goes hot, not because I fear we've been overheard by the gray-haired ladies at the table over but because she's right. Thomas has been up for the task since day one.

"Because it would complicate things when we get divorced," I stress. "I don't want to get . . ."

"Attached?" Janelle finishes for me, like she knows exactly what I'm afraid of. "Is it so bad if you do?"

"Um, *yeah*."

"Why, Stella?" she challenges.

Because I can't get my heart broken again.

"Because it's just not a good idea, okay?" I say instead. "What's next on your damn list?"

Janelle doesn't miss a beat. "Number two: It's clear that you already like him."

I shake my head, but I'm lying to us both. "I don't like him like . . . *that*."

"Oh, baby girl." A grin spreads slowly across her face. "You're fully sprung for that man."

I almost choke on the eggs I've shoveled into my mouth. It's a few seconds before I recover enough to speak. "I am *not*."

"You so are. I bet you're already thinking about what your little biracial babies would look like."

"Janelle!"

She shrugs and takes a bite of her food, chewing thoughtfully and then swallowing. "Number three."

"Oh, here we fucking go."

"No one said you *have* to get divorced."

I squint at her. "It was part of our agreement from the very beginning. Of course we do."

"Don't go acting like some oblivious little girl," she reprimands. "There's no reason this marriage can't turn into something real, even if it started out as a mistake."

I hunch in my seat. She's not completely wrong, but the idea of deviating from my original plan and allowing things to change along the way makes my skin crawl. Then again, didn't I tell myself to stop making plans?

"I don't know if it ever could," I admit. "I don't know if we could last in the long term. And who knows, this may just be a silly crush that will go away the next time I get laid."

Janelle considers for a moment, then levels me with a curious stare. "Should we do a pro and con list to see if this is the real deal?"

With our type A personalities, we both love a pro and con list, so I kick it off, even if I don't think it's going to help in this situation. "Pro: Thomas is so handsome it should be illegal."

She nods with solemn enthusiasm. "I love Ron with my whole heart, but . . . yeah, you're right."

"Con," I immediately follow up, "he's younger than me."

She scoffs. "By like two years, Stella, come on. He's old enough to eat corn bread without getting choked."

"Fine." I hold my fork up in defeat. "Pro: He's shockingly

nice. Just really, really kind. He actually cares about my opinion and how things make me feel."

"Honestly, that's a three-pointer. It shouldn't be so difficult to find a man who treats you like a real human being deserving of respect, but it is."

"Con: The other day he slapped his thighs and said 'Right' before he stood up."

She winces. "Okay, that's about negative five points."

"Pro: He found a nail place for me *and* a salon to get my hair done weekly."

"We're back in the positives, baby."

"And get this—he insists on paying for both every time."

Janelle leans back, pressing a hand to her chest. "I'd say marry him if you weren't already married."

I laugh, a little less burdened by heavy emotions. "I forgot to mention, he wants me to go to the Maldives with him and his friends for Christmas."

"You should go! Don't let Étienne overshadow the chance to go somewhere beautiful."

I shake my head. "I have so much work to do to get this new shop off the ground and keep the rest of the empire running. I don't have time for a vacation."

"Which is exactly what someone who needs a vacation would say," she points out. "Let him take you on a little trip. Get some sun, swim in the ocean, and give yourself a hard reset." She reaches across the table to grasp my wrist to drive her point home. "You deserve this, okay? I'd go so far as to say you need it."

A break from the stress of life and work does sound spectacular. And it's not like my company will tank if I take a week or two off, as I've already learned. What's the harm in giving myself a real break this time?

"Plus," Janelle goes on, "you clearly need some vitamin D. Firstly from the sun but also from Thomas's—"

"Don't you dare say it," I interrupt, but I'm already pulling my phone out of my purse with my free hand.

I unlock the screen and tap on my short chain of messages with Thomas. Janelle, as sweet and vulgar as she is, has a point. I deserve to have a hot man sweep me off to an even hotter destination.

I changed my mind, I type before I can think better of it. Let's escape to paradise, your highness.

# CHAPTER 26

THOMAS

Stella in a little white dress sipping an old-fashioned is alluring. Stella in a slinky gown while entertaining a group of people is an absolute vision. But Stella in the tiniest bikini the world has ever seen while smiling slyly over her shoulder? Fuck me for declaring that I was okay with being just friends—I'm not feeling *remotely* friendly toward her right now.

"I'm so glad you convinced me to come here," she says on a dreamy sigh, gaze drifting to the crystal-blue Maldives water. "This is so beautiful."

It's not nearly as beautiful as the sight of her standing on the deck of our overwater bungalow, but since saying that is verboten, I just mumble "Yeah" and shove my hands into the pockets of my shorts.

In reply, Stella playfully rolls her eyes and tosses her waist-length braids over her shoulder. *They're vacation braids*, she explained when she came home from the salon with the new look. *So I don't have to worry about my hair for the trip.* I didn't tell her I already knew that thanks to Amara's influence, because I love her little explanations of things she thinks I won't understand.

Two weeks have flown by since the gala, and with as busy as Stella has been, I haven't seen much of her. Honestly, our flight out here was the longest amount of uninterrupted time we've had together lately. She spent most of it passed out, though, too exhausted from the fifteen-hour workdays she's been pulling. When we landed and transferred to the seaplane that would take us to the resort—which I made sure was *not* an A.P. Maxwell International property—we exchanged a few words to check in on each other, but that was it.

My fingers are crossed that we'll get to spend some solid time together on this holiday, because I miss talking to her. I miss the jokes she cracks at my expense and how she can take it as good as she dishes it out. I miss feeling like I have a partner in crime.

"I'm gonna go for a swim," she announces. "Then maybe we could find something to eat?"

I nod. "Sounds good. Joshua and Amara should be here in the next few hours, so we'll meet up with them."

"Can't wait."

And then she dives into the water so smoothly that I need to ask if she ever swam competitively. There are so many things about her I still want to discover. I'm praying I'll get a chance to during the ten days we're set to spend here.

I almost regret booking us the two-bedroom villa. Maybe if we were forced to share a bed again we could have a little pillow talk or some late-night chats, anything to get her to open up to me. We were getting there before, and then I fucked it all up, but I'm determined to change that on this trip.

I'm determined to learn everything about her—because that's what friends do, right?

A few hours later, Stella is dressed in a floor-skimming cotton skirt and a tiny top that leaves the dramatic curve of her waist exposed, her hand resting in the crook of my elbow. Our arms look almost comical next to each other—Stella's shimmering brown skin has only grown deeper after hours of basking in the sun while mine still looks like I've never seen a ray of light before. I'll pick up some color after a few days, but for now, I'm content admiring Stella's glow.

Good God, man, stop being such a simp.

"I'm excited to meet your friends." Her grip on me tightens as she flashes a grin. "Mainly so they can tell me all the embarrassing stories about you."

I eye her, amused. "Is that why you won't let me hang out with you and Janelle? So she won't spill all your secrets?"

"Maybe," Stella says breezily. "Although you and the world already know about my worst moment, so anything she told you wouldn't be so bad."

We can relate there. There's nothing Joshua and Amara could reveal that would be worse than my Lorenzo rant. They could tell her anything about me and I think I'd be glad for her to know it. To know me.

"Is that them?" Stella murmurs as we step into one of the resort's many restaurants.

I stop and follow her gaze to the couple standing near the railing of the outdoor seating area. They're not hard to spot, because other than Stella, they're the only Black people here. "That's them."

"Fuck," she exhales. "We're not the most beautiful couple in the room anymore and that makes me furious."

That's one way to pay them a compliment, but Stella's right

no matter how she phrases it. Joshua and Amara are a striking pair.

"My conceited wife," I warmly tease her.

She turns that sparkling grin on me again. "If only you'd known what you were getting into when you married me."

"Oh, I knew from the start."

"That's right," she muses. "You did say you liked cocky women."

"I still do. Very much."

Our eyes lock and something charged arcs between us. It steals my breath for a second, tempting me to lower my lips to hers in an attempt to reclaim it—or at least steal hers too. Stella's not unaffected either. I can see it in the way her pulse flutters at the base of her throat, how she swallows hard, her gaze sweeping over my face as if she's searching for a reason to keep abiding by the rules we've set.

She must find it, because she clears her throat and glances away, snapping us both out of the moment.

"They know the truth about us, right?" she asks, nodding in Joshua and Amara's direction.

I don't miss the slight waver in the words, but I don't call her out on it, even though I'm desperate for us to stop ignoring the potent attraction refusing to ease, despite the lies we keep telling ourselves that we can move past it. We haven't yet and I doubt we will unless we do something about it.

For now, I play along. "They do."

"That's a relief," she says as I nudge her into walking again. "You know I can put on a show, but I hate lying all the time."

Then maybe we should stop lying to each other, I want to suggest, but again, I crush it down. "You can be as honest with them as you want."

Just a shame we can't do the same with each other.

As I suspected would happen, my friends like Stella more than
they like me. Tragic, but understandable.

I've been (happily) pushed to the side as they've gotten to
know her over the past couple of days. Stella and Amara have
practically taken up residence in the ocean, doing their best
mermaid impressions from sunup to sundown. They shut up
whenever I swim closer, giggling and snickering and making it
abundantly clear they've been talking about me. The only time
they separate is when Amara and I go off on Jet Ski or speed-
boat adventures, our spouses with less daredevil spirits left
behind to enjoy drinks on the beach.

Stella and Joshua always seem to be engaged in some sort
of deep conversation when we drag ourselves back to land,
but when Stella's attention finds me, she lights up so brightly
that it makes Joshua eye me in a way I can't quite decipher.

Christmas arrives with little fanfare, barely acknowledged
past the gifts we're exchanging before heading to dinner. With
a £20 price limit, the items range from useless and laughably
offensive—like the key chain Amara got for me from
D'Ambrosi—to actually thoughtful and kind—like the vinyl
record Stella gives Joshua from an Afrobeat artist that I told her
he liked . . . a full month before it's slated to even be released. I
don't ask how she pulled that off, and while the price tag *technically* didn't break the limit, it certainly required more work than
£20 could cover.

Her gift for me? A sunset-orange Stella Margaux's–branded
apron.

"You look good with my name on your chest," she teases as
she watches me tie the strings in a neat bow around my waist.

It's only fitting that I toss her a McMorris T-shirt with my name and number on it. "Then you better wear mine on your back."

She cackles and tugs it on over her dress, preening for Amara, who pulls out her phone and snaps photo after photo. As the women venture out to the deck for their shoot, Joshua shifts closer to murmur, "I get it now."

I cut him a look, but he's staring out at our wives pretending to be models. "Get what?"

"Why you married her."

I snort, rubbing my thumb over my wedding band. I haven't taken it off since the end of the season. "I don't think anyone knows why I did that."

"Then I get why you want to stay married."

"I never said I wanted to."

It's his turn to shoot me an unamused glance, seeing right through me. I know I've been transparent about my attraction to Stella, and I know my actions speak louder than anything I could ever say. He's never seen me this dedicated to a woman.

This isn't an argument I'll win, so I deflect. "Why do you think I want to stay married to her?"

Joshua pauses to consider his answer. "Because she makes you laugh."

"*That's* enough of a reason?" I scoff. "Come on, be serious."

"Not on its own," he clarifies, "but it's part of it. She . . . matches you. Matches your humor, your drive, your kindness. She's thoughtful in the same way you are. Supportive without expecting anything in return. I've never seen that in any of the other women you brought around. And certainly not from Figgy."

"Are you really saying Stella is my perfect match?" I press, incredulous.

But Joshua only shrugs, leaving the silence to linger and my thoughts to swirl. Honestly, some days it feels like Stella and I are polar opposites, two people from vastly different worlds and upbringings and life experiences. And yet I can see exactly what he means by us matching each other. We just . . . fit together.

"If the situation were different, she's the kind of woman I'd want to seriously date," I say before I can think better of the confession.

Joshua snickers. "Oh, so you're finally ready for a girlfriend now that you have a wife?"

"The irony isn't lost on me."

"So why don't you try?" he suggests.

"She doesn't want a real relationship."

"Are you sure?"

"Considering she has rules that have made it pretty clear, yeah, I am."

Joshua's hand clamps down on my shoulder, forcing me to glance over and witness the dismayed set to his mouth. "Since when have you been a devout rule follower? You've *always* searched for a loophole, Thomas. If you weren't a driver, you'd be the most brilliant solicitor."

"Glad you think I'm smart."

He squeezes harder, right in the tender part of my trapezius, clearing away my sarcasm. "Right now I think you're a ridiculous excuse for a man who can't pull his head out of his ass and make his feelings clear."

I wince, both from the physical torture method and his biting words. "God, you're sounding more and more like your wife every day."

"Love will do that to you." Finally, he lets up, slapping me hard on the back before returning his attention to the laughing women outside. "Seriously, mate. You'll never know what could happen if you don't try."

🏁🏁🏁

By New Year's Eve, I'm in hell.

I thought living with Stella would prepare me for a whole week of being together on holiday. How different could it be?

Vastly, as I've discovered.

Stella at home doesn't walk around nearly naked, sporting a new bikini every morning that makes me wonder if she's tormenting me on purpose. Vacation Stella has relaxed shoulders and easy smiles. She's loud and funny and quick to grab my hand to drag me off to whatever activity is slated for the day. She peacefully naps wherever she can find a space, whether that's on the couch in our bungalow or under an umbrella on the beach, curled up like a cat with her face burrowed in the crook of her arm. Sometimes I even tuck her braids behind her ear just so I can get a better view of the peace on her face.

Yeah . . . I'm not faring remotely fucking well.

Thankfully, we only have two more days here before we head home. I don't have a clue what our dynamic will be like when we're back, but it won't be as difficult to keep my eyes—and hands—off her once she's bundled up against the English winter. I almost miss her cashmere tracksuits, though I can't deny the sight of her in a white crochet bikini is dangerously appealing.

Tonight she's wearing some sort of tight black bustier dress that pushes her tits up and slightly over the cups, tempting me to press my face into their softness. She's done her makeup heavier than I've seen all week, darkening her eyes with shadow and winging out a line that makes every glance she tosses sultry. And her lips, painted wine red like the first night we met, are simply lush. If someone said they could bring the woman of my dreams to life, it would be Stella in this moment. Or really, Stella in any moment.

I fear if I tell her that, it will scare her off into the ocean, never to be seen again. So I settle for taking her hand and spinning her in a circle before saying, "You look stunning."

"You don't look so bad yourself," she commends, taking in my black suit and white shirt with a few buttons undone. "We match."

Logically, I know she's only talking about our color coordination, but I think of Joshua's words. *She matches you.* The more I've considered it, the more I've come to see what he means. We *do* match. We're alike in so many ways, and even in the ways we aren't, everything still aligns.

"We do," I agree. I press my luck and lace our fingers together. "Looking like a real couple. Who'd ever think this was fake?"

Stella gives me another one of those beguiling laughs from deep in her chest, and all it does is push me farther down the rabbit hole of desperation. I need more from this woman, whatever she's willing to give. I'd let her use me in return, let her sink her teeth into me and tear away whatever she wanted. She could burn through me and I'd fan the flame.

Again, Joshua's words haunt me. *You'll never know what could happen if you don't try.* There are options for what that could mean, some better than others. But *something* has to change— has to give. We can't keep dancing around each other like there isn't some sort of string tying us together, getting shorter and shorter by the day. I'm going to drive myself mad if I don't do anything about it.

"Hey, actually, can we talk?" I say as she recovers from her laughter. My heart picks up the pace, threatening to beat out of my chest, because what the *fuck* am I doing?

Stella glances at the clock on the wall. "We're already late for dinner," she says regretfully, clearly not knowing what's coming for her. "What about when we get back?"

That will be far past midnight, and who knows how many drinks we'll have had by then. It might help my cause, but there's a chance it could also lead me to say all the wrong things.

Still, I swallow hard and murmur, "Yeah. Sure."

But I don't know how much longer I can hold this in.

I want to be with my wife—for real. Even if it's just temporary. Even if it's just for a night.

Even if that's all I ever get.

# CHAPTER 27

STELLA

There's something off with Thomas.

I hate that I realize it. And I hate that I'm desperate to do something about it. I wasn't lying when I told him I like him better when he's smiling, even if it's for my own selfish reason of never wanting to see him upset, because I . . . like him.

Unfortunately, as I've come to realize over the past week, I am absolutely sprung for this man, saddled with a crush that can't be swatted away like an annoying fly. It's a devastating truth, but being with Thomas nearly every waking minute has shown me everything about him up close and personal.

My rules were supposed to prevent the development of any sort of feelings for him, but maybe I should have added *Don't look at me, don't talk to me, and certainly don't smile at me* to the list. Because even without sex, with limited intimacy and my attempts to focus mostly on work, he's still found his way under my skin and planted roots.

I just hope I can rip them up without damaging myself when the time comes.

He's quieter than usual through dinner, speaking only when

spoken to and nursing his whiskey on the rocks. I want to shift closer and ask what's going on. It likely has something to do with whatever he wanted to talk to me about earlier, and I'm kicking myself now for insisting we head to dinner instead of staying to hear him out.

Then again, I think I might have an idea of what he was going to say, because the same thing's been on my mind too.

Whatever this is between us is unignorable now, but I have to push it aside. Things will be easier once we're back in London and back to our lives—back to reality and all the reasons why we need to keep this marriage strictly platonic. The reasons might be escaping me now, replaced by butterflies and sparks every time he laughs, but they'll come back. I just can't make any mistakes until then.

Amara declares that it's time for dancing the second our plates are cleared away. Soon my hand is in hers as she drags me from the restaurant and out to the beachside bar, where a DJ and wide dance floor are set up on the sand. There are a few dozen people here already, most drinking, some dancing, and all enjoying the warmth of the night and the soft breeze that curls around us. It's the perfect way to say goodbye to the past year and ring in the next.

When the boys catch up, Thomas tries to slip to my side, but there's something in his eyes that makes me step back. I can't put my finger on what it is, but it's . . . heavy. Too heavy for the night that I want to have.

I hook my thumb over my shoulder in the direction of the bar. "I'm gonna go get drinks!" The music is loud, but I still say the words at an unnecessary volume. "You guys go grab us a place on the dance floor before it fills up."

Amara loops her arms around Thomas and Joshua with a grin, and I suck in a much-needed breath as I turn away.

Thomas and I can't have whatever conversation he's keen on cornering me for—not now and certainly not later when we're alone in our bungalow. We only need to survive two more days of this unbearable pull between us before we can escape. We can do that, can't we?

Slipping onto a stool, I lift a hand to signal to the bartender, who nods at me as he finishes up with his current patron. I keep breathing deeply as I wait, trying to bring down my anxiety, but it feels like a lost cause. I'm *nervous*. All because I can't trust that I'll make the right choice if Thomas confesses he feels the same way I do.

"You okay?"

I glance to my right at the question, finding a man leaning against the section of bar next to me. He's tall enough that I have to lift my chin to look up at him. Handsome enough too, but he doesn't hold a candle to—

Nope. Don't do it.

"Totally fine, thanks," I answer, polite but dismissive as I look away.

I haven't opened up any avenues for conversation and yet he shifts closer, his cologne tickling my nose. I don't care for the scent.

"You look tense," he comments, eyes flicking up and down over me. To his credit, his gaze doesn't linger on my pushed-up tits and his frown seems genuine, as if he cares that this strange woman at the bar is uncomfortable. "This place is too beautiful to be anything but relaxed."

I fully fucking agree, and I would be chilling if I wasn't so worried about Thomas.

I spare the man another glance and find him still staring at me in that earnest way. Ah hell, what's the harm in entertaining a quick conversation while I wait? Maybe it's the distraction I need.

And then he says, "Come on, baby, give us a smile."

I let my eyes slide shut for a moment, because of fucking *course*. Of course some man is telling me to smile, because what else are they supposed to do? Inquire into what has a woman upset? Listen attentively and nod in understanding? Actually *care*?

You mean all the things Thomas did when you met?

I swallow back what I really want to say to this man, things Mika would applaud me for but that might get me thrown off the resort property. The bartender thankfully chooses that moment to come over, and I order two double bourbons. One of them might be for Thomas if it doesn't end up in this guy's face first.

"I'm sorry," he says, laughing as if he knows the line was bad but not caring. "I just can't stand to see a gorgeous woman upset."

"Literally never said I was upset," I deadpan, back to staring straight ahead.

And *then* he has the nerve to put his hand on my shoulder, smoothing his palm down my arm. "I could just tell. You want me to cheer you up?"

The bartender sets the drinks down in front of me. Sorry to Thomas, but he's not getting this whiskey and I might be getting a one-way trip to a Maldivian jail cell.

I curl my fingers around the glass, ready to lift it.

"I'd advise taking your hand off my wife."

My head snaps up to find Thomas standing beside me. He's intimidatingly calm, giving off the kind of energy that has me setting the glass down in surprise. Even the man hitting on me draws his hand back with a quickness, blinking at Thomas like he's shocked to find him there. I know I am.

"Sorry, man," the asshole says, taking a step back. "I didn't know she was spoken for."

I lift my left hand to give him the finger—and to show off my ring glinting under the fairy lights. Before I can speak, though, Thomas inserts himself between me and the man, preventing me from throwing the punch I was considering. Still, the idea of my diamond causing some damage sends a thrill through me.

Thomas says something to the man that I don't quite catch, but it has Mr. Give Us a Smile nodding rapidly and stumbling away.

I scowl at Thomas's back. "I was handling it myself."

"I know you were." He turns around, taking up the spot the man just vacated, but this is a much better view. "I was saving him from the medical bills you were about to inflict." He nods to the rocks glass. "That for me?"

I nudge the bourbon in his direction, a reluctant peace offering. As he sips, I watch him from the corner of my eye, curious about something.

"Why did you come over?" I ask, then jokingly tack on, "Were you jealous seeing me with another man?"

"Of course I was." He doesn't hesitate to say it. "You're my wife."

I grab my drink, my reaction to the first half of his sentence tempered by the second. "That doesn't actually mean anything," I mumble into my glass. "This is fake."

Thomas doesn't say anything as I take a swig of whiskey, forcing myself not to wince as it burns its way down. When I look back at him, he's staring out at the dance floor.

"You know, I've never understood it," he says.

I squint at him as he sets his drink back down. "Understood what?"

"Men who are assholes to women and then expect them to fall to their knees with lust. It's bullshit."

It's always thrilling to hear Thomas swear, like my English gentleman has taken a little break. Still, I don't quite understand the shift in conversation, but I shrug anyway. "Some women like a bad boy."

"There's a difference between being a bad boy and a complete fucking knobhead."

Not the word I'd use, but I guess the sentiment stands.

"Now, this?"

I almost jump when his hand lands on my thigh, but I freeze when his touch slips under the hem of my dress.

"*This* is being a bad boy."

I'm sucking in a sharp breath before I can stop myself. Heat spreads over my cheeks and rushes through my bloodstream, notching up a degree with every millimeter higher his fingertips creep between my thighs.

"We're in public," I remind him, but the words are incriminatingly breathy. And I don't try to stop him.

"Isn't that part of your rules?" he murmurs. He's moved so that my legs are blocked from the crowd's view, giving us the tiniest bit of privacy. "That all of our affection has to be in public?"

When his touch ghosts over the lace of my panties, a whimper escapes me. "You're not wrong."

"Doesn't have to be that way, though."

Yes, it absolutely does, because otherwise things will go further than this. This is already more than enough, and yet not even close to what I really want.

His free hand cups my face, and he traces my cheekbone with his thumb. "You're blushing."

I blush harder. "I'm not."

"I can see it."

"No, you can't."

"Yes, I can." His fingers lightly explore across my face. "The bridge of your nose. The tips of your ears. The little spots at the tops of your cheekbones."

It's hard to keep breathing, but I'm somehow managing it. "You've really been looking hard at me."

"Of course I have, Stella. I want to learn every inch of you."

I swear I've just been sucker punched, every ounce of good sense knocked clean out. "You can't say things like that, Thomas."

"Why not?" he challenges. "Didn't we agree to not keep secrets from each other?"

He's got me there, but his taunting is infuriating. Instead of answering, I turn my head so his touch falls from my face, but I don't push away the hand that's still up my dress.

Walk away, Stella. Don't entertain this.

Thomas watches as I lift my drink with a trembling hand. His fingers trace small circles on the skin of my inner thigh, waiting for my final answer. I knock back the rest of the bourbon instead.

He starts retreating, fingertips slowly trailing back down, but I grab his wrist before he can get far. It's the answer I can't say aloud yet.

As much as I shouldn't, I want this. Want *him*. I don't know what exactly that entails, but I want to feel him, want to close my eyes and listen as he whispers all the things I've been desperate to hear. I want to stop pretending there's no sexual current running wild between us.

But I'm not ready to admit or acknowledge all the feelings behind these desires. I can't confess how much I've grown to care for him, or how my new biggest fear is that I'm already too attached to ever say goodbye. My brain is screaming at me to keep this surface-level, even if my heart has let him burrow in deep.

I can't go another night without discovering all the things I've deprived myself of with my rules. I have to do what feels right—no matter the consequences.

"I know I'm breaking the rules," Thomas murmurs when I still don't say anything, seeming prepared to make an argument for why we should break them a little more.

But before he can utter another word, I stand abruptly from my stool. He's about to take a surprised step back, but I cup his jaw to keep him there and declare, "Fuck the rules."

I drag his face down to mine until our lips meet, rough and crushing, letting him taste everything I can't put into words. He must understand, because his arms wrap around my waist without a beat of hesitation, as if he's been waiting for this—as if all that's been holding him back has finally snapped.

My body ignites as he pulls me flush against him, and I revel in the way we meld together, simultaneously hating myself for dodging and avoiding all the moments when I could've so easily had this. And as his mouth moves against mine, tongue sweeping across my bottom lip, I can hardly remember why I kept pushing him away. Why would I ever pass up a chance at this slice of heaven? Why would I act like this was anything other than inevitable?

I can't go back to my rules after this. Whatever tether I had to them is gone and I don't know if I can get it back.

But Thomas won't let me forget them, even if I want to act like they never existed. He reluctantly breaks the kiss, lips lingering by the corner of my mouth.

"You don't mean that." His hands slip from my waist to my hips, gripping hard. "Tell me you don't, Stella."

I nod, mind made up. "I mean it. No more rules."

But I don't know what their dissolution means or where we go from here. This first step is terrifying enough.

"God, I've been waiting for you to say that." Thomas exhales shakily as he stares down at me, searching my gaze. "You weren't wrong to put them in place, though. I know you did it to protect yourself. And I'm not . . . I'm not going to ask you to break them forever."

I frown, my pounding heart sinking like a stone. Is he *rejecting* me? Is this what I get for finally laying out my desires for him to see?

Thomas squeezes my hips before I can dive headfirst into a spiral of doubt. "What I mean is . . . I think we owe it to ourselves to finish what we started back in Vegas. But only for tonight."

"I don't—" I'm still not quite following what he means. "I don't understand."

"I want a night with you," he says. "The night we were supposed to have before we decided to rush off and get married. After that, we go back to following the rules. But I think we need this. There's this . . ."

"Tension," I finish for him. "And it's fucking suffocating."

"It is." He brushes his nose against mine, eyes closing for a moment. I can imagine the ache settling heavily in his chest, because it's doing the same in mine. "Do you want that, Stella?"

I hesitate. Not because I don't want it but because my heart has decided it wants *more* than that. But it's not allowed to run the show, and he's given me a solution to the problem that's been driving me mad.

We can both get what we want without suffering the consequences of entanglement. It's a get-out-of-jail-free card, a no-strings-attached agreement. Tomorrow, we'll have this out of our systems, the need to find out what could have happened that night finally satiated. The novelty will be gone and we can move on from it. It's a perfect plan.

At least, that's what I tell myself, even though it rings as a lie.

"One night?" I repeat, but my mind's already made up.

Thomas nods. "One night."

I take a breath and slip my hand into his. "Then we'd better make it count."

# CHAPTER 28

STELLA

"If this is going to be a re-creation of Vegas," Thomas says, "then we're going to need a bottle of whiskey."

Laughing, I cling tighter to his hand, practically running to keep up with his long, hurried strides on the decked pathway to our bungalow. "Whiskey is what led to us getting married," I remind him. "Maybe we avoid that."

Besides, I'm warm from the last round of drinks we had at the bar, ordered so we could toast to our agreement—and for a last hit of liquid courage. It's loosened us up and taken away the pressure of the situation. I'm giddy instead of nervous for the night ahead. And while this isn't how I expected to finish out the year, it feels fitting. We can have this indulgence and then leave it in the past.

Thomas makes a sound of grudging agreement as he slows, giving me a chance to catch up so he can pull me to him. I go willingly, our chests flush as his hands drop to my waist.

"You're probably right," he murmurs, eyes darker in the illumination of the pathway. "We'll have enough fun without it."

"Oh yeah?" I taunt. "Can you promise that?"

"I can't believe you'd doubt me, Stella." He *tsks* and dips his head, his lips finding my jaw, nipping at my skin in punishment. "You already know I can make you feel good."

I absolutely do, and a shiver runs down my spine at the memory of him touching me at the strip club. "I'm going to need you to prove it to me again."

"Gladly, sweetheart."

I let out a squeal of surprise when he tosses me over his shoulder, his hand gripping my ass to keep me from falling off. "What are you *doing*?"

"You're too slow in those heels," he says. "And I'm done wasting time. I want to fuck my wife."

He's a liar—I'm a champion in heels—but I'll let him have this excuse to touch me. Besides, time's ticking. We're only a couple of hours away from midnight—a few more from sunrise. When dawn comes, this is all over. I want to get my fill before then.

So I slap his ass in reply and grin as his laugh mixes with the sound of gently lapping waves on the beach.

Soon we're back at the bungalow. Thomas easily holds on to me as he unlocks the door and then kicks it shut when we're in. He doesn't ask which bedroom I want to go to, moving straight to his.

"I've been imagining you in this bed since the day we got here," he says as he carefully lowers me to the mattress. "I've thought about it every night. And every morning I've woken up with my hand around my cock, wishing you were there."

My breath catches as he pulls back, standing at the foot of the bed to stare down at me, like I really am a fantasy come to life.

"Am I living up to expectations?" I ask when I find my voice.

"You're better than anything I could have come up with."

I gaze at him, a work of art backlit by moonlight. "You're not so bad yourself."

His lips quirk, amused, but it doesn't take away from the intensity in his eyes.

"Take off your dress," he instructs. We're done with the small talk.

Heat floods through me and pools at my core. My instinct is to banter with him, to dare him to do it himself, but his tone has me sitting up and reaching behind me to grab the zipper. It's a smooth slide down, my fingers stopping at the small of my back. I let the material fall down to my waist, then push up onto my knees so I can wiggle it past my hips. When it's over my thighs, I lower myself again and slip it the rest of the way off. Thomas is kind enough to pluck it from the bed and place it on top of the dresser.

"So considerate," I muse from where I'm lounging on my elbows, the line of my body and lace lingerie on full display.

"Bra next," he says, ignoring my quip.

I comply, his deep voice and the breeze of the air-conditioning pebbling my nipples. Before he can reach to take the bra from me, I toss it to the floor. My own little act of defiance. I go for another when I hook my thumbs under the sides of my under-wear before he gives me the order to do it, dragging them slowly down my legs. It ends with me kicking them off the bed as well. And then I'm bare for him.

"You're such a brat." His eyes rove my body, drinking in every inch. "And you're fucking beautiful."

I bask in his admiration, chest lifted, knees parted so he can see exactly what's waiting for him. I'm soaked and aching, ready for this. I need him to satiate this craving so I can finally think clearly again without him being on the edges of all my thoughts.

"I'm better up close," I say, opening my legs a little wider.

The invitation is there, and I expect him to come to me. But instead, he starts to unbutton his shirt, taunting me back. Each move is unhurried and deliberate, and while I would love for him to pick up the pace, I'm enjoying the show. It doesn't matter that I've seen him in nothing but swim trunks all week— this is different. This is just for me.

His pecs and abs are perfectly defined. It's the body of an athlete, long and lean, honed over hours in the gym. It's the dedication that I respect more than anything. He's a man committed to his craft, determined to do what he can to be the best.

And I get to reap the benefits, so really, I'd say I'm the winner here.

When his shirt is off and has joined my underwear on the floor, he grips me behind my knees and yanks me down to him at the edge of the bed. I gasp, hands flying out to find purchase in the sheets as he kneels in front of my spread legs. My prince is officially gone. My rogue is back.

"Thomas," I exhale, moving to sit up, but he puts a hand between my breasts to push me back down. When he hooks my thighs over his shoulders, my mouth snaps shut, protests going up in smoke.

"You're right," he murmurs, stubble brushing against my skin. "Much better up close."

He bands an arm across the tops of my thighs, keeping my hips pinned as he bites and licks and sucks his way down to where I want him most. He takes his sweet damn time, savoring each taste and forcing me to tolerate the torture. Right when I think his mouth is going to give me relief from the building pressure, he switches to the other side and restarts his slow journey until I've found the edge once more.

I'm begging and swearing by the time he makes his way to the crease of my thigh for the second time. I'm whining, dripping for him, wound so tight that the second he *really* touches me, I'll combust instantaneously.

"You know, I'm glad we waited to do this," he says, breath ghosting over my slick skin. "I know you so much better now. What you like. What makes you tick. Better than being strangers with no concept of each other."

"I bet you would have done just fine back then," I pant, daring to lift a trembling hand to run my fingers through his soft hair. A desperate part of me considers pushing his face down between my thighs, but the way he's looking up at me, eyes full of worship, has me stroking his cheek instead. Damn this man. And damn everything he's made me feel.

"Is this still what you want, Stella?" he asks, as if he can sense the way I've softened for him. "One night?"

Right now, if he offered more, I would take it. But this is a heady reminder of our agreement. He's set the rules this time and I'm determined to respect them, just like he's done for me over all the weeks past.

"Yes," I breathe out, sweeping my thumb over his cheekbone. "I want this."

He turns his head to press a kiss to my wrist—and then his mouth drops to where I've wanted it all along.

The first swipe of his tongue has me nearly levitating off the bed, my hands back to clutching at his hair. "Oh *fuck*."

I'd be embarrassed by my moaned exclamation if I didn't feel the vibration of his own sound of pleasure against my clit. My heels dig into his muscular back as he tastes me over and over and over again, and I wish he didn't have me pinned so I could lift my hips and grind against his face. Even still, I writhe as he slips a finger into me, then another, crooking up to press on the spot that makes me clench around him. It's so good that I can't do much else but babble *yes* and *do it again* as he drives me to the brink.

I'm overheated and coming undone. It won't be long before I'm fully unraveled, and when it happens, it's with his name on my lips and a burst of light behind my eyes. I swear my soul has left my body, hovering somewhere above me as I spin my way back down.

Minutes or hours could have passed by the time I hear him murmur, "Sometimes I can't believe you're real." The sensation of him pressing featherlight kisses against my thighs finally returns me to my body. "How can someone be so perfect?"

This orgasm already has me fighting not to confess that I'm obsessed with him, and the last thing I need is more praise. I bite my cheek to keep from admitting something I can't take back—from myself or from him.

"I'm not real," I say, gently pushing him back so I can sit up. My head is still swimming, dangerous things threatening to leave my lips. "I'm a figment of your imagination."

I stop breathing when he lifts his wet fingers to his lips. "Then you're the best-tasting hallucination I've ever had."

"High praise." The words nearly come out as a moan. But I need more of him and I need it now. "Come here. Let me touch you."

I place my hands on his shoulders, then let them drag down his chest as he climbs to his feet. He tenses as my fingers dip between the hard planes of his abs, breaths stuttering when I reach the waistband of his pants. I pop the top button and make quick work of the zipper before slipping my fingers past the elastic of his boxer briefs, excited to feel the weight of him, wanting to know what my prize is.

When my palm wraps around his thick erection, I falter, my confidence drying up like a puddle in the desert sun. I've known since the night at the strip club he was packing something impressive, but fucking hell, he's easily bigger than anyone I've ever been with.

"*That*," I say, daring myself to run my hand up and down him, feeling every inch, "is a human rights violation."

A shiver rolls through him, but he still manages to tease, "Come on, sweetheart. I know you can take it."

I don't know about that, but I'm no quitter, so I'll certainly try.

But before I can do anything else, he pulls away from my hand and then moves to the dresser again, opening the top drawer. "Maybe it was presumptuous of me," he says, pulling out a foil packet from a box, "but I did bring condoms this time."

"*Very* presumptuous," I reply, sliding back on the bed. His heavy gaze tracks every move I make. "Also, is this a good time to tell you I have an IUD?"

Thomas freezes for a moment before stalking back over, tossing the condom to the bedside table as he climbs on top of me. His knees and forearms press into the mattress, and his thighs push mine open wide, the fabric of his undone pants brushing against my most sensitive skin. "Are you telling me we could have done this back in Vegas? That we could have avoided our condom run turned wedding?"

I scoff, pressing my hands to his chest. "Um, no. You were a stranger then, and I certainly do not fuck strangers without one."

"And now?"

"You're my husband." I brush my nose against his, not tempted to add *fake* to that sentence. "Whose health records I saw lying around in the office from your postseason exam and who I know hasn't been with anyone else in months."

"I could have been out shagging people," he mumbles, eyes dipping to my mouth. "You don't know."

"Oh, I think I do." I tilt my chin and kiss him gently, letting it linger. "You've been too busy thinking about me to want anyone else."

I mean it as a taunt, but these are my own feelings for him coming to light. How could I have looked at another man when he was right in front of me? Why would I even bother? Who else could possibly match up?

"Guilty as charged," he says with no hint of shame or regret. "I haven't thought about anyone else since the moment I saw you."

My heart twists. This is turning into a dangerous game. We keep pushing the limit, letting true feelings show in flashes and split seconds, then covering them up with searing touches and sharp humor. I should drop the act and let it all out. But I can't. I can't let this be anything more than we said it would be.

"Wish I could say the same," I murmur, breathless and unserious, needing to lift us out of these depths. "I can't stop thinking about Ed Sheeran."

A burst of laughter escapes him as he pushes off of me to stand. "Please, not my nemesis."

I grin along. "The heart wants what it wants."

And right now, my heart only wants the man in front of me.

It's a terrible realization, one I have to come to terms with some other time, because Thomas is taking off his pants and his boxer briefs, and I have to press my lips together to keep my mouth from hanging open in awe.

"It's impolite to stare," he chides, giving himself a long stroke.

I swallow hard. "Show-off."

"Only for you."

He's back on the bed before I can blink, planting his hands on either side of my shoulders as he leans in, pushing me down until my back hits the mattress. He kisses the hollow of my throat as if to praise me for complying. It's shockingly tender, but the nip he gives my skin next is anything but. I scoff at the move, though it's weak as he kisses down my body. His tongue swirls around one nipple, then the other, just enough for a taste of each, before coming back up to my lips.

"You ready?" he asks against them. The question is too quiet, too serious.

I nod and shift to turn over onto my stomach, not sure I can look him in the eyes for this, but he stops me with his hand on my hip and a shake of his head.

"No. I want to see you." His mouth drops to mine for a kiss, deep and lingering, and I'm panting when he pulls away. "I want to watch you come."

I spread my thighs wide, inviting him between them, savoring the way his hips press me open. Still, it's been so long since I've done this with anyone that I freeze for a second as I take him in above me. But the second I meet his eyes and find him staring back, checking once again that I'm okay with this, I relax into the sheets and reach for him.

The groan he lets out as I drag my hand up and down his length has me grinning in satisfaction, though it's quickly wiped away when his mouth crashes down to mine again. My grip loosens as our tongues brush, leaving his cock to slide through my folds, rubbing against my clit, my hips bucking as I chase the sensation.

Our kiss breaks when he drags his lips across my cheek to my ear. "This still what you want, Stella?"

"Yes," I gasp, wanting—*needing*—this. "*Please.*"

I can feel his smile even if I can't see it. I'd be mad at myself for begging if I weren't so desperate to get some relief.

He brushes my hand out of the way, gripping and guiding himself through my wetness. "Such a gracious girl," he murmurs. "I'll give you what you want."

The head of his cock nudges at my entrance and I clutch his shoulders, desperate to pull him closer, pull him all the way in. I'm impatient, breathing hard, and yet I press back into the mattress when he finally sinks into me. The stretch is both intoxicating and excruciating, and the moan that escapes me is lewd, bouncing off the walls and settling into the sheets with us.

"Fuck, you're so tight," he groans into my neck. "You've got to relax, sweetheart."

"You're not the one with *that* inside them," I gasp as he eases back out, only to give me a little more with the next rock of his hips. "Oh my *God.*"

He stills for a beat, giving me a chance to adjust to his size. "What did I tell you before?" he prompts, though it's more of a demand, expecting an answer.

"That I can take it," I whine.

"That's right. Now relax and let me fuck you the way you deserve."

He's left no room for argument, so I force myself to do so muscle by muscle until the pinch of pain subsides, shifting into something sharply pleasurable. When I'm ready for more, I dig my nails into his shoulders and lift my hips, drawing him farther into me. Moans mingle in the air as he strokes deeper, giving me a little more each time until we're joined completely. It takes a few more seconds of learning, but then we're moving with each other, setting a rhythm that's just right.

"That's it." His voice is lust-roughened, hardly more than a deep rasp. "Good girl."

I'm obsessed with this version of him, the one whispering in my ear how good I'm taking him. The one stroking so deep that he's hitting my G-spot each time. The one biting and sucking at my neck, ensuring that I'm marked.

"Harder," I plead.

"You must not want to be able to walk tomorrow," he says, but the next harsh snap of his hips is enough of an answer. "I can make that happen."

When he pushes one of my knees up to my chest I cry out at the new angle, back arching off the mattress. "*Yes*, like that." My hips tilt up to meet him, writhing, and I'm so full that I already know I'm going to feel empty when he pulls out again. "*Fuck*, Thomas."

Hearing his name uttered like a prayer makes him lean in to taste it on my lips. He bites at them, hard enough that I shudder and tighten around him involuntarily. It earns me another groan that compels me do it again, on purpose this time. But I don't get to gloat for long, because his hand slips between our bodies, thumb rubbing against my clit.

"If you're going to do that," he says in my ear, a breathless note to his teasing, "you might as well come."

I'm already trembling, the pressure building low and hot, threatening to spill over at any second. But I'm holding back, not wanting to give him the satisfaction, though I can't keep the orgasm from crashing over me for much longer. Especially not when he whispers, "Come all over my cock, Stella. Let me feel you let go."

I'm exploding in ecstasy, pulsing around him, head thrown back as my legs shake. My body is somehow weightless and endlessly heavy at the same time, dragged by a current yet floating across the waves. I'd cry out, but the air has been ripped from my lungs, and I'm left gasping as I finally reach the other side, the world slowly coming back into focus.

He's still moving—slow, steady, watching every expression that flits across my face. There's a quiet fierceness to him now that wasn't there before. I'm so wrecked that I can't do anything but cup his jaw with shaking hands, hoping he can see that I want him to keep going, even though I'm tender and sensitive. I want him to feel the same release, to fall off the same cliff.

He picks up the pace again, and there's less control to his strokes than there was before. The hand between us comes to grab my wrists, pinning them both above my head as he buries his face in my neck. There's not a single inch of us that isn't touching as I hook my ankles at the small of his back. The friction is so acute that I don't know how neither of us is on fire.

This may be about him, but there's a heaviness growing in me once more, building and building with each thrust. My body fills and blooms with heat until I'm tensing around him again. This time I'm so loud that there's no way our neighbors can't hear me.

The sound is enough to push him over the edge. His hips stutter a few times before he settles deep, body tensing as his cock pulses, spilling into me. When his grip relaxes enough on my wrists for me to slip them out, I run my hands through his hair, over his shoulders, and down his back, his skin slick with sweat. I want to touch every inch of him, want to burn it all into my memory so I never forget a single thing about this moment.

My chest heaves as I try to catch my breath, and when he

presses his palm over my racing heart, I want to tell him everything that lives inside it.

"Too much?" he asks, a breathless whisper against my skin.

My throat is tight. I'm being choked by a rush of emotion,
all the ones I'm not allowed to feel. "Just enough," I answer.

He kisses me again before rolling to the side and climbing
out of bed, heading for the bathroom. I press my hand to my
chest where his just was, trying to convince my heart to slow—
and to push him back out of it.

Thomas steps back into the room with a damp washcloth in
his hand and sits on the edge of the bed. He then presses my
knees apart and runs the warm cloth gently over my inner
thighs. It's so considerate and so *him* that I could cry.

"I'm not done with you, by the way," he murmurs after he's
finished. "I'm just giving you a chance to recover before we go
again."

I spare a glance at the clock, relaxing when I see it's still a
half hour until midnight. We have time. *We have time.*

"So nice of you," I call to his back as he returns the washcloth to the bathroom, and I admire his ass in the process. "But
it's not going to take me long."

His chuckle precedes him back into the bedroom, and it
wraps around me just before he does. I don't resist when he
hauls me against him, my thigh hooked over his hips, my head
resting on his chest. It's too intimate, and it almost cracks me
right open.

"You know," he muses. "Now that we've officially consum-
mated the marriage, we can't get an annulment."

I snicker and bury my face in his shoulder. "You do know
that's not how it works, right?"

"Hush," he says warmly. "Let me pretend I get to keep you."

I'm smiling before I can stop it, and the words I shouldn't

confess come with it. "I'm already yours, Thomas. No need to pretend."

My face immediately goes hot, mortification creeping up my neck. Worst of all, I can't think of a joke to follow it up with, something to make him think I'm just teasing. Instead, I dip my head so he can't see my expression and press a kiss to the space where his shoulder meets his neck, praying he won't take me seriously. That he'll brush it off and remember what this is—a one-time thing.

Blessedly, his chest vibrates underneath me as he laughs softly. "That's right. Even got the papers to prove it."

I nearly slump in relief, pressing another kiss to his neck in silent thanks. "Mm-hmm. That's right."

We lapse into an easy silence after that, his fingers drifting up and down my spine. My anxiety slips away bit by bit with each stroke. I don't realize I've been nearly lulled to sleep until his phone starts incessantly buzzing on the floor, still tucked into the pocket of his pants.

"Don't answer that," I mumble against his shoulder, but he's already rolling away.

Without him pressed against me, the cold reminder sets in that I've let myself get too attached. I've already discovered that this night won't do what I wanted it to, because there's no such thing as getting Thomas out of my system. My feelings haven't suddenly disappeared or become easier to manage. If anything, I've sunk deeper. I'm starting to drown.

I need to lock down my heart now or else I'll never get it back. If I don't, and if he breaks it . . . I know it will be the end of me. I can't risk disappearing into another man. I can't risk him turning out to be like Étienne.

He groans when he sees the name on the screen, then tosses me an apologetic look. "It's Maeve. I really should get this."

I want to tell him to ignore it, that *we* need to talk, but what good would talking do? We already have an agreement. We both just need to follow it and maybe—God, *maybe*—everything will turn out okay.

I motion for him to answer.

He winks before sitting on the edge of the bed with his back to me, taking the call in hushed tones. My eyes drift closed, and I'm vaguely listening, but it's his loud "Are you serious?" a few seconds later that has me paying attention.

Thomas mumbles a few more things before he hangs up. Still, a handful of beats pass before he turns to me again.

"What is it?" I dare to ask, but I already know our night together is over before he answers.

I already know that we're over.

"It's Lorenzo," he says in disbelief. "He's ready to meet."

# CHAPTER 29

THOMAS

Lorenzo Castellucci is just a kid.

If someone had said that about me when I was twenty-one, I wouldn't have taken it well. I was grown enough to have a Super License, a place in Formula 1, and more money than I knew what to do with. How could anyone consider me a child?

I understand it now, because I'm staring at someone who had the exact same privileges I did five years ago and had no idea what the universe could throw at him. He knows now, though. All too well.

The rehabilitation center is just barely on the Italian side of the border with Switzerland, tucked into the foothills in a quiet compound. I passed through at least three security checkpoints to get to Lorenzo's room, and there's a man dressed in black lingering outside the door, waiting to escort me back to the lobby when I'm done. There will be no wandering, not in a place where a private room costs nearly €100,000 a month.

But considering Lorenzo is standing—yes, *standing*—in front of me, the care must be nothing short of miraculous.

His hands grip a walker, tight enough that his pale knuckles are nearly white. My shock is certainly written across my face, because the first thing he says is, "Don't believe everything you hear about me."

I won't anymore, considering the last and latest reporting was that he was paralyzed from the waist down as a result of the crash. Maybe that was the prognosis for a time, until surgeons could carefully take pressure off his spinal cord and repair the surrounding damage. They must have succeeded at it if the sight in front of me is any indication.

I spent the sixteen-hour journey here wondering what version of Lorenzo I'd find, interspliced with gut-wrenching guilt for having to leave Stella the way I did. But I wouldn't be in Italy if it hadn't been for her machinations, combined with her literally pushing me out of bed to get here before Lorenzo changed his mind about wanting to see me.

"Come in." Lorenzo nods toward the two high-backed chairs by the wide window, overlooking the snowy landscape. "Have a seat."

I hesitate, waiting for him to turn and step in the direction of the sitting area first. His movements are slow and measured, supported by the walker, but he's managing it fine. He's walking on his own.

I want to ask if he's in any pain or if he needs help, and yet my mouth stays closed, not daring to accidentally say the wrong thing. I try not to stare when I do finally sit and wait for him to do the same. The lump of bandages underneath his T-shirt hints at a recent surgery, and the wince I see cross his face tells me his recovery hasn't been easy. This is a journey he's not far into, even four months after the crash that landed him here.

"Thank you for seeing me," I say once he's settled into his seat.

Lorenzo leans back, relaxing into the cushions, and quietly assesses me. "Thanks for cutting your holiday short to come here." Again, my surprise must show, because Lorenzo gives a weak snort. "You really think there aren't photos of you and your wife out on the beach? Paparazzi don't rest. You know this."

I do. It explains the high security here, and that in turn explains why we've seen neither hide nor hair of Lorenzo in months. He's stayed locked down to keep it that way. His circle must be small and loyal since nothing has leaked.

Somehow, I'm being let in.

"How is your wife, anyway?" Lorenzo asks, head cocking to the side. The motion makes him look even younger, dark curls sweeping across his forehead like a boy who refused to let his mother cut his hair. "Still strange that you even have one."

His Italian accent and inherent charm make the insult almost sound like a compliment. "I know it was surprising to a lot of people," I admit. "But she's good. Things are . . . really good."

Things might be better if we'd gotten a chance to speak before I had to jump on a plane. Her urging for me to go is why I didn't waste any time, and I try not to read into it too much. Did she push because she wanted me away from her? Or did she push because she knew how much I wanted—*needed*—this sit-down to happen?

I don't know. But I do know that the second I touch down in London, she and I are going to have a conversation about where our relationship is headed.

I thought one night together would be enough to break the tension. To make me want to back off from pursuing her. Extinguish the flame that's been steadily burning in my chest.

But I'm slowly realizing that one night with Stella could never be enough. I was a fool to think it might be. And more of a fool to even suggest it.

Lorenzo stares me down for a moment longer, unreadable. "I know you didn't come here for small talk," he eventually says.

"No, I didn't." I take a breath. "I mostly wanted to see how you're doing."

"Oh, is that all?" he drawls, the insult clear this time.

"It's the most important." There's no sense in being anything but up-front with him. "But I also wanted to ask a favor of you."

He's quiet, but he's not waiting for me to go on. His gaze trails to the window, jaw working, probably debating if he's made a mistake inviting me here.

"I already know what you want." His eyes drag back over and there's a resignation in their depths. An anger too, but I don't get the impression it's directed at me. "I'm sitting down for a major interview soon to clear the air. Make my amends—and do it publicly. People need to stop blaming you for something that was my fault."

My brow dips, but he shakes his head, staving off my questions.

"You shouldn't have said what you did," he starts, "but I shouldn't have given you a reason to say it."

I blink and let the words settle in. It's a huge admission—huge growth. Six months ago, he was laughing after he nearly killed me. Then he threw my apology for the leaked video rant back in my face, telling the media that if I was a better driver, I wouldn't have found myself in the barriers at the first sign of a little racing.

To hear him take responsibility for this is unexpected but not unwelcome. I just hate that it's the result of so much pain.

"I have to make up for what I did." He pauses, wetting his lips, and for a moment he looks so young and lost that I want to put a hand on his shoulder. But then he lifts his chin and it's gone; he's back to being the haughty contender to the throne. "Don't expect too much, though. Some people are going to hate you forever, even if I tell them not to."

I blow out a breath and nod, accepting that. That's a fact of life when you're in the public eye. But it's better when you don't give everyone a valid reason for it.

"Your teammate really fucked you with that one," Lorenzo finishes, shooting me a pitying look. "It didn't have to be like this."

I nearly nod again but freeze when the words register. "I'm sorry, what?"

The pity quickly shifts to confusion. "Did you not know?" He waits for me to shake my head before explaining, "Arlo Wood leaked the video." He says it like this is common knowledge. "Filmed it too."

"No, that's not—" I cut short, letting out a nervous laugh. "That can't be true."

Not just that, but it doesn't make *sense*. Why would Arlo jeopardize my career like that? We've been fine together as teammates for the past two years—not the best of friends and definitely still fierce competitors, but we've always worked well enough together. We've gotten along. So why would he not only do this to me but take the risk himself? What would he gain?

"Are you sure it wasn't our reserve driver?" I suggest, because that's someone with motive. "Finley Clarke?"

Lorenzo shakes his head. "It was Arlo."

The room is spinning, shifting on its axis as I try to piece it all together. But no matter what I try to force into place, none of it fits.

"You really didn't know," Lorenzo murmurs. "I thought it would have gotten back to you by now."

"Gotten back to me?" I repeat incredulously. "How did *you* even find out?"

His lips twist into a wry smile. "I may not love being the son of a world champion, but people tend to tell me more because of it. They think they're impressing me, trying to be my friend. Arlo practically bragged about what he did."

As much as I don't want to believe that . . . I do. Arlo loves to show off, loves to impress anyone he can, especially anyone he views as more impressive than him. And with him and Lorenzo coming in from F2 so close together, maybe he thought there was some sort of camaraderie there, something that Lorenzo is telling me never existed.

But speaking of camaraderie, maybe Finley didn't have his hand directly in this, but he could have had Arlo do this on his behalf. They were teammates before, after all, and with Finley desperate to get into F1, there's a chance this was a joint effort to push me out. Still, the blame lies at Arlo's feet.

Whatever it is, and whatever reason he had for doing this to me, the damage is done. If he did it to get me out of McMorris, he may still succeed, even with Lorenzo's attempt to help.

"*Fuck*," I exhale.

Lorenzo tosses me a vaguely sympathetic glance. "I'm sure next season is going to be interesting with you two."

I scoff a laugh. That's an understatement. I don't know how I'm going to look Arlo in the eye after this, let alone resist the urge to throttle him when we're back at the factory for preseason work.

"I'm almost disappointed I won't get to witness it."

The world stops spinning again at the reminder that there is no next season for Lorenzo. He may be up and able to walk, but that doesn't mean he can jump back into a car like nothing happened. I don't know enough about his injury or recovery to know if he even *could* race again. But that isn't the question I want to ask.

"If you could," I hedge, "would you want to race again?"

Lorenzo only takes a second to think. "No."

"No? Really?"

"It's a fucking cliché," he says, "but it was never my dream. It was my father's. He wanted me to carry on the legacy. He . . . expected it."

Lorenzo's behavior makes more sense now in a way I never thought it would. I can't imagine the pressure of being expected to live up to a four-time world champion's legacy, to bear the weight of the Castellucci name.

"I'm glad to have that off my shoulders," Lorenzo finishes, and while I don't doubt that in the slightest, the way he glances away makes me wonder if it's the whole truth. "Anyway. Reid will let you know when the interview's coming out."

The dismissal is clear. I hesitate for only a beat before pushing myself out of the chair. Lorenzo stays seated, his walker between us, but his eyes follow me up.

"Thanks for meeting with me." I consider offering a hand for him to shake but think better of it. We don't have that kind of relationship, that kind of understanding, and I doubt we ever will. "Let me know if there's anything I can do for you. And I'm still sorry for what I said. You didn't deserve that."

His smile barely lifts the corners of his mouth. Not a show of amusement, but acceptance. "You weren't wrong, though, were you?"

"Not about all of it," I concede, meeting and holding his gaze. "But enough of it."

There's a waver of something in his expression, a returned hint of that childlike vulnerability. It's crushing to see, and even after it's wiped away, it twists my stomach into knots.

I can only hope that whatever comes next for him is better than what's already come to pass.

▚▚▚▚▚

Stella's in the kitchen when I let myself into the house.

I have zero concept of time right now, but the hazy sun tells me it's morning, and my phone says it's just past eight a.m. on a Wednesday. With how jet-lagged I am, you'd never think I'd traveled before, let alone believe I flew across the world on a weekly basis.

It's like I'm walking into a dream when I step into the kitchen. Stella is bent over in front of the oven, wearing the apron she got me for Christmas. When she straightens, there's a muffin tray clutched in one of her mitted hands and a wide smile on her face. If someone had told me that coming home to my wife was going to be like this, I might have gotten accidentally married sooner.

"I hope you like blueberry muffins," she says, which isn't exactly the first line I'd want her to say if this was actually a dream, but I'll take it. "Thought you might want something special for your homecoming." She places the tray on the counter and pulls off the oven mitt, her engagement ring glimmering under the lights. "Sorry it's not spotted dick, but I simply don't have the moral constitution to make anything with a name that terrible."

The laugh that leaves me feels as natural as breathing, all because it's Stella who inspired it.

"You're forgiven," I tell her. "This is everything I could have wanted."

The only thing I needed was her presence. To see her here is more than enough.

"How did it go?" she asks as she pops the steaming muffins out of the tin one by one. The question is casual enough, but I can sense how anxious she is to know.

I pull out a stool at the island and sit. "It went as well as it could. I got to apologize, and Lorenzo did the same. He's doing an interview soon and said he's going to make it clear that he doesn't hold a grudge against me. Don't know if it's going to do much for my reputation, but I'm glad we got to sit down."

Some of the worry in her expression seeps away. "That's really good. And how's he doing, recovery-wise?"

"Better than I expected. He was up and walking. Certainly won't be driving an F1 car anytime soon, but it didn't sound like he wanted to stage a comeback anyway. He's done with racing."

"Wow." Stella wipes her hands across her apron before slowly untying it, like she's trying to wrap her mind around that. "Big choice to make, injury or not."

It is, and I spent plenty of time on the flight home contemplating my own desires to stay on the grid. Especially with the other bomb Lorenzo dropped.

"I learned something else interesting too," I say, and Stella raises her eyebrows, curious. "It was Arlo who leaked the video of me."

Her hands drop heavily to her sides, eyes wide. "Your teammate?"

"That's the one."

The apron is off and over her head. "That's it, I'm gonna kill that smarmy little shit."

Trying not to smile too widely, I hold up a hand to stop her as she marches around to my side of the island. "I appreciate your desire to defend my honor. But that's not necessary."

"Why? Do you have something planned for him? Have you already told the team?"

"No, and I'm not going to." At the way she rears back, I explain. "He'll get what's coming to him eventually. And who knows, maybe Lorenzo will say something. Best thing I can do is keep my nose out of it."

Stella doesn't look pleased, but nods nonetheless. "I guess the last thing you need is your wife going off on him," she grumbles.

A thrill goes through me at her mention of being my wife. The fact that she's said it and has welcomed me home so warmly, even if she hasn't tried to hug or kiss or touch me yet, means more than she knows. Maybe she wants me to be the one to initiate something, to see she's not the only one who's glad to be reunited.

I reach out and grab her by the waist, tugging her toward me until she's standing between my knees. With me sitting and her barefoot, we're exactly eye to eye, and I get to see every inch of the face that I've been desperate for the whole time we've been apart.

"I missed you," I tell her.

Stella smirks and puts her hands on my chest, but there's something distant in her eyes. "It was only three days."

"Three days too many. I didn't want to leave in the first place."

I didn't want to leave her in that bed, naked and satiated, looking like an absolute dream. I didn't want to give up our one night together. But what got me out the door was the hope that we could pick it back up—that we could turn it into something that would last longer.

"That's sweet," she says, but she doesn't return the sentiment. When she glances away for a brief moment, I'm hit with the feeling this isn't about to go the way I wanted.

"Can we talk?" I ask quickly, before she tries to escape. "About us?"

She's quiet as she holds my gaze, unblinking, a war happening behind her eyes that I can just barely see. And then she says, "I don't think there's anything to talk about."

I don't let her go, but my grip loosens. How can she say we don't have anything to talk about when we have a million things we need to settle?

"Come on." I scoff, trying to read her face for any sign that she's messing with me. But I see nothing. "We can't leave things like we did. We didn't—" *We didn't get closure. We didn't say where we're going from here. We didn't give ourselves a chance to explore all the things that should come next.* "We didn't even have a conversation."

"We didn't need to," she says gently, but it feels more like she's stomping me into the ground. "We'd already set the parameters of what was going to happen. Talking would have complicated things."

And not talking will make it *easy*? Can't she see that doesn't make any sense?

"We had our one night, Thomas." The pat she gives my chest is meant to soothe. To show me there are no hard feelings. Instead, it's like driving a chisel into the crack that's formed in my heart, splitting it down the center. "Let's leave it there."

"Fine." I don't mean to say that. I don't want to. I want to demand she hear me out. "I understand."

I get a tight smile in reply, the distance in her eyes growing. She's so far away that even when she leans in to kiss my cheek, I don't feel it.

"I've got to get going," she announces when she straightens. My hands fall away from her when she steps back and I wonder if that's the last time I'll touch her in private. "We're closing on the new Stella Margaux's location today. I can't *wait* for this store to be open."

She's acting like everything is perfectly normal, as if she hasn't stripped my world of the color and sound and light she's brought into it. I want to be happy for her, to be the supportive partner she deserves, but I can't bring myself to do more than stare and nod.

"See you later, yeah?" she says over her shoulder as she heads for the door.

She's gone before I can answer. But truth be told, I don't think she was ever here. The Stella I know isn't the one I just spoke to. This one was unfamiliar—the stranger I woke up next to in Vegas months ago. This isn't the woman who said she was mine.

And she's made it clear she never will be.

# CHAPTER 30

STELLA

Breaking your own heart is a hell of a drug.

I've been pushing, pushing, pushing for the past month to stop myself from thinking about the reopened hole in my chest. The wound is worse this time, aching and oozing, threatening to poison me. But as long as I keep going, as long as the adrenaline never wears off, I'll survive it.

Throwing myself into work was the easy thing to do. With the new store set to open by spring, the never-ending to-do list has kept me busy and given me a reason to avoid Thomas. I knew I was going to have to do it the second he kissed me goodbye in the Maldives and said we'd talk when we got home. If I didn't, it was going to be game over for me—I was going to fall in love with him.

I was going to lose myself again.

I've escaped that fate by a hair. Then again, maybe I haven't, if this hollowness in my stomach is anything to go by. I felt this way when Étienne left, but not so acutely. I'm blaming the fact that I never fully healed from the first go-round, and this second fracture on top of everything has compounded it all. It's no wonder every part of me feels wrong.

Dancing around Thomas has been torture, but it's the only way to survive this. Gone are our easy connection and budding friendship. In their place are stilted conversation and overpoliteness. We feel more like strangers now than we did the night we met.

Maybe if he hadn't left to see Lorenzo, if I'd told him to let the boy wait on us, things would be different. But I knew he had to go. That conversation was more important than anything he and I could have said to each other. And I knew we couldn't renege on the deal we made to go back to following the rules, or else I never would have been able to pull myself back out of the warmth of being with him.

So I watched him walk away and let everything come crashing down.

Now we're less than two weeks out from a wedding I'm not sure I want to have and I can barely look my husband in the eye. That won't be good when we're standing in front of the hundreds of people Thomas's mother invited, including my entire family, who already think I got married for the wrong reason. Who's going to believe we're madly in love when we haven't said much more than *hey* and *see you later* in weeks?

It's going to be a disaster. I've started dodging Janelle's and Mika's calls just to avoid having to talk about the wedding and my feelings about it, let alone my feelings for Thomas. I don't want to dig into it and face the possibility that I completely fucked up by putting distance between us. But what else was I supposed to do? Stick around and fall into the messiest situation possible? Let my heart guide me instead of my head?

Absolutely not. I did that once and it got me left at the altar. I'm not risking it again.

I may be avoiding my best friends, but when Amara texts me as I'm about to leave for my latest walk-through of the new Stella Margaux's and asks what I'm up to today, I don't hesitate to send her the address and tell her to meet me there.

We've talked about as much as Thomas and I have, which is to say not much at all. She, Joshua, and I all flew back to the UK together from the Maldives, but we've only exchanged a few texts here and there since, usually just holiday photos and memes we thought the others might find funny. Her reaching out feels like something I shouldn't ignore.

"This place is *gorgeous*," Amara gushes as she turns around the space, neck craned to take in the nearly finished mural on the ceiling. "How do you manage to make all your stores look like a dreamscape?"

"I hire people with more creativity in their pinkie finger than I have in my entire body," I reveal. "I tell them my ideas, and they bring them to life."

All of the Stella Margaux's locations have a similar vibe with their soft pastel decor, bespoke art reminiscent of Renaissance portraits, and pastry display cases where the sweets look like they're floating on little clouds. I want anyone who steps inside to feel transported to somewhere magical and dreamy, maybe even a little otherworldly.

"Smart woman," Amara commends as she lowers her chin to look over at me. "Thomas told me you've been working on the summer menu. Said he missed being your taste tester now that you've been working here instead of at home."

I try not to wince at his name and the heavy-handed hints she's dropping. I knew he'd come up in conversation eventually, but I hoped it would take slightly longer than this.

"Just finalized the menu, actually," I say, choosing to ignore the mention of him. "I'll send you home with some samples. There's this key lime pie one that I know you're going to love."

"Thomas said his favorite was the blood orange and vanilla cream one."

This time, the comment comes with a pointed look as she says his name. I can't believe I had the nerve to think she reached out just to be friendly, because that's not what this is. This is a fact-finding mission. And as much as I hate it, I respect it. I'd do the same for my friends.

I sigh and drop onto a plush powder-blue settee pushed against a wall. "We're going to have to talk about him, aren't we?"

Amara sits next to me, fingers playfully flicking my knee to get me to make room for her. "We wouldn't have to if you talked to him yourself. But it sounds like you're set on avoiding him."

"I'm not," I protest, even though we both know it's a blatant lie. "I'm just busy, as you can see. This has been taking up all of my time."

"So busy that you can't say more than a few words to your *husband*?"

I scrunch my nose, hating that she knows all of this, but she's one of Thomas's best friends. Of course he would have told her. If I weren't avoiding the judgment of my own friends, I would have told them too.

"We don't really have anything to talk about," I say weakly. "We're a strictly platonic married couple who live in the same house and have separate lives."

"You're a terrible liar, babe. Try again."

Groaning, I let my head fall back against the wall. "Okay, fine. Thomas told you about our last night in the Maldives, right?" I wait until she nods, and my face goes hot at the idea of her knowing anything about my sex life, but I'm certain Thomas wouldn't share any explicit details. "Well, we agreed beforehand that it was going to be a one-and-done situation, then we'd go back to following our rules. Which is exactly what we did."

Amara assesses me, dark eyes narrowed. "And is that what you wanted?"

"It's what we agreed to."

"That's not what I asked."

I bristle, tempted to tell her to mind her business. "Does it matter?"

Her furrowed brow softens. "Of course it matters. How do you feel about him?"

No one is forcing me to answer her questions, let alone tell the truth. But I've been pushing it down for too long and I'm ready to burst. "I like him, Amara," I whisper. "A lot."

She reaches over to squeeze my arm, pleased with my answer, though I know her blossoming smile is going to be wiped away when I finish my thought.

"But I can't risk this all going wrong." I swallow past the growing lump in my throat. "This marriage being anything but fake can't happen."

She draws her hand back like she's been burned. "You're taking the piss."

"I'm completely serious," I declare. "I had my entire life turned upside down by the last man I was with. If that happened again, especially so soon after, I don't think I—" I cut off, choked by impending tears that I have to fight to keep back. "I don't know if I'd ever be okay again. And I'm . . . scared. Fucking terrified, actually."

Amara sighs softly before gathering her knees up to her chest and wrapping her arms around them. She's silent, letting my confession settle in the room with us, and stares up at the mural again. I join her in it, grateful for the distraction as I admire the amount of work the artist has put into it. They aren't finished yet, but the work they've done thus far is magnificent—a beautiful work in progress.

"I know we're still learning about each other," Amara finally murmurs, "but I get the distinct feeling that you're trying so hard to be perfect. And I get it, because I used to feel the same way—that I had to be perfect in order to prove to people that I was worthy of their time or attention or admiration. To make someone want me."

I stay quiet as her lips twist into a wry smile, her words resonating deep within me, as much as I hate it.

"But, Stella," she says, "none of that matters. The people who want you in their lives will take you as you are. They'll cherish you the way you deserve. Anyone who doesn't was never meant to be in or stay in your life."

I blink a few times as I look back at her, clearing away the tears. "And you think Thomas wants me in his life like that?"

She snorts, breaking some of the tension. "Of course he does. The man's obsessed with you."

I suppose I can trust her opinion on the situation since she and Thomas are close. Then again, that only raises my suspicions about this meeting. "Did he ask you to come talk to me?"

This time, Amara throws her head back and cackles for so long that I almost start to worry. Finally, she wipes under her eyes and shoots me a *girl, you've got to be kidding* look. "If he knew I was here, he would kill me. And by kill me, I mean he'd write a very strongly worded letter and forgive me after a day, but to him, that's aggressive."

I wince a little because, yep, that's exactly the man I've fallen for. But I don't think I'd want him any other way.

"If he's so obsessed with me, then why hasn't he tried to fight me on this?" I press. "If he didn't like me insisting we go back to following the rules—which *he* suggested, by the way— he could have made it known."

Amara stares at me like I'm oblivious. "It's because he *respects* you. That's the kind of man he is. When you say no, he takes it as a final answer because he understands it's a complete sentence. But if you give him a single reason to fight, he will."

"And you don't think I have?"

She considers her reply. "I think you've been so firm in your stance that he believes he doesn't have a way to change your mind. That even if he told you how he felt, you wouldn't factor it into your decision."

My shoulders lift to my ears. "Okay, *ouch*. I'm not *that* bad."

But . . . maybe I am. There's a chance I've made him feel unheard and unappreciated. I mean, the rules were all my doing, after all, with little input from him. And maybe I've been bad at returning the moments of kindness and tenderness he's always shown me. If you add it up, I come off as the bad guy here—all because I was trying to protect myself from more heartbreak.

Lot of good that did ya, considering how shitty you feel now!

"Never said you were," Amara says breezily. "But you need to tell him how you feel so you can at least be on the same page."

It only takes a few seconds of reflection for me to groan and scrub at my forehead. "You're right."

"Of course I am." She lifts her chin, smiling smugly. "I've known him since he was an annoying little shit in short trousers. And if you're honest with him, I can guarantee your life will get so much easier."

I'm sure she's right about that too. "Okay." I exhale, steeling myself for what needs to be done. "I'll talk to him soon."

She arches an eyebrow suggestively. "Tonight, maybe?"

I slap her leg with the back of my hand before standing. "Don't rush me. Besides, he's busy with all the preseason stuff and I don't want to distract him. I've got to find the right moment, make it special." More importantly, make *him* feel special.

"God, you're even more of a romantic than he is," she groans. "You're a match made in soppy heaven."

Despite the dig, I smile to myself, turning away to hide it from her.

It's time for me to follow rule number one. It's time to stop keeping secrets.

⬛⬛⬛⬛⬛⬛

Another week passes before my chickenshit self feels even slightly prepared to speak to Thomas.

Between my cowardice and Thomas's suddenly hectic schedule, squeezing in an organic moment with each other has been impossible. He spends more time at McMorris HQ than he does at home, preparing for the start of the season at the end of the month. My work schedule isn't much better either. Add in dress fittings and a thousand other wedding details that Iris springs on me, and it's amazing I have a chance to sleep.

Tonight, though, Thomas will finally be home. And we're going to talk.

In the kitchen, I catch myself glancing at the clock nearly every minute, willing it to move along. Dinner's in the oven and Thomas's favorite dessert is steaming on the stove, because yes, I was also finally brave enough to try making spotted dick. I even spent an hour in Waitrose finding all the right ingredients. Honestly, who cooks with suet and currants in this day and age?

I'm about to start on the vanilla custard when my phone

buzzes in the pocket of my apron. Or really, Thomas's apron. I know I threatened several times to toss the Union Jack–emblazoned thing in the bin, but it's grown on me. Just like he has.

My heart skips a giddy beat at the idea that it might be him texting me. In another bold move, I messaged him this morning to say I'd be cooking tonight and that I wanted to chat over dinner if he was free. I got a reply less than thirty seconds later declaring he'd be home by eight.

It's seven now, so maybe this is a heads-up message that he's on his way. If it is, I appreciate the consideration so that I can time all of this perfectly. I want everything to be just right.

But when I pull my phone out, it's not Thomas's name that lights up my screen.

ÉTIENNE: Can we talk?

# CHAPTER 31

THOMAS

I'm going to be late for dinner with Stella and it's all Arlo fucking Wood's fault.

Normally I might respect his dedication to making sure he's informed about the car's specifications for the season, but tonight I want to slap my hand over his mouth and tell him to quit it with the questions. Preseason testing in Bahrain isn't for another two and a half weeks, anyway. We'll have plenty of time to talk to the engineers before then; none of this has to be discussed tonight.

I'd still want to shut him up even if I didn't have Stella waiting for me, mostly because his voice is the most irritating sound in the world now. It's my newfound distaste for him shining through, I know that, but he's like a little yapping dog who won't be quiet.

"We'll wrap things up there," our team principal announces, and I'm out of my seat at the conference table in a flash.

I don't care if anyone thinks I'm rude for striding out with only a half-assed wave goodbye, but I've got somewhere to be and a long-awaited conversation to have. Stella's text earlier nearly stopped my heart. To say it was unexpected would be the understatement of the century, considering she's been so hell-bent on avoiding me lately.

Part of me was tempted to ignore her like she's been ignoring me. It was petty and childish, not my usual style, but that's what her rejection has brought out in me—this unsettled desire to make her feel as uncomfortable as I do.

It was unfair, though, so I messaged back once the feeling passed to say I'd be there by eight. I've been staying at the team apartments for the past few days, and these evening meetings aren't a problem when all I have to do is drive ten minutes down the road, but if I want to make it back to London before eight, I should have left thirty minutes ago. It's seven now, so barring any traffic and a few—okay, *a lot* of—broken speed limits, I might get there just a few minutes late.

"Thomas! Wait a second."

I roll my eyes but don't slow at Arlo's shout. "I've got somewhere to be, Wood."

His sprinted footsteps follow, and soon he's falling in next to me. "My, my. Old man's got plans?"

"Something like that," I answer, eyes straight ahead as I push through the doors that lead to the lobby.

"Color me shocked." I catch his grin from the corner of my eye, but it flickers a little when I don't return it. "You all right? You're an odd one on a good day, but you've been off all week."

I wonder why you think so, you backstabbing gobshite. "Absolutely fine."

He eyes me cautiously, not buying it, but I don't care what he thinks at this point. My goal is to survive the season together, and if his role in leaking the video comes to light, he'll get his answer as to why I've been distant.

"Everything good at home?" he asks, like he's figured out

the reason for my discontent. "Trouble in paradise already? Didn't you two *just* get married?"

I don't reply. Partially because he's right but mostly because it's none of his business and I don't owe him a damn thing.

"Wait, don't you have another wedding coming up?" Arlo pushes. "I swear my assistant said she got an invitation. I can't believe you didn't hand deliver it to me. I'm hurt, Tommy boy. I thought we were closer than that."

My fists itch to wipe away his smug smile. How did I ever think anything about him was endearing? He's pure smarm hidden behind the facade of a racing driver.

But it's his mention of the wedding that has something deep in my chest twisting. The date looms ever closer. Five days from now, Stella and I will be publicly declaring our commitment to each other. Or at least I hope we will be, because with the way things have been, I don't know if she's going to want to go through with it. Hell, I don't know if she wants to even be in the same *room* as me.

Although, she wouldn't have asked me to come home for dinner if she couldn't stand me, would she? I don't know exactly what she wants to talk about, but I'm taking it as a good sign that she's cooking. A woman who hated me certainly wouldn't do *that* . . . unless she's trying to let me down gently before declaring she has no intention to meet me at the altar.

Fuck, I need to be home.

"Have a good night, Arlo," I say as I step out into the frigid February night.

Thankfully, he gets the hint and falls back, letting me walk off to the car park alone. I wouldn't be surprised if he had his suspicions about me discovering his misdeeds, but I won't say anything directly. He can sit and stew.

And sitting and stewing is all I can do as I make the torturous drive back to London, though with each passing mile, I swear my heart beats a little faster at the prospect of seeing Stella. I've *missed* her. I've missed our conversations and our easy mornings and our dinners together. I know it's not all down to her specifically avoiding me—our individual careers really have taken over—but I've been miserable without her infectious humor and unwavering belief in me. I want it back. I *need* it back. I need *her*.

By the time I park and push through the front door, I'm near to bursting with everything I want to confess. It all starts with us going through with the wedding and letting it mark a fresh start for us. I want it to be the beginning of us being together as a real couple, not as two people playing pretend. Yes, we have a legally binding contract tying us together in matrimony, but we could ignore that and just . . . date. Learn about each other organically, with no pretenses and no acts to put on. It would just be us. No secrets, no lies, and nothing to fake.

"Stella?" I call out as I set down my bags, but I get no answer.

I stride toward the kitchen, figuring she might be in there, considering she was supposed to be cooking. But the space is empty, save for the full dinner spread on the counter—including dessert. It's all finished and yet there's no sign of her.

Worry creeps across my shoulders, tightening the muscles, but I force myself to shake it out. She's probably just upstairs getting changed. Maybe she accidentally spilled something on herself and needed to put on something new.

I take the stairs two at a time, calling out for her again, figuring she didn't hear me. When I don't get an answer this time, the worry slowly morphs into dread.

It momentarily stops when I throw open the door to her bedroom and spot her, but it rushes in when I see the suitcase she's kneeling next to.

Her head snaps up when the doorknob bangs against the wall, and I hate the panic that lights her eyes at the sound.

"I'm sorry," I rush to say, but I stop in my tracks as I stare down at her. "What are you—what are you doing?"

Her gaze drops to the suitcase, hands returning to the task of putting items inside. "I have to go back to DC."

The words are quiet, nearly a whisper, and they're not said with her usual confidence. It's . . . weak. *She* seems weak, like something has beaten the life out of her and has left a husk in its wake. It's a Stella I've never seen before.

"You—*what?*" I shake my head, not understanding. Is this what she wanted to talk to me about? I know I'm late, but not so much that I thought she would give up on waiting and start on whatever plan she'd hatched without explaining it to me. "What's going on?"

She doesn't lift her head, just keeps steadily working, folding a blouse and pressing it into the case. "There are some things at home I need to handle."

Home. The last times she's said that, she's meant here, this house. Our home. But other than that throwing me, it's the timing of it all.

"Our wedding is in five days," I point out.

"I know."

I wait for more, staring slack-jawed. "Okay . . ." I try not to scoff, but the derisive sound escapes anyway. "Will you be back by then?" Or is this her way of telling me it's over? That we're completely done?

Finally, Stella looks up. The misery in her gaze catches me out, my breath hitching.

"I don't know," she whispers.

"You don't *know*?" I repeat incredulously. I let my hands fling out to the sides, silently begging for her to let me in and tell me what the hell is going on. "Stella, what—"

"I have some business to take care of," she interrupts, louder this time, but it's still not her voice.

I don't recognize this woman on her knees. And I don't know what could have turned her into—

No. I do know. If she's going back to DC and it's got her this wrecked, then it's because of her ex. Something has happened between her invitation this morning and her packing now, and I'm certain it has to do with him. The only times I've ever seen her close up and curl in on herself like this were when something I did reminded her of him or whenever I pressed too hard to share about her past.

The fight floods out of me, and then I'm on the floor in front of her, kneeling on the other side of her suitcase and trying to get her to look at me. "Sweetheart, talk to me. Please." I reach across to where her hand rests on a pile of clothes, covering it with mine. "Is everything all right?"

She's quiet again, fighting for the right answer. It's a long moment before she quietly settles on "It will be."

But that's not good enough. I need more. I need a real explanation of what Étienne has said or done to have her crawling back to America mere days before we're supposed to prove to everyone that our love is real.

"Stella," I hedge, squeezing her fingers, trying to keep her with me even though she's already slipping away. "You don't have to—"

"I need to go, Thomas, okay?" she cuts in. The words are rushed and her eyes are pleading. "Will you let me do this? Please?"

I want to tell her no, that I won't let her do that because I don't want her to leave our home to go see another man. But that's not my place. Stella doesn't need my permission for anything. She never has and never will. I'm certain she knows it too, so the fact that she's even asking in this roundabout way instead of just jerking her hand away and storming off is a punch straight in the heart.

She's said it without having to say the actual words—she feels for me as deeply as I feel for her. This is all reciprocal, a closed loop of respect and adoration, the start of something that's steadily building to more.

And now I have to watch her walk away from me.

I'm slow to draw back. Slow to stand. Slow to step to the side and watch her zip the suitcase closed. She keeps her head down, eyes low, lips pressed together hard. I'll break if I see a single tear slip down her cheek, but I doubt she'll allow herself that show of emotion.

I have to let her go and pray she'll come back. She's said her piece and I won't debate her on what she thinks she needs, because I get the feeling that what she needs is closure. Still, I can't stop from grabbing the handle of her suitcase when she moves for the door, stopping her.

"Do you want me to come with you?" I ask quietly.

It's a last-ditch effort to stay with her. Even if we can't stay here, we can stay together.

Her hesitation buoys my heart, but it's quick to drown under a crashing wave when she shakes her head and stares at the floor.

"I have to do this on my own." It's a firm statement. "And you have work to focus on. I won't ever ask you to put me before it."

I do have work, but I'd toss it all aside if she said she needed me. "I can—"

"Thomas." She shakes her head, telling me not to finish that sentence. "I need to go."

Please don't say goodbye. Please don't tell me this is the end.

I get my wish when she leaves without another word.

# CHAPTER 32

STELLA

"I can't believe you're actually going to talk to him."

I shoot Mika a look, not appreciating her bringing this up again when we've already been over it. I'm fresh off an eight-hour flight from London and back in the kitchen of my Alexandria house, drinking the last bottle of wine I left behind while my best friend berates me. It's not where I want to be, but even with her questioning my life choices, I was glad to find her waiting on my doorstep when I got here.

"I already told you," I say as patiently as I can. "Étienne and I have a lot of stuff to settle, including what the hell we're going to do with this house." I motion to the vast, empty monstrosity we're sitting in that I can't wait to get rid of.

Mika's still not having it. "Which could have been handled by lawyers without you having to leave behind your sexy-ass husband who's *clearly* in love with you, especially since he didn't want you to leave in the first place." She narrows her eyes, searching my face, and I wish I hadn't confessed the whole story to her. "Why are you doing this to yourself?"

It's a great question, because why *am* I doing this to myself? I could have ignored Étienne's message asking if we could talk, along with the five others that came in after it, all of them begging me to give him a chance to explain himself. I know now, though, that he wasn't begging. All those words, the *Please let me explain*, the *I want to do this face-to-face*, the *I just want you to come home so we can handle this* were demands wrapped in the shroud of a plea.

But last night, I couldn't see through it. The sick adrenaline rush of his name appearing on my phone after months of silence was enough to steal my breath, my confidence, and my good sense. Suddenly, I was back in the church, alone and grieving. The woman who waited for hours and days and weeks for him to return had finally—*finally*—gotten what she wanted. He'd come back.

It was what I wanted all along . . . except I didn't feel the relief or the comfort or the joy I thought I would. It was only soul-crushing guilt and self-loathing for staying with him for so long. And worse, for still feeling tied to him, for feeling like I had some fucking *obligation*. I couldn't say no to him asking me to come back, because our tie hasn't quite been severed yet.

The person Thomas saw on the floor of my bedroom was the worst version of myself, hollowed out by the man who I couldn't bring myself to tell him I was going to see. Yet Thomas knew without me even having to say Étienne's name, as if my reaction was answer enough.

I didn't want him to witness me that way, so broken and bloodied. But every horrible thing I'd felt in the aftermath of Étienne leaving was back full-force, and it made me hurt Thomas in a way I wish I could take back. I can't, though, so all I can do now is make sure it wasn't in vain.

Étienne made a mistake by leaving me on our wedding day. But he's about to discover that he's made an even bigger one by inviting me back into his life.

"Seriously," Mika pushes on. "What reason do you even have to speak to him again?"

"Because I need closure, Mika," I snap, setting my wine-glass down a little too hard. "Because I want to look into his eyes and finally ask him why he left me like that. I want this over with for good."

She's silent for a beat, head cocked to the side. "What if you don't like the answer?"

"There's no answer he could give me that I'd like." I take a breath to ease the anger in my chest, both at myself and at him. "But I need to hear it from his mouth so I can close this chapter of my life and move on."

"Move on with Thomas?"

I stay quiet, even though every cell inside of me is scream-ing, *Yes, with Thomas, if he'll have me.* I don't know if he will after the way I left. He may hate me now for all I know.

If you give him a single reason to fight, he will.

Amara's words ring through my head. So far, the only thing I've done is push Thomas away. I haven't given him a reason to fight, but I'm praying I haven't made him want to give up on me. I won't get the answer to that until I'm done here.

"We'll see," I say, sliding off my barstool and extending a hand to help her up. Étienne is supposed to arrive soon, and the last thing I need is for her to be here threatening to fight him, so she needs to mosey her way back home.

"Well, is the wedding still on?" she asks as she takes my hand. She's out of her cast and in a brace for the last bit of heal-ing her leg needs to do, but she's still wobbly on her feet. "You need to let people know if it's not. The whole family is flying out on Thursday."

My throat goes tight, wishing I could give her a definitive answer, but I can't. Not yet. Not until I talk to Étienne. I can't walk down the aisle again, even if it's all pretend, until I face my trauma from the last time I did.

"I'll let you know," I murmur. "Get home safe."

Mika's sigh does little to soothe me, but the tight hug she pulls me into does the trick. "You better tell that man to kiss your beautiful fat ass. And if he tries anything, I'll—"

"Kill him and make it look like an accident," I finish for her, suppressing a smile.

"Damn right." She gives me one last pat on the cheek. "Give ol' Frog Legs hell, baby."

The knock on the front door comes exactly fifteen minutes past the hour.

By Étienne's standards, it's early. But by my own, the ones I should have had when he and I were together, it's too god-damn late. If he had any hopes of this being a productive con-versation, then he's going to have to work harder to make that happen. This is another strike against him.

I'm surprised that my hands don't shake and my palms are dry when I pull the door open to find him on the other side of the threshold. And even when my eyes land on him, I don't feel any of the things I expected to. I feel . . . nothing.

Well, no, that's a lie. I feel the overwhelming urge to drive my fist into his mouth when his trademark smirk tugs up the corner of his full lips. He's an objectively beautiful man, but he has the most punchable face. How did I never notice that?

"Stella," he says, like he's greeting an old friend and not the woman he ran the fuck away from three months ago. "It's so good to see you. You look magnificent."

The effort it takes not to knock him out should earn me an Olympic gold medal, because the audacity of this man is unbelievable. "Come in," I force myself to say as I open the door wider. "We can talk in the living room."

He brushes too close when he steps inside, the musk of his cologne nearly choking me. The scent makes my nose wrinkle, even though I know it's the same one he's worn for years, the one that used to make me want to bury my face in his neck and inhale. Now all it makes me want to do is puke from how heavy and overpowering it is. It's nothing like what Thomas—

Now is not the time to think about him. Get through this first.

There isn't much furniture in the living room, but there's a couch and a chair, and I take the chair to prevent him from trying to sit next to me. Best if he stays at least six feet away; I won't be able to take a decent swing at him from there.

The rage simmering in my stomach is unfamiliar but welcome. I knew there would be some sort of anger, though I thought it might be drowned out by nostalgia and the past love I had for him. The heart's unpredictable, after all, but thankfully my brain seems to be winning out here.

"How have you been?" Étienne asks when we've settled into our seats. His posture is infuriatingly relaxed, legs crossed, an ankle resting on his opposite knee. He isn't wearing socks with his overpriced loafers and there's too much skin showing past the hem of his pants. Ew.

I scoff but hold his gaze. "You've got some nerve asking me that."

He puts his hands up to show he's not about to argue. That's new. His favorite thing to do was argue. I mean, I can give as good as I get, and I think he respected that for a while, but arguing all the time is exhausting. It got to a point where I had to practically tell him *I come in peace* before I started any conversation.

So I can give him the chance to explain himself, lest I be a hypocrite.

"I know," he says, slowly lowering his hands. "And that's my fault."

Is he . . . is he actually taking responsibility for his actions? Color me shocked. My lips part to give him a real answer to his question in recompense, but then he has to go and ruin it all by saying, "Although, you can't be doing too bad considering you're already remarried."

He says it lightly, like it's all a joke, but it slams any good-will that might have been developing out of me.

"Not *remarried*. Simply *married*," I correct sharply. "You know, considering you never went through with our wedding."

That gets him to blow out a breath, eyes dropping to the floor. He looks almost . . . guilty. Like he knows just how badly he's fucked up. But I've yet to hear an apology, so I don't put much stock in it.

"I guess I should explain what happened," he murmurs when he looks back up. His expression is open and earnest and yet I don't believe it for a second. "About why I left."

I just don't want to be with you anymore, Stella.

"You've already told me why," I say, stomach twisting at the memory of his last words to me. "What I want to know is why *then*? Why that moment? Why couldn't you have said something sooner, before we were in a church full of people?"

Why did you have to not only break my heart, but do it so publicly?

"Because I was a coward." It's a straightforward answer, said without blinking, and I grudgingly respect the bluntness. "We both knew something was wrong with our relationship before then, but neither of us wanted to say it. That was the last moment I could."

He's right that our relationship had been on the rocks and that neither of us had said a word about it. But that being the last moment he could have said something? Give me a break. There were better ways to handle it and he knows it.

"But the more I've thought about it, the more I've regretted it," he goes on. "Not just how I left you, but the fact that I did in the first place."

Well, I wasn't expecting *that*. My shock must be written across my face, because he takes that moment to uncross his legs and lean forward. If we were closer, I get the feeling he'd try to sweep me into his arms like the hero from a telenovela.

"I *miss* you, Stella," he says, just above a whisper. "Leaving you was the biggest mistake of my life."

The impact of the words pushes me back in my seat, but I don't actually believe what he's saying. He was out with another woman two weeks after our breakup—he couldn't have missed me or regretted his choices *that* much if he could move on so quickly.

Then again, didn't I do the same? Sure, mine was all in response to his shenanigans, but I still moved on with my life in the form of accidentally marrying Thomas.

Étienne seems to be waiting for me to say something. "I appreciate you saying that," I force out, but truthfully, I'm lost for words.

There's a strong chance he's lying to me, but he could also be telling the truth. I really don't know. And yet . . . it doesn't matter which one it is, because even if I haven't been able to admit it to myself until now, I've been done with this man for a long, long time.

He's not satisfied with my answer, though. The next thing I know, he's on the floor in front of me, down on his knees as he grabs my hands. A surprised "Oh shit, okay, here we go" leaves my lips, but it doesn't deter him any.

"I shouldn't have done it," he declares, gazing up at me like I'm his sun and moon and stars. "I shouldn't have said that to you and I shouldn't have left."

He's talking, but I'm still not hearing the words *I'm sorry*. Instead, I'm getting the dramatic performance of a lifetime.

"We should start over." It's a statement, not a question, as if he expects me to get swept up in his whirlwind. "We can put all of this behind us. It would be a shame to waste all the history we have together, wouldn't it?"

Maybe you should have thought about that before you did what you did, buddy, I want to tell him, but I'm too busy trying not to shudder from secondhand embarrassment. Like, honestly . . . is this man for fucking real? Does he really think this is going to have me crawling back to him, all because we have "history"?

I pull my left hand from his grasp and hold it up so he can see the ring on my finger. "I'm married, Étienne. There's no *starting over* for you and me."

He scoffs, some of the act falling away. "I've heard your marriage isn't real," he says, and there's a hint of a threat in it that I absolutely do not care for. "That you met and got drunkenly married in the same night."

Ding, ding, we have a winner! But just because he's correct in his assumption doesn't mean he knows anything about what's happened between Thomas and me since then.

"Maybe you need to stop listening to rumors," I shoot back, tempted to toe him in the ribs to get him to stand up. "Because my marriage is very much real."

In fact, I have the marriage certificate to prove it, sitting right on the kitchen counter, because Drunk Stella wrote down this address when filling out the license. When I opened it earlier and saw my name printed next to Thomas's, I cried because I missed him. Less than twenty-four hours apart and my ass was bawling.

If the certificate isn't enough to prove that it's real, then what I feel for Thomas is the smoking gun.

"Stella, you barely know the man." Étienne drops his voice, low and persuasive. "Be the smart woman I know you are and come home."

It strikes a chord deep in my chest. I want to go home. Desperately. But this isn't my home anymore. I don't think it was ever more than just a place I lived until I found where I belonged.

My home is in London with a man who knows I prefer gold jewelry. Who holds my hand even when my fingers are freezing. Who outfitted his whole kitchen with my favorite appliances in my favorite color and requested that I make the place a mess. Who let me leave to handle the things haunting me, because he would never stand in my way.

The life I built in DC was a beautiful one—until it all came crashing down. And I don't want to rebuild it on top of the ashes. I want that fresh start Étienne was talking about, just . . . not with him. I want it with Thomas. I want us to begin again as if none of this is fake. No rules or guidelines or mandates to follow. Just us. Together. Whatever that looks like.

"I'm getting to know him," I answer, tugging my other hand away so I can grab my phone. I've got a flight to book. "And I'm going to keep doing it."

Étienne lets out a mocking laugh and sits back on his heels. "You can't be serious."

"I'm a very serious woman, Étienne," I say as gravely as I can, though I'm seconds away from grinning in his face. "You know, you actually did me a huge favor."

His face contorts in confusion. "Excuse me?"

I nod and stand. It's like a thousand tons have lifted from my shoulders. "You left when I couldn't," I explain. "Don't expect me to say thank you, but it's the best thing you've ever done for me."

He makes a sound of offense, like he can't believe I'd ever be grateful that he did what he did. And while I don't love it, and I'll certainly carry the scars for the rest of my life, this really was for the best. He was never the man I was meant to be with. I just hope the one I want will wait a little bit longer for me.

Because I'm coming home.

# CHAPTER 33

THOMAS

As it turns out, it's difficult to have a wedding rehearsal without the bride. It's even worse when you don't know where she is or when she'll be back—if ever.

I've hidden myself away in the attic of the Cotswolds house, avoiding anyone and everyone. Fielding questions as to Stella's whereabouts from my mother and the wedding planners has been a nightmare, because there are only so many ways and times I can say *she'll be here* before people start thinking she isn't going to show. And there's a chance she won't. This could already be over without me even knowing.

Doesn't mean I'm not trying to find out, though. Her phone is either off or dead, because every time I call, it goes straight to voicemail. There's also the worse option, that she's blocked my number, but I'm trying my best to stay positive. Do I have any reason to? No, none at all, minus the fact that I don't think Stella would do that.

I just need an answer, a definitive yes or no. A *yes, we're still going through with this wedding* or a *no, and here are the divorce papers, goodbye!* I can't stand this limbo, but I have no idea how to break free.

In my hand, my phone buzzes with a text from Maeve. Found out Stella's at least in the country, the message reads. I very kindly asked her assistant where she was and I got a copy of her flight itinerary in return. She landed at Heathrow a couple hours ago.

Very kindly in Maeve's book means there were at least three threats of bodily harm, one attempt at blackmail, and a half-assed apology when the information she wanted came through. I might normally scold her for the actions, but the woman gets stuff done. And in this case, she did exactly what I needed.

I reply with my thanks and blow out a breath, my heart lifting ever so slightly out of the despair it's been simmering in. I want to be relieved that Stella's made it back to this side of the pond, but if she has, then where the fuck is she? She *knows* this is happening today—right now—and yet she still isn't here.

A knock on the door has my head snapping up, hope swelling in my chest at the thought it might be Stella. But it deflates like a sad clown's balloon when Figgy pops her head in. Great. Of course she's here. This whole second wedding is happening because of her meddling, so I should have expected it.

"I figured you'd be hiding up here," she says, pushing the door open enough to slip inside.

I appreciate that she's quick to close it behind her and keep my whereabouts private, but I'm in no mood to talk, especially not to her. Still, I grunt and say, "You caught me."

She glances around the space, past the old sofa I'm sitting on and the wooden wardrobes housing various antique clothes and keepsakes. When she realizes I'm alone, her brow scrunches in confusion. "Where's Stella?"

I could lie to her like I have to everyone else, and I probably should, considering the circumstances, but the idea of saying *she'll be here soon* one more time makes me sick.

"I don't know," I say honestly.

But Figgy doesn't seem to understand. "Don't tell me you're hiding from her too," she teases. "Not a good look from the groom, I must say."

"No, that's not—" I cut short and shove a hand through my hair, pulling on the roots. "She's not here, Figgy. Stella's not at the house."

Figgy frowns. "Well, is she on her way?"

Again, all I can say is "I don't know."

The words come out incriminatingly choked. She stares at me for a few seconds, trying to put the pieces together with the clues I've given her. Her frown deepens, but it's the genuine concern written across her face that forces me to look away as my stomach sinks to hell.

"Thomas," she says softly, stepping closer until she's able to crouch down in front of me. "What's going on?"

This is a glimpse of the Figgy I've always known, not the one who's appeared over the past few years as the pressure to land me as a romantic partner grew and grew. It's nice to see her again, and it makes me want to tell her the whole truth, even though this scheme with Stella was to get her off my back. Maybe I've underestimated her empathy and ability to understand the stakes. Deep down, I don't think she actually wants to be with me. She's been pushed toward the idea of me, of what I represent, of the things I could give to her.

Neither of us should be resigned to leading half lives in a loveless marriage, and even if things with Stella fall apart, I still want Figgy to find the person meant for her.

I must be taking too long to answer, because she reaches out and squeezes my knee. "You don't have to tell me," she murmurs. "And for what it's worth . . . I'm sorry."

My eyes lift from the floor to meet her gaze, a little stunned to hear the apology. "What?"

She blows out a breath, but to her credit, she doesn't look away. "I won't pretend I understand what the situation with you and Stella is, but it's clear you really care about her. Love her, even."

I've been telling myself not to use that word because it's too soon. It might scare not just Stella off, but me too. But that's what this is, isn't it? This gut-twisting, heart-aching, bone-deep pull toward her can't be anything else.

"That part, I get," Figgy goes on with a self-deprecating chuckle. "I knew the second you brought her here that my chances of us ever being together were gone. And it hurt, which is why I told your mother my suspicions. She might have planned this whole wedding to test your relationship, but anyone can see the way you look at Stella. There's nothing you need to prove."

She gives my knee one last squeeze before drawing back and standing. Her posture is stiff, like this is hard for her to admit. Despite the differences we've had lately, I'm proud of her.

"I'm sorry for the role I played," she declares. "I would *really* like to have my friend back. Shockingly, no one else will traipse through sheep shit with me just to watch the sunset."

That drags a weak laugh out of me. "I'll still happily do that with you." I sober again, really letting myself look at her for the first time in ages. She's not a bad person and never has been. She's a woman shoved into a role that she followed to the best of her abilities, who now has to figure out how to live without a map guiding her every step. "You're going to find your person, Figgy."

Her smile says she doesn't quite believe me, but she doesn't try to argue. "I'll do my best to stall your mother. And if I see Stella, I'll bring her up."

I nod my thanks before she turns away, leaving without another word. I'll have to step out eventually to explain that the wedding is off on account of the bride ghosting me, but for now, I'll sit and sulk.

I drop my head back against the sofa, eyes sliding shut, wishing this didn't burn me from the inside out. None of this was in my plans, from marrying a stranger to falling for her. I didn't think being without Stella for mere days would reduce me to such a mess, but she's burrowed her way into every aspect of my life.

But I have to face the facts—she isn't coming back.

Before I can convince myself to go downstairs, though, raised voices from outside catch my attention. There's only a small window up here, overlooking the front of the house, too high up for me to peek out of, but the thin pane allows sound to travel in. I can't make out the words, but the voices are both high-pitched and snappy. Probably my mother starting a fight with one of the vendors who isn't willing to put up with her bullshit. It's a sign I should get up and intervene. No one needs to suffer through Iris's control issues.

There must be anvils on my shoulders with how hard it is to stand, and even once I'm on my feet, I can't make them move. The noise outside seems to have stopped, so at least there's no rush to fix that.

I'm about to force myself into walking when the sound of footsteps thudding up the stairs reaches me. No, not thudding, *clicking*. The telltale sound of high heels. Figgy was wearing boots when she came in, and I can't imagine any of the vendors would wear heels while having to traverse the grounds. So unless it's Calais or Geneva or one of their supermodel friends, it must be—

A breathless Stella in all her stilettoed glory bursts into the room.

"Mother*fucker*," she pants.

As she bends over to put her hands on her knees, I stand stock-still, taking her in. Am I . . . Am I hallucinating? I don't think I've reached the level of desperate pining where I would imagine her bent over and breathing hard without me having something to do with it.

I blink a few more times for good measure, but Stella doesn't disappear. "You're here."

She's still breathing hard, hands moving to her hips as she straightens up, but she cracks a smile. "I wasn't going to miss out on a chance to have a party."

I want to laugh, to get out all the stress of the past several days, and yet I'm so shocked that I can't make a sound.

"I would have called," Stella rambles on, "but I wanted to surprise you. Grand gesture, you know? Also, I had to drive myself here from the airport—long story, don't ask—and . . . let's just say I should never be allowed to do that again. But then I got stuck in the worst traffic and I couldn't let anyone know I would be late because my useless American phone decided it didn't want to work, and—" She cuts short, sucking in another breath. "Whatever, it doesn't matter. I just couldn't miss this."

I have so many questions, ranging from the logistics of how she got here to why she came back. My lips part, waiting for the words to come, but all that leaves my mouth is a disbelieving huff.

Some of Stella's humor and frenzied energy drops away at the sound, her dark eyes turning pleading. "Thomas, I'm so sorry."

I want to tell her that she has nothing to apologize for because she's *here*. It seems like there were plenty of things that tried to keep her from me and despite it all, she made it, even sprinting those last few meters to pull it off—her, the woman who hates running.

I don't blame her for leaving and handling what she needed to, because it's led her back to me in the end. I just need confirmation that she plans to stay. Right now, that's all that matters. The rest is already history.

"I wanted to be back sooner," she continues, fingers twisting in front of her stomach. "I tried, but—"

"Did you speak to Étienne?" I interrupt. He's the reason she left; I have to know if that's resolved before I can let myself be too relieved.

Her brow creases in concern, like she's afraid of where I'm going with this. "I did," she answers slowly. "It wasn't a very long conversation. I already knew what I wanted."

Then why did it take you so long to come back?

The question must bleed into the air because she follows up with, "I couldn't get in to see my lawyer until yesterday, but she's handling everything now, including getting our finances separated and the properties sold. I won't be going back anytime soon."

My heart squeezes, praying she means what I think she does. "So . . . everything's sorted?"

She nods. "It is."

For a moment, we simply stare. We've both waited for this chance to be honest with each other, but now that it's here, neither of us quite knows where to start.

But I can't let her walk away again. I need a definitive answer so I don't have to hold back any longer—so I can finally stop keeping the secret of how much I want her in my life.

"I think it's time for you to decide whether this is real or just for show, Stella," I say, because that's what this comes down to, isn't it? Real or fake. Yes or no.

Stay or leave.

The flash in her eyes tells me she recognizes the words from our first night in Vegas. The context was different then, yes, but it still applies now, more so than ever.

And to my immense relief, her answer hasn't changed.

"I want it to be real."

She's in my arms before I know what's happening, and whether it was me who moved first or her, I couldn't say. But none of that matters. I only care that Stella's back where she belongs.

"I missed you," she says against my neck, her breath warm on my skin as she clings to me. "I thought about you every second I was gone."

"I haven't been able to breathe since you left." It's only now that I can inhale deeply, her sweet citrus scent easing the last of the knots in my chest. "I've been waiting for you to come home."

"I wasn't sure if you'd want to see me again."

Horrified, I draw back enough so that she's forced to look up at me. "How could you think that?"

Her dark eyes are anguished. "Because I hurt you and—"

"No, you didn't," I firmly cut her off. "You left because you had to clear a path for us. That didn't hurt me. The idea that you might not come back did, but you're here now."

"You really don't hate me for leaving?" she asks cautiously, but there's a hint of hope in her expression.

"I could never hate you." I tuck her hair behind her ear, fingers lingering on the corner of her jaw. "God, Stella, I'm fucking crazy about you. You must know that, right?"

Finally, the corners of her lips start to flicker up. "I'm starting to get the idea. But . . . maybe you could tell me more?"

There she is—there's my girl. "I'm crazy about your smile," I say, "your laugh, your fucked-up sense of humor. I'm crazy about how you come off so confident, even when you don't feel that way, but just by faking it you have the whole world eating out of the palm of your hand . . . Should I go on?"

She squeezes me tighter, gazing up into my face like she doesn't ever want to look away. "Keep going."

I'll happily oblige. "I'm crazy about how caring and considerate you are. How you've tried so hard to help me, to make my life better in so many big and little ways. How you always make me want to do and be better—to ask for better." Leaning down, I press a kiss to the spot right below her ear. It earns me that little shiver I love, but most importantly, it's a guarantee that she won't miss what I have to say next. "I'm crazy about everything you are, Stella."

She gives a small, contented sigh, melting against my chest. "So . . . does that mean you want this to be real too?"

That drags a laugh out of me. How could this mean anything else? But I'll give her whatever reassurance she wants and needs. I'll do it every single day until it soaks in so deeply that she never doubts it. "Yes, I want this to be real. I want us to give this a real shot."

"Good," she whispers, lips trailing up my neck. "Because I can't imagine my life without you anymore. No one else is you. And you're everything I want. Everything I could have ever dreamed of."

My head spins, blood rushing so hard and fast I can hear my pulse in my ears, spreading joy to every cell of my body. Still, I try to play it as cool as I can. "Then I guess we should go get

married. Again. Really solidify this commitment to a real relationship, you know?"

Stella laughs, and the sound settles around my heart.
"We've gotta stop doing all this stuff out of order," she says.
"So, what, we're getting married so we can . . . date?"

"You have something against dating your husband?" I ask
in mock offense.

She shakes her head, hands lifting to cup my jaw. "I would
love to date my husband. See where it goes."

I lean into her touch. "We don't have to rush into anything.
We can take this as slow as you want."

"I don't want to take it *too* slow," she warns. "We've been
waiting long enough for some things."

I agree, but I'll be taking this at Stella's pace. I'm content to
just be on the ride together.

"You're right," I murmur, eyes dropping to her mouth.
"There are some things we *really* need to do."

She's slowly dragging my face down, and I don't resist. Our
lips are bare centimeters apart when she whispers, "I think we
should start here."

I'm the one who closes the distance this time, our lips meeting sweet and slow. It's the perfect way to seal our promises to
each other. It's the taste of her I've been hungry for in the weeks
we've been strangers. It's everything I need.

And so is she.

CHAPTER 34

STELLA

"Can you believe this is your third wedding but still only your first marriage?"

I glance over at where Mika is lounging on the bed in the bridal suite—which is really just one of the many guest bedrooms in the Maxwell-Browns' manor—and blink as I take that fact in.

"Huh." I have to laugh, because, really, isn't that kind of outrageous? "Hadn't thought about it that way."

Also sprawled on the bed, Janelle smooths out her crimson matron of honor dress as she sits up. She may not have been in the bridal party of my first wedding, but I wasn't going to miss out on having her next to me at this one.

"And no offense to your last two weddings," Janelle says, "but this one is a hell of a lot better."

As much as it pains me to admit, considering I put so much time, effort, and money into my wedding with Étienne, Iris has planned an absolute masterpiece. When I stepped outside earlier to take in the multiple marquees, the overflow of fresh florals, and a glimpse of the Michelin-starred menus—yes, *plural*—I knew it was going to be the event of the season, if not the year.

"Our mother might not be good at much," Geneva drawls from where she's preening in front of the mirror, also wearing a matching crimson bridesmaid dress, "but when it comes to weddings and themed parties, she's the best of the best."

"Just wait until her midsummer fete," Calais adds, and I glance down to where she's kneeling at my feet, adjusting the hem of my flowing gown. "Pure bacchanalia. You'll need a week to recover."

The expectation that I'll be there fills a spot in my chest I didn't realize was hollow. As much as I don't view leaving my life in DC as giving something up, it's a relief knowing I have another life waiting for me here—one with family and friends and a man who worships at my altar. Even my career will be just fine. It's the sweetest of fresh starts, more than I could have asked for.

But the best part is that I *didn't* ask for any of it. There's not a single part of me that would have prayed to meet a pretty-eyed race car driver and marry into his elite, upper-crust British family. In fact, it sounds like a fucking nightmare on paper, and yet here I am, being dressed by one of my sisters-in-law while my mother-in-law wrangles vendors in order to make this the perfect day. I'm so happy that tears burn the backs of my eyes.

"Hey, no crying over inevitable orgies in the garden," Amara snaps at me, darting over so she can dab delicately under my eyes with a tissue. "I'm sorry, but that's just the kind of family you've joined. You know how these old-money people are. Wait until you hear about all the blood sacrifices."

I let out a watery laugh, eyes swinging to the ceiling so I don't ruin my makeup. "I guess I'll have to find a way to cope."

"We'll teach you the proper etiquette," Geneva teases.

"Nothing worse than not knowing the protocol for—" A sharp knock on the door cuts her short.

I glance over, expecting to find one of the wedding coordinators telling me it's time to get the show on the road. But to my surprise, it's Daphne standing in the doorway, lips pursed as she takes in the crowd. When her eyes land on me, some of the tension in her expression fades, though there's still something in her eyes that has me concerned.

She clears her throat. "Stella, can we talk?"

I could absolutely tell her to fuck off. I probably should. Instead, I find myself nodding and waving her in. Maybe it's morbid curiosity, or maybe I want the chance to threaten her not to sell any details of this wedding to the press, but we need to chat.

Daphne waits for everyone else to file out before primly taking a seat on the edge of the bed. Unlike my first wedding, I'm not wearing a massive ballgown, which means I can easily take a seat across from her at the vanity without looking like a fool. I'll probably need one last steaming of the perfectly tailored ivory column dress before I walk down the aisle, but even if I don't get the chance, the wrinkles will be worth it to have this confrontation.

"I didn't even know you were here," I say when Daphne makes no move to speak.

I don't necessarily say it to hurt her—I legitimately had no idea she was on the guest list—but I'm done playing nice with someone who has never played nice with me.

Daphne frowns. "Of course I am. We're family."

Not like you ever act like it.

"I would show up even if you were getting married in the middle of the Amazon," she goes on, probably having seen my doubt. "We've had our differences over the years, but we're still blood, Stella. I'm never going to stop supporting you."

A flash of anger surges through me. "Running to the press with every detail about me being left at the altar was you *supporting* me?"

It's the first time I've flat-out accused her and I wait for her to start spluttering and denying it. But Daphne sighs and lifts her hands in defeat. She's not denying anything.

My God, she really did it, and she doesn't even care that I know.

"I was trying to help you," she says, to which I give a scoff, leaving her to speak a little louder when she continues. "No, seriously, I was. And I *did*."

"Are you kidding me?" I shake my head, disgusted. "Fuck outta here with that. You haven't helped me at all."

"You can believe that all you want. But have you paid any attention to what's going on with Étienne lately?" she demands.

My lips part to retort, but I shut them again when I realize that no, I haven't, actually. At first, I didn't feel strong enough to look into him and his life without me, and once I was, I just didn't care anymore. I have literally no clue what's happening with him.

"Telling the world what an absolute sack of shit he is was the right move," she says firmly. "If it were up to you, you would have swept it all under the rug and let him go on his merry way, right?"

She pauses, giving me enough time to answer, but I keep my jaw clamped shut because she's right and I hate it. I wanted everything to blow over quickly and quietly, even if it meant no consequences for him.

Daphne correctly interprets my silence. "Well, I wasn't about to let him get away with that. Janelle was too sweet to do it, but I won't sit back and watch people I love get played without retribution." She sits up even straighter, leveling me with a hard stare. "I wanted that man ruined. So I told the press about what he did—how he left you in the worst possible way. It was never meant to be a slight against you. *You* didn't do anything wrong. He did. And now he's suffering for it."

It's my turn to frown, confused. "What do you mean he's suffering?"

Her brows knit together the best they can with the beautifully subtle Botox she's had. "You really don't know?" She waits until I shake my head before letting out an exasperated breath. "The man is destroyed."

If she means emotionally, then yeah, I saw that embarrassing shit firsthand. But in any other way? I have no idea what she's talking about.

"Janelle told me he came crawling back to you," Daphne goes on. "Did you ask him why?"

"No, I didn't." Because it didn't matter. I already knew what I wanted, and it wasn't him. I was only there to put the final nail in the coffin of our relationship.

"It's because he's losing money hand over fist and his reputation is shot." She leans forward, making sure I'm not missing a single detail of this. "He came back because he needs you to fix it all. Between how he left you and the fact that *you* were the reason his business stayed successful for so long from riding your coattails, he's cooked. And the fact that he tried to get you to forgive him means he knows it too."

Damn Janelle for telling her my business, and damn Daphne for punching me in the gut like this. Part of me already knew Étienne didn't come back solely because he missed me and couldn't live without me, but I didn't bother to interrogate it.

"He didn't even apologize," I hear myself say. "So he wasn't exactly begging for forgiveness."

Daphne stares open-mouthed at me for a moment. "Wow," she finally mumbles. "Fuck that guy."

"Fuck that guy," I wholeheartedly agree.

We're both silent again, processing, some of our animosity slowly drifting away.

"I'm sorry if what I did hurt you," she says after a few more beats. Despite everything, it's an apology I believe, even if I'm not ready to forgive. "And when I talked to the press after your second wedding—"

"I'm sorry, *what*?" I splutter.

Her face contorts in disbelief once again. "Do you seriously not remember?"

I almost snap that no, I definitely *don't* remember, but then I have to consider all the lies Thomas and I have told about what happened that night, including actually remembering it.

"I was there," she says slowly. "I was your witness, literally signed your marriage license. Were you so drunk that you don't even remember that?"

I'm kicking myself now for not looking closer at our marriage certificate, focusing only on Thomas's and my names together, not bothering to search farther down the page for anyone else listed there.

"Stella," she admonishes. "I can't believe you."

I hold up a hand to stop her incoming tirade of disappointment. "We can save the guilt-tripping for later. How did you end up being the witness at our wedding?"

Daphne looks like she wants to protest more but ends up huffing instead. "I ran into you and Thomas at the pharmacy," she explains. "You were just . . . all over each other." Her lip curls in disgust at the memory. "Gross as that was, I couldn't believe how happy you were. I hadn't seen you light up like that in ages, and the way he was looking at you . . . I'm sorry, Stella, but I can't think of a single time Étienne looked anything other than smug to have landed you. But Thomas was ready to worship the ground you walked on."

My throat tightens. I wish I could remember all of this, but the knowledge that Thomas has viewed me in such a way since the very beginning makes me all the more certain about being together.

"I don't know what led to you two talking about getting married," she says, "but you'd already made your minds up by the time you spotted me. I'm guessing you don't remember making fun of me for buying antacids because—"

"Because you're old and can't eat tomato sauce after nine p.m.," I finish for her, wincing. "It's coming back to me."

She rolls her eyes but thankfully doesn't dwell on it. "Anyway, you practically dragged me with y'all to the chapel, begging me to take photos so you could 'show your future kids,' which were your words exactly, by the way."

Okay, yikes at me getting ahead of myself on about ten thousand levels. "And you didn't try to stop us?"

Daphne barks out a laugh. "As if that was even possible. You were both dead set on doing it, there's no way I could have talked you out of it. And honestly . . ." She blows out a breath, starting to seem a little sheepish about her involvement. "I kind of wanted to see where it went. I wanted you to have something to rub in Étienne's face, to show off that you could move on from him. Something more than just a onetime hookup. That's why when the reporter approached me, I shared all the details. I wanted it to get back to him."

I want to be mad, want to yell at her for all her absolutely ridiculous machinations, but all I can manage to do is put my elbows on my knees and take it all in. She might not have gone about any of this in the right way, and she caused me more trouble than I ever thought possible, but when it really comes down to it all . . . Daphne did me a favor. She's the reason I'm even with Thomas today. Without her meddling, I would have gotten that annulment without a second thought and moved on with my life.

I wouldn't have had the chance to fall in love with my husband.

"Fucking hell," I exhale, resisting the urge to scrub my hands over my face. "So you knew the truth about that night all along? And you just let me lie about it?"

She nods, trying to tamp down a smirk and losing. "It was funny watching you keep trying to dig yourself out of it."

"God, you're such a—" I cut myself short before I say something too mean, then finish with, "Honestly, you're a conniving genius and you deserve a medal for this bullshit."

Daphne doesn't hold back a grin this time as she stands. "I'll settle for a shout-out in your toast at the reception." Her gaze drifts to the grandfather clock in the corner of the room. "Speaking of, it's about that time. You ready to marry this man again?"

That's not even a question in my mind. "Yeah. I am."

"Are you at least sober?"

"Not even a sip of alcohol today," I swear. "Learned my lesson."

"Good." She brushes off the front of her dress, letting the silence hang for a moment as an air of seriousness settles back in. "I'm glad you two found each other. Thomas is exactly who you needed."

I agree. It feels like sheer luck, and I'm glad that whatever force controlling it decided to be on my side. Because—as scary as it is to admit to myself—I've fallen for Thomas. I mean, I literally ran in heels for that man. You can't tell me that's not love.

"Congrats, Stella," Daphne says, softer this time. "Now go get your happily ever after."

▚▚▚▚▚

When Iris told me the wedding would be held on the manor grounds, I didn't think I'd be having another church wedding. But lo and behold, there's an old stone chapel not far from the house, surrounded by lush rolling hills and the best views millions of pounds can buy.

It's barely big enough to hold the hundred people invited to the ceremony, and certainly wouldn't fit the hundred more expected to be at the reception, but it's perfectly rustic, covered in ivy and flowers brought in from greenhouses around the country. It's nothing like the sweepingly modern church I chose for my first wedding, and yet this feels so much more like me.

Outside the chapel, I stand with my mom and dad on the narrow pathway leading down from the house, listening to the happy murmurings of the people already inside. I'm slated to make my entrance in a few minutes, and I'm using these last moments of peace to try to ease my nerves. Then again, I'm not sure how peaceful it's going to be with the way my mother is looking at me and wringing her hands.

We haven't spoken one-on-one yet, even though she's been here since yesterday for the wedding rehearsal and the dinner after. There have been plenty of opportunities, sure, but every time we face each other, the words die out for both of us. *I'm sorry for pushing you away*, I want to tell her. *I couldn't keep facing your disappointment.* But that sentiment won't leave me until I hear what she has to say first. I'm stubborn and I got it from her.

"I need to say something before we go in," she announces.

I try to share a glance with Dad to see if he can give me any hints as to what this is going to be about, but he's pointedly looking away.

"Okay," I exhale as I grip my bouquet tighter. "Go ahead."

Mom purses her lips for a moment, like she's trying to conjure something difficult. But then her expression relaxes and she's reaching out to grip my shoulders, pulling me in so she's all I can see.

"I'm sorry I doubted your feelings for Thomas," she says. "And I'm so, so sorry I made you feel like you couldn't talk to me because of that. I never wanted you to have to choose between him and us."

It's clear who I chose, though, considering this is the first time we've had a real conversation since Thanksgiving. But she's still shown up for one of the biggest days of my life and I'm just happy to have my mom with me.

"It's okay," I tell her, and I mean it. There's no animosity on my end, nothing that will overshadow my connection with Thomas. "I get why you doubted us. But you're here supporting us now and that's all I want."

She frowns a little, probably surprised that I'm letting this go so easily. When her smile lifts again, it's full of both love and relief.

"I hope he makes you happy," she murmurs as she pulls me tightly against her. "That's all I want for you, Stella."

I hug her back and whisper, "No one's ever made me happier."

When I pull back again, the wedding planner is standing off to the side, waving to get my attention. It's finally time.

"You ready?" Dad asks, eyes already shimmering with tears, but if he cries, I'll cry too.

"I'm ready," I reply, and then link my arms through his and mom's.

It's a tight squeeze through the doors of the church and down the aisle, but I barely notice. I'm too focused on Thomas at the altar—on my future in front of me.

We spent last night apart in a show of respect for tradition, and in the dark of my bedroom, I feared all the things that could go wrong today. What if he turned and bolted, just like Étienne? What if he wasn't there when I showed up? What if he stayed but obviously didn't want to be there?

All those concerns are out the window now as he smiles at me, practically bouncing on his toes, looking like he's trying not to run *toward* me. It's reminiscent of how Ron looked at Janelle on their wedding day, the same look I thought I'd never have. How wrong I was.

I try to focus on my parents kissing my cheeks and the wink Janelle shoots me as I hand her my bouquet, but all I want to do is turn to Thomas. When I do, it takes a ridiculous amount of effort not to giggle. God, who has this man turned me into?

As he takes my hands, I can't hide my grin. It mirrors his, wide and bright, and if this alone hasn't convinced everyone here that we're the real deal, then I don't know what will.

"Hi," he whispers to me as the officiant standing beside us loudly launches into his spiel.

"Hi," I whisper back. "If you have any plans to run away, would you mind telling me now? I'd like to be prepared this time."

His teeth sink into his bottom lip to stifle what was sure to be a guffaw. His shoulders still shake, which I'll take as a win.

"No plans to run." His ocean-blue eyes roam over my face like he's cataloging every inch of me and this moment. "Though, if you want to run together, we can."

I subtly shake my head. "I think I'll stick this one out. Don't want to disappoint everyone who showed up, you know?"

"You have to admit—it would give them quite the story to tell."

I'm sure it would, but the only show I want to put on is us looking like two absolute fools obsessed with each other.

"I'm good," I say. "I'm just glad to be here with you."

Thomas's grip on my hands tightens. I'd be fine if he never let go. "I'd follow you to the ends of the earth, if you'd let me."

I might not have a week ago. In fact, I didn't. Now, I'd let him follow me all the way, and I'd do the same in return. From here on, there's no keeping us from each other.

When it comes time to recite our vows—the classic ones, no extra bells and whistles—we do it quickly and efficiently, ready to get to the good part. I'm nearly bursting when the officiant proclaims that the groom may now kiss his bride, and the laugh I've been holding in finally escapes as Thomas sweeps me into his arms.

"I've been waiting for this," he murmurs, and then his lips are on mine.

This is the kiss the prince gives the princess at the end of a PG-rated fairy-tale film to seal their love, the kind where the scenery drops away and it's just the two of them in a haze of golden light, a gentle breeze blowing their hair. It's the kind that makes you close your eyes and let it sweep you off to some faraway place. My knees even go weak. If not for him keeping me upright, I'd be a puddle on the floor. It's perfect.

My eyes flutter open when Thomas pulls back. The rest of the world floods in again with a crescendo of cheers and applause.

"Think they bought it?" he asks, smiling down at me.

Between the kiss and his smile, I'm breathless, though I still manage to say, "Maybe we should do it again, just in case."

"Brilliant idea."

This kiss is less of the fairy-tale variety and more *save it for behind closed doors*. But I don't care who's watching—let them see how much I want this man. Let them see the electricity that arcs between us. Let them see how we've chosen each other.

Staying married all those months ago was a gamble with no guarantee of paying off. But now?

I'm pretty sure we hit the jackpot.

# CHAPTER 35

THOMAS

Three weeks later, March
Bahrain

This could very well be my last season as a McMorris F1 driver. In fact, I'm betting on it.

Stella sits next to me in the sports car on our way to the Sakhir circuit for the first race of the season. She's scrolling through her phone and rapidly replying to emails, keeping her empire afloat from afar. Honestly, she was right when she said she was more impressive than me, because I would probably lose my mind if I had to do all the things she does on a daily basis. I'll take driving around a track any day.

"You almost done?" I ask her as I turn onto a cordoned-off side street that leads to the car park. "We're nearly there."

"Just a couple more," she murmurs, eyes still glued to her phone. "Then I promise I'll be a good WAG for you."

I snicker, but I have no doubt I'll have all her focus when it's time. We've been inseparable since our second wedding, and she didn't hesitate when I asked if she wanted to come along to Bahrain. I warned her that I'd barely have any free time between preseason testing and the first race weekend, that the dates we'd started to go on every few days would have to stop for a while, but she wasn't deterred.

"I only married you so I could get more passport stamps," she teased before pressing a kiss to my jaw. "Ends of the earth, remember?"

It may not have officially been part of our vows, but it's become our promise to each other. Whenever we can, we'll put in the effort to be in the same place. Certainly makes this whole dating thing easier—which, I have to say, is going well so far. Who knew getting married first would lead to having the world's greatest girlfriend?

As I turn into the car park and pull into my designated spot, the beginning of an adrenaline rush starts to seep into my veins. In a few hours, after more team meetings and last-minute adjustments to the car, I'll be on the grid watching the lights go out. To say I've missed this is an understatement, and to think I ever considered giving it up . . . it's nearly unbelievable now. I'm determined to fight harder than ever. I'm going to prove I belong in this elite level of motorsport—and prove my worth to any team that might want me in the future.

While preseason testing last week was promising for Mc-Morris, Specter Energy and Mascort are still topping the time-tables, with D'Ambrosi not far behind. I slotted myself into a respectable P5 in qualifying yesterday, though with the talent ahead of me—including both of the returned champions, Zaid and Axel, and our newest championship winner, Reid—I don't stand much of a chance of finishing higher than that, especially if Dev defends hard in P4.

I won't waste my energy being disappointed by the result. More than anything, I'm pleased to see Zaid and Axel back and competing just as fiercely as they did before the crash. That seems to be the only thing that's the same about them both, though. Some of Axel's rough edges have softened during his time away, which I will never complain about. The guy needed to take his off-track aggression down a few notches.

Zaid, on the other hand, seems to have hardened. Not that he was ever light and bright and constantly smiling—like Dev, for example—but he always had a compelling warmth that drew people to him. I won't say it's completely gone, just . . . faded. There's a wall up that I don't remember ever seeing from my idol. But with Dev as his teammate, I don't know how much longer that wall will be allowed to last.

"You're not going to believe this."

Stella's voice draws me out of my thoughts. She lifts her phone, leaving me staring at Edith's name in the *From* line of a forwarded email sent to me and Stella. Reading on, I spot that it originated from A.P. Maxwell International—and it's something that certainly should *not* have been distributed to anyone outside of the organization.

The subject line makes me freeze.

[CONFIDENTIAL] PRESS RELEASE:
A.P. Maxwell International to Continue
Partnership with McMorris F1 Team.

My eyes go wide, then snap to Stella. "You're kidding."

"Keep reading," she urges.

Stunned, I return my attention to the screen, forcing myself to focus on the next line.

Pulled some strings, Edith wrote. The partnership is contingent upon you staying at the team, but the money will go wherever you go. Andrew won't fuck with this again. Expect an apology from him soon.

I reread the note again to make sure I'm not hallucinating.

"Holy shit," I breathe out. "What strings do you think she pulled?"

Stella shakes her head. "I don't want to ask and I don't want to know."

That's the best way to go about it, because it undoubtedly involved some sort of blackmail. My eldest sister is, as Stella would say, not to be trifled with. But never in my wildest dreams did I think Edith would do something like this for me. Then again, maybe she had a few nudges along the way.

I eye my wife. "Did you have something to do with this?"

She flips her hair over her shoulder, haughty and confident, my favorite version of her. "I will neither confirm nor deny." She pauses, hand dropping to her lap again. "Okay, I'm denying, because I deserve zero credit for this. But it may have come up in conversation when I talked to Edith last week about how pissed she was at your dad's choice to make Andrew CEO—"

"Wait, wait, wait. You talked to *Edith*?" I cut in. "Willingly?"

"We're both savvy businesswomen, Thomas, keep up." She winks to take the edge off. "But yeah, we've chatted. She's blunt, for sure, but she's pretty great once you get to know her."

I want to ask more, but motion from outside the windows distracts me, a reminder that we need to head into the paddock. My mind whirls in pure disbelief from both developments as I slip out of the car and move around to Stella's side to open her door.

In no world did I think my wife and sister would team up to make this happen for me, or that they'd even be able to make a difference. I'm sure the interview with Lorenzo that came out a few days ago helped their cause, since he essentially cleared me of all wrongdoing and revealed to the world it was Arlo who filmed and posted the video of my tirade. My teammate has been conspicuously absent from several team meetings since, and part of me won't be surprised if he's swapped out for another driver by summer break at the latest. And knowing that McMorris will get to keep the sponsorship money as long as they keep me . . . Well, it's obvious who their priority is, isn't it?

Stella slides her hand into mine when she's out of the car, lacing our fingers together and giving them a squeeze. "You'll be able to stay at McMorris if you want," she says quietly as we start toward the paddock entrance, ignoring the camera flashes as we go. "Keep performing as well as you have been and they won't even consider anyone else for your seat."

I dazedly wave to the people shouting my name from behind the barriers and nearly drop my pass as I tap it against the turnstile sensors. I thought I'd be happier about this news, maybe even overjoyed to know I have a guaranteed seat next year, and yet . . . I don't know how I feel. I really don't. And it's all because my goals have changed.

I want more than just a safe seat at an upper-midfield team. I want more than a podium or two all season, if I'm lucky. I want more than what McMorris can give me.

I don't realize I haven't spoken until Stella lifts my hand and kisses my knuckles, dragging me back into the moment.

"Yeah, I could stay," I say, but even the open answer doesn't feel quite right.

As we move through the crowds and past the team hospitality motorhomes, Stella asks, "Do you *want* to?"

There it is, laid bare. Do I want to stay at McMorris? Could I continue to push down my wants and dreams for that seat? This spark in my chest now reminds me of how badly I wanted a place here back when I was karting. Simply being in F1 was the dream, yes, but it was always more than that. It is for everyone before our expectations are tempered by age and experience.

But why temper them now when I could strive for more?

"I want to be a championship contender," I say loud enough for only us to hear. This time, the words feel right. "I don't know if I'll ever get that at McMorris."

Stella nods in understanding. "Where would you want to go instead?"

We're about to walk past the Specter Energy motorhome, the navy and neon yellow sign glinting under the floodlights like a beacon. There's a tug in my chest, like something seeding itself there. It's a big reach, but . . .

"I have a few ideas."

꧅꧅꧅

As predicted, I finish where I started.

It's not bad by any means and it's a great start to the season. It's even more satisfying because Arlo finished P11, barely a second behind the driver in front of him, and scored no points. I know I should want better for the team, but honestly, it serves him right.

Stella's waiting for me in the garage, a green headset around her neck and a wide smile on her face. Her arms drape across my shoulders when I approach, her amusement turning sly, but there's no missing the pride in her brown eyes.

"God, you're good," she says as I wrap my arms around her waist. "You almost had Dev at the start. Forced him to think quick to cut you off. It was *very* sexy of you."

If only I could have held him off, but alas. This season's Mascort is once again a feat of engineering that only Specter

Energy can contend with. It won't stop me from trying again next time, though.

"Still a loser," I remind her, but I'm grinning back. How could I ever feel like anything less than a prizewinner when I have her? "Have you decided if you're coming to Jeddah for the next race?"

The last time I asked a few days ago, she said she would double-check her calendar and let me know. Even though we did away with most of her rules, we still keep numbers one and two in place—no secrets, and no one's career is more important than the other's. I'd never ask her to stay away for longer than she could reasonably manage, and I'll always make an effort to be by her side when she needs me to stand there and look pretty.

Stella heaves a sigh, as if she can't believe I'd ask that. "What did I say about passport stamps, Thomas?"

"That they're the only reason you married me," I dutifully reply.

"That's right." I get a pat on the chest, quickly followed by one of her intoxicating laughs. "And that's a stamp I'm missing, so I'm coming with you. Hope you didn't think you could get rid of me that easily."

There's not a moment that could pass where I wouldn't want her with me. We may have decided to take this at our own pace, to not jump into anything too fast or too soon, but what-ever this is—whether you want to call it dating or marriage or simply just a committed relationship—it's amazing.

"I'd never be so presumptuous," I say, and even to my own ears it sounds intolerably posh.

Still, it earns me another laugh. "Good. Because I'm not going anywhere." She pauses. "Well, until you go to Australia, then I'm dipping. That flight's just too long."

"Whatever happened to the ends of the earth?" I tease.

Stella leans in, brushing her lips across mine and stealing my breath. "I'm drawing a new map."

I'd watch her draw one as long as it still led me to her. She could rewrite history too if she promised to still let it pair us together.

"And I'll be waiting for you," she goes on. "At home."

Home. Our house in London where her trophies now sit next to mine. Where the kitchen is full of appliances, both old and new, in her favorite shade of café au lait. Where I hope to always return to the scent of sweet citrus lingering in the air.

"Will you also be waiting with dessert?" I tease, closing the distance for another featherlight kiss.

She's the one breathless this time. "For you, Prince Charming . . . I'll make all the spotted dick you could ever want."

EPILOGUE

STELLA

Eight months later, November
Las Vegas, Nevada

The engagement ring on Willow Williams's finger keeps catching the light in such a way that I'm pretty sure everyone is going to go blind by the time dinner is over.

"Dear God," I murmur to Thomas, wincing when she throws her hand up again and the refraction hits me square in the face. "That thing's a weapon of mass destruction."

"It's nearly as big as she is," he whispers back. "How is she even able to lift her arm?"

I snicker. "She's small but mighty, I suppose."

Other than potential retinal damage, our anniversary dinner has been fantastic so far. Our friends and families have made the trek to Vegas to celebrate our first year of marriage in the place where it all started. Even a few drivers and their partners have joined us—including the newly engaged Dev Anderson and Willow Williams.

I say *newly*, but it's been over a month, though you'd think it happened just yesterday with how excited they both are.

"Dev's been *insufferable*," Thomas complained after the first race weekend back following their engagement. "We both know I'm obsessed with you, but that man? Sickeningly in love. I regret that we played a part in their romance."

"Ah yes," I mused. "Because me renting out the Manhattan Stella Margaux's location free of charge to him so he could propose was *your* doing."

Thomas lifted his chin, playfully indignant. "I'm the one who broached the topic with you, did I not? If I hadn't told you how he wanted to propose, I wouldn't have to listen to him wax poetic about how he can't wait to marry her. I've made a terrible mistake."

He may think it was a mistake, but I don't miss the fond glances he gives Dev and Willow across the table. My man's a sap underneath it all, just how I like it.

"Hey, when are you going to propose to me?" I ask, nudging his knee with mine under the table. "I never got to have that part."

"No, you just don't *remember* that part."

He grins and takes my hand, holding his fingers under mine so my own impressive diamond twinkles under the lights. Even though we've technically just been dating since our last wedding back in February, most days I swear we forget we agreed to being anything less than a married couple.

"Is that something you want?" he asks as he toys with my ring. "Because I can make it happen." He dips his head so we're eye to eye, and my heart picks up the pace. "Will you marry me for a third time, Estelle Margaux Wilhelmina Tyrrell Baldwin Maxwell-Brown?"

I pretend to consider it, pursing my lips before nodding. "Yes, I will. And you're in luck—I know a chapel we can go to. Might as well get that whole pesky wedding thing out of the way."

Thomas lifts my hand to his mouth and kisses my ring. "Actually, I have a better idea."

"Oh?" I arch an eyebrow. "What's better than marrying me multiple times?"

"Getting your initials tattooed on my finger."

I let out a surprised laugh and lean back. "Baby, I'm not sure that'll even fit."

"It will."

He says it so confidently that it makes my smile drop away. He's serious.

"*You* want a *tattoo*?" I press, punched by disbelief. "I know I've called you knockoff Harry Styles before, but I didn't think you'd ever go that far with it."

He shakes his head at my comment but blessedly ignores my quips. "I want a tattoo because I can't wear my ring when I'm racing," he explains. "And I want that reminder of you with me all the time."

I sway a little in my seat, possibly from the wine we've been drinking, but—nope, I'm swooning. This is a swoon, full-on, in action.

"Oh," I exhale, and even though I've known for ages that I'm in love with him, it still hits me with the force of a speeding train. "I like that."

He brightens. "Yeah? You do?"

"Mm-hmm." It's all I can manage because my throat is getting tight. But I make myself say, "And I love you. So much. Like, an absolutely ridiculous amount that I might be embarrassed by if I wasn't sure you felt the same and didn't listen to you proclaim it about twenty-seven times a day."

Thomas laughs at my rambling, then follows it up with a grin that reminds me why I fell for him in the first place. "Well, if you love me so much, why don't you get a tattoo with me?"

"Matching tattoos?" I scoff. "You don't think that's . . . tacky?"

"Oh, it absolutely is." He leans in, nose brushing the shell of my ear. "But isn't that what Vegas is all about?"

He's not wrong. I mean, we've already had a tacky Vegas wedding, so what's one more thing?

"Besides," Thomas continues. "You can't wear your ring because your hands are in dough half the time. It only makes sense for you to get one too."

"You think you're sly, don't you? You just don't want to do it by yourself."

"That may be part of it," he concedes.

I eye him for a moment. I've never been all that interested in tattoos, but if there's one person who could convince me to get one, it's him. "All right, fuck it, I'm in."

He doesn't hesitate to press his lips to mine for a quick kiss in celebration. "God, I love you."

"That's the twenty-eighth time you've said that today."

"And I mean it more every single time."

"I can't wait for twenty-nine, then."

"That'll come after my initials are on your finger."

I lean in for another kiss. "I bet you a hundred bucks you won't be able to last that long."

"You're right," he murmurs against my lips. "I love you, Stella."

I don't get to say it back because he's too busy kissing me again, but that's all right. He knows.

Our love is one thing that's not staying in Vegas.

ACKNOWLEDGMENTS

Even though she's not allowed to read this book, the biggest thank-you goes to Mom D. Your *Of course you can do it* attitude got me through the stress of writing on a deadline. I owe everything to you. I love you so much.

My agent, Silé Edwards. I live for your podcast-length voice notes and hope to receive many more in the future. You're the absolute best.

My editors, Kinza Azira and Mary Baker, deserve so much credit for making this book the best it could be and for all their comments in the Word document that had me cackling. Bon appétit!

Chloe, Ana, Carol-Anne, Rosa, and the entire Pan Macmillan team—thank you for welcoming me into your office and making the UK release of my debut novel such a dream. I'm hugging you all from across the Atlantic! Jessica, Tina, Kalie, Katie, Danielle, and everyone at Berkley, plus all my international editors and translators—I appreciate all the work you've done to bring these stories to more readers.

Leni Kauffman, for once again creating the most stunning work of art for the cover.

Soraya, for organizing events and being an amazing conversation partner (we've really got to get started on that podcast). Mahbuba, for being the absolute best hype woman and letting me come sign books at your store. And Teigan, thank you for being the bravest and marching up to booksellers to ask if I could sign copies of *Cross the Line*—I'm officially hiring you as my UK manager.

Zarin, Bei, Aaliyah, Kell, Moon, Ruqi, Ali, Alissa, Chloe, Norhan, Deidre, Nat, and Marina, for being such loud and proud supporters. And the Pit Wall Recs team, for hosting such an amazing watch party for the Monaco Grand Prix and inviting me to talk about *CTL*.

Val, Kristin, and Arzoo—I'm so glad our friendships made it out of college and survived these past ten years. Sorry it took so long for me to even tell y'all that I am a writer, but hey, glad we can all celebrate together now.

Sammy, you're the best sister-friend a girl could ask for. *CTL*'s UK release wouldn't have been the same without you. I'm still thinking about those meat pies . . .

"Well, at least he's not playing 'A Team.'" My A Team, I love you all and I regret ever saying those words, but I'm so glad we got to experience our namesake song sung live so many times by complete accident. And thank you to the Dublin Airport staff for playing Ed Sheeran on repeat for what seemed like hours; you have no idea what you've inspired here.

Flamingo House: Kate, I truly don't know what I'd do without you. Thank you for putting up with my tantrums, and then gentle parenting me into getting the work done. I cherish our pool chats and phone calls that are never any shorter than three hours. Natalie, my cool little sister who keeps me young, thank you for always being my cheerleader and being so proud whenever I (rarely) manage to be vulnerable. SWTM forever.

And Mom J. I wish you could be here to see this, but I comfort myself by believing you're the one making it all happen. Thank you.

Keep reading for a preview
of Willow and Dev's story in

CROSS
THE LINE

Available now!

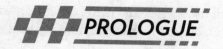 **PROLOGUE**

DEV

October
Austin, Texas

I've fucked up. Boy howdy, have I fucked *all* the way up.

My race engineer is in my ear, asking questions like *What happened?* and *Are you okay?* and, most importantly, *How much damage did the car sustain?* I need to answer him—need to reassure him and the team that I'm conscious after skidding through gravel and hitting a barrier at nearly a hundred miles an hour. For now, they'll have to trust my vitals displayed on the pit wall computer screens, because I can't seem to form the words to tell them. Not because there's anything physically wrong with me. It's just that my brain is . . . not present. It's taking a day off. Fully out to goddamn lunch. And it's not because of the crash.

"Dev?" Branny's voice breaks through the fog, his concern deep and clear over the radio. "Can you hear me? Are you okay? Repeat, are you okay?"

"I'm fine," I choke out, still clutching the steering wheel. My knuckles are probably white underneath my gloves. "Car's done, though. I'm sorry, everyone. This is on me."

Like any good engineer, he'll want to question what the

problem was, but he knows better than to ask it over the team radio, where anyone in the world could be listening. It'll wait until the debrief, and then I can get my ass handed to me by our CEO, our team principal, and my lead mechanic. And I'll deserve it, because this really was on me.

This was no fault of the car, the track surface, another driver, or a force of nature. No, I committed a mortal sin while behind the wheel.

I got distracted.

It shouldn't have happened. It's *never* happened in all my years of racing, and certainly not during the five I've spent in Formula 1. I've never let my mind wander so far that I braked too late and lost the back end. I barely had time to react before coming to a bone-shuddering stop in the barriers.

"Turn the car off and come back to the pit," Branny instructs.

I do what I'm told before I ruin anything else. I can only imagine what the TV commentators will report as they discuss the possible reasons for my crash. I can practically hear them saying, *It's such a disappointment, but what matters is that he's okay.*

But I'm not okay. I'm far from it. I screwed up big-time—and I don't mean the crash.

I can't stop thinking about it, even as I pull myself out of my ruined car and step away from millions of dollars of damage. If I'm being honest with myself, things may never be okay again.

Because I kissed Willow Williams last night. And now I'm a dead man walking.

# CHAPTER 1

WILLOW

Seven months later, May
New York City

I've nearly set my apartment on fire. Again.

Making macarons should not be this hard. They're small and cute, and the recipe calls for super simple ingredients—it's just egg whites, almond flour, and sugar. So why, oh *why*, can't I make a single batch without completely messing up?

"Oh no, oh shit," I mumble as I snatch an oven mitt off the counter and pull out the now-smoking confection. According to the timer, they shouldn't be done for another five minutes, and yet these are nearly burnt to a crisp. Either the recipe was wrong about the baking temperature, or my oven was sent straight from hell. I'm betting on the latter.

I'm desperate to re-create the infamous Stella Margaux Bakery's classic macaron because, as of a month ago, New York City's one location closed for renovations, and I simply can't live without them. The news was enough to make me consider moving back to the West Coast, where there's a Stella's practically every hundred feet.

Then again, I might not have a choice about returning to San Diego to live with my family if I can't find a job in the next couple of months. I came to New York four years ago for college and had plans to stay for possibly the rest of my life. My education was bankrolled by my amazing parents, with the stipulation that after graduation, I'd support myself. Truthfully, they'd have no problem continuing to help me, and they absolutely have the means, but it's the principle of it all. I made a promise, and I'm going to keep it. I just didn't think it would be this difficult.

I busted my ass during undergrad with a double major in communications and sports marketing, a minor in English, and a new internship every semester. With all that experience, I thought it would be easy to find a full-time position working in the marketing department of a professional sports team—a.k.a. my dream job. But after dozens of flat-out ignored applications, zero callbacks after interviews, and endless *We'll be in touch* lies, I'm still unemployed.

It would be so much worse if I'd graduated ages ago instead of just last week, but I've been applying for positions for months now, hoping to have a job in place by the time I was handed my diploma. My brother landed one in his field months before graduation, so I figured there was no reason I couldn't do the same.

Ha. Joke's on me, because here I am with no job, a dwindling sum in my bank account, and a two hours' drive from the closest Stella Margaux's. This is not what I call *living my best life.* But damn if I'm not trying.

"What's on fire?" Chantal asks from the doorway to the kitchen, grimacing at the smell.

I sigh and move to open the window, sparing a glance back at my roommate as I do. "My hopes and dreams."

"Figured. Smells awful."

Can't argue with that.

"This is the fourth batch I've ruined today," I lament as I shuffle over to her. Seeking comfort, I rest my temple against her upper arm. It's not quite her shoulder, since I'm five foot nothing and she's a six-foot-one angel. "The first ones weren't sweet enough. The second ones were flat as crepes. The third were underbaked, and these are—"

"On fire."

"*Singed*," I correct, pulling back and giving her a warning look. I can't be too mad, though, because they *were* kind of on fire at some point. "I can't get it right and I don't know what I'm doing wrong."

"Take a break," Chantal instructs. Her tone is firm, but there's a tenderness in it. "You can try again tomorrow."

She's right, and I'll absolutely pick myself up and dust myself off for yet another attempt, just like I always do. But she knows my frustration isn't just about macarons. She knows how badly I want my life to be perfect and how upset it makes me that I'm struggling to pull it off. As my roommate since our freshman year, she's witnessed plenty of my highs and lows, and is well-versed in all my hopes and dreams. I'm lucky that her own dream job as a financial analyst—go figure—is keeping her in New York, because I don't know what I'd do without her.

"I'll order takeout so no one has to enter this disaster zone," she says, pulling her phone out of the back pocket of her denim shorts that showcase her long, deep brown legs. "And check your phone, would you? It keeps buzzing in your room, and it's driving me nuts."

I flash her a bashful smile. "Sorry. I didn't want to get distracted, so I left it in there."

She cocks a brow playfully. "You mean you didn't want to risk dropping it in the batter again."

My face flames at the mention of that specific baking attempt. "It only happened one time!"

She flips her braids over one shoulder as she strolls out of the kitchen, the delicate beads at the ends clicking together as she goes. I helped her pick them out last week, the gold and deep azure perfect for the warming temperatures and one last hurrah before she starts her new job and has to have a "professional" hairstyle. It'd be great if the world could stop telling Black girls what's appropriate when it comes to our hair, but today is not that day.

Sighing, I undo my apron and hang it on the hook by the window. The pastel pink cotton flutters in the warm breeze, silently mocking me and my failure. I don't even bother looking at the charbroiled macarons as I leave the kitchen and pad down the narrow hallway to my bedroom.

I pass Grace's open door along the way, catching a snippet of the conversation she's having on the phone. Judging from the occasional groan and the (very few) words in Cantonese I understand thanks to the lessons she's given me over the years, she's talking to her mother. She's probably assuring her that she won't miss her flight to Hong Kong tomorrow, which she's done twice before.

She gives me a finger wave as I walk by, and I blow her a kiss in return before slipping into my room next door. The sun streams in through my gauzy curtains, casting short shadows across my desk. My phone sits on the surface, wedged between a few skincare products and a mug full of glitter gel pens. The screen is dark, but when I scoop it up, a litany of texts and missed calls, all from my brother, greets me.

Most people would assume there'd been some kind of emergency, but this is just how Oakley operates. If he can't get a hold of me—or anyone, for that matter—on his first attempt, he'll keep calling and texting until they pick up. There's no subtlety with him.

I don't bother looking at any of the twenty texts. They're probably just emojis and the sentence *Pick up!!!!* over and over again. Instead, I tap his name and put the phone to my ear, flopping onto my ruffled duvet to stare out the window at the brick apartment building across the street.

"Took you long enough," Oakley grumbles when he answers.

"I was busy," I say vaguely. If I confess my baking catastrophe to him, he'll never let me live it down. "What's up?"

"Do you want to go to Monaco?"

Another thing about my brother—he doesn't beat around the bush.

I'm used to it, but the question still throws me. "Monaco?" I repeat. "Like, the country?"

"*Yes*, Willow, the country," he mocks. "Keep up."

I roll my eyes, mentally flipping him a middle finger. "God, I was just checking."

"So?" I can imagine him prompting me by circling his hand in the air, ever impatient. "You interested or not?"

"I mean, yeah," I reply, even though I'm suspicious of the offer. "Who wouldn't be? But why are you even asking?"

"Because I'm going next week and thought you might want to tag along. Plus, it's a race weekend, and—"

My snort interrupts him. "I should have known this was a motorsport thing."

When my brother was a teenager, his life revolved around kart racing, which led to a successful but short-lived career in Formula 3. In the end, he gave it up to have a "normal" life and went off to college. Personally, I wouldn't have given up the opportunity to be a professional athlete for anything. But that's the difference between Oakley and me—he had options in life. I didn't.

"*And*," Oakley barges on, "my company is hosting a huge event. I figured you might want to schmooze with athletes, then watch the race from the paddock. I've got passes, courtesy of SecDark."

Part of that "normal" college experience for Oakley involved studying cybersecurity. He was recruited during the fall semester of his senior year by one of the leading companies in the industry, SecDark Solutions, and has worked for them ever since.

The business was so successful that they'd recently branched out into sponsoring various sports teams and athletes, a Formula 1 team among them, which would explain the party and paddock passes. If I wasn't so proud of my brother for working his way up the ranks of such a flourishing company, I'd be jealous as hell.

But considering I'm being offered perks from his wins, I can't complain that he's doing better than me.

"I know you're not having the easiest time finding a job," he says before I can ask more about the event, "but this could be a good opportunity for you to network. You haven't given up on sports marketing, have you?"

Rolling onto my side, I pull my knees up to my chest. I'm more embarrassed by Oakley's gentleness than I would be if he was making fun of me for still being unemployed.

A career related to sports has always been my dream. I grew up loving baseball and basketball, loved going to games with Oakley and our father, loved the electric energy of a crowd cheering for their favorite team. I was hooked from the second Dad took my hand and led me into my first stadium. There was no going back after that. I wanted to be like the people on the field and the court. I wanted to run bases and make half-court shots. I wanted to hear my name chanted, to have it echo throughout the stands and beat in the hearts of fans.

Unfortunately, my body kept that dream from ever becoming a reality. Even though it took years and countless doctors to get a diagnosis of hypermobility, I knew early on that I was different from other kids. That I'd never get to do some of the same activities they did.

My baseball career ended after a dislocated shoulder during my first T-ball lesson, and basketball was simply out of the question thanks to all the running and sudden stops that my unstable knees couldn't handle. Being an athlete just wasn't in the cards for me.

So, after years of watching and learning from the sidelines, I figured sports marketing was the next best thing. I could still be immersed in a world that brought me joy, and I could share that joy with others. At least, I could if I got a job.

"No, I haven't given up." I sigh. "I'm still waiting to hear back from a few places."

"Then come to Monaco in the meantime," he wheedles. "Like I said, the event will be perfect for networking. Or, fuck it, just consider it a vacation on my dime. A joint graduation gift and a super early birthday present."

"All in one?" I drawl. "Wow, you're *so* kind."

"Let's be real. I'm only offering because Mom made me."

"So, I should be thanking her for this invitation and not you?"

"Semantics," he says, dismissing my comment. Then he launches back into his pitch. "Just think of all the people you'll meet. You know how many athletes and their teams will be at this party? If you don't end up with a job offer at the end of the night, I'll cliff dive off the coast."

I snicker. "You'll do that even if I do get an offer." We both inherited the adrenaline junkie gene. I just know better than to act on mine.

"Probably," he concedes. "But seriously, Wills. This is a great opportunity. And you don't even have to lift a finger. I'll handle everything."

I shift onto my back and study the ceiling, twisting the hem of my sundress between my fingers. "You promise it's worth my time?" I hedge, but excitement is already starting to bloom in my chest. "I don't want to be away for too long and miss out on an interview."

"I promise. You can fly in on Wednesday and fly back Monday morning."

Holding my breath, I mull it over. He's right. It could be an excellent networking opportunity. And who wouldn't want to spend a few days in one of the coolest places in the world? Besides, who am I to turn down a free trip?

"Okay, fine," I blurt before my brain can catch up. "Take me to Monaco."

ABOUT THE AUTHOR

Simone Soltani is a romance author and former ghostwriter for a serialized fiction platform. Born and raised in Washington, DC, she holds a BA in geography from the George Washington University, which she likes to think comes in handy for world-building in her novels. When she's not writing, she spends most of her time planning vacations she'll probably never get to go on, reorganizing her many bookshelves, and watching sports while cuddling with her dogs.

Visit Simone Soltani Online

SimoneSoltani.com
 SimoneSoltani
 SimoneSoltani
 AuthorSimoneSoltani

Ready to find
your next great read?

Let us help.

Visit prh.com/nextread

Penguin
Random
House